SISTERS

OF

THE BRUCE

1292 – 1314

J. M. Harvey

SISTERS

OF

THE BRUCE

1292 – 1314

Matador
9 Priory Business Park,
Wistow Road, Kibworth Beauchamp,
Leicestershire. LE8 0RX
Tel: (+44) 116 279 2299
Fax: (+44) 116 279 2277
Email: books@troubador.co.uk
Web: www.troubador.co.uk/matador

ISBN 978 1780885 018

British Library Cataloguing in Publication Data.
A catalogue record for this book is available from the British Library.

Typeset in 11pt Book Antiqua by Troubador Publishing Ltd, Leicester, UK

Matador is an imprint of Troubador Publishing Ltd

Printed and bound in Great Britain by
TJ International Ltd, Padstow, Cornwall

For my mother & grandmother

CONTENTS

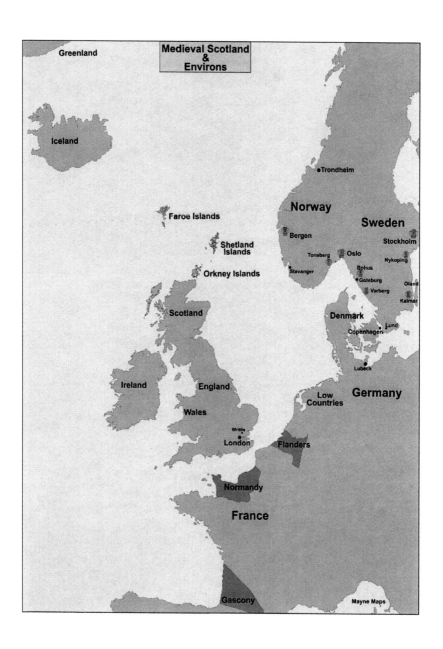

Earldoms of Scotland

Battles   Castles

Westray
Roussay
Skaill
Hoy
South Ronaldsay
Pentland Firth
Cape Wrath
CAITHNESS
Lewis
The Minch
L Broom
SUTHERLAND
Fearn Abbey
Delny Castle
ROSS
Moray Firth
Forres
Elgin
Banff
Dingwall Castle
Avoch Castle
Nairn
Pluscarden Priory
BUCHAN
Skye
Inverness
MORAY
Slioch
Uist
Castle Urquhart
L Ness
Kildrummy
MAR
Inverurie
Aberdeen
Rum
Barra
L Ericht
The Mounth
Castle Tioram
Coll
Brechin
Montrose
Tiree
Dunstaffnage
Dunkeld
ATHOLL
ANGUS
Forfar
Arbroath Abbey
Brander
Mull
Scone
Dundee
Argyll
MENTEITH
L Tay
Methven
St.Andrews
STRATHEARN
Perth
FIFE
Jura
LENNOX
Kinghorn
Dumbarton
Stirling
Firth of Forth
Dunbar
Islay
Glasgow
Falkirk
Edinburgh
DUNBAR
Lanark
Roslin
Berwick
Loudoun Hill
Melrose Abbey
Roxburgh
Kintyre
Irvine
Arran
Douglas
The Forest
Isle of Rathlin
Dunaverty
Dundonald
Jedburgh Abbey
L Foyle
Ayr
L.Doon
Tibbers
Alnwick
Antrim
Turnberry
Lochmaben
Ulster
L Ryan
CARRICK
Caerlaverock
Lanercost Abbey
Newcastle upon Tyne
Glen Trool
Dumfries
Hexham
Larne
Galloway
Buittle
Holm Cultram Abbey
Carlisle
Carrickfergus
Wigtown
Durham
Hartlepool
Guisborough Priory

Ireland

Isle of Man

York

Dundalk

Mayne Maps

Chester

x

PREFACE

Medieval Scotland was a wild and perilous place: only the tough survived. In this fictional narrative, the five sisters of Robert the Bruce speak to us from the past. Their remarkable story deserves to be told, so that they might no longer be 'unwept, unhonour'd and unsung' – to borrow a line from Sir Walter Scott.

Many years ago, a snippet of information caught my eye. Robert's sisters, Isabel and Christina, were believed to have corresponded during their divergent lives and Isabel, in her role as Dowager Queen of Norway, contributed a contingent of Norse soldiers to the Battle of Bannockburn. The seed of an idea took root and this novel, a social history of the times, flourished as a result, backed by a decade and more of research and travel. The tale has many parts: some based on facts upon which even historians cannot agree; others upon legend; the rest flows with the broad brush strokes of imagination.

Within the novel are letters by Robert the Bruce, written by a mystery contributor – a Scot by birth – but adapted by me to fit in with the story's timelines.

There are many gainsayers regarding the Bruce family. Ideally, Robert's actions should be reviewed within the context of the times, given the social and political landscape of medieval Scotland and its competing cultures – the ancient Celtic clan system with its Gaelic language and the French-speaking, Anglo-Norman society, structured upon strict feudal principles. Inherent in this conflict was the deep prejudice literate societies often hold against oral cultures. On many levels, they were incompatible. For those families straddling the two societies, the choices cannot have been easy. Underpinning this story is the survival of not one culture over the other, but the melding of these societies into one, which endures today.

Alba gu Brath – Scotland Forever

PROLOGUE

Scotland

July 1306

A rider thundered along the track as if the very hounds of hell growled and slavered at his heels. Fiery rivulets of light streaked across the midnight sky. The air fizzled and spat and the heavens howled in despair. Now the rain came as horizontal shards biting into his skin. On he rode, driven by the horror of what lay behind him.

The rutted track came to an abrupt halt. The walls of the castle loomed large. Through smoky arrow slits, faint lights glowed. He clattered across the drawbridge, the beat of his horse's hooves ringing in his ears. Manoeuvring his way through the small gap between the creaking oak gates, he fell from his mount. Though his skin was lathered with sweat, the man's belly churned with an icy terror.

"A great host approaches!" he croaked, his voice barely audible.

From the guards nearby, a frantic shout rent the air: "The English are coming!"

The ashen-faced household stumbled from their beds. Standing in tight-lipped silence, they looked to the chatelaine of the massive fortress of Kildrummy.

"We will deal with this! To your posts!" Kirsty Bruce cried and swept out of the bailey, her cloak dragging in the mud as she turned sharply on her heel. She masked her fear well – a few short weeks past, the Bruce kinfolk had only just managed to evade capture after the rout at Methven. Their desperate return brought tears of relief and sorrow to the Kildrummy household.

Now, the anticipated news had come. An enormous English host was pillaging Scotland. None would be spared. All knew the command to 'Raise the Dragon' had been given. It was imperative: the kinfolk of Robert the Bruce, crowned King of Scotland and foresworn enemy of the brutal Edward I of England, must reach safety.

The adults gathered in Kirsty's solar. At the window, Queen Elizabeth, Mary Bruce and Isobel of Buchan peered into the gloom. A streak of light caught Niall Bruce's strained features. He must play for time and hold the castle steadfast. Some of the household would dress as Robert's sisters so the Earl of Pembroke would not be alerted to their escape. Once again, Kirsty blessed these loyal souls who were as family to her.

"We leave at first light." The others nodded as Kirsty gave the sombre order. Like vanguards of doom, the heavens rumbled a low, menacing response.

A few hours later, the women and young Marjorie, the king's daughter, led their horses, hooves slipping on the wet cobblestones, down through the dark, vaulted tunnel.

Farewells were quick and muted. Fears lay unspoken, but none could hide their raw devastation. Niall's sisters hugged him, aware only of the unstinting strength he offered in return. Marjorie clung to him in desperation. Wiping her tears away, he pulled her close. "Courage, lass," was all he said. In the eerie half-light, they escaped through a fine veil of mist and fled north. Niall remained, grim-faced and silent, until a deep sigh escaped his lips. With a heavy heart, he made his way up once more to the battlements.

Who knew what lay ahead for any of them?

PART ONE

PART ONE

Scotland

Turnberry Castle

1292

Upon a headland of low cliffs and grassy links in the far southwest of Scotland, a castle stood firm before the elemental forces of sea and sky. Above the turreted towers, the Bruce standard of blue lion on white endured a frenzied whipping by the autumn gale sweeping in from the west. A large internal cavern beneath the thick walls allowed vessels to offload cargo safely and, now, wave upon crested wave flooded this space matching the raw emotion of all those who called Turnberry home.

As rumour and fact collided and sparked along the darkened corridors of early morn, the household's high-pitched keening rose above the moan of the wind. Shock waves emanated throughout at the passing of the Countess of Carrick overnight. For Lady Marjorie's ten unruly children – from crawling infants to burgeoning teens – the loss of their mother created a chasm of disbelief and sorrow which could not be bridged easily by their father, Robert Bruce; the Earl of Carrick was an austere, industrious man who, if truth be known, preferred to be well away from the clamour of royal courts and the intrigue of shifting alliances. Dreamers and schemers were incomprehensible creatures to him. In the mayhem that was Scotland, he managed the complex demands of the Bruce estates, which ranged far and wide across Scotland and England. That was enough for him and he did it well. It was also a matter of some pride that he had fathered a male heir with ease and a great brood of sons and daughters followed. Oft-times, Robert returned from a sojourn to find his wife, pale and weary, smiling with pride at the new babe she held in her arms. Marjory's stamina for life was remarkable. Soon, she would be back upon her favourite palfrey, riding across Carrick's rolling countryside, enjoying the freedom and excitement of the hunt.

Robert felt well-blessed to have such an engaging wife and so many fine children, all of whom flourished under the nurture and care provided by the household. But few would have found the earl's life an easy road to travel, for his greatest detractor was his powerful, irascible father, the Lord of Annandale. The latter's claims to the kingship of Scotland following the death of King Alexander foundered now on his advanced age and his assessment – that his son and heir had neither the fire in his belly, nor the warrior skills to win the crown in his own right – brought with it increasing frustration and rage. Robert bore the brunt of these confrontations with an icy bitterness; no matter how hard he tried, he could never please his father. During these battles, the countess proved his most loyal ally and Robert depended upon her skilful negotiations and humour to bring peace to the troubled relationship with his father.

Now grey-faced and sleepless with shock, the earl could offer his children nought in the way of comfort. Marjorie's sudden absence from his life was almost beyond his ken and the bitter gall of regret for a lifetime of missed opportunities rose like loathsome bile in his gullet. Unable to breach their father's stony silence, the older children left him alone in his solar staring blank-eyed at the empty hearth. Remnants of a jug lay shattered and a scarlet trail seeped along the cracks between the broad flagstones. Overhead, heavy clouds settled and sleet spattered through an arrow slit to land on the stone floor. Robert cast a baleful look, as some of the pellets skidded and flipped into a dark, viscous pool. Heaven's tears of ice, Marjorie had called them long ago and he caught a ragged breath at the thought.

Remembering the night's events, Robert's scowl deepened. Unable to prevent Marjorie from leaving them, he had entreated God and the saints for their mercy. The physics bled her. It was all to no avail. The fever ran its course and her last breath came as a sigh, so soft he almost missed it. The emergence of the serving women carrying the shroud sent him stumbling up the stairs to his tower chamber, anger coursing through his veins at God's abandonment of them all.

A gust of moist, salt-laden air extinguished the candle on the nearby trestle and shadow enshrouded the earl's hunched figure. All strength departed from his limbs and his body trembled with the biting cold. As a wave of scalding anguish swept all before it, Robert held his head in his hands and wept for all he had lost.

For a century or more, Scotland's relationship with England had been amicable with intermarriage between the royal families an accepted practice. But Wales now bore the imprint of the oppressor's heel upon its back and it was clear to some King Edward was set upon absorbing Scotland into his kingdom either by law or conquest.

When Alexander died, Scotland lost a fine king. In time, his heir, the little Maid of Norway – the child of his daughter and her husband, Eric of Norway – followed him to her grave. Who would lead Scotland? One who could see beyond futile despair was Robert Bruce, Lord of Annandale. As a competitor for Scotland's vacant crown, he brought a great deal to the table: his lands, of course, but also his skills and unique abilities. His capacity to see the world from a broad perspective allowed him to reach beyond the fine mesh of details, which often stymied the progress of others. With his Crusader past, immense wealth and powerful oratory, this remarkable man was well-equipped to accomplish much in the political arena.

Thirteen claimants presented their case. After lengthy deliberation, only two remained. Both shared close ancestry with King David I, but the Bruce hereditary claim proved less substantial than his opponent's and his assertion – that King Alexander named the Lord of Annandale as his successor in the absence of a royal heir – was dismissed.

As a primary adjudicator by Scotland's invitation, England's astute monarch was well-placed to stem the advancement of the powerful Bruce family. And when Edward chose John Balliol as the new King of Scots, the latter's supporters and Comyn kinfolk – enemies of the Bruce family – knew only relief and gratitude.

Who was this great ruler, Edward of England? Longshanks they called him, and his presence cast a pall across the north. Bold as a hollow-bellied lion, he could scent weakness and the thrill of pursuit sent his fiery blood coursing through his veins. Could King John withstand such an opponent? Robert Bruce knew it was only a matter of time before the fragile crust of peace crumbled and Scotland became a bloody quagmire.

Undeterred, the Lord of Annandale forged ahead to bring the plan, which lay at the core of the Bruce family's long-held aspirations, to fruition. For his oldest grandson, he held a vision for the future – and determined the lad's father would have to make of it what he would.

Anger niggled at the earl's composure. Once more, he was found wanting by his father, the old Competitor, and the public shame amongst their friends and supporters at being passed over for the potential role of king was irksome in the extreme. As proud as Robert Bruce was of his young son, there was guilt there too, for he resented his many talents. Must he forever walk in his shadow? The solution came to him one dark and fretful night. If he could not *be* a king, then a king-maker he must be.

So it was that three generations of the Bruce family gathered in a shadowed chamber, after negotiating a fragile alliance of sorts. Before the hissing flames of the fire, they stood, united at last in a common goal. All shared the Bruce family name of Robert, though each was quite different in nature, purpose and ability. Given their noble past, none doubted it was their just right to acquire the crown, but force alone would not win this prize. Careful timing and the strategic use of their resources might just tip the scales in their favour.

Over time, the Competitor passed his lands and title as Lord of Annandale to his son, Robert. The latter had obtained the earldom of Carrick by marriage and now with Marjorie's death, he passed this title to their son. The old man then relinquished his claim upon the crown in favour of his eighteen-year-old grandson, Robert. Elation shone across the young man's face to have been offered such an opportunity, though it was tempered by a healthy dose of awe, for this quest now rested upon his shoulders alone. Indeed, Lady Marjorie would have been pleased tonight to see her eldest son, the new Earl of Carrick, so honoured. Firelight flickered across hopeful faces as they raised their goblets to Scotland and its crown.

It is as well that foresight is denied mere mortals. Had they known the terrible price they would have to pay to achieve their goal, their steps may have faltered and turned from such a perilous path; their actions would ultimately fracture their beloved family and the country they so revered.

CHAPTER TWO

Scotland

Turnberry Castle

1293

Seated before a wooden trestle, upon which lay a burnished mirror and a basket of hair pins, Isabel Bruce smiled at her sister's reflection. Using a slow, steady rhythm, Christina ran a gap-toothed comb through Isabel's long tresses. Behind her, the slanting westering sun struck the rich colours of the hunting tapestries covering the stone walls. Set high in one of Turnberry's towers, the chamber held a fireplace already set in preparation for the evening chill. Far below, the measured cadence of waves on rock and sand offered a soothing backdrop, pierced at times by the sharp, fleeting cries of gulls as they dived and fished deeper waters. The briny-sour tang of sea wrack lay heavy upon the air, a reminder of the unseasonable summer storm the previous night.

A younger, fine-boned version of her sister, Christina applied herself to the task with immense concentration as if she might imprint this memory forever. She knew time was precious. Soon, Isabel must dress for the farewell banquet before the hazardous journey on the morrow crossing faraway oceans with their father. Marriage to King Eric of Norway awaited her. Isabel should have felt happy at such an esteemed match, but trepidation at the thought of leaving home and what lay ahead filled her heart.

It was less than a year since their mother, the Countess of

8

Carrick, had died. Since then, intolerable sadness filled their lives. Memories, whilst sweet, brought inconsolable pain. As the eldest, Isa had comforted the tears and night fears of her young sisters. Now, she was leaving. It felt like a betrayal although it was not of her doing. Sensing her sister's sadness, Christina put down the silk glossing cloth. Her long, tapered fingers rested around Isabel's head framing an attractive face, so like her own. Both had thick, lustrous hair, copper-chestnut or russet depending on the light. Their strong features were firm without being sharp with high foreheads and aquiline noses, slightly freckled by the summer sun from days spent rummaging along the shoreline. Both became infinitely more beautiful when they smiled and laughed; Isabel's quick wit, always a source of amusement.

For the sisters, these happy times had been frequent when their mother was alive. Indeed, her mere presence could ease the darkest mood and make the shadows recede. So alive was her memory, it seemed as if she might walk in through the heavy door to their chamber – laughing, flushed from the hunt, smelling of horses and hay and something she had trodden in far below in the stable. Now she was older, Isa wished her mother were here to talk of marriage, life at court and the complex role of managing the family estate.

Over the past few weeks, the girls had begun to speak wistfully of times past: stories embedded within the fabric of the family's long history. When the winds blew and flames sent shadows leaping across the chamber, their gatherings were the richer for such tales shared.

It was clear to Isabel that a feast of joyful memories, though poignant, might sustain her in the lonely times ahead. One by one, she began to pack them away, as one might vestments and apparel, into that compartment of her mind where her rich inner life flourished. Wit and self-effacing charm came to mind, when Isa recalled her mother's stories.

Most children gain pleasure hearing of a parent's youthful transgressions and the sisters were no different – their incorrigible mother never did things by halves. Her unseemly wooing of their father earned the ire of the king and was the talk of the court! Their grandfather intervened lest the couple be banished from the kingdom. Blaming their indiscretion upon youthful passion, he obtained clemency through payment of a hefty fine. In the process, he forgave his feisty new daughter-in-law, but not his imprudent son – sometimes, their grandfather's memory seemed quite inconclusive when it suited him. It was at *his* suggestion, that his son ride with due haste to Turnberry Castle to inform the heiress of the ancient Celtic earldom of Carrick that her crusader husband, Adam of Kilconquhar, had departed the earth not of a battle wound, but the bloody flux in faraway Acre. Implicit in the suggestion had been that Robert secure the widow *at any cost* or so he had thought; it was not the first time the son had misread the father and suffered his temper as a result. Widows, comely or otherwise, who were heirs to a fortune, must be brought to ground just as stag or boar, not overly for their flesh, but for dynastic power and mighty wealth and before others sought to do the same.

Marjorie knew eligible men further afield could kidnap her and force marriage, though another danger lurked; a noblewoman, new to her widowhood, became the chattel of the king. In due course, he would marry her off to a knight of *his* choice; her wealth, just reward for past deeds and continued loyalty. Was it any wonder she wooed the gentle, unassuming man who rode into her lonely existence? Overhead, storm clouds, scudding in from the northwest, foretold of fierce weather. Marjorie offered the generous hospitality of Turnberry Castle and, in time, took the handsome young man not to ground, but to her warm, goose-down bed. Wondering again at how his son had so easily lost his wits and become the quarry, their grandfather despaired at the calumny wreaked upon the family.

In reliving the tale, Isabel saw again how her mother's eyes twinkled at their youthful effrontery, but it was short-lived. A veil of sadness fell across her face.

Marjorie's first child had been born some time before Sir Adam left for the Crusades. Prior to his departure, the knight had organised the betrothal of his heir to Sir Thomas Randolph of Lanark. The Bruce siblings knew they had a half-sister, but the lass had lived away from Turnberry and departed this earth after giving birth to a son.

For Isabel, her mother's worldly experience and wisdom lay buried with her beside the cold chapel wall. The sisters had to rely on information gleaned from their serving ladies, Bethoc and Aiofe, as well as their long-time cook. Mhairi was as bountiful a source of knowledge as she was a provider. In the warm fug of the kitchen, she served up tantalising snacks – doocot pies and the like – at night to sustain them till the main meal of the following day. If their mother had known, she had never spoken of it, allowing them their youthful fun. Now, Mhairi, who often smelt of freshly baked bread and honey wafers, was a welcome source of discreet, floury hugs within her soft, enveloping body.

Breaking the silence, Christina sought to lift Isabel's spirit. A merry dimple creased her left cheek as she bowed low. "Soon, you shall be a queen and a fine gold crown will rest upon your head. Lavish delicacies will be offered to your grace from silver platters. Your gowns will be draped with pearls and rubies from afar. Oh aye, it will be a grand life! Promise me, Isa, you will write!" The soliloquy ended far more solemnly than it had begun.

11

"I am certain of it, Kirsty! There will be so much to tell," Isabel replied, touched by the note of yearning in her sister's voice; the words hung in a shadowed space caught somewhere between thought and feeling. Their attempts to lift each other's spirits fell far short, but were saved from drifting lower. The heavy oak door responded to the well-aimed thrust of a boot. In came a gaggle of limbs and skirts as Mary, younger than Isa by a few years, crossed the threshold carrying a squirming bundle: a round cherub of a lass, new to walking – Margaret, the baby of the family. From the stairwell and nursery several levels below, Mathilda emerged panting; an impish grin concealed beneath a mess of tawny ringlets. Efforts to hush them failed, until Isa consented to tell them *the* story.

"In a far-off land called Norway, there lives a handsome king named Eric." The strange name, now heard many times, was still the source of much amusement. "In the moonlight, his castle shimmers silver and gold and the turrets are so tall, they are crowned with stars. The stable holds a magical black steed. Whenever I am forlorn and want to come home, I shall leap upon that horse and fly far over the sea at night to see my little ones. What shall I call him?"

"Brandubh, swift as the black raven!" Came the chorus.

Margaret let out a wail as a ragged creature, large of limb and body – Onchu, one of the pups of their wolfhound – shot through the gap in the doorway. Shortly thereafter he was followed by Thomas, Edward, Niall and Alexander. Throwing themselves on the beds, already in disarray from the piles of linen and silk undergarments being sorted through for the journey, the brothers set about wrestling until one rolled and landed, yowling, on the floor with a crash. Adding to the din, Onchu barked and fell upon his stunned victim delivering a bristled, soggy assault. Impetuous as ever, Mary grabbed a tousled feather pillow and began beating Edward around the head until the other three boys leapt to tackle her. The game

12

ended in wild, muffled cries and calls for "Pax! Pax!" Margaret's cries gave way to wide-eyed delight as Kirsty danced about the chamber, a small child under each arm, trying to avoid the mayhem. Fortunately, there were no adults to admonish them for the maids were far below out of earshot. Standing well out of harm's way, Isa had a moment to consider her future. Being so far away from her siblings *would* be difficult but, as the noise grew louder and her brothers' antics more outrageous, a small ingenuous desire surfaced for some longed-for privacy. Surely a queen might do as she wished? The foolishness of her presumption brought a wry smile to her face; men made the decisions and, as far as she could see, had a fine time in the process. For a start, her brothers' lives had proved far more fascinating than her own – up till now. She wondered what mark they might make upon the world.

Edward was newly arrived from Islay in his role as squire to Donald, Lord of the Isles. Always second to Robert in looks, achievements and prospects, he was by nature less secure and given to bleak bouts of jealousy, but all knew the affection he felt for his family held neither boundary nor condition. If there was an adventure to be had, Edward would always be in the forefront, for his greatest foes were inertia and boredom. Danger held no fear for him and he followed his older brother with a true heart in all family endeavours. Isa suspected he would continue to do so with the highest of spirits and utter determination.

Their father had placed younger brothers, Niall and Thomas, in fosterage from a young age as was the norm. She wondered how much trouble the irrepressible pair, both wicked mimics and mischief-makers, found themselves in at Dundonald Castle in deepest Ayrshire. As youngsters, they once tormented Mhairi and the kitchen maids that a bevy of rats had got into the oats stored in the larder. Before beating a hasty retreat, the lads helped themselves to bramble tarts cooling on the scrubbed oak table. Most recently, they had returned to Turnberry in the company of their lord, Sir James Stewart, who held the royal hereditary role of Steward. The administrator wished for important talks with their father.

Serious in nature, much like his father, Alexander exhibited a studious bent and spent much of his time with the monks at Crossragruel Abbey. The brothers knew a passionate temper lurked beneath Alexander's quiet veneer, though it took a long time on the simmer before it boiled over and one of them received a vigorous clout. Right now, it was Thomas who was on the receiving end, as Alexander sought to restore order by removing a pair of leggings from his younger brother's head. Isa joined in the laughter. Despite the chaos, the lads' high spirits acted as a balm and salve to her inner turmoil. Of her five brothers, she felt closest to Robert and missed him. Since being made Earl of Carrick, his comprehensive duties took him across the Bruce estates in Scotland and England and he was rarely at Turnberry.

Brought back to the present, Isa heard Aoife's sharp call well before the maid entered the chamber. When the boys leapt up from behind the beds, her shriek delighted them all, but her Gaelic scolds fell upon deaf ears. Down in the bailey, excited voices rose when Robert and their grandfather galloped in to the courtyard. Hounds bayed. Horses snorted and stamped their hooves on the cobblestones. Whooping down the curved stairwell, the brothers tumbled over each other in their desire to be first to reach the bottom; each as competitive as the other. Muttering at life's injustices, Aiofe departed for the launder room, her arms filled with muddied linen.

Bethoc sang an old Gaelic working song as she climbed the stairs. Her weary face softened at sight of the youngsters. Ignoring the mess of tangled clothes scattered about the room, the maid's soft brown eyes caught and held Isa's steadfast blue-green gaze.

"Time to get ready, Lady Ishbel," she said, her voice gentle with the lilt of the Isles.

In the tower chamber, dust motes drifted and tiny goose feathers danced in stray shafts of sunlight. Outside, seabirds wheeled across the waves, their cries melding with distant echoes. With her sisters' departure to see the new arrivals, peace reigned at last. Isa lowered herself upon the cushioned window seat. Taking up her embroidery, she paused, allowing her eyes to pass over the familiar sight of blue-grey waves and distant coastline. Mesmerised by the rise and fall of the sea's swell, her thoughts drifted and tarried, seeking an escape from the pressing demands of the day. As she settled upon her childhood memories, one event in particular rose to the forefront. Its impact upon the family had been extraordinary! Exhaling with relief, she closed her eyes, enjoying the restful glow of the late afternoon sun...

On long winter evenings at Lochmaben, their grandfather often sat with his grandchildren around the fireside recounting stories from the past. One macabre tale held them spellbound, so potent was the impact of a certain St Malachy, which even a century and a half later could not be dispelled. During a visit to Annan, site of the earliest Bruce castle in Scotland, the Irish priest pleaded with the Lord Robert of the time to spare a thief's life – successfully, or so he thought. Upon seeing the felon hanging from a gibbet the next day, Malachy cursed the family. In brutal consequence, the Bruce line would wither and die. Shortly thereafter, a flood washed away the castle and a plague followed. Within the settlement, many died and the accursed tale became magnified for posterity. Shifting away from the unpredictable watercourse, the Lord of Annandale built a new castle on a high motte at Lochmaben.

So intimidating was the threat of calumny upon the family, their grandfather made an extraordinary journey to the abbey at Clairvaux in far-off France to visit the saint's grave on his way home from the battles against the Saracen horde. That was many years ago. At this point in the story, the old Crusader often became morose. Drawing gnarled hands through his silvered mane, he reflected upon the growing divide between Scotland and England. For the family to remain strong and secure, a fine balance was necessary between opposing forces, but the reality seemed as precarious as riding a great destrier without benefit of a saddle.

A look of resignation flitted across his grizzled features. The tasks required were complex indeed and danger lay ahead. He was sure of it! Growing ever more pensive, he stared at the dying embers, the flickering hearth light mirrored in his rheumy grey eyes. As if tugging his forelock to fate, the old man's thoughts often found their way to his beloved priory at Guisborough, source of the family's devoted patronage since its inception so many years before. "All the Bruce ancestors have been buried there and I will join them one day." His words hung expectantly; the warm embrace of death and the loving welcome he would receive, foremost in his mind.

With the sea's breath cool upon her skin, Isa remembered his words. A shiver of apprehension stiffened the tiny hairs on the back of her neck. Life without her grandfather was unthinkable. She thought of her mother so white and still beneath the ground. Perhaps old Malachy's cold, spindly fingers had reached out from the grave after all.

Day turned to night, and Isa wished she could make time

stand still. The ordeal of the farewell banquet lay before her. She sat in her hip bath, filled with steaming hot water hoisted up the narrow stairwell by Earchann, her servitor, from the launder rooms far below. Humming softly, Bethoc busied herself with the final packing of the wooden chests in the chamber. On the morrow, they would be hoisted onto the vessel waiting at the castle's dock.

Isa's greatest fear, piercing and visceral in its clarity, was that she might forget her family and her old life. Irrational it might be, but such an eventuality was frightening. Irritated by her own weakness, she splashed her face, knowing it would take more than water to wash away the pain of the forthcoming separation.

Beside her on a cornice shelf, wax candles glowed; their flaring incandescence cast oblique shadows which reached out to dispel the gloom. Isa allowed her thoughts to drift in the perfumed warmth. Across her face, lines of tension softened. Her breathing slowed and tiny flickers of movement rippled imperceptibly beneath closed lids…

On occasions, the family made the long journey to the Bruce estate at Writtle in Essex in the far south of England to visit their father. With a baggage train of servants and essential household goods, it took months of rough travel along rutted, muddy tracks, before they reached their destination. Their grandfather's attorney, Adam de Crokdak, helped them settle into the thatched manor house, once a substantial royal lodge. Some of the local household snickered behind their hands at their strange accents and different ways, but Master Adam cuffed the worst offenders, banishing them to scullion duties. Busy servitors scurried off to unpack, whilst groomsmen led the oxen and exhausted sumpter ponies over to the cavernous, oak-roofed barn for a welcome feed of hay.

Exploring the many outbuildings and rich farmland –

siblings-in-tow – Isa missed the wild, rocky shore of Turnberry and the relentless cry of seabirds. In time, the rich colours and softness of the countryside calmed her spirit and soothed the aches brought on by the long journey. Nearby, at their other estate close to the village of Hatfield Broad Oak, they played in the forest surrounding Brunesho Manor. Master Adam showed them an enormous oak within whose rounded, empty bole they could hide. Small roe deer, an occasional badger and numerous hares passed though the silent glade – alert and tentative – but, inevitably, one or other of the brothers would whoop and scare the skittish creatures.

Later, the sisters hitched their skirts and linen shifts and climbed the sprawling branches of forest trees, jumping on the boys as they wandered by absorbed in their own exploits. Afterwards, they laughed and rolled in the thick, soft grass. Warmed by the sun and with the scent of the abundant, mellow earth about them, the girls lay there long after the lads departed. With hair and clothing askew, they gazed up at the scant scraps of deep blue sky filtering through the leaves. In hushed tones, they spoke of all that was wondrous in their lives, blissfully content to be so free and unhindered. They knew it would not always be this way.

Turnberry was their home and primary residence, but much time was also spent at Lochmaben Castle across the hills to the southeast near Annan. Set on high land and surrounded by a cluster of lochs, its watery domain was the ideal place to play in coracles and watch the teeming fish, caught so easily by their brothers with spears in the shallow water and nets in the fast-flowing channels. Isa and Kirsty joined Mary and the boys to hunt on foot with the hounds and catch the wild geese which flew from the north to tarry awhile before heading south; their arrow formations, straight and true. When not in tutorage at Turnberry, Isa learned to gallop on her mottled-grey pony beside her mother's chestnut palfrey.

During infrequent visits home, the boys raced their horses across the hills, whooping wildly as they flew past a hawking party, disturbing the highly-prized birds and bringing down upon their heads their mother's wrath. Lady Marjorie's passion for hawking had passed to her daughters. One year, she gave Isa a most precious gift: a merlin, whose slate-blue back was cool and silky to the touch. Isa marvelled at the skill and lightning speed of the bird, which brought sudden death to hares and other small creatures, providing food for the pot. Her father said she could take Luag in a cage to Norway, but Isa feared he might wither in such confinement. In the end, she gifted him to Kirsty. She felt sure her mother would not mind if he remained here free to hunt and roam the skies over Turnberry.

Hearing a gull's staccato call, Isa's reflections took another turn. Along the rocky shoreline, the siblings had entertained themselves for hours exploring the shallow caves, devising adventures of knightly valour or defending themselves against vicious predators upon their sea girt kingdom. Rob and Edward were well known for their pranks, especially after shore bound explorations. Isa caught herself almost chuckling, as another memory hove into view.

High up on the windy ramparts, fires lit by the guards sent thin beams of light filtering through the narrow window across the silent, shadowed chamber. Worn out after a long day, Isa had clambered into the large curtained bed she shared with Kirsty and Mary. Stretching deep within the linen sheets, the girls' small feet slipped into a mess of slimy tendrils and the sharpish spines of a starfish reached up to spear their soles. How their screams alerted the castle! Alarmed guards shouted and, from all directions, sleepy-eyed servitors came running, tripping over each other in their haste. Meanwhile, the perpetrators fell about laughing – almost piddling their braies, so it was said later. Rarely though was punishment meted out in full, for the lads were never at home long enough. Soon, they returned to their various places of fosterage: learning the many tasks of page and squire and, over time, the crucial arts of attack and defence, and the skills of the tourney to ready them for manhood with its inherent adventures and responsibilities.

Isa allowed her thoughts to wander at will. Turnberry was always busy with important folk coming and going, each with their large entourage. On occasions, the family went by boat to visit kinfolk or friends across in Bute, Arran or Kintyre. These highly social visits were reciprocated; it was far easier to travel by sea than land. Some warm evenings, after the guests had departed, they wandered amongst the links, enjoying precious moments of their mother's complete attention. If the mood took them, they lay down on the grassy banks to observe the constellations or watch the moon's silvery trail across the sea.

Their father was often away, sometimes across the Solway in England or elsewhere in Scotland. Upon his return, he gathered them round and told stories of faraway places: the royal palace in Edinburgh; the wild, rugged mountains of untamed Wales or the heaving, malodorous crush of London. Of war and intrigue, he rarely spoke and an impenetrable mask slid across his features when pressed by his sons for gory battles tales. Then, their mother would intervene, sending the lads off to bed, heedless of their groans and pleading. She loved to make their father laugh, to soften the hard shell of duty which so often encased him.

Isa knew that she and her siblings had enjoyed a privileged childhood, but it was the love and laughter she most remembered. As if from a distance, she heard her maid's soft call. She lingered, ending her bath with a languorous stretch. The shadow of a wistful smile played upon her lips. There was pleasure and pain in her exploration, but she was sure now – the memories held close to her heart would never fade.

Isa stepped into the warm linen wrap held out by Bethoc. Beside the glowing fireside, she dried herself and slipped on her gown over silk undergarments. Sage green was a favourite colour of hers and Bethoc's addition of red braid at the hips made the perfect contrast. All in all, it was very pleasing. She nodded at the maid who beamed with delight. Kirsty returned, ready to provide the quiet strength her sister needed, but when Mary arrived soon after, her excited chatter fractured all peace.

Isa and her sisters entered the Great Hall, thick with smoke and dust and raucous anticipation. Along the tapestry-hung walls, members of the Bruce household and numerous visitors crammed the long trestles. All were placed according to status, though disputes broke out here and there to be quelled by stewards, meting out rough justice. On an elevated platform at the head of the hall, significant family members and esteemed guests dipped their hands into silver bowls of briar-scented water. A brood of young pages stood in readiness with steaming cloths.

Tonight, three generations of the Bruce family entertained their most powerful friends to farewell Isabel and her father, and the diplomatic entourage which would accompany them to Norway. It was a banquet to honour Isa's new status but subtle undertones marred the festivities for her immediate family. Once she began her new life, it was likely they would never see her again. Outside, Lady Marjorie's grave was a grim reminder of the wanton fickleness of fate. Isa lifted her chin, squared her shoulders and made her way to the dais. A twisted gold filet held her shining hair in place and she felt confident the sleek lines of her gown looked well upon her. Pleased with her grace and elegance, her father rose to greet her, aware of the appreciative glances flickering across faces around the hall. With a solemn tilt of her head, Isa acknowledged the guests –

the very image of a noble, young queen – until she caught the glint of humour in Rob's eye. For a brief second, her heart lightened and she felt her old self returning as her brother winked at her.

The hall bustled with activity and the din grew. Through the doorway from the kitchens below, serving maids trailed back and forth delivering trenchers of food. Trying to avoid the sweaty, wandering hands of the lesser nobles, the women dripped juices from serving platters over the herb-strewn floor, whilst lewd comments followed in their wake.

Burly, scarred knights in stained tunics were served by pages: some barely past their seventh year and in need of sleep. Picking at pimpled faces with absent-minded devotion, squires leaned against the walls, awaiting their orders. Having caught the rich scent of meat, several hounds loped into the hall, settling under the tables to scratch at their ragged pelts and await scraps from the meal. These soon became the object of a scuffle. A booted foot found its snarling target and a tight yelp was heard above the music and ribald laughter. Something rustling under a stool caught the intense gaze of a large mouser. Her tail flicked once, twice. She lowered herself, quivering with desire. Isa watched as the creature melted back into the shadows – a small rodent, dangling from her clenched jaws.

Making light conversation with James the Steward and Domnhall, the Earl of Mar from Kildrummy Castle in the far northeast of Scotland, was not onerous. Both old friends of the family, they had known Isa since she was in swaddling. Tonight, nerves curdled her stomach and her head ached with the noise and commotion. She ate lightly of the rich fare and was relieved when the meal was finished and greasy trenchers removed. When the magnates departed for their formal consultations with her father in his private solar, the atmosphere lightened. The dancing could now commence.

High up along the walls, oil-soaked rushes flickered and smoked from the draughts through the narrow windows. With determination, Isa committed to memory this dear scene. The rhythmic boom of the waves entering the cavern far below served as a reminder of many such dinners with her siblings in various stages of growth and the tiny babes which appeared with marked regularity. Now, most of them were full-grown; their mother, gone.

Isa's attention was caught by her brother, Edward – his squire's tasks finished for the moment. Following one of the buxom maids who had caught his eye, he sidled along the far wall towards an exit. Niall and Thomas were trying to avoid the watchful eyes of the Steward's older sons, sipping mead and arm-wrestling on the back table. If their mother were here, she would have chastised them and sent them on their way. This thought brought with it such a pang that Isa forced herself to concentrate on the musicians; the plaintive notes of harp and short pipes were matched by the quick muffled beats of the bodhran. Groups of dancers formed quatrains, attempting a fast-paced reel, until they fell laughing against the walls, too exhausted to continue.

Isa's thoughts passed onward to her younger sisters. They had supped in their chamber and were, by now, lulled by the rhythm of the waves and Bethoc's lullabies. Isa realised she would miss their little bodies, deliciously warm and creased from sleep, but not the moment when they scrambled into bed with her as soon as the sun's rays pierced the early morning gloom.

In a far corner of the hall, Mary and Kirsty stood together, eyeing a group of nobles, lean and boisterous as young colts. Long ago, powerful marriage alliances had been arranged for the older siblings, but Isa resented the fact she could not marry for love as her parents had done and was a pawn in the game of political strategy. With her mother gone, it was harder to argue with her father's blunt political needs, particularly with the escalation of conflict between their family and the Comyns.

After the death of King Alexander, their grandfather feared their enemies would take control of the crown by force before legitimate consultation occurred. In his estimation, attack was always the best form of defence. Now John Balliol, ally and relative of the Comyns, was king, the Bruces were in a hazardous position for raiding the Comyn's castles in Galloway. Retribution was bound to follow.

Tonight, this noble daughter of Scotland wondered what this royal alliance might gain for her family and what it would cost her. She felt an urgent need for fresh air to clear her mind and made her way up one of the winding stairwells to the battlement walk. Guards nodded deferentially, allowing her to wander at will. The moon would soon be visible through the clouds over Ailsa Craig, the granite monolith which rose dome-shaped from the sea a little to the south. Its bulky form dominated a landscape as familiar to her as her own face. Oft times, gannets and puffins found their way, along with their eggs, onto the menu whenever the lads sailed over to explore the cliffs.

The sky darkened and the beauty of the moon's reflection in the sea's swell caught her off guard. It seemed to epitomise all the wonder and, by default, all the losses in her life up to this point, bringing to the fore the lump in her throat she had been fighting all day. With difficulty, Isa forced herself to make out the faint outline of Arran to the north and, beyond it, the long landmass of Kintyre. In the far-off distance, Antrim and the Irish coast were just visible in the deepening night sky. Her reveries were cut short as her oldest brother appeared quietly at her side.

"Isa, the time has come for our farewells. There have been too many of them; Mother, friends who have died supporting our cause and, now, you are leaving us. I know you are loath

to go. Soon, each of us will depart. Nought remains the same."
Following his sister's gaze out across the shimmering sea,
Robert paused.

"The betrothal contracts between Bruce and Mar are
finalised. Isabella is to be my wife and Kirsty will wed Garnait,
next year. Strong links are needed to offset Comyn territories
in the north. Kildrummy will make a fine home for Kirsty.
Such a massive stronghold will be easy for us to defend if
necessary. No! She does not know all the details, as yet. Leave
it, if you can, for Father to talk of it. Each of us must do what
we can for our family's cause."

His last words held an edge which her ear caught, just
before the soft sea air stole them away – fierce ambition and
elation at the forthcoming challenges. She also heard
something deeper, hidden in the night's shadows; a youth's
whispered fear of failure.

Isa had no words which could alter her future. She
remained silent, her eyes glistening in the dark. When Rob
placed his arm around her, she rested her head upon his sturdy
shoulder. Focusing on the faraway moon's gentle sheen, she
silently prayed for its peace and harmony to surround them
all.

CHAPTER THREE

Norway

Bergen

August 1293

My dear Kirsty,

I write this missive seated at a trestle in my solar. Beside me, the window embrasure looks out over the harbour in Bergen. Father's vessel nestles nearby. Across the grey expanse of water, the carved masts of so many Norse longships look like a strange sea-bound forest. Bergen is so wet, even in summer. I have yet to see the sun.

Our journey here was eventful. When we departed from Turnberry's shore, my heart felt as if it would shatter into so many pieces it could never find repair – much like Mhairi's precious salt urn that Thomas knocked over all those years ago. As we gathered speed, I wrapped Mother's cloak close around me, hoping desperately it would offer both comfort and courage in equal measure. With so many eyes upon me, I did my best to appear resolute, but as we passed around the southernmost tip of Kintyre, the view of our dear coastline was lost to me in the sea's deep swell. I felt crushed and looked to Father for support. His stern expression showed there was little point in bemoaning my fate. Swallowing my fear, I faced the chill wind and braced myself for our strange adventure.

To my shame, I acted out my own distress and cuffed Aoife for wailing that we would all die and the fish feast on our flesh. She stopped eventually, though spent the best part of the voyage snuffling or churning her guts over the boat's edge. Such was her fear of the sea it seemed she might die by her own actions. Out of spite, I told her so. From then on, she made an effort to drink the ale Father brought with us. It seemed to give her some colour; the dried venison and salt cod needed to be washed down with something. What I would have given for a crisp-crusted pie, steaming hot from Mhairi's huge ovens!

For an unusually long time, sea creatures followed our vessel and I could not keep my eyes from their sleek forms and gentle eyes. I hoped they might travel back to you and whisper in their strange tongue that all was well; that these things indeed shall pass.

Beside us, the large galley belonging to the Lord of the Isles sank and rose with the swell. Edward shouted and waved to me, and for a fleeting moment it felt like old times when we used the sea to visit friends. Our first night was spent at the lord's castle. At first light, we left overland for the harbour. For a long time, Edward remained on Finlaggan's battlements, until the haar stole him away from me. After this brief respite, our birlinn passed the Isle of Jura whose bare mountains, the Paps, reminded me of dear Mhairi's voluminous bosom. Bethoc laughed when I made mention of it.

Avoiding the rocky shoals, we headed into deeper, darker waters. Fearghas, our captain, told tales of a giant whirlpool, Corryvrekan, where vessels and crew were sucked to their death by an enormous sea creature. I was so fearful that Father spoke sharply to him. We were far away from this dreadful place and so no harm would befall us. Aoife did not believe him. Muffled from within the stinking shelter, her moans and pitiful retching went on for hours. Days were spent at sea passing countless isles, some large with jagged, black mountains and high red-stained cliffs. At smaller ones edged with white shell beaches, villages close to shore offered up fresh victuals and ale. Father was careful that we did not stop too long lest our enemies, the Macdougalls of Lorne, attack us.

With the deep rolls of the vessel threatening to empty us into the monster's gaping jaws, we endured the rough weather around the northwest cape. It was impossible to sleep, and with the barest minimum of privacy, attention to our physical needs before so many men proved to be a trial. Never have I been so relieved, as when we drew anchor off the low, treeless isles of Orkney. Father's friends welcomed us. Next day, we passed by the bay where the Maid of Norway died. Accompanying us on our voyage was a former cleric, Master Weland, and his brother, Henry. It was to prove fortunate indeed, for Weland, as he graciously requested I call him, had been a member of the official delegation on the voyage with the maid and recounted the fateful tale. The tragedy was brought home, as fast as a crossbow bolt fired at great speed. Not for the first time, I wondered if King Eric blamed the Scots for his daughter's illness and death during the voyage to Scotland, though it was nought but a cruel twist of fate. Would the shadow of her passing mar our new life together?

The winds blew and the rolling sea carried us on our journey ever eastward, following in the wake of the Fionnghals: those white strangers from the north had been consummate mariners. Their sleek, clinker-built vessels journeyed back and forth across this rough, grey expanse of the North Sea. Families followed in sturdier craft to settle the lands, pillaged and plundered so wilfully. Father reminded me, just three decades ago, that the Battle of Largs was fought off the west coast of Scotland. His grandfather had been there. A great storm weakened the mighty Norse fleet and the Scots claimed victory. Later, King Haakon, my betrothed's grandfather, sickened and died on Orkney. In time, the great northern nation severed ties with their lands, acquired through death and destruction. The Hebrides, which we passed much earlier in our journey, and Man, an isle in the far south, were exchanged for gold. Never had our violent past seemed so real. If I was to flourish as Queen of Norway, it would serve me well to follow Grandfather's creed. Fierce courage had been his greatest defence.

With a strong westerly sweeping us before it, our vessel reached the Norwegian coast. At first sight it was cloaked in a fine, watery haze. Time slowed as we manoeuvred our way through the islets. My gut churned with unease until it became obvious the king was not in the quayside party of dignitaries. Far from taking offence, I was relieved and hoped there would be an opportunity to wash and dress before seeing him. Perhaps Bethoc's salves, packed away in error, might resurrect my lips and face, chapped red and dry by the cold winds.

When we alighted, Aiofe fell to her knees. Blessing all the saints she knew, she bent and made to kiss the dock's dirty planking, much to the amusement of the crowd. Cutting short the keening wails which were about to echo forth, Father spoke harshly to her in Gaelic. Chastised, she rose and with mighty sniffs followed our bedraggled entourage up the platform to a massive, grey stone tower. Our apartments stood near the thick harbour wall in an area called the Holmen. After a welcoming meal of hot cod cakes and crisp flatbread, we were shown to our chambers. Huge tubs of hot water awaited us. It was blissful to have Bethoc wash and brush my hair till it shone. I closed my eyes and thought of you, dear one.

In the Great Hall, hung with colourful banners, our entourage was met with the eerie, haunting sounds of curved animal horns blown by courtiers. Fair maids with ample bosoms slammed huge tankards and platters onto the benches. Men shouted and called to one another. The commotion proved overwhelming. Acrid wood smoke stung my eyes, and the stench of unwashed bodies and greasy fare made my stomach churn. When the king raised his hand, all turned. A deafening silence reigned. Father escorted me down the long central walkway between the crowded trestles. I tried my best to perform a deep curtsy to King Eric. My legs wobbled, boneless like the eels we used to catch in Loch Doon. Fright may have played its part as well. Never have I seen such fearsome, helmeted warriors. In a line along the walls, they stood tall, armed with double-headed axes, spears at the ready. Dressed in leather jerkins and tightly-strapped leggings, the men were fair with shaggy, unkempt beards. Thick, curved bands of silver encircled heavily-muscled arms. Father steadied my forearm, so I might stand with dignity.

I wish I could say King Eric matched the tale the children so enjoyed. From on high, he gazed at me as one would appraise a new palfrey. I wondered if my teeth and legs met with approval. After some time, he gave a perfunctory nod and motioned for me to sit beside him in a large throne-like chair, carved with strange dragons and writhing serpents.

With my lack of Norse and the king's ability to speak little in the way of French, Gaelic or broad Scots, our conversation slipped and faltered until we found a few words in common of Latin and Lowland English: the language influenced as it was by so many years of Norse occupation. One of the bishops translated for us and a brief, stilted conversation ensued. With so much to comprehend, I grew tired and was permitted to retire. Sleep came quickly, aided by the luxury of soft linen and the lustrous cream pelt of an enormous creature.

Today, it seems the king is keen for our marriage to proceed at the beginning of the next moon's cycle. A part of me hoped otherwise, but father is well-pleased. The creases have left his brow and he hugged me in a brusque kind of way. Soon, I shall write of the wedding and all that entails in this peculiar, faraway land.

The weather has turned foul and it may be some time before I can find a trader to take this missive. Know that not an hour passes when I am not filled with an unbearable longing for you all at home.

Your loving sister

Isa

Norway

Bergen

September 1293

My dear Kirsty,

I am now Queen of Norway! It seems like a dream from which I will awake and find myself once more at home with the family. The service was held in a stone cathedral with painted central beams and carved wooden settles.

After much consideration, I chose the deep-crimson gown with its tight bodice and flowing lines, which you thought looked well on me. Added to this, a long silk veil, transparent as gossamer, was held in place by a finely-worked, jewelled crown. To my dismay, my Norse ladies-in-waiting, Thora and Gundred, placed a thick, twisted-silver torque around my neck and many heavy gold chains as well, so much so it was an effort to walk. It seems the practice reflects the Norse love of adornment and functions not only as a sign of wealth and prestige, but as currency as well. The gold was a gift from the king, so I was advised to wear it. Every last piece! At my shoulder, an ermine cloak was fastened by a large oval brooch; its raised surface, embossed and set with precious gems.

Outside our apartments, a small wagon of dark, richly-glossed wood, carved with swirling creatures and strange bearded faces, awaited our presence. It was a gift from the local craftsmen and traders. Attached to the open carriage was a fine black pony with a feathered headpiece of red velvet, upon which were attached many gold coins. When he tossed his head, the large feather swayed and bobbed whilst the coins jangled and glittered in the sun. A groom calmed him until Father and I were seated upon the padded benches ready to depart. Townsfolk arrayed in their best clothes waved and cheered as we made our way through the large gate in the perimeter walls and around to the church, a short distance in reality, but an inestimable journey in terms of change: innocence to knowledge, youth to adulthood.

With Father, handsome in his finery, walking beside me up the long aisle, I hoped to glide along in my soft leather boots, but I bobbed and swayed until I learnt to centre the heavy weights. On cue, the angelic voices of the choir soared into the lofty realms. The bishop intoned copious blessings. King Eric seemed as relieved as I when the service was over; it seems he has little time for priests and the like. Unbelievably, the celebrations continued in the Great Hall for the moon's full cycle with much consumption of sweet-honeyed mead night after night. Our entourage enjoyed the generous hospitality of the royal court, but I tired of the noise and throng after just a few days and longed for the peace of our royal apartments at day's end. Eric has been a kindly husband, for which I am most grateful. He is endeavouring to teach me some Norse words, so I am able to understand more of what is happening around me. Strangely, they have chosen not to adopt a more formal language like Latin and Norse is the language, both oral and written, of the court proceedings.

With your betrothal to Garnait, how goes it between you? Your marriage vows must be soon. Kildrummy is a fine castle, but will you miss the sea being surrounded so by hills and mountains? It, too, is a long way from home.

Another grand event was my coronation. When Bishop Narve placed the golden crown upon my head and handed me my sceptre, I saw, out of the corner of my eye, Father's eyes glisten and his chest swell with pride. In a quiet sort of way, we have become tolerably close since our journey together. He remains unsure of himself, angered by Grandfather's gruff criticism and weighed down by his burdensome tasks. Sadly, he cannot show his affection for me in public without feeling weakened.

You will all be pleased to know Aiofe has settled somewhat – since she determined we will not be slaughtered in the night by the ferocious guards or the sinuous monsters she envisions lurk in the slick, undulating sea beside our apartments. The fickle, flighty creature puffs herself up and lords it over the other servants just because of her long term of service with me. Bethoc has grown to tolerate Aiofe's brittle nature and quick outbursts and remains devoted to my welfare. I have also had assigned to me a skilled seamstress, Eithne, the daughter of some Irish thralls and a Gaelic speaker. Eithne and Bethoc have become allies in league together against Aiofe's sharp tongue.

I am fortunate to have made a dear friend – grey-haired Bishop Narve. His sharp wit and intellect belie his age. Having been educated at the universities of Paris and Bologna, he has a breadth of knowledge about the world and a keen legal mind, being both administrator and churchman. The king is not impressed, but I expect Alexander will be. The bishop's quiet strength and deep understanding of the people have been a great joy and aid to me. He and Master Weland often play chess together. Their battles of will and wit are entertaining to say the least.

Turnberry seemed a world away until yester eve, when my wedding gifts arrived with a German trader. Bethoc and Aiofe unpacked the trunks, filled with so many treasures. We could scarce conceal our delight. I was stunned by the sheer opulence of the gowns, and the fur-lined capes will keep me warm throughout winter. Father exhorted us to contain our excitement, but he is well-pleased all arrived in good order. Already, the scarlet bedcover looks impressive in the royal bedchamber. The magnificent silverware holds great value for the king and will be used on occasions of state. I was humbled Father had gone to such great expense for my trousseau. When I thanked him, he replied in his usual terse manner that it was not pure extravagance, but essential to establish our credentials as a family more than worthy of this royal connection. He gave a wry smile then, for he could see it was not me whom he needed to convince. You know how much he decries ostentation.

It surprised me to see one of Father's clerks, Neil Campbell, on board the trading vessel. He had been sent by Robert to ensure the gifts arrived safely given their great value. If I was hoping for some news of home, it was not to be, for the taciturn soul, having completed his task, conferred only with Father and Master Weland. The latter is now one of King Eric's trusted royal officials. This pleases Father for the doughty, plain-speaking fellow and his brother are supporters of our family.

Weland was a cleric at Dunkeld Cathedral before his skill as an administrator brought him to the attention of King Alexander. After the king's sudden death, the cleric's outspokenness saw him expelled by King Edward's administrators at the same time as many churchmen were removed from their positions – some found their way to France. Weland was welcomed into the realms of Norse diplomacy as a royal councillor. King Eric required someone with his discernment of Scottish affairs. A role was found for Henry, who functions as a trusted courier. Father believes Master Weland will be of great assistance to me in my new role and will be able to offer guidance in matters of state. Sometimes, our father chooses to forget I have a mind of my own, one that I fully intend to use. Yester eve, he told me I was far too much like Mother: her obstinacy, the bane of his life! He so rarely talks about her, but when he does, the sun shines on the past and warms our memories.

After his consultations, Father's clerk took a berth on a passing trading vessel and sailed forthwith, carrying messages of support on our behalf for the exiled Scots in Paris. I yearn for news of the family and know much is happening in our troubled land, but hear few details. Father tells me he wishes to remain until after the winter to consolidate our royal connections. He also seeks to avoid paying homage to Balliol at the ceremony at Stirling when Robert is confirmed as Earl of Carrick. No doubt our brother will need the firm guidance and support of the Steward and the Earl of Mar who are to act as his sponsors. I wager the parliament will be fraught with intrigue.

At last, the rough seas have settled. The festivities have come to an end and the many guests are departing. Both missives will be sealed with my new wax seal, which I keep, along with my writing tools and parchments, in the kist Rob had made. It has pride of place in my solar and reminds me always of home.

Isa

Scotland

Turnberry Castle

December 1293

Isa, dear heart,

It is indeed a challenge to write this missive, huddled as I am beside the hearth in our solar; any closer and my gown may start to smoulder. The fuel is damp; the flames, pitiful and the shutters do little to keep out the brisk wind. One of the maids just brought a hot stone for my feet. Such blessed relief!

Yester eve, we welcomed the arrival of the captain's vessel – especially since we had begun to have serious fears for its safety. The galley encountered a gale and suffered much damage. With its wool sail in tatters and walrus hide ropes lost overboard, the ship and its crew were fortunate to make it to one of Orkney's harbours. Timber for repairs had to be brought from Norway. All the same, we are grateful Turnberry continues to be a part of the captain's normal trading route.

Fearghas appears so fierce with that jagged scar upon his cheek. He reeks of tar and ale but has a kindly look to his eye. As you requested, he delivered your letters to my hand. So relieved was I to hear from you I both laughed and cried, confounding the gruff old fellow. Strange as this may sound, a cold, solid weight lifted from my chest. After you left, we were all so miserable, and then the weather turned foul for weeks. When the boys left to go to Dundonald, the corridors and stairwells, which had echoed with their laughter, were silent and empty. I could do nought but stare out to sea, praying it would deliver you safely to your destination. Alexander stayed on for a bit to read and coax us out of our dark thoughts, but in the end even he gave up and went back on his garron to his studies and the strict routine of the abbey.

On the first sunny morn, Mary and I rode our ponies up to the hills. The fresh air was so crisp and clear it was possible to see far-off Antrim. Luag lifted off my gloved hand and his slate-blue feathers rippled in the sun. For some time he did not return, until I began to fear he had flown off to find you. Then, his faint cry answered the groom's call and he returned with a young scaup duck – its crushed neck, bloody in his beak. Mary's goshawk flew low and fast over the woodland to snatch its prey: a fat, grey pigeon in blundering flight. Both would please Mhairi. Garnait was expected that night from

Lochmaben having become Grandfather's squire and thus allowed the occasional visit to me, his betrothed. Indeed, we have known Garnait for so long, Isa, from his frequent visits with his father, that it seems passing strange to imagine sharing a marriage bed with him. At least he is neither old nor toothless with foul breath and temper to match. Thank all the saints, he is gentle and kind, and his smile warms my heart. Sometimes Garnait's cough bothers him and I have taken to mixing him a soothing honey salve.

It will surprise you to hear Mother's morning room is still in use. Do you recall Floraidh, the midwife and healer from Lochmaben? Grandfather brought her here to help with the household's ailments. At her direction, Mary and I have gathered herbs from hill and shore. In a small closet we found some notes Mother had made. Now when I pound and mix the potions, I sense her standing nearby watching over me. The stillness and earthy smells of the chamber are much to my liking. It feels peaceful. From where I am sitting at Mother's trestle, I can see the sea and imagine it ebbing and flowing all the way to you, dear one.

We are in good health here apart from old Earchann, who injured his back after slipping on a waxing cloth left on the stairs by one of the maids. He lies now on a makeshift cot beside the kitchen fire enduring the ministrations of Mhairi. Ever fond of him, she tends the poor man as if he were a helpless bairn, feeding him wholesome broth and sweet possets.

When she can escape from our new maid's stern eye, Mary prefers to be down in the stable grooming the ponies or out in the fields watching the tiny new conies run about their burrows. It bothers her not they will end up as supper. Yester eve she was late back having gone out with old Fionnlagh to check on some ewes up in the corries. Grandfather says she should be full of shame coming back covered with hay and

37

muck and grass seeds in her rich brown hair, but he is secretly pleased. It seems she is much like his Isabel – our grandmother. For her lateness, Morag gave Mary a good shoogle and a tongue-lashing she will not forget soon, and added an extra piece of embroidery to finish for good measure. What with lessons from Father Dughlas over from the abbey, she is always amidst some vexatious discord. Her Latin is slipping and he is ill-pleased with her wilful inattention to algebra, so ready is she to run off in search of adventure. You remember how much she detests the effort of writing, preparing vellum and sharpening quills. Never have I seen anyone make such a mess with our precious ink. As usual, Mary is content for me to be the one to write and sends her love.

Morag cannot comprehend why we have lessons at all and would rather we were tutored in music, dance and the like. She was a maid in Queen Yolande's court and carries a vastly over rated opinion of herself. When King Alexander's widow left to go back to France, the household was dispersed amongst the Scots' magnates. In a fit of largesse, Grandfather offered her a place at Lochmaben, but even he grew tired of her elevated ways and acerbic tongue. Now, she graces us with her presence. Such a face she pulled when I told her the countess requested her daughters have lessons. Admiring Mother's thoughtful assessments and her skilful way with words, Father often bent before her strong will and agreed his daughters would do well to develop their minds. Morag proceeded to goad me even further and gave an indifferent shrug. As she walked before me down the stairwell, the desire to give her bony shoulders a shove proved a sore temptation.

Tomorrow is Yuletide. I wonder how you will be spending this special time in your new life as queen. We will do as we have always done, share gifts on the eve of Christ's birth and burn the Yule Log. Mhairi will prepare mulled wine. Grandfather will drink far too much at the banquet and fall asleep, mouth wide open, snoring loudly in his chair. The children will stay up to see the entertainment he has organised for them – a travelling mummer's show with puppets and the like. The following morn, we will walk across the bailey, our leather boots crunching on the white, frosted grass. In the small chapel, we will gather and say prayers for our mother's soul, our father's safe return and your continued health and happiness.

I have read your letters to the children. Mathilda insists on keeping a handful of hay under her pillow, perchance Brandubh is hungry after his long journey! I shall pass this missive to the captain. He will return to Norway as soon as the weather settles, after trading the rest of his cargo of furs and timber down the coast to the Isle of Man and across to Antrim. God speed!

Kirsty

CHAPTER FOUR

Norway

Bergen

March 1294

My dear Kirsty,

Your news filled me with longing. In my mind's eye, I could see all as you described. Indeed, our sister, Mary, is as contrary as ever. I do hope Grandfather is well and Earchann recovers from his injury. I was aggrieved to think of you all in our simple chapel with Mother's grave nearby and me so far away, but I took heart remembering our many happy times together. Here, a huge service was held in the Kristkirke. I felt so alone in the vast crowd.

Winter was relatively mild, but wet, of course, without the heavy snows the rest of the country endures. The old mariners say a warm current passes by the coast from far off in the west. It brings the rain and tempers the weather. You will not be surprised to hear our Yule festival was notable for its revelry.

With the short, dark days, I felt irritable and restless confined so much to the royal apartments. Now, it stays light and we are able to get outside more. It is pleasing to hear Luag is providing meat for the larder. Many birds of prey are exported from here – only by the king's regulation mind – so it was not difficult for me to choose one: a young, snow-white gerfalcon. Maon was bred by the king's falconer and is a most precious gift from my lord husband. Sometimes after our rides out hawking in the hills, I whisper in Brandubh's soft, sable ears. When he hears of the hay which awaits him at journey's end in far off Turnberry, he whinnies with pleasure. Father is due to depart soon. At our farewell, he exhorted me to be strong and bring honour to the Bruce name. It is indeed a struggle.

Isa

Scotland

Turnberry Castle

April 1294

Isa, dear heart,

Blustery winds brought Father's ship scudding across the waves. From atop the battlements, Mary shouted for us all to come and see. The chapel bell was rung and its deep peals echoed around the castle. What a welcome our guests received down at the dock! Everyone was calling out. Onchu barked and leapt over the boxes being off-loaded, almost knocking the captain into the water. A frenzy of activity erupted. Shouting at the scullions and serving maids to move their rear ends, Mhairi threw herself into a fluster, preparing a feast at short notice. From the launder room, young Dughall carried steaming pails of water for baths whilst other servitors struggled, heaving wooden trunks up to the hall and onto various chambers.

Now, slower moving, but of sound lungs, Earchann chided and harried the household, turning chaos into purposeful activity. With much ale consumed by the crew and the castle's retainers, the banquet was a merry event. Before departing for bed, we gathered in Father's solar to hear about far-off Norway. His tales were thrilling, though he must take greater care, lest the young ones conjure up warriors and savage beasties in their night's dreaming. He seems well-content your marriage brings such prestige to the family, and believes you are strong and will flourish if you set your mind to it. Later in our chamber, I read your letter once more, feeling at times forlorn, bemused as well, by the strangeness of your new life.

Rob is well and sends his love. He plans to depart soon to Ireland for a year or more to build our kinship networks inherited from Mother. Now Father is home, I expect we will see more of Thomas and Niall when the Steward comes to call. Alexander has procured two new manuscripts, one about the stars' constellations and the other on continental law. He is kept busy at the abbey. No doubt Father will venture forth soon to Crossragruel; he will want an update from the abbot as to how well our brother attends to his studies.

Grandfather is as choleric and irascible as ever. Red of face and in a temper, he fumes, grumbles and shouts about the developments here in Scotland. Most lately, he has been of an even more vexatious disposition and has taken upon himself to secure for his clerk, Thomas, the bishopric of Galloway: normally a Balliol patronage. What torment will befall us from this offensive, only the good Lord knows!

France is on the boil, as well, I hear, and King Edward's alliance is deteriorating into war over the status of his duchy in Gascony. While the mouser is away, the wee mice come out to play and the intrepid Welsh have risen against the English again. Our only grace is that Edward's cool grey eyes are not looking our way for once.

On a brighter note, I am to marry Garnait in the spring of next year and will leave for Kildrummy shortly before. Our hearts and minds are ever with you.

Kirsty

Norway

Bergen

October 1294

My dear Kirsty,

I received your letter from the hands of the captain, thankful his vessel carried everyone safely home and he continues to trade across the seas despite the rough conditions. He tells me the risk is great, but so is the financial gain when stocks are scarce in the winter months. The king was most appreciative of the grain and wool Father sent, knowing Norway produces so little of it. Our father's safe arrival was indeed a blessing, as the weather has been, at times, wild and ill-determined. No doubt he will be pleased to take over the reins once more to re-establish his control and mandate – especially with Rob away over to Antrim. All sound well, for which I give thanks.

Our lives have settled down now into a quieter routine. The king meets with his councillors and a large assembly known as a Ting is held when the freeman landholders come for judgements on issues of conflict. Bishop Narve is often present, but treads wearily as my husband does not welcome interference from clerics. Obtusely, he does not seem to mind Master Weland's input. The latter has shifted into his role of royal councillor with consummate ease. More often than not, the king is surrounded by a cohort of his personal guards and I have grown used to their powerful, silent presence. In the past, the huskarls would have served in wars, but now they are sent on diplomatic missions or to collect monies owed to the crown. I wager payment would be prompt! German merchants have been given royal permission to sail as far north as Bergen. These merchants have extensive influence on the continent and wish to establish themselves here. King Eric would like the benefit of their trade but is wary all the same. You might recall Father speaking of the Hansa, a conglomerate of traders from German towns like Lubeck, who are well settled at Berwick.

Recently we had some fine autumn days, clear and cool. I was able to explore the town precincts on foot along the sturdy, wooden planking with my lady-in-waiting, Thora, and, for safety, a brawny, helmeted huskarl by the name of Hauk Olafsson. Over a white linen shirt and a tunic called a kirtle, he wore a thick-pelted, brown bear skin. A silver amulet – the hammer of the pagan Norse god, Thor – hung on a leather thong around his neck. At his waist, a sharp seax was sheathed in a small scabbard, intricately carved and lined with wool. At first sight, Hauk appeared most fearsome, but I have seen him grow red-faced and bleak-eyed around Thora, the comely, fair-haired daughter of one of the king's administrators and widow of a trader lost at sea. It amuses me to watch them out of the corner of my eye, engaged as they are in the painful, awkward dance of early courtship. Perhaps, if Hauk were to don a thick woollen cloak instead of his bear pelt with its strange, musky odour, Thora's ardour may quicken!

Parallel to the harbour wall, there runs a long curved road named Ovrestretet. It is flanked by sod-roofed stalls where all manner of goods are crafted and displayed. Closest to the castle are the gold, silver and coppersmiths whose booths have earthen floors for fear of fire. Located at the far end of the narrow road just before the malodorous tannery, the ironmongers are deemed the greatest fire risk of all the crafts with their furnaces and bellows smelting ironstone from the bogs into transportable iron bloom, and fashioning so many utilitarian goods out of base metal. Bishop Narve recounted how the town, with its excess of wooden buildings, experienced the devastation of two fires, earlier in this century and the one prior. A deafening throng of patrons and servitors line the road, engaged in gossip and barter with the craftsmen. Such an array of crafts abounds: toggled, leather boots and carved belts; clinker-built pails and intricate, studded reindeer combs. Household goods, amulets and trinket boxes are carved from soapstone, reindeer, whale bone and the most costly, 'fish teeth' – the ivory tusks of the huge walrus, a creature from the far frozen north. Seated on stools in front of broad looms weighted with heavy stones, women weave imported wool into cloth, rich with the colours of moss, bracken and tree bark. Beside them, an old man fashions gaming pieces and boards out of slate and ivory, whilst his neighbour creates intricately-carved door frames.

At Bryggen harbour, only the traders in their tall, narrow buildings are permitted to sell the goods from the knarr, the wide-bellied vessels which trade from as far off as Byzantium. At my request, Thora purchased some fine fabric, vibrant silks and plush velvets, as well as tools for sewing: ivory pins, whalebone needles and two pairs of razor-sharp spring shears for cutting cloth. Sometimes three stories high, the cog-jointed, half-timbered shops have a shop at the base, an expanse of storage in the middle and accommodation for the trader's family at the top.

Alleyways, parallel to each other, link Ovrestretet to the busy harbour which reeks of tar and brine, overlaid by strange oriental aromas. Beside the water's edge, a baker and fish smoker sit cheek by jowl with the fish market, which sells peculiar bulbous-eyed fish and huge crustaceans, white bellies exposed and claws imprisoned by hempen twine. Barrels of codfish are salted and stored, while smaller fish lie in tubs, pickled in brine. The aroma of fresh-baked pies of smoked fish and eels curl and steal around empty bellies, appetites sharpened by the brisk sea air. All manner of goods can be found for sale: wool and flax; walrus and whale hide ropes; wooden clinkers for boat building, as well as tar and moss fir for calking.

The making of arms such as swords, round shields, the distinctive conical helmets with long nose shields and double-headed axes, are made by the ironmonger – to be sold at the king's discretion only, so Hauk tells me. The harbour teems with vessels. Sailors and warriors; farmers and tailors; bakers and launderers; butchers amidst bloody carcasses hanging from hooks; brewers of ale and mead – all rub shoulders in a heaving melee of sound above which cries of seabirds drift. Seeking snippets of food, urchins and curs wind their way through the crowd, whilst wiry black rats, their big ears twitching, sidle from ship to shadowed shore.

At night it is not safe to wander the alleyways – so I have been told by scrawny, skellie-eyed Ansell, one of the grooms. Beneath the smoking rushes, women ply their wares and disappear into the shadows for quick, furtive assignations with sailor and trader alike. Of course, Ansell tells me he tarries not, but wanders on in search of an ale and good company.

Bergen is astounding with its abundant trade offering the riches of the continent. It pulsates with life and colour. Truly, it is soft upon the eye, surrounded as it is by mountains. Some are so steep as to be almost vertical, such as the one behind Ovrestretet. Clothed in firs, larch and pine, the surrounding forest is a glorious, verdant place filled with noisy birdlife and small forest creatures, many of which I have never before witnessed. Beyond lie the wild valleys and mountains, home to wolf and brown bear. In the far north, the huge white bear lurks, hunting walrus, fat seals and beached whales. In the east, the sun rises over a treeless land of endless bog and rock-edged lochs. The bishop tells me Bergen means 'meadow surrounded by mountains'. With its islands and waterways, it is fair, but never as fine as home.

Your loving sister

Isa

Norway

Bergen

November 1294

My dear Kirsty,

Two weeks have passed and my parchment still rests within my kist. When the weather turned foul, the captain delayed his departure. The sky, bruised and black, shed a torrent of rain. The harbour was a heaving mess of masts, as vessels were tossed on waves so high sometimes it seemed they would vault over the rock walls. Peace reigns at last.

On the morrow, Fearghas expects to leave, so I must share my unrest with you in a brief despatch – just for yourself and Mary mind. Now, we reside in the royal apartments atop the tower and Aiofe spends her time staring from the windows. Silly dolt tells me she keeps watch lest the sea monster writhes over the sea wall and slithers, one can only guess, up the stairwell to tap on our door with a slimy tentacle. As if I am not taxed enough by my predicament, my patience wears thin and I have sent her to the harbour for some hairpins of which I have no need.

I am not yet with babe though am asked on a regular basis by my husband. He tells me his councillors have requested he make a greater effort. A son is required. I fear this will become a sore trial if I am not with child soon. My womb has bled so heavily on occasions Thora asked the midwife to check my body. This is far better than enduring the ministrations of the burly court doctor and his grimy, kneading paws. The king tells me he prays to Frey, god of fertility, and for me to do the same, but to Freya, his twin sister, goddess of love and sex.

This does not sit well with me. I go to the Kristkirke to pray to St Sunniva, whom the bishop assures me will offer help and guidance. Her story is most curious. Having escaped from danger in the lands to the west, she sailed across the sea and made landfall on an island near here. When warriors appeared, she hid with her retainers in a cave and, it is said, prayed the rocks at the cave's entrance would crash down which they did, saving her initially. Much later, a strange luminosity was sighted over the island. The king and local clerics went to investigate. Upon opening the cave, they found her body perfectly preserved! Her body was brought to Bergen, canonised by the Pope and here she rests.

Being a countrywoman, I hoped she might aid me and I implored her for help. My knees are red and swollen from kneeling so long in the cold, empty cathedral and my back aches. Gundred whispered she knew a volva, a seer who lives on the other side of the hills. She has amulets for just such things. Did I wish her to go there for me? If only Mother were here, she would know what ails me.

Isa

CHAPTER FIVE

Scotland

Turnberry Castle

February 1295

Isa, dear heart,

The winter tempests have proved unrelenting. Father welcomed the captain's safe arrival, for he had held grave fears for the ship's safety. Fearghas said his crew developed the flux so he put into the Shetlands. A priest aided them with fresh victuals and ale as the food on the vessel was rank and maggoty, spoiled as well by rain and seawater. In time, the captain took advantage of a break in the weather and made for Skye. The shelter provided by the many isles in the vicinity enabled the galley to continue southwards.

Your letters brought joy regarding all the new and different things in your life, but sadness as well. Mother is sorely missed at these times with her great experience. Mary believes riding a horse could be harmful. She could add nought else. So I knew none to ask, but Floraidh whom I took aside in confidence. She recalled a physician suggesting the placement of a warm poultice on the woman's belly and for her to rest and avoid distressing sights. Perhaps, Bethoc might help with the poultice and to keep Aiofe at a distance.

Grandfather released Garnait from being his squire. We make ready to depart and the long, daunting journey by horse to Kildrummy is ahead of us. Father arranged for Morag to attend me. I requested Dughall's sisters, Seonaid and Marthoc, go in her place. He raised an eyebrow but approved the request. Mary and the girls will visit us later in the year. I am to wear Garnait's mother's wedding dress, an odd request from his father who has had it locked in a trunk since her death. In case the moths have nibbled upon it, I am taking a silken gown which will do very well. Perhaps, if I beseech St Sunniva...?

I wonder how we might continue our correspondence. Alexander thinks mendicant monks travel across the northeast between the abbeys. They might consent to take my letters. Surely Garnait's father will have some contacts amongst the traders setting out from Aberdeen or Arbroath to Bergen.

Be brave, dear one. Perhaps the blessed St Sunniva will hear both our prayers?

Yours aye
Kirsty

Scotland

Turnberry Castle

May 1295

Isa, dear heart,

I bear sad tidings. Grandfather collapsed onto the floor of his solar at Lochmaben. Shortly thereafter, he breathed his last. It was Easter Eve. Fearghas stayed his departure for the funeral and is now ready to leave with the tide. We are all asunder, already missing so much: Grandfather's strength, his astute eye and robust voice. Only dim echoes remain. Who will guide us now? Rob returned from Antrim and at the funeral spoke of all the things Grandfather achieved in his life: feudal lord of many estates, Lord of Annandale and Hartlepool, a justiciary, constable of both Scotland and England, regent of Scotland and a Tanist for the throne of Scotland. Christina, Grandfather's second wife, of whom we have heard or seen so little, came to the funeral, but had words with Father. It would be about the will, I wager. Soon after, she returned to her home in Ireby across the Solway. Rob and Edward are to take his body, once treated, all the way to Guisborough. Despite the ruinous state of the priory from the fire, which raged some decades ago, Grandfather will be content at long last to sleep beside his ancestors.

Wish me well, for I leave on the morrow for a new life.

As ever

Kirsty

Scotland

Kildrummy Castle

June 1295

Isa, dear heart,

It has been a long time since we have heard from you. Perhaps the role of queen occupies you overmuch? It is what I tell myself, for I cannot bear to think any harm has befallen you.

I have much news to share about my new home. Surrounded by forested hills and with the bare mountains beyond, Kildrummy Castle is well-situated above a ravine. At first sight, it took my breath away. It *is* beautiful. Garnait hoped I might love his home as much as he does and his eyes shone with pleasure at my response. Though similar to

Turnberry, it seems more imposing. The walls are the palest gold in colour – much like Mhairi's finest oatmeal – and its shape follows that of a broad shield. At its most rounded point, enormous oak doors are flanked by two sturdy towers and a large drawbridge crosses a steep-sided, dry moat.

Our chambers lie atop the Snow Tower, five floors up. I can see forever across the countryside, but it is most strange. I miss the briny freshness of the sea and the shore to wander upon. The first night, sleep evaded me. Peculiar noises punctuated the darkness. The bark of night-creatures competed with the hoarse, throaty calls of the frogs in the ravine far below my window. The hooting of owls in the forest floated above the usual castle sounds: hounds howling, horses stamping on the cobblestones, the guards' rumbling laughter and the chink of armour upon stone. For hours I lay awake, trying to gather the memory of rolling waves and the drifting cries of gulls close to my breast. All the while, the north wind continued, weaving its mournful path around and through the tower. Eventually, it soared away into the darkness. Only then could I rest.

One of the intriguing aspects of my new home is within the Snow Tower. It was built over a small well and running up through the central winding stairwell is a sturdy pulley system, enclosed for safety, with a pail that can be filled with water and hoisted upwards. Such convenience is a boon.

As I hoped, Garnait is a gentle, loving husband despite being susceptible to chills and what not. Sometimes I seem more nurse than wife. While I go out hawking, he is content by the fire in his solar with manuscripts brought over by monks, the source of much of our news, on their rough, sturdy garrons. You will be pleased to know Luag is flourishing, having recovered from being caged for so long during the journey here. He is still as sleek and supple as he always was, bringing down items of small game with great accuracy and swiftness.

St Sunniva's blessings were unnecessary in the end. Though cream with age, the silk gown was trimmed with lace from Flanders; its bodice shimmering with silvery pearls. A little tight, it fitted me well enough and in all the right places according to Garnait's father who was brimming with mirth and mead. Aglow in a pool of soft sunlight filtering from the three tall chancel windows, Garnait and I exchanged vows to the cheers and murmurs of the family and household gathered in Kildrummy's chapel. A fine repast followed in the Great Hall with the sweet music of lyre, harp and flute floating down from the gallery above. Rob will be coming north soon to marry Isabella, and will bring Mary and the girls with him. Thank the Lord, for I have sorely missed the family! Hopefully they will be permitted to stay awhile in these troubled times. Father has gone south to Essex with much to do sorting through Grandfather's estate with his executors, John de Tocotes and old Master Adam, now Sir Adam de Crokdak.

Tomas, a thin, grey-haired monk who acts as a courier, passes on a roundabout journey through this area from the priory of Pluscarden on his way to Arbroath Abbey. He has agreed to carry my letter with all haste and care. The abbot, he says, will seek out a vessel carrying cargo to Bergen. Tomas will call again upon his return and take my letter to the harbour closest to his priory in the north. With silver coins jangling in his leather purse, a bag stuffed full of fine victuals and sufficient ale for the journey, he awaits my sealed parchment. Dear one, I long to hear your news and to know you are well and untroubled.

Kirsty

Norway

Bergen

July 1295

My dear Kirsty,

It was passing strange to receive news of Grandfather's death so long after it happened. Since then, my troubles have worsened. I can scarce believe it. Some months ago, after many hours of travail, I delivered a babe. No sound did he make and the smiles and joyful murmurings, which should have welcomed him, were painfully absent. Little enough chance either to even gaze upon his small, perfect features before his tiny body was ripped from my arms and placed – who knows where? Not I that is for certain! I am angry beyond bearing and know not what I have done to bring this fate upon such an innocent. St Sunniva must be asleep in her shadowed tomb, deaf to my pleas. At night, it angers me to see the stars flash their hard, glittery eyes. Daytime brings the sun. It, too, mocks me, shining its brazen light so wilfully through my window. With all hope departed, its warmth cannot penetrate such grey despair.

The king will not speak of the dark vale between us and avoids my eye, but our bedchamber is busy at night. It is a sore trial, indeed. He seeks another child sooner rather than later. Have they no sorrow in their hearts, those high and mighty men of the king's court?

I am desperately weary, and the hours pass by slowly. Bethoc sits with me, speaking little. She is content with her embroidery and her presence is a comfort. Yester eve, Gundred hung an amulet on a leather thong around my neck. I wonder? Will it aid me?

Isa

Scotland

Kildrummy Castle

September 1295

Isa, dear heart,

Your torment and despair have brought such sadness. Though months have passed and the leaves are turning, I pray your heart and body have healed. I lit a candle in the chapel for your little one and hope our prayers find him, safe and warm in the arms of an angel. Isabella, Robert's new wife, and our good sister, was with me and lit one for our brother. He is now far away.

So much has happened here. Scotland has festered and the pustule burst. War is upon us! Father swore fealty to King Edward of England and is now constable of Carlisle Castle, as was Grandfather many years ago. Mid-year, in a constitutional revolt, the Scottish parliament resolved to take the government out of Balliol's hands due to his incompetency. A council of twelve was elected in his stead. Now, the Guardians formulate a treaty with Philippe, King of France. In the event of an incursion from England, the French are to come to our aid or at least provide a diversion. Furious at such collusion, Edward gathers his forces. He is close to destroying the Welsh, inch by inch, having constructed mighty castles to defend his bloody territory. The English war machine now wends its way towards Scotland.

Father will not support the Balliol pretender, as he calls him, and refused to attend the Scottish host with troops from Annandale. In doing so, he protects his estates in England, but what of our homeland? In anger, King John Balliol gave Annandale to our staunchest enemy, John the Red Comyn. His troops have despoiled our family home, as have the English soldiers in turn.

The Abbot of Crossragruel arranged for Alexander to travel south to Writtle, where he will remain under the care of Grandfather's attorneys. With Cambridge University not too far away, he may be able to pursue his studies. Niall and Thomas have been sent to Mother's kinfolk in Antrim, out of harm's way until they are of an age to fight. Our brother, Edward, is with Rob at Carlisle. Of the household, Dughall and the servitors have gone south to Carlisle with the troops, whilst Earchann arrived here with Mhairi, Floraidh and the maids just this morn, worn and weary from the long, dangerous ride on their bony garrons. Morag's bitter complaints still ring in my ears. If only she had been required in Carlisle – anywhere, but here! Thank the Lord, Garnait was too unwell to go to war, but his father departed with his troops to join the Scottish host as they head to Carlisle. Grandfather would be twisting in his grave, ere he knew Bruce and Mar fought on opposite sides. Our prayers are with all our menfolk regardless. Scotland needs your prayers, Isa. We all do.

Be strong of heart, dear one, for I must also tell you Robert's Isabella is with child, due in the new year. I was loath to write of this, but the news has brought such joy to us all here.

Your loving sister
Kirsty

Norway

Bergen

October 1295

My dear Kirsty,

Forgive me! Such a mess I have made in my haste. No time for repair – Fearghas is due to depart with the tide. He will carry my letter to Aberdeen and assures me it will reach you. You will be relieved to know the cloud of darkness which so troubled me, has lifted. I know not where my grief has gone, perhaps to some quiet, shadowed corner of the soul to settle and mourn in peace. My life is drifting back into focus. No longer do I feel so cold as if the marrow of my bones, having turned to ice, is now experiencing some strange, internal thaw.

You may wonder what occurrence could presage such change. Perceptive as ever, Bishop Narve bought me a gift which he had purchased from a Byzantine trader: a tiny, orphaned canine from Pomerania. When the little mite's pink tongue licked my hand, the world seemed to come back into focus, alive with colour once more. At the sound of my laughter, warm smiles blessed the faces of my companions. With his curly tail askew, this pug-nosed ball of golden fluff is my joy and constant companion. I have named him Solas. Much to Aiofe's disgust, he piddled on her shawl which she had left lying beside the settle and chewed one of her leather boots! So not only is he beautiful, but a fine judge of character.

Yours aye
Isa

Norway

Bergen

November 1295

My dear Kirsty,

Once again, our letters have crossed. Many tears have I shed for our family, torn as we are from our beloved lands. Isabella's news was painful to read, but I do wish them well. Rob must be content to have a child, hopefully an heir, so soon into his marriage. Father *will* be pleased.

Apart from what Fearghas gleans from harbour taverns, I hear little, save Carlisle is still in English hands. After his last visit to Turnberry, he departed at night lest his cargo be taken without payment by the troops. Taking pity upon my distress, my lord husband advised of recent developments with King Philippe of France. A pledge has been made. Norway's part is to aid our joint friends, namely France and Scotland, and hinder their enemies rather than invade England for that is beyond this country's capacity. A large fleet of Norse galleys is to be sent to supplement the French fleet; some of which Philippe has already sourced from Genoa whilst others are being assembled in Normandy.

Master Weland tells me the barons have a powerful influence upon my husband. It is to Scotland's benefit in support of an alliance: Scotland's agreement with France stipulates King John Balliol's son, Edward, is to marry Jeanne, the niece of King Philippe. Such a threat could not be borne by the English and so King Edward, too, makes treaties, this time with his allies in Germany, Spain and the Low Countries. It seems my husband is no longer on good terms with the English monarch.

Regards our family's allegiances, I am uncertain, awash

with disbelief if truth be known. Father seeks to protect our lands in England and plays a dangerous game with King Edward. Will the hare outwit the sleekit fox? Disquiet fills my heart for I know Scotland will be forever home.

Isa

CHAPTER SIX

Scotland

Kildrummy Castle

February 1296

Isa, dear heart,

I have delayed writing to you – such is our news. I had best begin at the beginning. A few weeks before New Year, after a long night and day of birth pangs, Isabella gave birth too early. Despite being bruised and battered, the babe continues to thrive. Rob called her Marjorie – a name we all cherish. Sometime later, Isabella faded from our lives; her blood staining the bed linen and running onto the chamber floor. Our brother was as pale as the snow-covered ground in which we buried Isabella. Entrusting Marjorie to our care, Rob left us after the funeral. Fate has dealt him a heavy blow.

Yuletide was a silent, gloomy affair as you can well imagine. At its end, our relief was palpable. A wet nurse sees to Marjorie's needs. Strangely, our lives are uplifted by her precious birth. Mathilda plays with her and Margaret tries to carry her with swaddling, dragging and catching on the rushes from cradle to bed. Mary inspects her daily as she would lamb or calf and assures us of her fine condition. The poor bairn puts up with my feeble attempts at the old Gaelic lullabies. Usually, she ceases her fearsome wails and focuses her dark eyes upon me, intent upon the strange warble issuing from my lips.

Eager to escape his own despair and the grieving household, Isabella's father left to attend the Scottish parliament where the treaty with France was ratified. Dire times lay ahead. Some of the Scots went on raiding missions across the English border to Wark Castle where they undertook a surprise attack; unsuccessfully, it seems. Others moved south, burning, killing, pillaging as they went on their way to capture Carlisle Castle. Without siege engines, it was an impossible task. You may have heard Father and Robert commanded the garrison. Believe me when I say they had no choice. The Comyns would have every Bruce dead or in exile. Thus for a while, we fight for the English king, if only to survive.

After only a day or two, the Scots' earls retired, some going to their own territories in the north. Full of bile and impatient to redress these perceived betrayals, Edward moved his armies north. On 30th March, Berwick, that most industrious Scottish border town of traders, merchants and artisans, was placed under siege. Edward's massive army poured over the defences, a paltry ditch and palisade, and entered the town on a rampage of slaughter. The king ordered the sack of the city. No townsfolk were to be spared. Some eight thousand citizens – men, women and children – were killed; their bodies left to rot in the streets. Some were deposited into hastily-dug ditches or thrown into the sea. Seeking sanctuary, Flemish traders barricaded themselves into their headquarters. When soldiers set the Red Hall ablaze, those within perished.

The garrison commander, Sir William Douglas, realising the siege could not be withstood, parleyed for an honourable surrender. But, when the castle's gates were opened upon his orders, most were put to the sword. Stout-hearted Sir William is lucky to be alive, after the tirade he launched upon his captors. Berwick's fate caused many a proud heart to harden against King Edward. Northwards, King John's army crossed to Dunbar Castle where the earl's wife hoaxed the guards into opening the gates to the Scots, whilst her lord husband was away supporting the English.

In April, Father was summoned to attend King Edward at Salisbury to swear fealty and gather his troops; Scots once more fighting Scots – the downfall of our country! At Dunbar, the army was routed with many killed and captured. It is known now as the Dunbar Drave. Afterwards, almost one hundred nobles were sent to the Tower of London. Chief amongst these were the Earls of Atholl, Mar, Ross and Menteith, who led the force which occupied Dunbar Castle.

Garnait was overwrought to learn his father awaits his fate in the Tower. The veritable heart of Scotland has been clawed out, Isa, and flung as carrion to the crows.

Kirsty

Norway

Bergen

April 1296

My dear Kirsty,

Poor Isabella – to die after so much pain! A sore blow indeed for Rob and the child! It is difficult to comprehend the extent of our country's ruination after Dunbar. Words fail me! All I have are prayers for the living as well as for the dead.

Isa

Scotland

Kildrummy Castle

September 1296

Isa, dear heart,

Your prayers are needed. The events of the last few months have left us drained and fearful. After the debacle at Dunbar and in the face of King Edward's might, the community of the realm began to crumble, at least on the surface. The Steward surrendered Roxburgh Castle. Edinburgh held out for but a week and Stirling, abandoned by its garrison, was left empty; its gates open to the invaders. Weakened and humiliated, King John Balliol was impelled to resign his crown at Brechin Castle in July. The royal tabard was ripped from his person, and his seal shattered. They mock him now as 'Toom Tabard' or 'empty coat'. King Edward stole our most precious relic, Saint Margaret's Holy Rood of the Cross, as well as the royal regalia, jewellery and much silver plate.

Most telling of all was the theft of the Stone of Destiny, removed from its resting place in the abbey at Scone. Scotland's ancient tradition of royal enthronement on the Stone will be forever denied if Edward has his way: he plans to have a wooden throne constructed over it, so his dominion of our country will be complete. With Scotland beaten and despairing, the vultures have flown in. Nobles in Edward's army are rewarded with the lands of Scottish lords who were present at the defeat of Dunbar. Widows of those killed live in dire poverty, having lost their lands and livelihoods. With husbands imprisoned, many are forced to petition the English courts with little success. Despite this, most remain steadfast in their loyalty.

August found our father and brother summoned to Berwick Castle to renew their pledge of homage and fealty to Edward. We are an embittered, divided people. Our lord father is less than contrite, believing he could not fight for King John Balliol who is supported by the Comyns, our mortal foe. Nor could we win against Edward's enormous war machine. Rob remains silent on these divisive issues. Perhaps he will come soon to visit his daughter.

Instead, venal Edward gloats over our lands and people. For two days, his army camped around the castle and we were forced into polite, strained submission. I was thankful Mary held her vengeful tongue. With Garnait's father and so many friends in the Tower, it was imperative we avoid giving offence that might imperil them further. Providing food for the horde left us almost without supplies. I swear they would have eaten the horses had not word come for them to move on. Relief only came when they rode away, the tension in my head and chest lifting. It was like having a viper in my bed.

King Edward installed Hugh de Cressingham as his treasurer in Scotland. The people call him 'the treacherer', for the man bleeds Scotland dry in order to fill English war coffers. Though fortunate to be so isolated, we feed many of the homeless here at Kildrummy, those who cannot afford the high taxes. Tomas reports much poverty and distress on his travels, especially around the towns oppressed by sheriffs and the like. Pray for us and Scotland.

Yours aye

Kirsty

Scotland

Kildrummy Castle

October 1296

Isa, dear heart,

In a curt dispatch, Father relayed that the lordship of Annandale is back in his hands. From his tone, our lack of support continues to vex him. That cannot be gainsaid.

An agreement was reached regarding the dower lands of Grandfather's widow, Christina of Ireby; an irksome task, out of the way. Most astounding of all, Father says he has wed again – to a Lady Eleanor. How strange it is that we now have a stepmother!

Kirsty

Norway

Bergen

November 1296

My dear Kirsty,

Saddened though I am by your news, I feel a sense of wonderment. In early spring, I am due to give birth. The king is much relieved and most felicitous of my welfare. To whom I owe this blessing, I know not; St Sunniva or the seer over the hills? Bless them both!

Oft times, I wonder how our brothers fare. I miss seeing you all and can scarce believe we have a stepmother. Pray God keeps you all safe.

Isa

Scotland

Kildrummy Castle

December 1296

Isa dear heart,

One last missive before year's end! Your news was received with joy and prayers – for your continued good health and a safe delivery. You will be relieved to know Marjorie continues to flourish, as do both Mathilda and Margaret.

Heralding a brief respite from the harsh realities of this year, Robert and Edward arrived to spend Yuletide with us and brought news. I fear Rob is much changed. Now wary of slights, imagined or otherwise, he is short of temper. Anger and frustration lie just below the surface. It never was his way to be so ill at ease with his family, nor to smile so rarely. Much of his time has been spent with Garnait, who has such an easy, perceptive way with him. But during quiet times, Rob and I found time to talk, often beside the hearth with some wine to ease the conversation.

As the head of the family, Father has a rightful hold upon our oldest brother. With the yoke of filial duty heavy around his neck, Rob says he now knows how an ox must feel, yoked to a plough and caught within a deep, endless furrow. The past year has lain such a heavy toll upon him he is fit to burst, to escape the path upon which he has been set and is at wits' end to avoid direct engagement with our countrymen. This has grown more difficult with each passing day. When the Scots' army, under the foolhardy leadership of the Comyn, besieged Carlisle Castle, this task was rendered impossible.

Carrick's lands lie destroyed; its people oppressed and

despairing. Worst of all is the disgust Rob sees in their eyes, mirroring his own, even though many of our nobles have vacillated and changed sides. He is tortured by the path which lies before him.

Our brother knows full well the Scots cannot win against the might of England on the battlefield. Only a fool, he says, would underestimate King Edward's power, but many have not seen it firsthand as he has and think bravery will win the day. If Edward has his way, Scotland will be crushed. There has to be another path! We cannot succeed without monies from our estates to fund these wars. Thus, keeping our lands is pivotal and we cannot win unless we are united. Bruce and Balliol cannot work together. Therefore, one must triumph over the other or come to some arrangement or we wait. And this waiting, shifting allegiances, sliding from one side to the other, is most galling.

Father tells Rob it is the same as in battle: to survive above all else you must stay on your destrier, moving this way and that, to avoid your enemy's lance. If you or your horse falls, you will most certainly die and your dreams with you. But Father is, by nature, a cautious man and our brother, a warrior, full of the vigour of youth. He would prefer to kill the enemy outright in a fair fight and be done with it. Rob worries at these issues, like a starving hound gnaws at the hind bone of a deer, and his sleep suffers. I fear it will be awhile before any resolution is reached.

Despite the chill wind and flurries of sleet, Edward went hunting with Mary in the forest to the north of us. He has his eye on young Isobel, the pretty daughter of Sir John, so they found themselves at Strathbogie Castle and stayed awhile. It was late when they returned home. I had grown anxious, for many dangers lurk in the forest. They both laughed and scoffed at my weak spirit. Being skilled hunters, they chided that no harm would befall them. At least the hunt was successful; the stag they brought back with them will be essential to our survival.

Edward seems older and more sure of himself now, but it is just an illusion. Living in Rob's shadow, he masks his insecurities and petty jealousies behind a wall of rash bravado. About his person, there is none of Robert's prudence or self-awareness. For Edward, much like Mary, there are no greys, only black and white. How much simpler would the world be if it were so?

Rob has written to you and is hopeful the letter arrived safely. He seeks for us to understand the challenges he faces and hopes we continue to hold him in high regard, trusting his judgement, strange and contrary though it may seem at times. From the boys in Antrim, he brought news. They are in fine fettle and find the Irish women much to their liking! Both are honing their skills ready for the call they know will come. Alexander has requested entry into the University of Cambridge for next year's intake. We are so proud of him.

Father spends his time either with his new wife at Lochmaben or at Carlisle Castle where he is governor. Robert could tell me little about our new stepmother other than she is plain and thin, but makes the old man laugh. Always a good thing, I should think! Edward described her as an insignificant widow of a lesser noble, but could tell me nought else. Here is a quarry of information and our menfolk do not seek to mine its depths! Our family trips and stumbles along a fateful path. Who knows where we will all be at winter's end?

Kirsty

Norway

Bergen

December 1296

As the year drew to a close, Isa received a letter from Robert. It was the first time he had written to her since she had left Turnberry over three years ago. Clutching the fine, calfskin parchment to her breast, she made her way over to the window embrasure where the light was marginally better. Solas jumped up on the padded seat and laid his head upon her lap. Outside, it was a grey day and a soft mizzle was falling. The sea smelt stale, full of the refuse thrown into it; the tide had yet to wash it clean. Above the gentle lapping of waves, the relentless cry of sea birds could be heard. Nestled within her thick woollen shawl, Isa broke the heavy seal and began to read, oblivious to all but the words before her.

London

October 1296

Dearest Isa,

This letter comes to you by the hand of Jan Falko, a trustworthy merchant within the Hansa group, who hails from the German town of Lubeck. The Bruce contract for our English wool exports has been with his family for many years. Forgive me for not writing sooner, but I have been wary lest my words fall into the wrong hands. As you know, English ships patrol our waters seeking to cut off our trade with other countries and to prevent any aid reaching us. My seal is in lead, so it can be disposed of overboard on the journey if necessary. Equally, please burn this missive after reading it.

It was Jan's brother, Otto, who brought you our wedding gifts a couple of years ago. I hope you liked the presents we sent you. The girls had the capes fur-trimmed, as we knew Norway would be cold, but I doubt the wintry conditions would be much of a shock to someone reared at Turnberry. We hoped the bed linen, coverlets, silver plate and dishes would be of use in your new life. The kist was from me. I had it painted in red and gold for Bruce and Scotland, with a sprinkling of Lions Rampant to remind you that you may be the Queen of Norway but you are first, and always, a princess of Scotland.

Our fortunes are at low ebb. I speak both of Scotland and Bruce. As you know, we could never pay homage to King John Balliol or his Comyn kinsmen. Nor could many of our friends and allies accept this hopeless man as King of Scots. It was an intolerable situation. In January, we received a summons from Balliol. We refused to raise our forces and, in consequence, lost our Scottish lands at one stroke. I took fifty men from Carrick and Annandale and a dozen knights only. These I led to Carlisle, where Father had been appointed governor. All our other men were instructed to stay home, guard their possessions as best they could and wait for our return. Edward of England was marching north and there was little doubt Balliol would be destroyed. Carlisle was besieged by Alexander Comyn, Earl of Buchan, who had been given Annandale by Balliol. He had no siege engines. We manned the walls, using the citizens of the town and my men. After a poor attempt to rush the gates, they fell back, burning and murdering on the way.

This folly left Edward of England a free hand to lay siege to Berwick, which he did with his usual efficiency and brutality. When it fell, there was butchery for two days. It turned my stomach when I saw the destruction and death:

many thousands, slaughtered. Edward then turned the place into his base for the invasion of Scotland and brought English settlers north to replace those many good Scots, so cruelly murdered. Before I arrived, he had struck north and met Buchan and the Scottish army at Dunbar. It was all too easy for the English when Buchan let the Scots attack off the hill to the west of the town. It was utter folly. By night on 27th April, the majority of the Balliol/Comyn faction was either dead or in the hands of the English. I care not about their fate, bar many of our friends like Mar and Atholl who sided with Balliol. Too many good, ordinary Scots folk would grieve that day as well. I then accompanied King Edward north, turning off to reoccupy our own lands of Carrick and Annandale (and repair some of the damage left behind).

In July, the English monarch caught up with 'King' John Balliol at Montrose. It was pathetic. He yielded not only himself, but also Scotland to Edward, muttering about evil counsel and his own simplicity. He had the royal arms of Scotland torn from his tabard and trampled on the floor. 'King Nobody', 'Toom Tabard', is king no more. After a leisurely progress to Elgin, Edward returned via Perth where he removed the Stone of Destiny from Scone.

By August we were back in Berwick, where every landowner in Scotland was forced to swear fealty to Edward. He let it be known there would be no other King of Scots. When Father spoke with him, Edward said, "Have we nothing else to do, but win kingdoms for you?" Thus, it was clear he means to incorporate not only Wales, but also Scotland into one kingdom. Englishmen have been appointed sheriffs all over Scotland, supported by thousands of English soldiers. The Earl of Surrey acts as viceroy whilst Cressingham is treasurer; Amersham, chancellor and Ormsby, chief justice. Effectively, Edward means to abolish Scotland. Father had pinned his hopes on Edward and has now returned to Hatfield in anger; his bleak spirit overwhelmed with hopeless despair. For myself, I will bide my time. Edward means to spend next year campaigning in France and the Scots may yet prove less pliant to his will than he expects.

Kirsty told me about the loss of your son and that you are once more with child. I pray all goes well for you. We have both had our share of sadness; for you will know I married Isabella of Mar last year and she is already dead, leaving me with a daughter. Marjorie has a mop of black hair and huge dark eyes. Luckily, our sisters have time for the babe. I have hardly been able to see her. She will grow up in better hands than mine, thankfully, and I can only hope she knows her father loves her, though he shows it poorly. What it is to be a Bruce! I wish we were back on the links of Turnberry, but I fear such happiness will never return at least to me.

Your loving brother
Rob

CHAPTER SEVEN

Norway

Bergen

March 1297

My dear Kirsty,

Two weeks past, my daughter entered the world. The wind howled and sleet battered the windows. I neither knew, nor cared, caught up as I was with birth pangs. Sigrud, a haggard-toothed crone, coaxed her out with the most gentle of hands boasting as she did so that she had delivered half of Bergen. With her was a lass, whose infant had succumbed to a fever. Now the girl seeks relief from her swollen breasts and welcomes the coins her wet nurse tasks will bring.

Gundred ventured the babe looks like the king, but she reminds me of Mother. Something about the firm, little chin stirs a memory in me. Her father named her Ingeborg after his mother. Though the name means 'beautiful one', it does not sit well upon my tongue, so I shall call her Inga. My lord husband withdrew after our child's birth – after the councillors who were present showed their displeasure at my failure to provide a male heir. It angered me to hear he had gone hunting with them but yester eve, he came to visit and stayed awhile. As he waved a wooden rattle in front of Inga's tiny face, a bleak smile creased his face. I feared his disappointment more than I can say, and was relieved to learn his sadness came from the past: our daughter reminded him of his little Maid so much that he shrank from contact. Memories of her loss and the death of our son reside with him still, though he speaks not of it. For a long time, he held our child in his arms and gave voice to a grief long buried. It was a special moment for us – a family, at long last.

It is the custom here to baptise royal babies in the Kristkirke. Bishop Narve was kind enough to warm the water in the baptismal font so Inga would be at peace when he bought her into the fold. When comments came afterwards that she was such a good baby gurgling with pleasure during the ceremony, he winked at me and smiled.

Forgive me for being so caught up in my own affairs that I have not made mention of the news in your last correspondence. Our family mire seems to have thickened, though Rob may surprise all and break free to be his own man. Assure him my trust and affection remains as steadfast and resolute as ever. I pray he and our brothers remain safe.

Your loving sister
Isa

Scotland

Kildrummy Castle

July 1297

Isa, dear heart,

Words cannot express how relieved and elated we were to hear your news. We pray all is well with you these many months on.

It is midsummer and the hills are bathed in purple heath. The children spend much time out in the sunshine, riding their ponies around in the bailey or plowtering about floating leaves and sticks over the waterfalls in the ravine under the watchful eye of the guards and the sonsy sisters, Marthoc and Seonaid. Somehow, the wee girls always come back up to the postern gate happily droukit. During a patch of bad weather, Tomas consented to teach Mathilda the rudiments of writing. She is clumsy still and unable to fashion letters, her hand tiny around the quill. For the most part, she slaisters herself with ink or tickles her sister with the feather's tip. The old priest is a patient teacher and ignores the giggles. He is somewhat hard of hearing and his sight has dulled with the years. Surely a blessing in this case!

Marjorie smiles often. She loves her bath and the wooden toys, a bird and otter, carved by Earchann. We have to watch her on the winding stairwell as she has had some tumbles crawling after the children. I imagine by now Inga will be sitting up and teething. How Bethoc must love having a bairn to sing to sleep with her soothing lullabies. Margaret is besotted with Marjorie and follows her around, copying Morag who tuts and huffs if the child falls in the dirt. Whenever Morag is not looking, Mhairi smothers her with kisses and feeds her sweet possets. Ne'er have I seen two grown women vie so fiercely for the affections of a bairn. Isa, we are as happy as we can be given the times we live in.

King Edward and his host have not come back this way. It is probably just a matter of time. In May, an insurrection began over in Lanark with the first blow struck by William Wallace, a giant of a man with a grudge against an English sheriff, William Hesilrig, whom he slew in revenge for the death of his wife. Oppressed and angry, a host gathers behind him. Even Sir William Douglas joined his band after his escape en route to the Tower from Berwick. Andrew Murray, another escapee – this time from Chester – led the townsfolk of Aberdeen to Loch Ness and an assault on Castle Urquhart.

Next, Garnait heard that Robert wilfully failed to deliver the son of William Douglas to the king's officials and then joined with Wishart, the bishop from Glasgow, and Sir James Stewart over in Irvine. After breaking free of Father's tight reign, Rob found to his frustration that the two elder statesmen planned to capitulate to the larger English forces after drawn-out negotiations, allowing Wallace time to create havoc further in the east. This worked for a month or so until Percy and Clifford demanded Marjorie as a hostage. Under the cover of darkness, Robert and his men departed in haste.

Along with Sir Alexander Lindsay, the bishop and the Steward were taken into custody as sureties until Robert delivered up his daughter; the hapless group knowing hell would freeze over before this would happen. Sir William Douglas was taken as well. King Edward has pardoned the Comyns, John of Badenoch and John of Buchan, for their recent transgressions with the proviso they not serve England's enemies over the sea. They returned north, but did little to halt the spreading chaos. Insurgents seized a number of English-held castles including Inverness, Elgin and Banff.

Wallace carried out many audacious raids as far as Carlisle and Newcastle, but with little real success lacking siege engines to batter impenetrable castle walls. By the time Robert joined him, the raids were smaller, intent on harrying the officials, sheriffs, bailiffs and the like, preventing the raising of revenue for Edward's French campaign.

Garnait is brimming with news. Our oppressors are scurrying back to England. Tomas stands by to take my parchment. With our area in uproar, he has waited until now for the dust to settle before venturing north.

As ever
Kirsty

Norway

Bergen

September 1297

My dear Kirsty,

Your news intrigued the king. Wallace holds the power of the people. Do the nobles accept him? Are they outlaws, now, living in the forest? And Father? Is he still at Carlisle? Now Robert is beyond his influence, our father's wrath will be something to behold. It would be as well if Rob made himself scarce. Thank the Lord our younger brothers are out of the country.

Forgive me, for I must be completely selfish and share Inga's news. Almost eight months old now, she crawls everywhere and is the delight of all who see her. Solas is her devoted companion. He sits when she sits, moves when she does, and cares not if she pulls his tail. It amuses her no end to see it spring back into its tight round curl. My lord husband is keen for her to become accustomed to sailing in his galley. For safety, she is tied onto Eithne's back with a long sash looped around her midriff. Like her father, Inga is happiest on the water.

On fine days, we sail to nearby islands calling in on some of the farms belonging to Eric's kinfolk. Beneath sod roofs, the boat-shaped longhouses are partitioned, with sections for sleeping and entertaining and a byre for the animals. Outbuildings contain looms, lathes or iron works and fish dry on tall, triangular wooden forms. As we troop from sandy shore to farm, Eithne hums the old songs from her childhood. All the while, Inga is enthralled by the animals, birds and butterflies. At day's end, with squawking sea birds following in our wake, we sail back to the harbour and moor at the royal wharf in front of the great tower.

Adjusting to this new life has been an immense challenge, but it is not without fascination. Here, I am feted as a queen. Women of high status are treated lavishly in Norway. It has taken a while to appreciate I am more than just a noble brood mare and must participate in the affairs of state. Learning the Norse language has been an important task for me.

Mother would be pleased, having been brought up in the old Celtish way in a society where women had more of an equal footing with men. Some in the old days even stood side by side with their menfolk in battle. Not that I have any such plans, though now you have married into one of the oldest Pictish earldoms in Scotland, the Mormaerdom of Mar, more might be expected of you, dear one.

Isa

Scotland

Kildrummy Castle

October 1297

Isa, dear heart,

We are safe for the time being in our mountain stronghold. From my window seat, I can see the far hills. The heath is tinged with russet, and the fields around the castle lie shorn of their harvest. As skirmishes turn to open war, we stock our storerooms in case of need. It is hard, relentless work. At night, many come to seek sanctuary, wary of remaining unprotected with their families and stock in isolated shielings.

When last I wrote, Rob had refused to hand over Marjorie as a hostage. We would never have forgiven him had he done so. The timing was right for him to join forces with William

Wallace, but in retaliation for his defection, the English commanders who hold the castle in Ayr, ordered our lands in Annandale to be burned and laid waste. Over on the east coast, Wallace was busy laying siege to Dundee Castle. You queried if he had been accepted by the nobles. He has by some, the Steward for example, though few would doubt he is more than capable of playing a greater role in the community of the realm.

By summer's end, two separate events of import occurred: Bishop Fraser died at Auteuil near Paris, and King Edward departed for Flanders, intent on resolving the troubles in Gascony.

No one believed it could come to pass! Wallace's name is on everyone's lips, praised by poor man and noble alike. On 11th September, history was made. With Sir Andrew Murray, harrier of the north, Wallace joined forces and made a stand at a narrow bridge, gateway to the rest of Scotland, which spanned the river near Stirling. I have a vague memory of it from a visit we paid many years ago.

On one side of the marshland in sight of the castle was the Scots' army; on the other, the much larger English cohort with its armoured cavalry on their war horses and well-equipped foot soldiers. They were led by Sir John de Warenne, Earl of Surrey, and the treasurer, Hugh de Cressingham. Wallace taunted the enemy troops and their commanders. One even slept late! Before the day was out, the English army was routed with men and horses, killed in the battle or drowned in the muddy, churning waters. Warenne is reported to have ridden all the way to Berwick, stopping neither for food nor water, such was his fear. Cressingham, the hated 'treacherer' and cause of so much cruel oppression, did not fare as well. In the frenzied aftermath of battle, he was skinned and dismembered – trophies of war. Parts thereof have been sent around the country. Thus are legends made!

The Scots jeered at the English, calling them 'tailed dogs'. Now the English have heaped invective on Wallace, calling him a monster, a bogle and brigand – morbid fascination vying with outright fear. Andrew Murray died after the battle and his son was born posthumously. With his father dead and grandfather imprisoned in the Tower, another family has been destroyed by this savage war. With the momentum of victory, Wallace continues his raids into north England. Mary is all for riding to his encampment just to lay eyes on the man. I told her being a camp follower was beneath her, but she just threw back her head and laughed. The brazen hussy is so like her mother! After Robert left to join the rebels, Father was removed from his role as governor of Carlisle and has gone south to Essex. With his plans thwarted, he will be disheartened and angry. Rob's apparent disobedience has hurt and shamed him. No news from our brothers. Pray they are safe.

Kirsty

Scotland

Kildrummy Castle

November 1297

Isa, dear heart,

The old earl is thought to have perished in the Tower. Garnait is full of anger and grief, fuelled by guilt. He believes he should have been the one to fight at Dunbar rather than his aging father. It is not the first time his poor health has caused him shame. If this news is to be believed, I am now the Countess of Mar.

As ever
Kirsty

CHAPTER EIGHT

Norway

Bergen

February 1298

My dear Kirsty,

Please pass on our deepest regrets to Garnait. Our family has lost another good friend.

Bad weather delays the departure of Fearghas's vessel. While he waits out the rolling line of storms, the captain stays here as my guest. Over time, he has become less able to deal with the harshness of life at sea and suffers from painful, swollen joints. Some days he cannot even pick up a mug of ale! Murchadh, his son, is eager to take over as captain.

The victory at Stirling brought a mixed response here. For the Norse, it has always been the highest honour to die in battle. The female Valkyries search the battlegrounds and select the dead to join Odin in his great hall at Valhalla. Thanks to Hauk, shadowy wraiths in flowing gowns haunt my dreams. Bishop Narve frowns at such mention, but he knows the huskarls revel in the pagan gods. Even the king is not averse to revering the old ways, whilst paying lip-service to the gentle Christ.

At night, my lord husband tells tales of the war god: how he forfeited an eye in return for a drink from the well of wit and wisdom. With two ravens, Hugin and Munin, bringing him news of the world, he knew all there was to know. A god of poetry as well, Odin inspired the skalds to sing their sagas around warm hearths. It is easy to see why Hauk is so impressed by the tale of 'the treacherer' being skinned. Such tales enliven the darkest night!

Regardless, a victory for the Scots is wondrous news. May there be many more of them!

As ever

Isa

Scotland

Kildrummy Castle

May 1298

Isa, dear heart,

Last week, an unexpected visitor arrived. After a vicious squall and near collision with a whale, his vessel sustained serious damage, only just reaching the safety of Aberdeen. With ample time to spare due to the extensive repairs, Murchadh borrowed a palfrey and rode to Kildrummy to deliver your missive himself, and to see the family his father served so diligently these many years. Despite having broken his nose, he is a handsome lad and his brawny girth proved of great interest to the sister maids. We are sorry Fearghas is no longer well enough to continue in our service, but Murchadh impresses as a man of his word. Now Marthoc packs him a fine repast for the journey ahead, whilst Seonaid mends his tunic, ripped in places in the storm.

You will be pleased to know Scotland's great warrior was knighted by Robert and elected as sole Guardian of the community of the realm. Ever humble, Garnait said, he had to be persuaded to take the office. Without a strong leader, we would be in deadly peril. In early March, King Edward sailed from Flanders, taking with him many of the Scots' magnates – prisoners from Dunbar – who had agreed to fight on the side of the English in return for their freedom. Many defected to the French king. A terrible retribution will follow all this. Mark well my words! For the humiliation suffered by England at Stirling and elsewhere, Edward means to grind Scotland into submission and out of existence.

Fearful times aside, our lives follow the peaceful rhythm of the seasons. The girls are growing into fine young children, ever into mischief. Marjorie is walking and repeating words, some of which she has picked up from the guards for which she gains a sound chastisement from Morag.

After so many years, I am with child, due at year's end, so our dear Floraidh tells me. We are blessed! I wish so much for peace to surround this isolated haven and for the safe return of our brothers. Perhaps Odin could send Hugin or Munin to tell me what is happening elsewhere.

As ever
Kirsty

Norway

Bergen

June 1298

My dear Kirsty,

Bethoc and Aiofe send their love and greetings. We are overjoyed at your news. It is as well Murchadh came to meet you. You may have need of him in the future, especially if war is being waged around you. You must come to us here.

Besides, I desire nothing more than to welcome you to safety and to show you my home, though I expect you might find Bergen a busy place. Almost seven thousand souls reside here plus many foreign visitors and traders. This fact was mentioned by one of the king's administrators in a report he delivered to the councillors; a most tedious document from a dreary, irksome man.

Now would be as good a time as any to tell you about an unusual craftsman who brought his wares to the castle. One day, a knock sounded on my solar door. "Entrez!" I called, expecting it to be one of the maids. To my surprise, in came a man with a wolf-grey thatch of hair, dressed in an old, dusty surcoat and carrying a large leather satchel, which he proceeded to lay down upon a trestle beside the window. His face was a most arresting sight. A wiry, black moustache drooped around his mouth down to his jaw line, giving him the look of one with an unhappy disposition. When I caught the glint of humour in his eyes, I realised this was not so. His name was Erling Kappen.

On a piece of rough, brown fabric, he laid out a range of combs, large and small, made from the antler of the reindeer. They were beautifully crafted: each section cut with the grain of the antler, rather than across it, and riveted together for greater strength. On my last visit to the market, Erling took note of my passing interest in his stall. He hatched a plan to bring his wares to me, knowing full well this was frowned upon by the king. Once one had access, all would demand it and the traders would harry the king for their loss of profits.

Canny as a fox, he created a diversion with a young lad chasing a cur into the castle grounds. Once the guards were fully occupied, the craftsman slipped through the gates, edged around the bailey's perimeter and stole up the tower stairwell. Knowing not which door to seek, he sent a fervent plea to Frey, the god of all abundance. Hiding in the shadows along the corridor, he saw a maid leave a chamber, carrying a velvet gown and silk undergarments for laundering. Frey had smiled upon his venture. With his heart hammering in his chest, he knocked and boldly entered. Chuckling at his own brilliance, he paused in the telling – just as the door was pushed ajar. Soon, the trestle was surrounded by my serving ladies, examining his intricate wares. Seated by the hearth with a beaker of ale in his hand, Erling recounted the history of this style of comb and its connection to Bergen.

High on the mountain plateau of Hardangervidda, a trapping system existed of stone cairns and fences, which led the reindeer onto a spit of land out in a lake. Here, they were killed on the beach beside a rough shelter, home to the trappers for many months of the year: Erling's father and his father before him. It was a massive production, gathering meat, bone and antler all to be sold in Bergen, the headquarters of the trade. Indeed, the craftsman boasted he pioneered the riveting process of the reindeer antler to make the combs so strong.

Unravelling my coiled plaits, Bethoc began to work one of Erling's combs through the rough tangle of hair. It remained true to its function! Well do I remember the trouble we had as young girls. Then and there, I determined to send the good women of Kildrummy a bundle of these precious combs: a small gift, to cheer you in such dark times.

Your loving sister
Isa

Scotland

Kildrummy Castle

August 1298

Isa, dear heart,
    Great adversity has befallen Scotland! After King

Edward's return from France, he began his own meticulously-planned war by relocating his entire administration to York. As the massive army lumbered northwards, his ominous intent could not be mistaken. In desperation, the inhabitants of the border lands fled to the hills. With their supply ships delayed, the army lived off the land, but when relief did arrive, empty bellies found little sustenance in the plentiful cargo of wine. Rebellious Welsh troops, threatening to desert to the Scots, became embroiled in a fight and a few English priests, protesting at the drunken disorder, were killed. More fighting broke out and eighty or more Welsh died in reprisal. Amidst the chaos, fortune smiled upon the English king; news had come, the Scots were camped not far away at Falkirk.

On the feast day of Mary Magdalene, the mismatched armies met. With only hand weapons and little in the way of cavalry, Wallace made use of the lie of the higher land and marshy ground below, aiming to trap the heavily-armoured destriers of the English knights. Formed into four great schiltrons of men armed with outward-facing spears, lances and halberds, the Scots' hedgehog formations were held in place by rope and stakes in the ground. Between each group, Wallace wedged the archers of the forest.

By day's end, the Scots' army faced annihilation, unable to withstand the might of Edward's war machine with armoured cavalry and an untold number of foot soldiers. The powerful range of the Welsh longbow and the lethal bolts of the French crossbow made short work of the Scots. It seemed only two English knights, both Templar commanders, lost their lives, but more than one hundred horses lay dead or dying; evidence, it is said, of Wallace's rule to maim the horse and unhorse the knight. This time, his strategy failed. Instead, innumerable Scots lay dead or dying. Notable amongst the dead was Sir John Stewart of Bonkyle, a quiet and sincere man whom I recalled from a visit he made to Turnberry with his father.

With the battle lost, our nobles panicked and rode away to hide in the forests and hills. Despairing, Wallace followed them into the anonymity of Tor Wood and escaped the horror amidst its dark vales, leaving behind the stench of the battle ground and the ever-widening circle of raptors. Though we had sound information from the Abbot of Arbroath Abbey, garnered in turn from his peers at St Andrews, none knew of Robert's whereabouts at the time.

Battles can be won or lost, but the strategists busied themselves in the background. In place of Bishop Fraser, Master William Lamberton, a staunch supporter of the Scots' cause, was elected as the new Bishop of St Andrews. He and his colleagues canvassed the Pope and the French king, who both wrote letters to King Edward, mid-year, urging him to release Balliol from custody in the Tower and cease his attacks upon our countrymen. This had little impact, so we heard some time later.

Edward continued his victory march, confined to south of the Forth – thankfully nowhere near us. When the English king arrived in Ayr, it seems Robert had already evacuated the town and burned the castle to stop King Edward from retaking it. The latter then pushed onto Lochmaben, which his forces took with ease. It is as well Grandfather was buried in Guisborough, otherwise English soldiers would have been tramping o'er his grave. After all this, William Wallace, heavy-hearted from defeat, felt compelled to resign his role as sole Guardian. Where all this will end, the good Lord only knows. We mourn the dead as does all of Scotland.

Kirsty

Scotland

Kildrummy Castle

November 1298

Isa, dear heart,

Autumn's end is nigh. In the distance, the mountains lie beneath heavy cloud. Mist weaves around dripping trees, standing bare and chilled in the grey light. Despite this dreich weather, my heart is joyful. Last Tuesday past, Floraidh helped my bonny lad enter the world. How quickly do our minds lose the memory of searing pain and find, in its place, overwhelming happiness? Named after his grandfather, young Donald brings such contentment to Garnait and I, filling a gap we knew not was there, so used to its hollow emptiness were we. It is strange to have a babe back in the Snow Tower. Young Marjorie is now in her third year. It seems only yesterday she was in swaddling.

Margaret lost two of her front teeth and is troubled by her new cousin's name. Poor mite, we laughed at her attempts and she got quite cross, freckles standing out red across her little snub nose; notwithstanding, she croons snatches of songs to him in her lisping lilt.

Mathilda's news is that she has mastered her letters – thanks to the patience of Tomas. He consents to stay on here as chaplain and tutor and the priory is pleased to receive a retainer for his services to our family. In his stead, we have Drustan, a sturdy, cheerful lad who loves to be free of the confines of monastic life, travelling the hills and vales on his garron as a courier. Tomas speaks well of his loyal dedication to duty. Having been left at the priory's doorstep in a small crib, the young man knows nought else, but the Order.

On broader matters, Rob is now a joint Guardian of Scotland, but his partner in this role is the younger Comyn,

John of Badenoch. The tension between them is appalling. With full knowledge of our bitter family rivalry, Bishop Lamberton is keen to make the arrangement work, but will have to step in to settle the inevitable disputes. I expect all of this took place deep in Selkirk Forest. Despite the beating received at Falkirk, the rebellion grows. One story surfaced of a woman who gave succour to Sir Simon Fraser after a raid on the outskirts of Edinburgh. The Constable of Edinburgh Castle accused Margaret of Penicuik and son, Hugh, of sheltering Scottish miscreants. Somehow, she escaped the constable's men; having lost her home, perhaps she now resides in the ancient forest.

Of Father, I hear nothing, though rumours abound he provided troops at Falkirk as part of the English host.

Isobel Strathbogie brought news: she is with child and wished to know Edward's whereabouts. As she spoke, her eyes were bright with unshed tears. I could have cheerfully wrung our brother's neck at that moment. This is far too close for comfort. The Strathbogies are our neighbours and kin by marriage to the Mar family. Apart from his daughter's misfortune, Sir John has suffered enough with his capture after the Dunbar Drave. He spent a year in the Tower before being released to fight in Flanders with King Edward. In a rare show of spite, Garnait raged; the Earl of Atholl at least had a life to live, unlike his father who perished in captivity. Isobel's brother, David, is keen to redress the dishonour done to his sister. Edward will need to proceed with caution.

The poor lass had hardly left our solar before Mary responded. Her surly declaration – that Edward had dipped his quill once too often – was surely loud enough to have reached Isobel's ears. Such an observation comes too late to be of any value. It would have been far more helpful had she kept him within sight the last time they ventured to Strathbogie. Instead, she covers for the rogue. They are both incorrigible! But her taunt did make me laugh, especially in this case where neither she nor Edward holds any affinity for writing nor indeed love sonnets!

When displeased, Mary scowls. She looks so much like Father. That amuses me even more and usually earns me a cuff or two, unless I am quick upon my feet. The child is due quite soon, it seems. Despite feeling ill at ease, I shall offer Isobel the services of Floraidh, if she is willing to accept our assistance. Any redress will be up to Edward. Isobel seeks the bonds of marriage, but I cannot be sure our brother will be so inclined. Right now, he is a penniless rebel.

Your gifts were received with pleasure and interest by us all. Whenever I use my comb, I shall think of you.

Yours aye

Kirsty

Norway

Bergen

December 1298

My dear Kirsty,

You have written of so much – some that is indescribably sad, but much which is joyful. How proud Garnait must be with an heir at last. By now, even Edward will have a child!

Since hearing your news, I am adrift in a sea of peevish despair for my lord husband desires a son above all else. Sadness for the child lost to me is like a weight dragging me down, till it feels as if I might drown. Reproach me not, for at the same time, dear one, I am content both you and the babe are safe and well.

Your loving sister

Isa

Norway

Bergen

December 1298

A letter arrived from Robert. It was precisely the distraction Isa needed. She smiled; inordinately pleased he had found the time in his chaotic existence to write to her. During their youth, they had always been close. When their father was being difficult, it was to Isa that Rob had turned, for she could always interpret the situation with insight and compassion. It had been penned in Carrick in October.

Dearest Isa,

I send this letter to you through our network of friends in the Hanseatic League. They have been buying honey, wool and salt from northern Cumbria. Their ship will soon return to Bergen, and then go onto Lubeck. I write to give you an account of our doings in Scotland. I have no doubt many English-based lies are circulating abroad, although I believe the Pope is well aware our community is sore pressed by the English tyrant.

Two years ago, Edward of England returned south, having thought Scotland was crushed. Whilst we were silent, we had not forgotten who we were or what had happened to our nation. I was with him when he crossed the Tweed and heard him remark how good it was to leave this dung heap behind; such is his opinion of Scotland and its people. It occurred to me how a foul-smelling turd has an awful habit of sticking to your boot long after you think it gone. So it proved with our fellow countrymen. You know how thrawn we can be.

Andrew Moray escaped from the English at Chester and got back to Inverness, where he raised the men of the north in revolt. In the south, William Wallace, a tenant of the Stewart from Renfrew and a man who had not surrendered at Berwick, began a personal war of revenge against the English. This was triggered by the brutal murder of his wife by Sir William Heselrig, the English sheriff of Lanark. First, Wallace killed Heselrig and then ambushed William Ormesby, the English chief justice. Sir William Douglas joined the revolt. It was only at this point Edward bestirred himself and ordered the Earl of Surrey, the so-called viceroy of Scotland, back north from his estates. Not only that, he ordered Father, still his Governor of Carlisle, to arrest Douglas.

This translated into Father sending me with five hundred men of Annandale and twenty of our knights to Douglasdale. On my way north at Moffat, I received a letter from our friend, Robert Wishart, Bishop of Glasgow, regards James Stewart who had gone into rebellion against the English and summoned his men to Irvine, north of Ayr. By the time I reached Douglas Castle, I knew what had to be done. It was May 1297. Calling my men around me, I told them, "No man holds his own flesh and blood in hatred. I am no exception. I must join my own people and the nation in which I was born. Choose then whether you go with me or return to Carlisle and my father." A dozen of our knights with lands in England chose to return to my father. The rest headed with me and the Douglas men to Irvine, where we joined Bishop Wishart, James Stewart and Alexander Lindsay.

Edward responded by ordering his northern levies into southwest Scotland, led by Henry Percy and Robert Clifford. They arrived at Ayr in late June 1297 with five times our force, and a heavy dominance of knights. Our only course was to parley, whilst Wallace and Moray cleared the northern parts of Scotland of English power. By July, we had to sign a treaty.

The bishop, the Stewart and Lindsay all surrendered on the basis of keeping their estates, subject to the provision of hostages, whilst William Douglas refused to supply hostages and was arrested. They wanted little Marjorie as my hostage, and this I also refused, but was able to get away into the hills in eastern Carrick, and defy them from there.

The Earl of Surrey raised a great force and joined with the English troops led by Cressingham and Ormesby in the Lothians. By this stage, Moray and Wallace had swept the English out of northern Scotland, and so the choke point at Stirling was vital if we were to hold the English off. Without command of Stirling Bridge, the great English force would not be able to cross into Strathearn and Fife. Moray and Wallace set out their troops, almost all on foot, at the northern end of the wooden bridge. From there, a ridge of dry ground runs back to the Abbey Craig and the Ochil Hills. It was that ridge which was defended by our pikemen with only a few knights and caterans from the Highlands guarding the more marshy land off the ridge on either side.

On 11th September, the English began to send their vanguard of elite knights on horseback over the bridge but were unable to deploy on the other side. Moreover, within the caterans were picked men who headed for the exit point of the bridge and seized it. The vanguard were now cut off and slaughtered; the bridge being demolished plank by plank in their rear. Surrey escaped, but Cressingham died as did most of the English knights. I was by Loch Doon in Galloway when I heard the news. A great victory won by the common folk of this realm. They were proving themselves to be better patriots than their nobles.

That winter, I was mostly in Annandale and twice survived raids by Robert Clifford. This was as a result of being warned well in advance by our people, whence I retired into the hills.

William Wallace, though no nobleman, is a great man in all senses. He is six feet six inches, with a mane of wild black hair, an enormous double-handed sword, and he carries a great hatred for the English. More especially, he has the loyalty both of the church and the adoration of the ordinary folk of the kingdom. As poor Andrew Moray had died of his wounds in the spring of this year, there was no doubt Wallace should be proclaimed Guardian of the kingdom. This he accepted in the name of John Balliol, the only king we have at present though he is a broken reed in exile. Wallace fully deserved his knighthood, which I was honoured to give him at a parliament at Selkirk.

King Edward agreed a truce with the French and returned to attack Scotland. In May of this year, he moved his government from London to York and it was clear he meant to crush us once and for all. By July, two and a half thousand knights and twelve thousand foot, including three thousand archers, were at Edinburgh. They had heard the Scots' army was at Falkirk, less than twenty miles away. Wallace waited for them on an open field with four great schiltrons of Scottish pikemen with stakes in front of them, archers between each and a small cavalry force under Stewart and Lennox behind them.

I was holding the southwest of Scotland and was not present, but I heard our pikemen stood their ground for many hours, even after the Scottish archers were ridden down and the cavalry put to flight. Several schiltrons moved back into the wood. Many escaped. Others eventually crumbled under the hail of arrows and were butchered. Thankfully, Wallace was among those who escaped. King Edward had no means of pushing northward though. His army was too large to feed for long and he tried to trap me in Ayr. Before he could reach me, I burnt the town and castle and then retired into the hill country. Here, the English numbers are dispersed and I am safe. He did capture Lochmaben from us before retiring over the border. I hear he has summoned a new army to assemble at Carlisle in June of next year. Have no doubt we continue to live in difficult times. William Lamberton, the new Bishop of St Andrews, has written asking I meet with him along with William Wallace and John Comyn of Badenoch at Glasgow. I cannot conceive anything good might come our way if John Comyn is involved. Nevertheless, if Lamberton thinks the matter worthy, then I will attend. God grant me patience.

I hope and pray this finds you well. Father is in Huntingdon presently. I hear misery lies heavy upon him and he rarely leaves his hall. As for the rest of our kith and kin, you may know more than me from your correspondence with Kirsty. Only our brother, Edward, is with me and he is in boisterous good health. Believe well of me and pray for Scotland.

Rob

CHAPTER NINE

Scotland

Kildrummy Castle

March 1299

Isa, dear heart,

It took courage for you to speak thus. Donald prospers and I am thankful for the precious gift of his life. Perhaps, in time, another child will come to you as well to bring you joy and peace.

In the face of famine and the growing restlessness of his nobles, King Edward left Scotland. Before leaving, he issued a summons for his host to reassemble in June of this year. At least till then, we shall have some peace.

Yours aye
Kirsty

Norway

Bergen

May 1299

My dear Kirsty,

At the end of winter, my lord husband contracted a fever after being out on his vessel in the bay. He coughed so much he spewed blood. His rigors were such even the royal physician could not calm his wracked body. The sweating fever raged until he cried out in pain and breathed his last. How can a life end so, Kirsty?

It is now the middle of spring and yet I still feel the shock and horror of that last night. The memory of his burning hands searing my skin stays with me. New life abounds everywhere: buds unfurl, animals give birth, but the king lies stiff and cold in his grave at the Kristkirke. Inga cannot comprehend where her father has gone. I believed myself so strong, Kirsty, but when tested, I cannot answer, so wrought am I. Bishop Narve told her about heaven. She laughed and pointed towards the harbour. Does the bairn think we might sail there?

Eric's brother, Haakon, is king and the wedding to his betrothed, Euphemia of Riigen, took place much sooner than anticipated. Being in mourning, I attended neither wedding nor coronation banquet. I hear King Haakon means to replace Bergen as the royal capital with Oslo. Its location is more strategically placed to stabilise our relations with the Danes to the south and Swedes to the east.

I know not what my future will hold. As Dowager Queen and mother of the late king's child, I expect I must remain here. With my ladies-in-waiting, I retired from the tower to our former apartments down beside the harbour. Bethoc and Eithne now sit quietly beside me, working away at their mending, whilst Aiofe maintains her steady vigil by the window. Though my heart is heavy, each day my mind finds greater clarity. Rob has corresponded once again. By all the saints, he is as stubborn as Grandfather. I wish it could be otherwise, this path he has chosen.

Isa

Scotland

Kildrummy Castle

October 1299

Isa, dear heart,

Murchadh took the longer route via Orkney rather than run the gauntlet of the English blockade. Rob entreats us to remain vigilant and to continue to use lead seals at all times so our letters can be disposed of easily at sea, if necessary.

To hear of the death of your lord husband was indeed a shock, but a king is as mortal as any man. We are concerned for you and Inga. Have you found peace or security of tenure? Rest assured dear one, you will always have a home at Kildrummy.

An early blanket of snow fell last week. It is quiet, as if the land lies in a deep trance. Yet while nature sleeps, our country's turmoil persists. As you know from the past, Scotland has a history of being better at diplomacy than war. The sustained efforts of the bishops and magnates to sway Pope Boniface in Scotland's favour brought about a response from him. This past summer saw King John Balliol released from the Tower into papal custody at Cambrai in France. A small, but sweet victory!

King Edward has been busy this year. He made a treaty with the King of France. In return for handing over Flanders to France, he received Guienne. Also, he married again – this time to King Philippe's sister, Margarite; a beautiful, young bride who should keep him otherwise occupied. Garnait tells me the Scottish parliament is much committed to getting the government's administration functioning again. To this end, the Guardians, Robert and the firebrand Comyn, signed charters across the country from Glasgow to St Andrews. In August, they made forays into the forest and planned to attack

Roxburgh, but found the castle and town heavily defended. Instead, they moved through Galloway, so hostile to Carrick and the rest of Scotland, cleansing that festering sore.

Some days past, Robert rode in with his retainers. Weighed down by all that has happened, he is thin, Isa, and ever fearful that people do not trust him. I tried to imagine what that must be like and could not. Frustrated at every turn, his goal is far from reach. It galls him beyond bearing. Mary asked where Wallace was now. Rob had no answer. The man seems to have gone to ground. How such a giant of a man could disappear, I know not.

Marjorie carries no enduring memory of her father at his visits. She consents to sit upon his lap, but sees him as a kind stranger who brings gifts from time to time. Ever present in her daily life, Garnait is more of a father to her. Rob thanked him for taking such fine care of his child, but it grieves him all the same.

This may interest you, Isa! Rob queried if Garnait had news of Lady Elizabeth de Burgh, daughter of the Earl of Ulster. The earl's sister, Ergidia, as you know, is married to Sir James Stewart. Garnait could offer no explanation as to Rob's interest and, much to my chagrin, he showed no inclination to enquire further!

Kirsty

Norway

Bergen

November 1299

My dear Kirsty,

Thank you again for your news. Our lives are more settled. A very generous, annual endowment has been allotted to me, along with lands and houses here in Bergen and elsewhere. Regarding the management of my own affairs, I am assured of my independence. Most relieved am I some man of wealth and status is not to be given my hand in marriage to gain his loyalty for the king. I might even select my own husband, should I choose to do so. It is beyond belief!

It is only where Inga is concerned, I need consult the king. You asked if I could return home: the answer is yes – I am free to leave at any time – but not with my child. Norway is Inga's home and her royal heritage must be cherished. In truth, it is no hardship for me to remain here. I have a fine life and want for nothing. With the fear of war ever present, I could not bear to live in Scotland now. My words will sadden you, but that is how it must be.

On a happier note, Euphemia, wife of King Haakon, is a kindred spirit of sorts. We have much to speak about – world affairs, literature and poetry. Fluent in several languages, Effie, as she likes to be known, is keen to teach me the Danish and German tongues. Already, she assembles a mighty library of tomes from far and wide, which Bishop Narve and I are bursting to access.

Fortunately for Effie, the king is a learned man and plans to establish clerical schools both here and in Oslo, the new royal capital, and to compile a royal archive. A gifted leader, he holds a firm vision for Norway. He is concerned about the German traders, whom he believes my lord husband allowed to siphon off much of Norway's trading wealth, depleting the nation's coffers. Apart from his inherent dislike of clerics, Eric was easily swayed by his advisors, much as a reed bends before the wind. Haakon intends to take on the barons and reduce their power. Already the sparks fly between them. One in particular, Auden Hugleiksson, would be wise to tread warily with this new king: he is no swaying reed, and a new wind blows through this land. With threats from the north, east and south, Haakon is on edge about the precarious defence of his kingdom. Effie says he will build a series of forts to prevent the Finns, Swedes and Danes gaining strength over Norway. Always, I am reminded this country's violent past is a mere shadow's breath away.

Time is slipping away, and Effie's move to Oslo draws close. Any visits will be by sea and only in good weather, for Norway's new capital lies at the head of a fjord, well beyond the high plateau of bogs and lochs to the east. Till next time.

Your loving sister

Isa

Scotland

Kildrummy Castle

December 1299

Isa, dear heart,

Do not trouble yourself. I understand your new life has a stronger hold than the old. We are forged anew from our experiences. God willing, I will look upon your face once more. When that might be, I know not, but it pleases me we remain in touch.

This year, we experienced a stronger sense of security, but not so, those further to the south. Most recently, a siege took place at Stirling. Young Moreham commanded the force that regained the castle for the Scots. A strange story is told of how he ambushed the Dowager Countess of Fife, kin of King Edward, on her way to Edinburgh. He carried her off and tried, without success, to force her to marry his brother, Thomas of Castlerankine. Given our musings of late, her tale resonates.

Garnait relayed our lord father remains firm in his loyalty to King Edward and is back at Lochmaben, rebuilt now as a fortress on another part of the loch. Grandfather's home is in ruins. The townsfolk raid the old castle and repair their houses under cover of darkness. I believe our brother to be at Turnberry. He must be close by Galloway, for his goal is to gain the trust of the people or harry them, wiping out pockets of disaffection. Such are these strange times. So far he has avoided direct contact with Father, despite the fact his men laid siege to Lochmaben – without success, I might add. News filtered through – Sir William Douglas, veteran soldier and patriot, died in the Tower. I cannot bear to think of the poor man's suffering. His young son, James, is now without a father.

For us, life goes on with fulfilment and joy. The children are flourishing. Excitement abounds concerning the gifts they hope to receive on the eve of Christ's birth. Donald continues to be a healthy babe, for which I am most thankful.

Despite the cold, the day is crisp and clear. Mary hawks on the Don with our Strathbogie kin who are spending the festivities with us. Isobel seems in good spirits, having come to some arrangement with Edward. She brought along their babe: Alexander is dark-haired and wiry like his father and cannot stay still for long.

Despite the disarray and extra work visitors always bring, we are determined to enjoy this special time. Mhairi works well with the Kildrummy cook, old Aonghas, and the two are preparing a grand feast. I can smell the delicious aromas wafting up the stairwell. Yuletide blessings from us all!

Yours aye

Kirsty

CHAPTER TEN

Norway

Bergen

April 1300

My dear Kirsty,

How I longed for spring's warm, dry breath upon my skin! The cold, dark months dragged on endless and dull, but now the countryside awakes. On my walks, I see many small creatures, martens and black foxes, and hear the songbirds in the fir trees. Along the shoreline away from the harbour, otters play in secluded rocky streams, safe under the leafy haven of birch, alder and aspen. I implore them to take great care, lest they end up on some tanner's slab.

The king and queen planned to sail up the coast to Trondheim on affairs of state. When Effie asked me to accompany them, I agreed immediately, relishing a break away after the challenges of the past year.

At dawn, we arrived at the quay. Moss-green ripples foamed white beneath the royal dragon-ship as it strained against the ropes. Unfurled, the heavy sail soon caught the breeze. When granted the freedom of the sea, the vessel shot forth, much like a stallion released from its halter. I had to hang on for dear life.

With their experience of wave patterns and tides, the crew managed the vessel with skill and determination. Keeping well out of harm's way, I watched their activities with great interest. Closer to shore, depth is measured by casting a lead-weighted line overboard. Keen eyes watch out for trunks of trees and massive boulders washed down the rivers in spate from melting snow. In deeper waters, extreme care is necessary, sighting air spouts of whales and manoeuvring the galley away from their path before the creatures breach the surface and slam down their tails. Skerries and bergs of ice add to the danger. Whilst there was much talk and laughter, we remained alert for cries from the sharp-eyed lookouts.

Along the serrated coastline, fishing villages dotted amongst the isles welcomed our contingent. Lavish banquets followed Tings where the king adjudged issues of conflict or concern. At one longhouse, Haakon was gifted a whale's skull and at another, a silver-rimmed drinking horn. Our journey took us to a substantial community on a northern inlet. Rivalling Bergen as a royal capital in the past, Trondheim has a magnificent cathedral, Nidaros, so called after the town's much older name; Bishop Narve speaks of St Olav, it's patron saint, in awed tones.

Accompanied by the most ill-tempered huskarl, we left the king and his entourage with a noisy throng of councillors. Along the cobbled streets and busy market, many treasures were to be found. Effie was first to sight some elegant leather boots for herself, whilst I found a pair of bone skates for Inga. A rectangular smoothing board made of dense whalebone with carved handles – dragon heads turning to face each other – proved an ideal purchase for Eithne, whose task it is to care for my wardrobe. Other items were more decorative in nature: a necklace, of brightly-coloured beads for both Bethoc and Aiofe; in line with their status as ladies-in-waiting, embossed silver brooches will be most suitable gifts for Thora and Gundred. No doubt Aiofe will bicker at the injustice of it all, for she adjudges herself to have the higher status. Whilst all these deliberations were taking place, Ottar grumbled into his beard with each new purchase adding to his already cumbersome load. Only when treated to a beaker of ale or two at one of the many stalls, did he finally thaw and lose his fearsome frown.

On our journey home, the galley turned into a fjord where sheer cliffs were drenched by roaring mountain streams, falling to the shadowy waters below. Effie urged the crew to take us as close as possible to the surging water. The boat rocked, unsteady in the rough and one of the lads toppled in. We laughed, exhilarated by the noise and cool, moist air. Behind the walls of water, lush patches of emerald-green ferns clung to the darkened rock and when the sun shone, silvery-pink and blue arches shimmered amidst the spray drift. In time, the king motioned for us to move deeper into the inlet. With fertile land in short supply, intrepid farmers and fishermen had built longhouses on perilously narrow strips, cleared from the surrounding dense forest. Below these plots, precarious paths – their steps incised into the rock face – wound their way down to small boat sheds which clung, tenacious as barnacles, to the shore's edge. Now, I understood the impetus, felt by many a younger son, to go hosting for the land and riches denied them here.

One last piece of news! The queen is with child, due sometime in the new year. She asks I attend the birth. Naturally, I feel some trepidation but am deeply honoured. Becoming more agitated by the second, Murchadh is standing by. He insists the tide waits for no man – or woman in this case.

As ever

Isa

Scotland

Kildrummy Castle

July 1300

Isa, dear heart,

Just a quick note! That ill-advised partnership between

Robert and the Red Comyn has fractured beyond repair. So often, temper overcame reason. In despair, Rob resigned. At the Rutherglen parliament, the Comyns' kinsman and ally, Sir Gilbert de Umfraville took his place. Up until May, Robert was believed to be in Galloway trying to bring those wild souls into some kind of peace.

Not much to tell as news is sparse. Drustan was recalled to the priory for a misdemeanour; he found an orphaned fox cub lying on a bleak hillside and brought it back to his cell, concealed beneath his cloak. Such an ill-fated secret could never be maintained for long. The keeper of the priory's geese complained. Drustan took umbrage and heated, unseemly words ensued. Garnait has since had to negotiate with the prior to allow Drustan to return to his duties as courier.

Our life is calm and peaceable at present. All are well and send their love. The children are out on their skates at every opportunity. Mary and I pin our cloaks with the gold brooches to much interest and acclaim. Thank you!

As ever
Kirsty

Scotland

Kildrummy Castle

November 1300

Isa, dear heart,

Scotland is back in the midst of war. Fortunate are we such mayhem is far to the south. I know not how our family fares. Midsummer, King Edward amassed his host and moved north of the Solway, making camp at Annan. Led by Robert

Cunningham, the garrison commander at Caelaverock Castle, the Scots attacked Lochmaben Castle.

King Edward veered west to relieve the beleaguered fortress and then moved onto Caelaverock, which sits within a deep, broad moat near the mouth of the River Nith. The English host surrounded the triangular castle. Incensed that the Scots' garrison sought an honourable surrender guaranteeing their safety, Edward brought into play the powerful battering rams and trebuchets. When it was all over, the bodies of the garrison swung from the nearest trees. After that success, Edward held a parley in the area with the Scots' leaders, Buchan and Badenoch, but angrily refuted their terms for surrender: restoration of King John Balliol and lands previously lost to the English to be restored to their rightful owners, the Scots' magnates.

In August, a skirmish took place across the Cree. Longbowmen shot arrows at the Scots milling on the other side. The next day, the English returned in force. When the tide turned and the cavalry crossed the estuary, the Scots found themselves ill-prepared; this led to the capture of Sir Robert Keith and others. With many leaving their horses behind, the Scots took flight into the hills. After bringing an army the size of the one at Falkirk at great cost and effort, King Edward grew disheartened with the lack of substantial engagement. Adding to his frustration, he received a Papal rebuke, albeit a year after it was written, concerning English aggression against Scotland.

In autumn, formal truce in hand for the period of October until May next year, King Edward returned to England. For the Scots' magnates present at the negotiations in Dumfries, the king's ominous vow, that he would be back to lay Scotland waste from sea to sea, echoed in their hearts and minds. That aside, we at Kildrummy wished the viper good riddance!

Garnait tells me plans are afoot: Wallace is to go with a delegation to the continent to plead Scotland's case for peace.

With the forthcoming change in the weather, Drustan wishes to ride onto his abbey sooner rather than later. I must finish now.

Yours aye
Kirsty

Norway

Bergen

November 1300

My dear Kirsty,

I long for something more hopeful from you next time. My news may surprise you! I have arranged Inga's betrothal, albeit with King Haakon's sanction. Not long ago, the Earl of Orkney came seeking a bride of royal birth. His first wife had died after the birth of their son. Forgive me, dear sister, a wicked part of me is flushed with pride at being able to choose my daughter's husband. I am well-pleased, for Jon Magnusson is a thoughtful man of some elegance and wit.

Master Weland was most helpful with the legal processes inherent in such an important betrothal. As a secular administrator, he did much of the negotiation concerning the marriage contract and dowry. When Inga is of an age to marry, we shall travel to Orkney for the wedding at the great cathedral in Kirkwall.

Yester eve, news came of a Scottish ship. William Wallace was on board! We rushed out to stand on the wide stone wall of the harbour outside our apartments. Off in the distance, I could see a tall, bearded man with a shaggy head of black hair, standing with some notables on the traders' wharf. Before long, the group boarded the waiting galley, which headed out over the choppy, grey waters. How I longed to be on that vessel. With only sea birds for company, I stood for a time, gazing at the sea and sky, my woollen cloak wrapped tight against the breeze.

Later, a most welcome visitor knocked on my door. Master Weland bristled with excitement. Unable to relax and sit by the hearth, he paced about my solar. The sparse hairs on his head stood on end and his eyes shone beneath his spiky brows. I could not recall seeing him so animated.

To avoid being captured by English ships, the vessel had sailed further north via Orkney and onto Norway. Only by a whisker, it seems, did they evade capture and avoid disaster. Now, safe passage was sought through these northern waters. For a time, Bergen seemed to fade into the background and we were both back home in the thick of intrigue and conflict. Pray God, the delegation arrives unharmed.

Another snippet of news regards my good sister; her babe arrived sooner than anticipated. After a long struggle, the midwife delivered the child and a great relief it was to hear the bairn's exhausted cry. Had it been a boy, I am unsure how I might have felt. Bishop Narve performed the baptism in the mighty cathedral and the celebrations went on for days. Meanwhile, my hands and arms still bear the bruises from Effie's iron grip.

Your loving sister

Isa

Scotland

Kildrummy Castle

February 1301

Isa, dear heart,

Mary was enthralled with your news. She tells me she would have swum out to the ship, had she been there! You know how prone to exaggeration our sister can be!

That you were permitted to arrange such a powerful betrothal was a surprise. Less pressure is upon us now to seek early betrothals. Many noble families have lost lands and wealth. The old ways are fast disappearing.

Heavy snowfalls keep our servitors busy, clearing pathways. Daggers of ice hang from the eaves of buildings. I tell all to stay clear, lest they pierce those foolish enough to stand beneath. With the bitter cold, heating the large chambers proves a great challenge. At night, the eerie wind howls like mournful *bean shidh* calling up the dead. Most young men have gone south. Many have died in battles or skirmishes. Of those that remain, some are in hiding, whilst others return to find ruined homes and family members killed or maimed. One of the lesser consequences of this unrest is that we now have only a small group of older retainers. In fine weather or foul, they gather logs from the forest.

Accompanied by guards, Mary takes two of the servitors with her to hawk or hunt along with our massive wolfhound, Brude, who enjoys the chase. Even with just one good eye,

Nectan, a skilled bowman, is able to pick out a deer from the undergrowth in the dappled light. Wiry Talorc has a strong throwing arm so is handy with a spear. The hunters often return flushed with victory: a deer or boar, slung on a pole between two horses. Poor Luag injured his wing some time ago in a scrap with a larger bird of prey, but Mary's goshawk still brings in grey hares and pheasants – all welcome additions to the pot.

The children have built a snowman in the bailey and decorated it with clothing found in the wooden trunks up in one of the tower attics. A velvet bonnet with its upright pheasant's feather and a moolie plaid belonging to Garnait's grandfather were put to good use. They dress up as well and build fortresses to hide within, removing them from the worries of the world. But try as they might, they cannot evade Morag.

From my window seat, I can see our jaunty friend; a neep for a nose, cones gathered from the firs across the ravine for the eyes, red and green plaid pinned at the shoulder and a velvet cap askew on his broad, white pate.

Over by the studded-oak gates, our small group of guards, most of whom have seen better days, stand around a brazier, stamping their feet. Steam hazes from their mouths into the frosted air. To fill their time, they attend to their weapons, complete repairs around the castle and practice manoeuvres down in the bailey, but if an army were to present itself, Isa, we would be hard pressed to defend ourselves.

Garnait and I have planned for a siege, filling any spare chambers with grain and other comestibles lest such a terrible event takes place. In the morning room, I prepare salves and evil-smelling concoctions, storing them for any eventuality. Old clothing and linen are ripped into bandages. Have I mentioned before that Kildrummy has spinning wheels and a loom? One day, not long after we arrived, a woman of muckle girth, middle-aged and newly widowed, came to the castle gates from a nearby farm; her cart loaded with wool from a flock of hill sheep. Cloth had always been purchased at Turnberry from passing traders. The widow, Shona, and her pretty young daughters, Affrica and Catriona, knew how to transform the wool which they did in the small living space in their croft. An arrangement was made for the sisters to set up a loom and spinning wheels within the safety of the castle's walls and to teach some of the maids in the process. In return, men from here shear the family's flock and the women receive a generous retainer. As I write, I can hear the whirring hum of the wheels and clatter of the loom weights in the distance.

A few days past, Tomas returned to the priory with Drustan for the consecration of a new building. With their tutor gone, the children are up to all sorts of mischief. Yester eve, they played hide and go seek; running along the endless passages and alleyways, up and down winding stairwells, hiding under curtained beds or behind doorways, shrieking when found. Close behind was Morag, like an old clucking hen whose wayward chicks paid no heed.

Of late, the girls can be found down in the stables helping Talorc groom their ponies. He gives them fish oil to rub into leather saddles. It troubles them not, grimed as they are with hay and manure. Often they lie in the hay plaiting long, thin lengths of leather into harness strapping listening to the groom's stories. As a young man, he fished the coast for herring. A fierce storm wrecked the family's boat, injuring his father. Talorc found work on the land lest his family starve. Ever patient, the groom listens to the girls' endless tales of Brandubh, the magical horse which flies at night all the way from the north lands, ridden by their brave sister, Queen Isabel.

It will surprise you not to hear the children spend many hours down in the great kitchen, so cosy on a sleet-ridden day.

Rosy-cheeked from the warmth, Margaret watches Mhairi bake griddle scones, brown-crusted pies and tarts filled with fruits preserved from the summer harvest. Sometimes, the ten year old attempts to grind oats and barley on the large quern stone, but Aodh, the scullion, soon takes over the heavy task. At the far end of the oak table sits Marjorie, now in her fifth year. She scratches away on an old slate tile lost in a world of shapes and stick figures. In the corner of the vaulted space beneath a set of smoking rushes, Mathilda sits at a trestle with her lanky legs drawn up beneath her. Brow creased in concentration, the eleven-year-old tries to beat Aonghas at games of skill and chance using the carved chess men or domino slate pieces. Sometimes, the old cook lets her beat him.

Donald is too small as yet to go off with the girls, so Marthoc takes him away to the nursery where he rides an old hobby horse with horsehair mane and tail. Whinnying and clip-clopping, he goes afar on a magical journey of his own making. When he tires of this, the bairn wobbles over on his chubby, wee legs to his wooden blocks, or pootles about in the trunk of toys until he finds his spinning top; all crafted by Earchann. Oft times, Marjorie joins her cousin in the nursery and plays with her wooden peg dollies, for which Seonaid made a little toy trunk of clothes. It seems the children are happy and at ease within our strong walls.

On a broader note, Scotland has a new chancellor, Nicholas Balmyle. Garnait thought it might be of interest to Master Weland and the king in future dealings. The three Guardians, Bishop Lamberton, de Umfraville and Comyn, have resigned – another partnership fragmented by conflict. In their place, one man has risen to the challenge, Sir John de Soulis. His castles, Hermitage and Liddesdale, control one of the strategic routes into Scotland. Pray he has a steadier hand on the rudder. In his new role, the Guardian wrote a letter to Pope Boniface updating him on the affairs of Scotland and King

Edward's disregard of the Papal rebuke. These protests fall on deaf ears, it would seem.

I have saved the best news till last. I am with child, due in just a few short months. Garnait is fearful for the child's future, but I seek to enjoy this happy time. Who amongst us knows how long it will last?

Kirsty

Norway

Bergen

May 1301

My dear Kirsty,

I pray you have a healthy babe and are faring well. When anyone asks Inga how old she is, she tilts her head and puts up four fingers. Just now, Bethoc plaits her long fair hair into braids over which she will tie a fringed scarf. In her white undershirt and dark blue pinafore, she looks a typical Norse maid, albeit in miniature. Soon we are off to the royal apartments in the tower, to visit the queen and six-month-old Ingebjorg. My daughter is taking a painting she did of a dragon ship as a gift.

In summer, we are hoping to go out in our own boat. As part of my dower, I received a vessel of my own. The crew is captained by Kettil: with a scar running from eye to jawline, he is not a pretty sight, but he adores Inga and she delights in being carried about on his shoulders. Do you remember Hauk? After a slow, tortuous courtship, Thora agreed to be his wife. In taking this step, the young man gave up much for only single men can remain in the world of the huskarl. In view of the couple's loyal service to the crown, King Haakon offered them a longhouse and farm up in the Sognefjord, a stunning area to the north of Bergen. Meanwhile, Thora's father gifted a vessel suitable for fishing or trading to supplement their income. Thora has asked us to visit her soon. She will be lonely, living so far away from all she knows.

Some weeks back, a peculiar tale of some intrigue came to light. Many folk believe King Eric's first daughter did not die, but was kidnapped! Stranger still, a young woman arrived from Germany claiming to be the, now adult, Maid of Norway. Down by the harbour, crowds gathered to talk and wonder. King Haakon ordered her execution and the site of her death has become a place of pilgrimage. It is a strange tale, especially in light of the fact that Eric viewed Margaret's body before she was buried beside her mother. Could grief have clouded his sight? At last, Inga and Bethoc are ready to depart. Stay safe, dear ones.

Isa

Scotland

Kildrummy Castle

November 1301

Isa, dear heart,

Forgive me! I was remiss not to pass on our congratulations to the queen on the birth of her daughter. It is hard to believe Inga is now four years old.

Keeping everyone safe during these trying times – bellies full and bodies warm – these are our challenges. A few weeks back, a dark-haired mite arrived one still, clear night. Garnait blessed her with his mother's name. Praise God! Ellen and I remain in good health.

In May, King Edward wrote a letter of rebuttal to the Pope concerning Scotland's *claims* of independence. Despite alarming bouts of ill-health and a growing weakness in his chest, Garnait raged about this news. The document was full of untruths meant to defend Edward's policies of aggression. Meanwhile, another delegation departed en route to the Papal Curia. Later in the summer, King John Balliol was released from Papal custody and allowed to go with fewer restrictions to his family home, Bailliol-en-Vimeu. Mid-year, Edward's army returned for yet another campaign. This time the host was split in two: the larger group, which met at Berwick, was led by the monarch himself. It moved up Tweeddale, taking the towns of Selkirk and Peebles in an attempt to seal off the forest, home to our rebels.

In the west, Prince Edward led a smaller army from Carlisle up into Dumfrieshire and Ayrshire. Supply ships from English bases in Ireland sailed up the Cumbrian coast into the Solway to keep the troops well-fed and resourced. Trying to keep the pressure on Edward's host from the north, the Scots were out in force around Stonehaven under Fraser, Abernethy and Moreham. The king planned to build such strength in the southwest that communications with the rest of the land would be severed. But Prince Edward's army, having kept to the coast to maintain contact with his supply ships, proceeded only as far as Whithorn before being harassed by the rebels.

With the Scots worrying and nipping at the perimeter of the armies, the planned pincer movement almost failed, but, in September, Bothwell Castle fell to King Edward. Somehow, the prince's army forged north capturing our beloved Turnberry, moving on to join his father's host for the winter in Linlithgow. Starving foot soldiers were deserting unhindered and a truce from October's end till next May was set in place. Longshanks rode back to England. Wallace's strategy of burnt earth had paid off; our enemies unable to live off the land.

Deep snow drifts delayed Drustan's passage and my parchment gathers dust. To the south, famine ravages the land, despoiled by troops of both sides. Farmers and townsfolk were told to carry what they could and move stock up into the hills and forest. Starvation and sickness are rife. Now, the weary trek home to burnt-out farms and buildings has begun.

Robert and Edward rode in two days ago with their men, bone-thin and reeling with fatigue. Floraidh and the maids attended to their weeping sores and lice-ridden bodies. Overseen by Mary, Talorc moved into the stables to be close to the men's horses, which are in a desperate state. They require much attention lest they become food for the hounds. In the group was one we had not seen for a long time, the brother of Seonaid and Marthoc, whom we all thought dead. Such a welcome Dughall received from his sisters! When Mhairi and Aonghas saw the sorry state of the men, they rushed to the kitchen. In the Great Hall, the men ate their fill of neep brose and honey wafers. For once, silence prevailed. Most notable, perhaps because of his height and girth, is fair-haired Christopher Seton whose ready smile and kind eyes caught my attention. This morn, the aroma of beef and barley broth and bannocks wafts about the bailey. Our hoarded supplies are being put to good use.

Subdued and wary of the strange visitors, the children stay put in the nursery engrossed with a new set of puppies: tiny replicas of their wolfhound mother. It is indeed comforting to have Rob and Edward at Kildrummy – if only they could stay until after Yuletide. The rift with Father festers like a vicious thorn embedded in flesh. How can one family be so torn apart? Despite all of this, the lads are safe. They send their love and blessings to you and Inga, as do we all.

Kirsty

Norway

Bergen

November 1301

My dear Kirsty,

A short despatch! Murchadh is eager to depart before the weather changes. I was relieved to hear of Ellen's safe arrival and that you survived the ordeal. It seems strange to me that mother experienced so many births, though each one must have weakened her. I fear I do not have such strength in me.

How frightening are the events unfolding in our land! It is as well our brothers sought respite. Pray God the good care they receive from you all will keep them strong.

Your loving sister

Isa

CHAPTER TWELVE

Scotland

Kildrummy Castle

March 1302

Isa, dear heart,

Despite the wintry conditions, we manage to stay warm. Ellen holds her head up now and takes an interest in her surroundings. A bonny lass indeed; her first smile was as sweet and tentative as a new bud unfolding.

Of late, we have had a sad time of it. Old Aonghas died in his sleep. Silent and pale as a wraith, Mathilda packed away the gaming pieces as if all childhood games were but folly and required burial. Mhairi, too, was red-eyed and distracted. Some of the meals she prepared left a lot to be desired, especially when she mistook the spices: even the guards refused their food and poor Aodh bore the brunt of her temper.

Drustan brought news from the Abbot of Arbroath: a truce has been arranged by King Edward for nine months. Robert and many of the magnates submitted to the English monarch. I knew when our brothers came last year they had had enough. It was not only their wasted bodies; the lingering shadow of defeat was evident in their eyes. After all they have been through, it is devastating. Rob feels it most for the people of Annandale and Carrick, now either slaughtered or starving. Hope is a luxury he can ill-afford.

It is impossible to imagine the dark place in which our brother finds himself and, more frightening still, where the journey might end. England is far too powerful for Scotland to overcome on the formal battlefield – for now, anyway. Rob tells me he can no longer countenance sacrificing his followers, his lands and himself for a false ideal: the return of King John Balliol. Rumours abound the latter will return with an army of French soldiers.

At any rate, our country is too impoverished to fight a war. The nobles cannot gather revenue from their tenants; these poor folk are now starving or diseased; their animals eaten in the famine. Fields are burnt; farm buildings destroyed with implements, lost or stolen. In February, Bishop Lamberton returned from Paris after trying to broker peace for Scotland. The struggle continues, but without any firm commitments. With our brother no longer in the picture, John Comyn was elected Guardian of Scotland.

Despite his painful, laboured breathing, Garnait managed to attend the parliament. Upon his return, he took to his bed; frustrated, sore of heart and weary beyond belief. It pains me to see him so unwell. With Robert back in the English king's peace, he received a summons to the royal court in London. King Edward prefers to keep his enemies close and to buy their loyalty. Ever the viper, he entwines and twists his will around their hearts and minds. One prize offered to Rob is the hand of Lady Elizabeth de Burgh, daughter of the king's close associate, the Earl of Ulster. The feisty Elizabeth has been in the forefront of our brother's heart and mind for some time.

If Rob is ever to be king, a wife he must have – to bring riches, a powerful bloodline and useful alliances. In the case of the fair Elizabeth, her family's Irish connections would be advantageous to the Bruce cause; her beauty, a welcome bonus. Rob plans to meet with our lord father at Writtle in an attempt to resolve the schism within the family. To be sure, our brother will need to be strong; ere his spirit will be even more bruised and battered. Our father feeds and cossets his grudges better than a muckle-breasted wet nurse tends a babe.

As things stand, Rob is unlikely to receive any revenue from Father's estates. To survive and rebuild his shattered lands, he will be forced to rely on King Edward's goodwill, especially with a forthcoming marriage and the need to setup a home, in London, I expect. With Cambridge so close, perhaps Rob might call to see how Alexander fares. News from our erudite young brother would be most welcome.

I must digress a little! Drustan brought with him a strange tale concerning Robert and the monks of Melrose Abbey. The abbot received a missive from him containing an apology to the tenants of the abbey, for having called them out to fight in his wars when a nationwide call-up had not been issued. He then promised this would never happen again – unless *it was for the common good of the whole realm*. Is this some ruse on Rob's behalf? Should the English king ask him to rally an army, he will have fewer men to draw upon. It seems to all of us here that Robert seeks to minimise any actions taken by him on King Edward's behalf. Our brother Edward is in an awkward position as well, having been admitted into the household of the king's wayward son. Once more, Isa, our family teeters on the edge of a deeply-shadowed, echoing abyss.

Yours aye
Kirsty

Norway

Bergen

May 1302

My dear Kirsty,

Our brother is now under Sassenach control, but, in truth, it is more of a truce. Many will be as shocked by this turnabout as was I – at first. Robert will be sore at heart and the recent family meeting will have ignited further bitterness.

But I wager our lord father will be well-pleased with Rob's impending marriage to the daughter of Richard de Burgh. Mother once told me how the earl, along with Mar and Stewart and several of our Irish kin, magnates all, visited Turnberry after King Alexander's death. Grandfather sponsored the meeting to build alliances in the region but also, in part, to garner support for our family's claim to the Scottish throne. Our countries had been at peace for many a long year, and the meeting was held within King Edward's good grace. That once neighbourly king then turned his back upon our family, having set his sights upon ruling Scotland himself.

With Rob's options so diminished, our brother has little choice, barring poverty or death, to place himself within reach of our most dire and formidable enemy. Elizabeth may prove a strong ally for Robert, especially if she reciprocates his esteem. For sure and certain, he needs someone of strong mettle to match his own spirit and the challenges that lie ahead.

Your loving sister
Isa

Scotland

Kildrummy Castle

May 1302

Isa, dear heart,

Several weeks past, Garnait returned from a meeting in Scone. Pale and weakened, he rested for a few days. Then, his breathing became even more constricted. Nothing Floraidh or

I concocted seemed to work. One night, he flailed around in our bed, unable to take in sufficient air. A bluish tinge touched his lips. His chest heaved and convulsed. An alarming dusky hue stole across his face and then, my dearest Garnait collapsed, breathing his last; a limp mess of clammy limbs and tangled sheeting.

Two days ago, Robert arrived for the funeral. He brought with him a letter from King Edward, advising that our brother is now Donald's guardian; my son being the new Earl of Mar and of a tender age. We could have lost all if the king had given Donald's guardianship to one of his cronies to bleed us dry until Donald comes of age. Now, Edward uses it as a bribe for Robert's loyalty. Bereft though I am, I can still see reason, but it causes me pain to see this wrangling over Garnait's beloved Mar. Thank God our brother was well-placed enough to be able to advocate for our advantage. We are in safe hands.

As ever
Kirsty

Norway

Bergen

June 1302

My dear Kirsty,

At the Kristkirke, prayers have been said for Garnait's soul. How I wish I could be with you! It is as well Robert was able to guarantee Donald's inheritance, for the security it offers. Curiosity bids me ask, did Rob's new wife attend the funeral?

It has been a tumultuous time here. The king had one of the most influential barons executed. Audun Hugleiksson was a particular favourite of my lord husband, but King Haakon vowed to rid himself of the powerful magnate. It seems he overstepped the mark and spoke out against the king to his peril. Strange rumours also abound of his involvement in the death of the Maid of Norway. Surely, such treachery cannot be true. Regardless, his death is a powerful reminder to all in the kingdom. Stay safe, dear ones.

Your loving sister

Isa

Norway

Bergen

September 1302

My dear Kirsty,

It has been many months since we have heard from you. I pray all is well. Our news may be of interest, if only to serve as a distraction.

One day in late summer, we chanced upon a period of fine, clear weather to visit Thora and Hauk. In the dusk of early morn, we trailed down to the wharf with baskets laden with victuals to break our fast: eggs in their shells, boiled till hard; brine-pickled herrings and thin slices of oven-crisp bread. With the large, square sail taut in the breeze, our vessel moved with ease up the coast and, much later, into the broad Sognefjord. Inga is now quite mobile and likes to climb; safety requires she be tied to her maid's wrist. Thus it was Eithne sat up near the rudder, so Inga might be close to her hero, Kettil. The Irish lass did not seem to mind, but I noticed Gundred flash tight, narrow-eyed looks in her direction. Oblivious to the subtle drama, old Fearghas, whose health has improved somewhat, chatted away with Kettil discussing tide times, wind directions, ice floes and the possibility of whale sightings.

It was a long time before we reached our destination down a much narrower fjord. On a flat piece of ground above the tiny hamlet, our friends' sod-roofed longhouse looked out over the steep-sided inlet. At the wharf, Hauk waited – a broad smile of welcome across his handsome face. He invited us to follow him along a snaking path. It led upwards past some flat ground yielding small pastures of hay and, further on, a large plot for root vegetables, cabbages and tiny, tart strawberries. Above us on the hillside, curly-horned goats and sheep fed upon sweet grasses. The off-beat sounds of bleating and the chime of bells floated down across the sun-filled glen.

Beside the house were a number of fruit trees hung with plums and cherries, beneath which chickens and geese searched for windfalls. In the main area of the house, a central soapstone hearth contained a large cooking vessel hung from a sturdy tripod. Around the perimeter of the spacious room, wide wooden seating doubled as beds for guests. Delicious aromas teased our bellies as fresh-baked loaves were brought forth. Thora's serving girl began to lay a trestle with platters of food: grilled trout and smoked salmon; a glutinous fish stew; chunks of meat simmered in rich gravy and two types of local goats' cheese. Lastly, she added a large bowl of tangled, wild flowers. From times past, I knew their delicate shapes and hues offered Thora both pleasure and inspiration for her embroidery.

From the byre at the far end of the house came a faint, earthy undertone. Here, several cows and a horse sleep at night, particularly in the colder weather. Sometimes, all the grazing animals are brought in if wolverines or bears are about. A work room at the opposite end of the building contained Thora's loom with its heavy stone weights and spinning wheel. An open ladder led up to a sleeping

125

compartment. Behind the longhouse, nestled under a fern-clad rock wall, a small, enclosed building contained a flesher's slab. Left to cure and develop their distinctive flavours in the cool mountain air, a variety of meats and fish hung from the walls and ceiling on metal hooks. A large barn stood nearby for storing tools and a trestle provided an area for woodworking. Attached to this was another enclosure, where Hauk smokes fish and various cuts of meat over a small fire of juniper or birch branches. Every vantage point afforded breathtaking views of the fjord and village below.

Soon, it was time to begin the long voyage home. Thora requested we return, perhaps for an overnight stay with a smaller group to enable a trek further along the valley where an intriguing church, a century old or more, stands in isolation. With news and gifts exchanged, our friends walked down with us to the wharf. Attached to the bollards, fishing vessels bobbed in the cool grey waters. On the shore, large triangular frames held lines of fish, which hung by their tails to dry in the breeze. Fishing nets lay spread about, ready to be mended. Creels for catching the big, white-bellied crustaceans stood in stacks waiting for the next trip. For a long time, Thora and Hauk stood arm in arm, watching our vessel glide away into the haze.

The wind was not with us on our journey up the narrow inlet. With the leading crewman beating the metal gong to establish a rhythm, the crew rowed for the better part of the journey until we reached the wider fjord. As if cleft by a sword, shoals of fish fled before us, their rhythm severed. Curious seals disturbed on the sparse rocky shores moved off in flowing unison. Once out to sea, the galley's woollen sail grew taut in the breeze and we gathered speed. Kettil and Fearghas scanned the sea for skerries lying close to the rippling surface. In the inky-blue waters, blunt-nosed dolphins – sleek, grey horses of the sea – leapt out of the cresting waves or glided along beside the vessel. High above, the sliding notes of the gulls drifted on the wind, whilst terns and razorbills swooped, mining the ocean deep for herring. Though it was night, the sky remained pale and silky; faint stars sought to guide us home. Cradled between the mountains and the sea, the town slept. Wispy spirals of smoke drifted upwards from roof vents. A few rushes lit darkened alleyways.

Wedged between two seats, secure against the rolling swell, Inga slept wrapped in a seal skin, snug and dry. At journey's end, Kettil carried the lass into the dower apartments to her wooden sleigh bed. Eithne and Bethoc fetched the gifts from our hosts: a smoked shoulder of lamb; a container of fruit and vegetables resting on new-mown hay; brown eggs packed in wool in a reed basket and a softly-coloured shawl for Inga's bed. Till next time.

Isa

Scotland

Kildrummy Castle

September 1302

Isa, dear heart,

Mary and I wished we could have made the journey with you. Gliding up a fjord suits me well enough, but I think Mary would prefer to be at the helm steering the ship, telling boastful tales to the crew. Your adventures in Norway hold great appeal for our wild and unruly sister. Sometimes I catch an edge of envy in her voice. Mary sees herself as a warrior queen, but it could never end well. More likely, her forthright opinions would fuel a war and her head be loosed from her shoulders!

By comparison, our life is mundane. I cannot recall my last visit to the market in Aberdeen. How I miss Garnait's presence at my side! So often, Isa, I yearned for a strong and virile husband. I see now how much we talked and laughed together, making light of irksome tasks.

Each week, accounts must be sorted through and decisions reached. Our administrator tuts and purses his lips, just so, and seems to frown over much. I am sure he believes me to be a wastrel, but I attend to every penny. Perhaps I shall have Mary sit with him next time! That might hurry his deliberations.

Our country's complex affairs cause many visitors to pass this way, some of whom we must entertain in style. I tread warily with those whose support lies with Balliol and his kinfolk. They come seeking news of our brother, but cloak their queries in sly banter and jests. All of this comes on top of managing the household. Floraidh is unable to keep pace with the sickness – belly cramps and the like, brought in by their servitors. Now it spreads amongst our own. You can tell I have not slept well of late. Irritable words form so quickly upon my tongue, I am hesitant to speak freely lest they offend.

Garnait's passing brings other pitfalls, about which I must keep my wits. Five-year old Donald is argumentative and resentful, unable to comprehend how his father could leave him. A child's ill-formed sense of betrayal burns in his small chest. Under the sad, careful eyes of the guards, he watches from the battlements for his father's return. Ellen is too small to know any difference, but it pains me to think she will not remember Garnait's easy smile or the way his eyes softened at the sight of her. Marjorie spends most of her time down in the stables with Talorc, avoiding me, as if I have secreted Garnait away out of spite. I truly have done nothing to deserve her ire, irrational and passionate as it is. Perhaps, in time, I may be forgiven.

Cocooned in the warmth and comfort of the great kitchen, Margaret is cosseted by Mhairi and the maids. Several years her senior, Aodh is an undemanding companion. As a much smaller lad, he stood in the huge fireplace turning the roasting meat on the long spits. His turn-brochie hands bear the scars of many burns. Now, those hands show Margaret the art of whittling soft wood into the shapes of animals; a skill he learnt from old Aonghas. In the sewing chamber, Mathilda finds solace in the peaceful company of Seonaid who has been altering gowns and tunics to fit a newly blossoming body.

With the passage of time, the bulbs I planted on my dear husband's grave blossom beautifully, as if fed from beneath by the goodness of his spirit. Being of a practical nature, Mary helps me a great deal. We sort through Garnait's manuscripts and letters and put away his precious objects and clothing into chests up in the attic. In doing so, some of the heaviness lifts from my heart. Life goes on, Isa, as you know full well.

In midsummer, Scottish magnates, both here and in France, grew disheartened at the news of a battle lost by the French against Flanders at Courtrai. So many French knights died, they are calling it a massacre. No longer will King Philippe be in a position to offer aid to Scotland and he may well seek a truce with England. For the good men who have striven at home and on the continent to manoeuvre a peace with England on our terms, all has been in vain. Thank the Lord that Garnait is not here to see this. It would have put him in a vile temper. Of late, a large and powerful delegation of Scots' barons and bishops has departed on yet another mission to Paris to see what can be salvaged from this debacle. Pray they find a solution.

When I look around me, I see the trees are gilded copper-red. The autumn air is crisp and pure. Snow dusts the mountain-tops. Before the weather changes, we pitch in to gather the harvest. In the empty fields, the scarecrows made by the children look strange, devoid of purpose. The crows – their black, upright shapes in sharp contrast against the gold-stubbled hay – strut and lurch, while warbling their ancient songs of death and destruction.

Outside the castle walls, a small hamlet develops as families, farmers, traders and craftsmen move closer for our protection. We now have an additional tanner, carpenter and ironmonger. Structures of thatch and daub have been erected by those who lost their homes and farms due to the high taxes imposed by the English when their power extended to the north. A fisherman hawks smoked fish and fresh salmon, whilst a brewer makes batches of welcome ale. Nearby, a cooper set up a stall selling barrels and pails. Few bother to make the journey over to the midden and the grounds around the castle stink with carcasses and refuse left lying about. The tanner, in particular, will be moved on soon enough, if he does not comply with my requests.

A while back, you asked about Rob's new wife. I still have not laid eyes upon her, but he sent news. They set up home in London at our family's manor house in Tottenham. Father softened and offered it as his wedding gift. Through one of the traders at Aberdeen, I sent a set of fine Flemish linen as well as blankets made by the household. It was part of our precious store, but it seems we may be safe for a while with Rob's successful attempts to gain King Edward's patronage. Some days ago now, I received a few words of thanks from Elizabeth, our new good sister. The missive was brief, but gracious, enquiring after the well-being of our families; she hopes to come north to Scotland to meet her dear husband's family. We look forward to such a visit.

As ever
Kirsty

Norway

Bergen

December 1302

My dear Kirsty,

The cold, dark winter months are upon us and the days are short. Has the weather been kind to you? With Yuletide just a few weeks away, I wish you peace and joy.

Bishop Narve arranged for a monk from the Mariakirken to teach Inga her letters. She is as happy as can be sitting now by the fireside with her slate. Earlier today, we dressed in our warmest cloaks and furs and wandered down to the fair. Many people came by boat or cross-country in sleighs or on skis to purchase gifts for the celebrations over the festive New Year period. Big bowls of warm glogg, a blend of fruit, ground almonds and spices, were for sale. Food stalls displayed mutton ribs steamed over branches of juniper, glutinous fish stews, roasted grouse and special sweet buns and biscuits.

Many Norse folk have a cheerful disposition, ready for a laugh and a drink. Today was a merry occasion. Erling gave us a hearty wave as we passed by his stall. Even the thin, fine-boned jeweller, Ottar Skjeggen, was keen to grab my attention and show me an ancient gold brooch inlaid with pearls and red almandine, which had come into his possession. From a wooden chest beneath his trestle, he brought forth his treasures: Frankish beakers made of green and blue patterned glass; a bronze and silver bracelet decorated with bands of gold foil and an exquisite, ornate necklace he crafted from opal, amethyst and garnet. As I placed it around my neck, Erling appeared behind me and whispered in my ear, "Be wary, your grace. Make sure it is not styled after the famed Brisingamen – lest it cost more than you think!" Full of mischief, he winked at the craftsman before returning to his stall where several women were trying out his combs. I turned to the jeweller to see his response. Poor Ottar stuttered and stammered and packed away his wares. Nothing more would he say, apparently severely mortified.

Later, upon our return home, I asked Kettil, who was sharing some refreshments at our hearth, what he knew of the Brisingamen necklace. It was ill-timed to pose such a query, for he proceeded to choke upon his ale and sprayed out a large mouthful onto my prized Byzantine carpet. After wiping his wet beard with a voluminous, red cloth, he recounted the story of Freya, goddess of love. So enamoured of the famed Brisingamen necklace was she, that she begged the makers, four dwarves, to give it to her. The price, they said, was she had to sleep with each of them – an offer she accepted without a second thought! I was sorry I asked. Till next time.

Yours aye

Isa

Norway

Bergen

December 1302

It had been a dreich day indeed. After so long sitting beside the hearth, Isa felt the need for some fresh air. She had used the last of the woollen thread for her current project: an embroidered cushion for Effie to sit upon at the window in her library. Pulling on thick leather gloves, she placed her warmest cloak around her shoulders, gathering the fur-lined hood well in under her chin. Dodging puddles of mud and ice, Isa and her maid wandered down to the harbour and the busy stalls.

Isa sighted Otto's ship pulling into the crowded wharf. He saw her waving and raised his hand in acknowledgement. It took some time before the crew disembarked. Under the trader's arm was a rolled parchment with its distinctive lead seal, obvious even at a distance. Leaving Aiofe to continue with the task at hand, Isa returned home at some pace, eager to read her brother's news.

Turnberry Castle

Dearest Isa,

I hope this finds you well in Bergen. It is now October and, by this time, you may have heard I have turned traitor and am back in the peace of Edward of England. I hope you know me better than to believe I would ever give up my country, but it is true I concluded an agreement in February of this year with Edward. For the present, we do not fight the Old Lion. As you may have guessed, this is all because of the Comyns and their machinations to destroy us. Bear with me, for to give you a more fulsome picture, I must backtrack a little.

After Falkirk, Wallace gave up the Guardianship. I was asked to take it on jointly with John Comyn of Badenoch. Bishop Lamberton persuaded me it was in the interests of Scotland to balance our factions in government. I knew from the first it was a mistake to have to work with those rogues and so it proved. Having made a mess of an attack on the English garrison at Roxburgh Castle, we met in Council at Selkirk. One of Comyn's men tried to claim the lands of William Wallace on the grounds he had left the country without permission. When I defended the Wallace position, John Comyn grabbed me by the throat. Luckily, Lamberton intervened, or I do not know what might have happened. The Council ended with Lamberton joining us as a Guardian and at least I did not have to talk so much with Comyn. We tried to arrange a truce with the English at the end of 1299, but Edward refused. Worse still, the Comyns stirred up the tenants of Balliol in Galloway to attack both Annandale and Carrick. As a result, I was forced to defend our people directly and thus resigned from the Guardianship; I knew, effectively, I was at war with Comyn.

We beat off an English invasion in 1300 and also heard the work of the Scottish church was rewarded with a Papal Bull which ordered Edward to leave Scotland in peace. Not that this convinced Edward to leave our lands for long. In June of 1301, Edward invaded again with two huge armies. Whilst Sir John Soulis slowed the main host – led by the king himself as it trundled forward from Berwick towards Edinburgh – I commanded my own men who fought the forces of the Prince of Wales. We checked the prince's momentum and he was forced to give up Carrick and head for the east coast and his father. Equally, Edward had failed to cross the line of the Forth, and, by the late autumn of 1301, was back in England.

1302 started well – with a truce for the year. It soon became apparent the Comyns were planning for the return of 'King' John Balliol. He had been placed in the hands of the French king by the Pope and, now, the Comyns were working to bring their cousin back to the Scottish throne. As you can imagine, this would have been the end of the house of Bruce in Scotland. Balliol had already tried to wrest Annandale from us in 1295, and it was likely he would proscribe us all on his return from France. This meant I had no choice but to sign an agreement with Edward if we were to survive. I was able to do so, as Edward also feared a French invasion via Scotland. Moreover, I gained the wardship of poor Kirsty's young son, now Garnait is dead. I will ensure he is safe and will protect the boy and his mother of course. That is the least I can do for such a good man.

I was able to get the permission of the Earl of Ulster to marry his daughter, Elizabeth de Burgh. You will know this already, having heard it from Kirsty. I had first seen her all those years ago at the English court where Edward and her father were just back from campaigning in France. Now, she is my wife. I wish you could meet her just to see how happy we are together, even in the midst of all this mayhem and worry. She is a great strength to me, and wise in many ways knowing Edward so well. He holds her in great affection, which I think was mutual – until I came into her life. It irks me to say this, but Edward can be a fine and generous man to those who are no threat to him.

Elizabeth sees him for the black-hearted devil he is and how he means to crush Scotland – and me with it – into submission. I expect the king thinks her family ties will bind me closer to him. We shall see, but first there remains the problem of the Comyns. I miss your laughter and wise advice.

As ever

Rob

CHAPTER THIRTEEN

Scotland

Kildrummy Castle

February 1303

Isa, dear heart,

Norway seems a world away, when the days are long and dark. Then, I am filled with a desire to talk and laugh and ponder life's mysteries together, as once we did. Who knows if we shall ever meet again?

Kirsty

Norway

Bergen

March 1303

My dear Kirsty,

Have you fared well with the passage of time? I am now of an age where a wimple is most welcome to keep out the chills and hide those wiry, hearth hairs, as Gundred calls them, which appear overnight.

But none can hold back time. Certainly not poor Fearghas! Bethoc nursed him, but today he breathed his last. Now, the old captain sails his galley o'er the River Styx.

Your loving sister

Isa

Scotland

Kildrummy Castle

April 1303

Isa, dear heart,

From outside my window, I can hear the infernal dripping of ice and snow. Down in the orchard, buds unfurl on our precious fruiting trees, and it is a relief to know we have survived another winter. I wonder how our country will fare as this year unfolds.

King Edward's truce expired in November last. Unable to campaign himself until May, he sent a force to reconnoitre the land west of Edinburgh; three brigades of knights led by Sir Edward Segrave. Upon hearing the English were near Roslin, Comyn and Fraser mobilised their men to ride through the night all the way from Biggar to launch a surprise attack. The next morning, they attacked one of the brigades capturing many knights as well as Segrave who was badly injured. Killed in the fray was Ralph Manton, the king's clerk and cofferer of his wardrobe. The loss of many items necessary for the health and well-being of an armed force will prove irksome to the king. Soon after, they captured the Peel of Selkirk. A buoyant feeling surrounds us all with these small successes.

A letter arrived from Robert regards his visit to Cambridge. When he saw Alexander after so many years apart, Rob barely recognised him, but the warmth of his welcome was real enough. Stocky in build with brown hair and beard, Alexander is now quite tall, though shorter still than Rob. He sports the same earnest expression he always wore as a child. With great pride, Robert gave the traditional feast at his inception into

Master of Arts. Robert Mannyng, a Lincolnshire canon with a talent for poetry, later applauded Alexander's acumen and ability as the best student who had ever read Arts at Cambridge; high praise indeed!

Do you recall when Alexander tried to discuss logic with Grandfather? The old man would screw up his face and bellow that the only logical thought he had in his head at that moment was to take the shears to Alexander's hair. This always caused such a furore. Now, Rob declares, those locks are neatly trimmed as is Alexander's beard and, befitting his new status as a master, he wears a velvet academic gown over his tunic. I wonder if he still takes himself so seriously.

In an aside, Robert made mention of some land near Wigtown. I hope our younger brother is wary of such gifts from the English king. As Sheriff of Lanark and Ayr and Keeper of the Castle, Rob received an order to call up one thousand hand-picked men from within the sheriffdom of Ayr for Edward's summer campaign. It seems our brother means to tarry. A dangerous game for him to play!

As ever

Kirsty

Scotland

Kildrummy Castle

October 1303

Isa, dear heart,

Fearghas served our family faithfully and well for so many years under such extreme conditions. At first I was fearful of him with that fierce scar upon his face, but it was his kindness that endeared him to me.

Autumn is fast turning into winter and the walkways have been repaired in preparation. Mud lies thick down in the bailey. The children slip and career about, in fun no doubt, but their clothes are caked and stained. I fear they are ruined. It takes forever to get the mud off their boots, so, of course, they do not bother and traipse it all through the corridors and stairwells. Earchann will do his best with a hog hair broom, once it is dry, whenever that might be. Morag grumbles as she tries to rid the Great Hall of its stale smell. With new rushes and strewing herbs to be cut, the task is never-ending.

It was always Mother's dream that Alexander would excel in the world of academia. How proud she would be of his achievements at Cambridge! Our father, too, will be satisfied his financial investment has brought its rewards. I hope Rob's presence at Alexander's feast will have given our younger brother much pleasure.

As usual, Scotland is paying for its optimism earlier this year. In May, the Scots' magnates received the news they had been hoping would not come. England and France had made peace. Despite all his promises, King Philippe left Scotland excluded from the peace and out on a limb. All the while, Scots' negotiators have hung onto the ideal of Scotland's legitimacy, but, when it most mattered, they were betrayed. In spite of this, a letter was sent thereafter by Bishop Lamberton urging John Comyn, Scotland's Guardian, not to give up hope that justice would prevail in the end. Blind faith will get us how far in the end, I wonder? In a mood to avenge the Battle of Roslin, King Edward began his expedition, moving inexorably north. This time, though, he planned well ahead. Three prefabricated barges were floated up from Kings Lynn to serve as bridges for his troops to cross the Forth. Upon reaching Edinburgh, the army did not stop, but marched onto Perth; avoiding Stirling Castle, manned as it was by a Scots' garrison that had refused to surrender. Onwards, the king's army trudged through to Dundee. Brechin Castle was placed under siege for three months and, when the commander of the garrison was killed on the battlements, the garrison yielded. Meanwhile in the central south, Comyn, the Guardian, along with one hundred horsemen and one thousand foot soldiers, was raiding up into Lennox. Regardless, the English host continued on its relentless path up through Montrose and Aberdeen, and onto Banff and Cullen until it reached Kinloss Abbey before heading south.

Unfortunately for us, he chose to come via Kildrummy, to threaten and intimidate. His visit gave me nightmares for weeks after. We are thankful that he did not pillage the area, but his host moved over our dear land, like a proverbial plague of vile, greedy locusts consuming everything in its path. With the ritual humiliation complete, the all-conquering army moved onto Dunfermline where the king plans to over-winter. May he roast in hell instead!

Kirsty

CHAPTER FOURTEEN

Norway

Bergen

March 1304

My dear Kirsty,

With the winter gales thrashing the seas, Murchadh took a much-needed break after the death of his father. Your last missive recounted such a tale of horror and woe. Your own safety may soon be threatened and I urge you to devise a plan of some sort, lest you find yourselves in a dank, airless prison. Murchadh could bring you here or, if this is too far, another alternative may be possible. Do you recall all those years ago, when I was brought here, we were given respite from our journey on Orkney? It was at the Kirkwall manor of Jon Magnusson, Earl of both Orkney and Caithness; a strange mix having two masters, Norway and England. After King Eric's death, I organised the betrothal of Inga to the widowed earl, but the poor man died, and King Haakon passed the wardship of his son and heir to Master Weland. It was a great honour and a measure of the king's trust and respect for his royal councillor. The latter then engineered an accord with King Edward to regain control of the earldom's lands in Caithness, but I wager the Norse king brought his considerable charm and ability to bear upon the matter. Most fortunate are we to have such a strong ally on Orkney. Surely Weland can find an isle where you would be safe from prying eyes. Consider this well, dear one, sooner rather than later.

Isa

Scotland

Kildrummy Castle

March 1304

Isa, dear heart,

You are right: our lives have become less predictable, but I cannot leave here without Donald and, given he is the Earl of Mar, he should not leave his people. If Garnait were here, he would agree with me. If it comes to it, the children and whoever else would wish to leave may go with Murchadh to a place of safety. I cannot speak to Rob concerning Marjorie, but trust he would want her kept out of harm's way.

When the time comes, I shall make the necessary arrangements. Should I be unable to put pen to paper, I will contrive, somehow, to send a sealed parchment containing a bird's feather. If you or Murchadh receive this sign, I ask the brave captain to proceed with all haste to Kildrummy.

Kirsty

Scotland

Kildrummy Castle

April 1304

Isa, dear heart,

Sad tidings! Father is dead. He lies now at Holm Coltram Abbey in Cumberland. I am adrift in a sea of memories and pray that Father finds peace.

Given our family's vulnerable standing in England, Robert requested that the Honour of Huntington be assigned to him as the rightful heir. King Edward is known for following lawful proceedings, but if our brother makes a misstep, our estates at Writtle and Hatfield Broad Oak could be parcelled off to one of Edward's knights. These are perilous times.

As ever

Kirsty

Norway

Bergen

May 1304

My dear Kirsty,

I hope Father finds solace at last. To inherit Grandfather's flinty character, but none of his flair or charm was truly outwith his control. Beyond the family, few warmed to him, driven as he was to prove his worth and safeguard our heritage. And so critical of Robert he pushed us away, expecting us to take sides.

Such a rift brings only sadness now. I remember his gentle storytelling all those years ago and the way his eyes softened when Mother walked into a room, and how proud he was of me on my wedding day.

Is it known what ailment caused his passing?

As ever

Isa

Scotland

Kildrummy Castle

May 1304

Isa, dear heart,

I wager it was Father's heart which brought about his sudden passing. Much like Grandfather, he grew more choleric with the years and the rift with our brothers irked him to the point of rage and despair. His attorney was present, but could do nought to save him. I assumed Father would be buried at Guisborough Priory. Perhaps this way will suit him best, not having to spend the rest of eternity with Grandfather. I am saddened as are you, but Father died some time ago now, and life goes on apace.

Under strict guard, the girls ride their ponies outside the castle walls. One day, they alerted us to a large group of riders coming our way. Mary and I rushed to the battlements. Fear soon turned to relief and elation. Robert was across from Ayr Castle to see to the management of the earldom. This time he brought his wife with him, as well as his supporters including Sir Christopher Seton. Most wonderful of all Thomas and Niall rode in with them; they have changed from the annoying pranksters of my memory into adventurous, charming young men. Niall is so handsome he had the eyes of all the women in the castle upon him, their chatter quelled momentarily. Whip-slim and wiry still, Thomas accepts the effect his brother has upon women, but remains good hearted, almost whimsical about it. Cheeky, guileless banter was ever his most endearing feature. Both lads have spent time between Ireland and the west coast working for our family's interests, they said, but were intent on keeping their heads down. Somehow, they seem to be operating under Robert's protection, but have avoided coming under King Edward's direct scrutiny.

You will want to know about our other important visitor. Elizabeth is fair of hair and face, fine-boned and slender, but well-proportioned with it. Robert is smitten, though it is her mind which intrigues him. So quick-witted is she that she makes him laugh. Her soft brogue reminded me a little of our gentle Gaelic speakers; it seems she was born of a large family like ours in Ulster. For a long time up until her marriage, she had been staying at Alnwick Castle in Northumberland with her Percy relatives while her father had been on campaign with King Edward. How strange it is she speaks of our enemies with such fondness. For the most part, I found our good sister to be quite personable, if a little shy, as would only be natural under the circumstances. Elizabeth may well have thought us barbarians, but had the good grace to say nothing.

This missive has been in my trunk for some weeks now, but for good reason. Christopher Seton requested my hand in marriage. Despite his formidable size, he is a man of great gentleness, good-humoured as well and possessed of a bright, shining integrity. Rob esteems him well and gave his support, wishing only I could be as happy and content as he is with Elizabeth.

Our marriage vows took place with Tomas presiding just a few days later in Kildrummy's chapel. A most joyous feast ensued though from where Mhairi purloined all the provisions at such short notice only the good Lord would know. To loud acclaim, generous piles of roast suckling pork and venison were carried in on platters and placed upon the trestles, along with jugs of thick gravy and enough trenchers for all. Steaming pies followed, filled with the tender, simmered flesh of pheasants, and deftly shaped into their form. Next, servitors offered platters of salmon and crisp-skinned, speckled trout. Sweet meats followed; ground almond pudding – Rob's favourite;

bowls of fresh cream, oatmeal and early brambles; apples and pears poached in syrup. All washed down by ale brewed outside the castle walls and Earchann's mead made from the honey gathered from our hives. Without jugglers or bards to entertain, it fell to Thomas to tell tales of us as children. Guests rolled about in laughter; some overbalanced and landed in a tangled heap. Music and dancing followed: energetic jigs, ring dances and the like well into the long summer night.

The gallant Sir Christopher has permission to stay until Rob's return visit in a month. The household will have to look after itself. I shall be otherwise engaged! I dearly missed your presence here at my wedding. Even after all these years, I still long to see you again – to laugh and talk late into the night. Do you remember how Mary used to snore and the time you pulled the coverlet over her head? Our brothers enjoyed hearing all your news and send their love, as do we all.

Yours aye

Kirsty

Norway

Bergen

July 1304

My dear Kirsty,

Well do I remember Mary's snoring! What a crabbit minx she was when she awoke! She kicked me so hard I rolled over and you fell out of bed turning your ankle. Weeks later, you were still hobbling about, whilst our dear sister was off having a fine time out riding. How happy am I for you that our brothers could attend your wedding. Alas, I am so far away!

It seems timely to tell you about Effie. A great patron of

literary works, in particular romantic ballads, she is keen to cultivate continental culture within the Norse royal court to counter its violent past. To this end, she authorised a translation from German of an eleventh century tale of knights and their chivalric code. After this, two more are to be completed. I hope to send you copies. 'The Euphemia Ballads', as they are now known, are quite dissimilar to the boisterous sagas of the skalds, the old storytellers. I wonder if they will become popular here. Do you recall the stories Mother told us of Eleanor of Aquitaine, the famous French queen? My good sister is cast in her mould.

King Haakon is caught up with the power struggles between Norway and Denmark, and the contentious brothers of the Swedish king who seek to challenge his authority. At one time, Duke Eric, the second eldest, led insurgents across our borders. These were repelled of course, but Haakon's broader strategy of negotiation aims to bring some long standing equilibrium to Norway's eastern borders. Perhaps to maintain peace and stability on the home front, he is more than happy to commission the queen's projects.

Effie engaged several monks from the University of Bologna to search out tomes for her. Alexander will be impressed for they cover religious texts, philosophy, logic, rhetoric and more. Fortunate am I to be invited to the special chamber in the royal tower where the books are stored. Sitting in the dull light on the padded stone seats of the window embrasure, Effie reads passages to me as if I am a child new to learning and explains in simple language the gist of the tale. It is necessary for, apart from French, my continental language skills are by far poorer than hers, but it does amuse me no end.

Here, I am reading about knights in courtly tales, whilst you, dear Kirsty, are blessed to be in a tale of your own making. I am a little jealous, if truth be known.

Isa

Scotland

Kildrummy Castle

August 1304

Isa, dear heart,

Your world seems so much larger than mine. Sometimes, I do not want to see the world beyond these walls.

Last week, Rob returned. With his tasks complete, he departed today with my lord husband. Bereft though I am, I am well-pleased with our precious time together. The children had an opportunity to get to know Christopher under less formal circumstances. Given his immense size, Donald and Ellen were wary at first, but thawed, especially when he let Ellen ride upon his back in the nursery. I heard nary a complaint from him and can only presume he was enjoying himself. On one occasion, Chris chased them around the castle in a game of hide and go seek. Ellen went missing! We searched for hours, only to find the bairn blissfully asleep in a trunk in the attic. She had wrapped herself in one of Garnait's old cloaks; the vision pains me still.

Endless battles took place. Chris taught Donald to feint and parry whist manoeuvring around obstacles, leaping over trunks and the like, up and down stairwells, along walkways – all without losing concentration. Next, he crafted a bow and a set of feathered arrows. Some of the guards grumbled at this, for an earl to fire arrows is considered unseemly. Chris bade them consider otherwise – the winds of war ride upon the back of change, he said – but the men were none the wiser.

Donald is down in the bailey; I can hear the dull thud as an arrow finds its target. He will miss 'the big man' he said; not yet willing to acknowledge someone who might replace his own father in his affections, nor would I wish it otherwise, though he sorely needs such a figure in his life.

Nearly all the Scots' barons defeated last December in a brutal skirmish at Stirling, capitulated in February of this year and entered into King Edward's peace, barring those two stalwart patriots, Wallace and Fraser. At a parliament held at St Andrews, freeholders wishing to have their lands restored had to submit to King Edward. His advice must be sought before the passing of laws. Worst of all, he has brought in his nephew, the Earl of Richmond, to head our subordinate government. So, the puissant English monarch continues his dominion of our good land.

Since May, the Scots' garrison at Stirling Castle had been under siege, but in July it fell. Despite the garrison's request for an honourable surrender, the English king continued the pounding assault with his trebuchets; he has added a new toy to his collection, an enormous siege engine known as 'Warwolf'. In a vicious mood as usual, he threatened the defeated garrison with drawing and hanging, until they were beside themselves with fear. It was only the intervention of his close associates that restrained Edward from making real his threats. Instead, the large group of weakened, injured men were sent off to prison, perhaps to die a more prolonged death. Wallace was involved in a skirmish and has now gone to ground. I fear he has lost heart. Rob spoke of a pact of friendship with Bishop Lamberton, to forfeit ten thousand pounds if breached. I can only assume from this that Grandfather's dream still burns strong and bright in his breast.

Drustan awaits my assistance; his finger retains a bramble thorn and is now swollen and sore. A poultice is required. Till next time

Kirsty

Norway

Bergen

December 1304

My dear Kirsty,

Bishop Narve died yester eve, the day after Christ's Mass. I can scarce believe he is gone. No longer will he sit by my hearth on wintry afternoons, musing upon the history of the world.

I recalled a story he once told me; it was before his time here. Some forty years ago, the churches in Bergen did not welcome the newly-arrived Dominican mendicants. Jealous of their popularity, one clerical group even sited their dung heap high on a hill above the Dominican church and cemetery, so the folk might be put off by the excrement running down the hill – not to mention the smell – and fail to attend services. Can you credit that! Now we have so many German traders living here, the Dominicans hold even greater popularity. In the town of Lubeck, the original home of many of the traders, a similar conflict occurred between the secular church and the newcomers. Upon the traders' arrival in Bergen, Bishop Narve welcomed the men and sought to gain support for them with my lord husband; no easy man to deal with at the best of times! The Dominican church prospered from the traders' donations as they grew in wealth.

Bishop Narve was a most humble man. To my surprise, he confided one day how he was once full of youthful pride and ambition; desiring above all things to be the Archbishop of Trondheim. After much lobbying, he achieved the role, but five years later, his appointment was overturned. Embittered at the loss of such a substantial post, he came to Bergen as its bishop.

Staring deep into the flames, he paused in the telling. A gentle smile reached his eyes.

"If our Holy Father had not brought me here, I would have seen neither the settlement of the church conflict nor the growth of this city as a royal capital. I would not have blessed the little maid when she drew her dying breath in Orkney nor would I have met you, my dear. If God in his grace had granted me another path and given me a daughter, I would have wanted her to be just like you."

May you find peace and great joy, dear Bishop Narve.

Isa

CHAPTER FIFTEEN

Norway

Bergen

March 1305

My dear Kirsty,

With the brighter days, Inga and I walk around the shoreline with Solas in tow. Oft times, the lazy mite flops down and we must carry him. Still it drizzles, but the weather grows less oppressive. A fine, fresh smell hangs upon the air.

The inauguration of the new Bishop of Bergen, Arne Sigurdsson, took place at the Kristkirke. He is quite an aloof man, full of his own self-importance, so I do not anticipate any profound discussions on long, wintry afternoons. Many notables came from all over Norway and, of course, Haakon and Euphemia arrived in great style. Determined always to minimise her own heritage, Effie insisted I wear a traditional outfit similar to hers though she, of course, sported a gold crown. Over a garment of soft white linen, a royal blue pinafore was wrapped around my torso, resting just below my armpits. Attached were wide shoulder straps held in place over each breast by an oval brooch raised like a tortoise. A third brooch, a disc of gold trefoil, hung down, suspended by a chain encrusted with beads. Such a weight to carry! Over this, I wore a cloak with another brooch fastened at the shoulder. I much prefer the simpler gowns of my youth.

Master Weland was a most kind and considerate escort, holding my arm much as Father did all those years ago at my wedding. The sweet, painful memory caught me by surprise.

Since the death of my lord husband, who earned the sobriquet of 'priest hater', I work hard at maintaining a good relationship with the clergy and have made many donations. In return, the church offers me properties in the area for which they no longer have a purpose. Inga continues with her lessons arranged by Bishop Narve. One of the queen's ladies-in-waiting is teaching her French and German as well as the delicate skill of needlework in which the Norse excel. Much of the clothing here is rich with decoration. With the long dark winters, a useful project is necessary to help pass the time. As you would expect, Princess Ingeborg has a surfeit of toys and Inga is often invited to play with her cousin in the royal apartments. For the most part, the queen is engrossed in her manuscripts and her father, away, seeing to fracas in his kingdom.

Yester eve, I had that conversation with our friend. He queried how many packages might need to be placed in storage. I told him no one would know until closer to the time.

Eithne is quite unwell. She sickened after our trip to Sognefjorden. Gundred claims my maid ate too much fish stew. This does not sit well with me. In summer we will pay another visit to Thora. Some weeks back, Hauk called by to tell us she is with child, due now in a few months. Never have I seen a man look so delighted, his days as a fierce huskarl long behind him. As a youngster, he must have practised scowling and curling his lip into a frightful sneer. It seems foreign to him now, especially with his hair and moustache trimmed so neatly by Thora. That dreadful bearskin seems to be a thing of the past too. He now dons a serviceable, woollen cloak. Till next time, stay safe.

Isa

Scotland

Kildrummy Castle

April 1305

Isa, dear heart,

My news first! I am with child, due in a few short months. My lord husband visits Kildrummy, when Robert is permitted to leave his post at Ayr Castle to attend to his role as guardian. It will be Christopher's first child and he is ecstatic. Donald and Ellen seem pleased enough, though I am sure they hold those jealous self-doubts about being replaced in my affections. It is such an effort trying to reassure them, especially Donald, and maintain all my other tasks as well.

Robert advised Grandfather's wife has died. As yet, no details are available. Our Lenten parliament received an instruction from King Edward for a constitution to be drawn up. To this end, Robert, Bishop Wishart and Sir John Mowbray (an earl, a bishop and a baron as per the usual practice) requested of the king that ten elected parliamentary representatives be given the task. They will reassemble in May. It irks our leaders we must crave the English king's pardon and seek his wisdom, such that it is, when we have managed our own affairs for centuries.

Wish me well, dear one.

Kirsty

Norway

Bergen

July 1305

My dear Kirsty,

I pray all is well with you. Your delivery must be soon, as contrary weather delayed the arrival of your letter.

Some weeks back, my concerns about Eithne's health rose to a peak. I asked my midwife to cast an eye over my maid, but Sigrud could find nothing overtly wrong. Could someone have put a curse upon her, she queried, merely in passing; an odd assertion, but in this strange and mysterious country, anything is possible.

For some reason, I grew suspicious of Gundred, though I could see nothing unusual about her care. If anything, she seemed more solicitous. In the end, I confronted her. In a trice, she broke down, overwhelmed as she was with guilt. I gave her such a shake her teeth chattered and her eyes rolled alarmingly in her head. She was jealous of Eithne and Kettil's interest in the pretty young Irish lass. One day, Gundred said, she visited the volva, the soothsayer in the hills, who handed her a grubby piece of parchment upon which was written a spell. Following instructions, Gundred stood over Eithne whilst asleep and recited the words. Now, the lass is deathly pale and as weak as a tiny babe. Even Gundred is concerned, for Eithne was not meant to die, only to be so unwell she could not go on any seabound excursions. "Show me the parchment," I demanded, but its destruction had been an explicit requirement of the spell.

Kirsty, I have never been as angry as that day with this foolish woman's meddling in what she did not understand; thoughts of St Malachy's curse on our own family whirled around my head.

Throwing a cloak over my shoulders, I bade her do the same and we departed forthwith to visit the volva. Following the shoreline around the harbour, we rode in my wagon up through the hills until reaching a secluded valley. Leaving Brandubh tethered to a tree at the start of a rise, we went the rest of the way on foot along a path lined with ferns and brambles. Down beside a rocky stream and surrounded by undergrowth was a small, wood-slabbed cottage with a ragged, sod roof. Smoke rose in a lazy, twisting spiral from its smoke vent.

My hand went to knock on the old carved door. I hesitated. A low voice behind me made me jump, I swear, clear out of my skin. Gundred babbled in fright. A large striped cat, its muddy fur full of tangles, brushed past my ankles, causing the hackles to rise on the back of my neck. I caught a glimpse, not of a wizened crone, but of a fine-looking lass, with long wavy hair the colour of a summer's sunset and the most striking green eyes. At this point, the picture became distorted. As she turned to face me, I saw running down her cheek and neck, a scalding, blood-red birthmark. She seemed ill at ease. We moved aside to let her pass. Within the cottage, benches held jugs and pails of wild flowers. From the wooden beams, bunches of tangled blossoms, the seer's tools of trade, hung drying and the air was thick with a strange musky scent. The brindled feline leapt onto a stool and began to knead an old cushion, before turning full circle, curling itself into a ball. One amber eye remained open to the proceedings.

On the kitchen table, central to the room, were a number of small wooden boxes containing amulets, a mess of owl pellets and most intriguing of all, pebbles and stones wrapped in the gut of a small creature. Against the far wall, various skeletons were arranged on a trestle. The most prominent was the angular jaw of a pig which lay beside the fine-boned form of a pigeon. Above them, dried entrails hung from a hook. At one end of the chamber, a wooden stand supported a raven whose beaded eyes never left my face. It flapped its ebony wings and the air became a shroud of dust and debris. At a word from its mistress, it settled, still and brooding.

The volva poured a liquid into thick mugs from a kettle which hung over a fire in the corner of the room. I began to disclose the reason for our visit. She cut me off and pointed a long finger, dirt well-ingrained into the cracked skin, at Gundred. "It is you who are to blame!" she said in a low voice which held an otherworldly chill. "Now, I must undo this foul mischance."

Much like an owl before it sweeps down to devour its prey, she turned her head and examined me in full. An unnerving silence filled the room. Words began to tumble ill-formed from my lips. With a scowl, she indicated I drink from the proffered cup. When I had drained all but the dregs, she held out her hand, swirled the cup and tipped the remains onto a platter.

"I see great pain ahead for you, my lady: war, death, knives, blood, much blood. I see strange cages swinging; hear them creaking in the wind. I smell fear." I was desperate to know what fate would befall me, but she shrugged. "Not you, my lady, nor your precious girl child, but those of your blood. Much suffering there will be, before the world is righted once more and peace comes."

Her voice wavered and then faded, as if heard from some far-off distant shore. She closed her eyes and rested her head upon her chest. Her breath came slow and steady, whilst I could scarce draw breath. Part of me prayed she would not say another word: the rest of me begged to know more. What could be done to avert this calamity? Would my family even heed such a warning? Whatever it was, her vision was over. As she raised her head, the birthmark seemed to bleed down her face and neck into the creases of her body. The volva, for I knew not her name, turned her attention upon the hapless Gundred, whose red-rimmed eyes were wide with terror within her pale, clammy face.

"I should place the curse upon you, dolt, but my eyes tell me you have suffered already. Go both of you. By the morrow, the maid will begin to recover." Again, she pointed the accusatory finger at Gundred. "Never pass this way again! Now, begone!"

What had started as a hiss became a roar. We stumbled out of the cottage, falling over each other in our haste. Behind us, the heavy door slammed shut as if a gale had been unleashed within.

After tripping and skidding along the wet path, we came to Brandubh; his tether still in place. For a moment, I cradled his warm forehead against mine and breathed his earthy scent. Our ride home was accomplished in silence except for the snivelling of Gundred. An expression of shame and guilt stole across her bleak, pinched features, so appalled was she that her crime had been exposed.

I felt stunned, but a perplexing question tugged and fretted at my thoughts. How did the seer know I had a daughter?

There you have it, Kirsty, a strange tale indeed. Eithne did indeed recover her full strength. And Gundred, you may ask? Well, let it be said Gundred is busy elsewhere. Iceland is a fine place this time of year, so Effie tells me.

Your loving sister
Isa

Scotland

Kildrummy Castle

August 1305

Isa, dear heart,

My daughter made her presence known on a warm summer's day. Meg proved to be a large babe and the birth was a long, hard tussle, but the good Lord saw fit for us both to survive. Floraidh already had a wet nurse in mind – young Marthoc, from whom she had delivered a set of twins; one had perished within the womb. No one came forward to claim Marthoc's infant as his own, though, the other day down in the bailey, I saw several strained faces amongst the garrison men when she passed them. Brave girl, she held her head high and clutched her babe to her breast. Now, with more than enough milk for two, she will move into the quarters near the nursery.

How I despise the binding of my breasts! Sometimes I envy the wet nurse, though who would want breasts that hang like the saddle bags on an old garron when the feeding is done? It is enough my belly has more lines and ridges than the face of an ancient crone. Pain, suffering and ugliness; are they all a woman can aspire to?

I rejoice that I did not receive your missive until after Meg's birth, for I would have been even more affrighted than I already was. I will speak to our brothers, but do not see them taking much heed. How can we avoid battles if we are at war – a war for our country's survival and our own freedom? That is what they will say. As for the cages, who knows what that is about? Stay well clear of this seer and her strange predictions, Isa, lest your wits become addled!

As ever
Kirsty

Norway

Bergen

September 1305

My dear Kirsty,
It was a grave challenge to put the foreboding I felt at the

seer's words from my mind. Many prayers have I said to the Holy Mother, in the hope both you and your babe might survive the ordeal. When I read that you were spared, tears of relief wet my cheeks.

Once Eithne made a full recovery, we sailed again to Sognefjorden. Kettil consulted the runes, those ancient markings, for an auspicious journey. I would have preferred he check the sky, the waves or even the flights of the birds. Being early autumn, there was a fair chance the weather might hold for our excursion. Our group was smaller, more intimate, this time. Kettil planned to explore the closest fjords and return in two days time. Hauk decided to go with the crew, many of whom were friends from his huskarl days.

Our first afternoon was spent in time-honoured tradition – admiring the infant, giving gifts and discussing the birth in all its gruesome detail. For a first babe, Halldora came in a rush; too quick even to call the midwife in time. Thora admitted she ignored the niggling pains and ache in her back which had gone on for some hours before. Hauk made sure his farm work never took him too far from the house and when he heard Thora's agonised cry, he dropped his tools on the workbench and ran to find her lying in a puddle of fluid on the floor of the work room. The maid had already gone for the midwife who lived on the other side of the village on a ridge, not far as the raven flies, but a fair distance there and back on foot. By the time Hauk reached his wife, her body was arched and contorted with pain.

In record time, the infant slid into view, streaked with a bloodied, white slime. Thora knew enough to tell her pale, clammy husband to cut the cord with his seax and knot it. To her surprise, the young man slid onto the floor beside her in a faint. It was a blessing she did not bleed as some women do, when a birth comes too fast and death follows soon after. When the midwife arrived, she found Thora suckling her child. Hauk

160

sat upon a chair; his head hung between his long legs. He knew all in the village would hear soon enough how he had disgraced himself. Later, with a container in her hand, the midwife took the afterbirth outside and instructed Hauk to dig a deep hole wherein she placed the bloody mess, muttering prayers of thanks to Freya. The woman then wrote a rune sign in the covering dirt to protect the birth matter from wolves and foxes, as it, in turn, needed to feed the earth. A cycle complete!

Now, Halldora grows into a fine, healthy bairn. Whilst Thora attended to her hungry daughter, our small band spent the afternoon wandering around the fields, picking bunches of delicate wildflowers and fruit from the orchard. Inquisitive geese and a throng of noisome goats followed our progress. In the barn, an early chick poked its tiny head out from under its mother's layer of brown feathers as we gathered eggs. On our return to the house, Groa used them to whisk up some soft, flower-shaped waffles. At night, an aromatic salad of herrings, cucumber and onions followed by a thick, savoury stew proved most satisfying.

Around the fire, stories were told of trolls, giants and elves. The further away we were from Bergen, the more believable were these tales, for the midwife was an accomplished storyteller. At each pertinent observation, her brows arched and her eyes widened. Some characters were described with such affection and clarity they seemed merely to be recalcitrant members of the community living about the hills and vales. The ugly trolls are long-lived, she said, up to a hundred years or more! You might recognise them by their crooked noses and bushy tails, but close investigation of their hands will show each lacks a finger. Irritable by nature, they have a particular dislike for church bells and a total dislike of billy goats which they enjoy harassing.

Elves are a different kettle of fish: some good, some bad. As if to reinforce her words, the woman shrugged her shoulders. They live in the deepest forests beside streams, she said. At night, they come out to dance and in the morning their playgrounds can be identified by strange rings of luxuriant grass. Groa nodded; her dark eyes huge in her fair, round face. She was sure she had seen such a thing down by the water over near the spinney of birch and larch. Other elusive creatures included the hulder who steals milk from animals; the draugen, a wailing, headless fisherman who foretells of drowning; and the vetter, guardian spirits of the wildest coastline. With Aiofe's aversion to sailing, I was relieved she had chosen not to make the journey. By night's end, her wild-eyed ravings would have caused my head to ache. Despite my first exposure to these strange creatures, I slept well.

Early next morning, after breaking our fast, we made the journey by horse and cart along the busy trade route. Thora wished to finalise arrangements for a formal baptism. Halldora had been blessed when the priest came to call, but children could fall prey to disease and greater protection was required. Whilst she fulfilled her tasks, we explored the church. It was constructed of black, tarred, wooden staves. Each of its sharply-sloped roofs rose atop the other, ending in a fine, elevated point high up in the sky. On the roof finials, carved wooden heads of creatures, bearing a strong resemblance to those on Norse ships, rose up in defiance.

Large wooden doorways double the height of a tall man stood adorned with the Yggdrasil: the sacred ash tree, whose sinuous branches were believed to span the cosmos. At ground level, an open veranda with wooden balustrades surrounded the building. Inside, thick beams painted with swirling figures supported the roof and flat, wooden benches lined the walls. It was so unlike anything I had seen before. Outside in the surrounding field, stones outlined boat-shaped graves and the sticky reek of tar lay heavy upon the air. During the journey back to the longhouse, our chatter was quelled as we reflected upon the church's brooding atmosphere.

Next morning came too soon. Our vessel raced homebound on the fast-running seas. The brisk, cold air was bracing. Empty bellies rumbled and the tang of salt upon lips kindled memories of succulent fish, steaming hot from the early morning hearth. With ties loosened and lost forever on the wind, meticulous coils of hair unravelled and flowed. Freedom's soft mantle – warm as a new-cut fleece – offered protection from all our woes. Dear one, if only such peace could be yours in these troubled times.

Your loving sister

Isa

Scotland

Kildrummy Castle

October 1305

Isa, dear heart,

Your journey proved a powerful distraction. The dark church intrigued us. Our simple chapels, both here and at Turnberry, offer tranquillity to all who enter. But such peace is fleeting.

King Edward harangued his men to capture Sir William Wallace, offering bribes and threatening the Scots' nobles who have gone over to the English side. He wishes him eradicated, like any dangerous animal. Robert tells me he and other nobles did everything in their power to avoid finding the elusive warrior.

It could not last. A garrison soldier, imprisoned after the surrender of Stirling Castle, told of a brother in the Wallace camp. In exchange for his freedom, he gave information. Wallace was taken to Sir John Menteith, sheriff of Dumbarton.

In London, Edward's court convicted him of treason. By 23rd August, Scotland's hero lay dead.

It is hard for me to write of this, but I must for all should know the depravity with which we are faced. The poor man was drawn on a rack behind a stallion, hung but not unto death; his manhood, hacked away; then he was gutted and his entrails burnt in front of his eyes. With his body quartered, the parts were dispensed around the country for display at various castle entrances. His once-proud head rests atop London Bridge. King Edward hoped to make an example of the brigand – as he called him – but for the Scots, his actions had the opposite effect. Simmering hatred, dormant for safety's sake in the face of English aggression in our home country, now sears the breast of many a patriot. In time, Edward may rue the day he created such a martyr.

Our family is deep in mourning for Sir William. Embittered and grievously angry, Mary withdrew, not speaking for days, riding alone for hours on end. When Robert arrived yester eve, our sister spoke to him with such harsh disrespect in the Great Hall, blaming him for not having done more to save Wallace's life. I saw looks of discomfort flicker across the faces of our household and was distressed by her behaviour. As ever, Rob would take on this shame – and the guilt of all his peers even. I have pleaded with him he must not, lest his spirit be crushed with the weight of such despair. The rift will heal no doubt between them, but not for some time with Mary's opinion so firmly embedded in righteous disgust.

Dark days are upon us. Only weeks after Wallace's execution, the Westminster parliament passed the changes made to the Scottish constitution, highlighting for all to see Scotland's loss of independence. In the eyes of King Edward, his overlordship has been ratified. The community of the realm is no more.

Kirsty

Norway

Bergen

November 1305

My dear Kirsty,

Prayers have been said for the great man's soul in the Kristkirke, so all here know what scandalous events are taking place in our country. Pray God keeps our family safe.

Isa

Kildrummy Castle

December 1305

Isa, dear heart,

A few days ago, as if the devil himself was after them, Robert's cohort thundered in through our gates. Elizabeth was marrow-frozen and exhausted. Children and geese scattered in fright. Guards shouted in alarm. With a huge cry of relief, Christopher slid from his lathered horse. He swung me high in the air, almost squeezing the breath from me, but I will tell more of him later.

This eve, Rob came to my solar. Anger and relief slid across his strained features as he recounted the events which led to their flight. At Bishop Lamberton's urging, our brother had relented and gone to see John Comyn, especially since John Balliol had retired to his French estate. In an attempt to settle their troubled relationship and rival claims for the throne, Robert made the Comyn an offer: all the Bruce lands in exchange for his opponent stepping down from his claim to the Scottish crown; or the reverse – Robert would receive all the Comyn's land and, in return, refute the Bruce kingship claim. By far more interested in owning the wealthy estates of the Bruce family, Comyn agreed to stand aside in favour of the Bruce. They formalised this arrangement in a document, a signed copy for each of them. To seal the pact, Robert broke a gold coin with the heavy shaft of his sword. One half he kept for himself whilst the other he handed to Comyn, his rival no more.

Strange doings were ahead. King Edward sent a missive to Robert advising him to put the castle of Kildrummy in the keeping of such a man, to whom he would be willing to answer. Did he no longer trust Robert? The next cause for concern was the king's action revoking the lands of Gilbert de Umfraville, which he had given to Robert when he came into his peace. Not long thereafter, our brother received an urgent summons to attend the king's court. Uneasy thoughts of the grave peril which might await him rippled through his mind, but he dared not refuse. Elizabeth accompanied him, hoping her presence, usually favoured by the king, might alleviate the dire situation.

For days, Rob hung about the court waiting for the expected meeting to take place. It did not augur well and despite his calm exterior, anxious anticipation vied with choking humiliation. A week past, the couple were in London in their lodgings when a discreet knock sounded on the heavy door. Startled, Robert enquired as to the owner's identity. It was not the king's men come to arrest him, but the servant of one of Robert's friends at the court. The man handed over a leather pouch containing silver coins and a pair of spurs. The clandestine message offered clues, for the coins sported the head of the king, whilst the spurs suggested a journey. The servant bade them go tonight, if possible. Rob looked well into the man's eyes and saw his sincerity. In haste, they roused their men. Within an hour, they were past the gates of London;

Robert having commanded they be opened in the name of the king. Without hesitation, the stunned, sleepy guards obliged.

At first, they made for Lochmaben. As luck would have it, they came across a courier wearing Comyn colours, coming from the direction of Carlisle. A fight ensued when the foolish man refused to hand over his satchel. Enclosed was a copy of the pact made with Comyn – now on its way to King Edward; proof, it would seem that the Bruce's trust had been betrayed. For some time, our brother had felt King Edward's suspicions lying loose around his neck. Now, the hangman's noose tightened inexorably. Rob choked on his words as he spoke and reached for his goblet. He took a mouthful then shook his head in disbelief. The letter contained his virtual death warrant. There was no going back. With Lochmaben so close to the English border, the fugitives rode on to the safety of the mountain fastness and Kildrummy. In their mad flight from danger, they scarce ate or slept. Running his fingers through his hair, Rob paused in the telling, unable to go on. He paced the floor seeking the words to describe his anguish. All his plans for the future were damaged beyond repair. I could do little but listen to his tirade. What could any of us do?

The weather is closing in. It is Yuletide. I must see to the preparations, but Chris is demanding my attention. Having not seen me for months, he is worse than the children! Meg looks like her father with her fair hair and open, smiling face. So different is she in temperament to Donald – such an obstinate lad. Our interactions always leave me feeling wrong-footed, despite my attempts to the contrary. The harder I try, the worse it gets. And distancing myself from him only seems to make matters worse. His sister, on the other hand, is a more forgiving child. Thank the lord, Ellen does not begrudge me my every word or action and takes pleasure in my company.

Mary no longer spurns Rob's presence as she did last time,

though, I wager, has yet to appreciate the strange complexities of his life.

Margaret and Mathilda are blossoming into lovely young women. Marjorie is much younger, unable yet to bridge the gap and is sometimes excluded for it. Though still shy and reticent, she shows signs of enjoying her father's rare visits. Rob cherishes these occasions and works hard to maintain their tenuous relationship. To her credit, Elizabeth, a most generous-hearted woman, gives him the space to do so.

The children are excited about the forthcoming festivities. Accompanied by guards, they went out today into the soft blanket of dry snow seeking a Yule Log. What a commotion they made upon their return: children laughing; horses blowing hot air through hairy nostrils; men cursing when the trimmed branches stuck fast coming through the gates; the dull thud of axes, followed by cheers. Peace, that most precious gift, surrounds our haven once more.

Yours aye

Kirsty

Norway

Bergen

February 1306

My dear Kirsty,

Our brother's life is filled with danger and uncertainty. How difficult it must be to watch these events unfold. Stay strong, dear one.

Some weeks back, Erling offered to take us up to the snowline to skate on a frozen loch and go on to the bog-ridden plateau where the reindeer herds roam. His sister, Jorunn, has a farm up that way. At the longhouse, we received a warm welcome. During the afternoon, Inga played with Jorunn's daughter, Arnora, over in the barn where several small reindeer, rescued from heavy drifts of snow, were receiving care. Jorunn's young sons were out collecting fuel, but would return soon. For supper, a platter of roast reindeer and spiced cabbage was followed by stewed moltboer, delicious amber-coloured berries which grow on open, swampy ground. A wild winter storm crackled and boomed overhead.

In the warm glow of the central hearth, Hrolfr Haraldsson relished telling the old tales, often finishing with a loud slap on his thigh and a rumbling belly laugh. Jorunn had long since given up trying to quieten her husband and the children slept through these drinking sessions. Inga was not so fortunate. She dozed on a pallet with Solas, alert-eared at her side. Over time, I had learnt about Odin. Now, the story of Thor – the noisiest god of all – was told by the barrel-chested Hrolfr, whose mass of fiery red hair acted as a flare within the smoky darkness. Armed only with his magic hammer, the god of thunder rode upon his eight-legged steed, killing giants – deceivers all – wherever he went. He was straightforward and reliable, as well as being game for anything. In a drinking contest, some giants gave him a horn – concealing the fact that its tip lay in the sea. Regardless, he outdrank his companions, draining the sea so much that the tide ebbed. During battles, the thunderer claimed the lower echelon of society, slaves and the like. Thus, he became every man's hero. A memory surfaced of the amulet Hauk wore around his neck. At the same time, it was clear the huge impact Christianity had upon these farming folk. A wooden crucifix hung loosely around Jorunn's neck. In darkness and in light, fearful horrors lay in wait. All protection was welcomed.

Next morning, Jorunn's prized berry patch was our destination some distance from the longhouse. Under a clear sky, the high plateau glistened with crystalline patches of snow. Soon, it was time to depart for home with myself in the back of the cart. Inga lay asleep beside me, whilst Solas curled his snug, little body around my feet. Beneath the light of the swaying lantern, Bethoc sat with Erling, huddled against the chill. In the dusk of early afternoon, the craftsman began to hum his country's ancient songs – his voice, deep and melodious. Bethoc's notes came as sweet and pure as the crisp, clean air.

In time, only the sound of the horse's hooves striking rocks on the path broke the silence. Somehow, I slept. My dreams took me to Turnberry under a pale, moonlit sky with silver-shot waves rolling onto the rocky shore. From somewhere deep within, a searing pain surfaced. Bitter tears stung my eyes. My fingers sought the warm comfort of the gold crucifix at my neck, but upon my lap, a tiny metal hammer – a gift from Hrolfr – lay enclosed within my palm.

Isa

Scotland

Kildrummy Castle

February 1306

Isa, dear heart,

Good news at last! Our brother, Alexander, has been appointed Dean of Glasgow with the whole-hearted approval of Bishop Wishart. Braving snow and sleet, he came to tell us himself. Mhairi was especially pleased to see Alexander and made his favourite dishes for the banquet. Mary is back to her old self. She went out hunting with Christopher, bringing down a hind for the celebration. Needless to say, the long respite has done all our guests good as spirits were at breaking point.

A few days past, Rob and Alexander took the children skating on the frozen Dee and thence to the slopes where they carried old wooden sleds and careered down. Donald and Marjorie collided, and the outing ended with scraped skin and damaged pride. Rob carried Marjorie home on his back, cradling her injured knee with his great warrior's hands. Despite the bitter weather, he and his troops plan to go south soon. He seeks to confront the treacherous Comyn.

Of his own plight, Rob spoke with ill-deserved harshness. "Grandfather would have raised merry hell by now, but I – Earl of ancient Carrick and a contender for the Scottish throne – sit here in fine comfort, allowing fear to curdle belly and soul; much like Father would have done!" Since then, his men have begun a punishing regime of training to regain their fitness for whatever challenges lie ahead.

On his way home, Alexander stopped at Guisborough to pay his respects to Grandfather. At Holm Coltram Abbey, he stood by a lonely grave. In the borderlands of Scotland, the charred ruins of the beautiful old abbeys – Melrose, Dryburgh and Jedburgh – lay empty. Some of the monks had fled to the hills; others were not so lucky. Not that England escaped either with Scottish raids into Northumberland and Yorkshire wreaking havoc. Even so, it was the destruction of our homeland that caused Alexander the most despair. He called to see friends in the area only to find farms burnt, homes destroyed or in grave disrepair. Starvation and illness have finished what the war started. His beloved abbey, Crossragruel, founded so long ago by the Earls of Carrick, had not escaped desecration. Soldiers stabled their horses in the church. In the melee, some of the monks died – even Father Dughlas, our old tutor – in a vain attempt to prevent the destruction of the library by fire. With his journey home, our brother travelled more than miles. His youthful beliefs fractured and were forged anew.

With great affection, we joined in celebrating Alexander's success and bowed our heads at the banquet as he blessed the abundance set out before us. When he departed to take up his new role as Dean of Glasgow, we wished our brother well.

Yours aye
Kirsty

Scotland

Kildrummy Castle

March 1306

Isa, dear heart,

A dreadful event has taken place. At Dumfries, Robert went to confront the Comyn regards his treachery. Involved in some legal disputes being heard at the judicial court, Comyn was lodged at Greyfriars Kirk. It was upon this neutral ground the pair met at Robert's request. An argument ensued. Both men drew their daggers. In front of the high altar, they struggled. Comyn fell to the ground. When his uncle rushed to his aid, Christopher struck the older man with a blow to the head, killing him. The friars carried the younger man into the vestry. Shocked, Rob ran outside, whilst some of his men went back in to make sure the Comyn was dead. Chaos followed!

With many rallying to his banner, Robert's force took Dumfries Castle. In fear, the justices barricaded themselves behind the doors of the great hall where they had been holding the Assizes Court. Our brother threatened to burn the place down. Surrender was prompt!

From February through to March, the fiery cross was carried from hillside to hillside across Scotland alerting men to raise arms, this time for the Bruce. Castle after castle fell to Robert and his men: Dumfries, Tibbers, Dalswinton and Ayr. Across the Firth of Clyde, Robert Boyd took the circular, moated castle – Rothesay – on Bute and then placed Inverkip under siege. Through the exchange of another, our brother gained Dunaverty Castle on the tip of Kintyre. Our own castle on the islet in Loch Doon was placed in the hands of my lord husband. With a defensive ring of fortified castles in place, Robert hoped to protect the western seaboard, thus curtailing the movement of English ships based at Skinburness. Only then might our allies from Ireland travel with impunity. Without success, Robert sought the surrender of the great rock fortress of Dumbarton on the Clyde.

Despite a murder having been committed on holy ground, Bishop Wishart exhorted his flock to rise up and support Robert. The old Celtic process of tanistry had run its regrettable course, especially when all attempts at reasonable compromise had failed. March saw our brother swear an oath before the bishop to fight for the freedom of Scotland and uphold the liberties of the Scottish church, long overpowered by Rome and Avignon. Notables from all over the country headed for Scone.

Our contingent arrived, relieved to be attending the royal coronation of one of our dearest members given the desperate and unforeseen events which had unfolded. Meanwhile, the erstwhile Bishop Lamberton escaped from Berwick under cover of darkness. By taking the ferry from North Berwick, he reached Scone in time for the coronation. Nothing, he said, would have kept him from witnessing Scotland's destiny take shape and form. Where possible, all royal traditions were to be maintained for this great event and, when Robert was crowned king, he sat upon a large block of stone on Moot Hill.

It was rumoured some months before the theft of the Stone of Destiny that a replica of the ancient stone seat was secreted in its stead by Scone's canny monks. If it were so, then it seemed the English king was none the wiser.

I wish you could have been with us, Isa. No one, not least Robert, liked how it had come about, but all were euphoric and willing to go with the grandeur of the occasion. All through the night we banqueted and danced. For a brief time, our country's woes were pushed from the foreground of our thoughts. Only Elizabeth, our new queen, her mood sombre and restrained, reflected on what the future might hold. Across her strained features, expressions of fear and worry jostled with pride and love. King Edward was known to be a cruel, unforgiving man to his enemies. In his wrath, he would unleash the full force of the mighty English host upon her lord husband and his beloved Scotland. This Elizabeth understood. Once, she told me, she prayed they would come to an understanding, but, now, she knew their differences could only be decided by war; Edward could never grasp how the community of the realm mattered so deeply to Robert. At its core, this Celtic belief was at odds with the feudal superiority of the English king. Ultimately, it set Robert apart.

The next day, a small party of horsemen rode in to Scone, their gasping mounts lathered white. Concealed for safety within the group was Countess Isobel of Buchan, wife of the earl who was himself a firm supporter of England. She escaped her husband's harsh care to ride to Scone to fulfil the ancient role belonging to the Earls of Fife – her own family line – to crown the Scottish monarchy.

Keen to uphold tradition and legitimise his new status, Robert had a second crowning take place to great acclaim. With the ceremony complete, our family accompanied the king to Kildrummy where Mhairi and the household had prepared a great banquet. How proud you would have been to see our household gathered in the Great Hall, cheering our brother; mugs of wine and ale raised to his health and happiness. You were sorely missed, dear one.

Kirsty

Norway

Bergen

March 1306

My dear Kirsty,

How proud I am of Alexander's achievements. He has done so well to become Dean of Glasgow. Despite all that has happened, Robert has earned the right to be king in my eyes. Long live the king

Isa

Norway

Bergen

March 1306

Isa heard a sharp knock. Reluctantly, she put down her beaker of warm, spiced wine and crossed the chamber, making little sound on the stone flags with her soft leather boots. Beyond the arched, stone doorway stood the quiet, intense trader whom she had known for some time. Otto leaned forward. Thick, greasy locks of fair hair fell across his eyes as he placed a parchment in her outstretched hand. From a small leather purse dangling at her side, she retrieved several gold coins. With a shy nod of acceptance, he turned. His sturdy footfall echoed as he retraced his steps down the dark, winding stairwell. Here was someone she knew instinctively could be trusted – a reassuring trait, Isa mused, in this contrary world of danger and subterfuge.

Lifting the iron poker, she stirred the embers until flames leapt and flickered. She edged closer to the hearth. The day was moist and the chill air penetrated her bones. Savouring the moment, she breathed deeply, inhaling the complex aromas of dried calfskin and the bitter gall of ink. Once broken, the lead seal was heavy in her hand. Slowly, Isa unrolled the parchment. Tilting it to the sparse light, she began to read. A warm smile lifted her strained features.

Scotland

Lochmaben Castle

16 February 1306

Well Isa lass – it is done! The game is afoot and this time there can be no turning back. Either Scotland stands free as in the past – its own kingdom – or it disappears into the swirl of English possessions. Either Bruce rises to resurrect the crown of Scots or Bruce will lie destroyed. And I am heartily glad of it. There will be no more playing with talk of constitutional reform to suit the English perspective. No more pretending to answer the summons of Edward Longshanks when he calls. In the name of the dead and murdered Wallace, I swear to resurrect the ancient kingdom of Scots and restore the freedoms and rights of the people. I am to be crowned within weeks and then no doubt, Isa, we will need your help and support, and that of our good friends in Norway against Edward of England.

As you know, I had been spending more time in England after Father's death a couple of years ago. It was clear Edward knew of my connections with Wallace. Things began to go badly for our family at the English court. At the New Year festivities, Edward ignored my presence. I began to suspect Comyn had betrayed me, because we had signed a bond in October, which promised Comyn all the Bruce lands in Scotland in return for his support for me as King of Scots. Comyn had signed this when Edward was sick, but he had recovered and, now, I began to wonder if Edward knew of our plans. Ralph de Monthermer, acting as Earl of Gloucester for his stepson Gilbert Clare, sent me word treachery was afoot. John Comyn had revealed the agreement to Edward and was sending south his copy as evidence. I was in our

London house. Gloucester sent me a purse of twelve silver pennies and a set of spurs. My arrest was imminent and Ralph was repaying me for our long friendship as boys, when we were squires together. With just a few retainers, we rode for home. After five days, we were fifty miles south of Carlisle when we spied a messenger heading south on the same road. I could see he wore Comyn colours and spurred across him. He had an axe and swung at me, but one of my men intercepted the blow and I killed him with one thrust. In his saddle-bag I found the agreement and, also, a request for all Bruce lands in Scotland and England to be given to him after my execution. We made for the safe haven of Kildrummy.

Accordingly, I sent a message to Comyn to meet me at Greyfriars Kirk in Dumfries. When he appeared, all swagger and fawning friendship, we withdrew to the area of the High Altar for privacy. I then took out the bond and threw it at his feet. His treachery was clear and his immediate response was to draw his dagger and lunge at me. I swayed backwards and then struck him under his arm. John Comyn fell to the ground, bubbling blood, and Robert Comyn rushed towards me with his sword drawn. Luckily, Chris Seton was faster. Robert Comyn fell beside his nephew. We left the church, and Roger Kilpatrick and James Lindsay ran towards us seeing the blood on our clothes. I said to Kilpatrick I thought I had killed Comyn. His only reply was: "Then I'll mak siccer." And he did make sure. The die was cast. Our party rode for Dumfries Castle, seized it and ejected the English garrison. All is now in play. Our Church remains loyal to Scotland's cause, and, now, I have the backing of the Bishops of St Andrews, Glasgow and Moray. While I can count on the Earls of Atholl, Lennox, Menteith and Mar, as well the Clan Donald in the Hebrides, the friends of Comyn and Balliol are many and there will be a violent reaction from London. The old lion is not yet dead and will want the Scots utterly crushed this time.

I aim to be crowned king at Scone on 25th March 1306, which is ten years to the day since we first took up arms in defence of our community of Scotland. Ten unhappy years it has proven to be. Now, pray for us all in our time of need. If Scotland is not to disappear, except as a legend of an ancient people sorely troubled by a more powerful neighbour, then we will require many prayers indeed. I hope you have not forgotten all your Gaelic: Alba gu brath!

Your brother

Rob

Scotland

Kildrummy Castle

April 1306

Isa, dear heart,

Dire times are upon us. Robert and his men departed Kildrummy for Aberdeen, but will return once they have gathered more troops in the north. At the beginning of April, King Edward sent Aymer de Valence, the Earl of Pembroke, to Scotland, to burn and slay. To our horror, the command to 'raise the dragon' has been given. No mercy will be shown to any of us. They have burnt Sir Simon Fraser's lands in Tweeddale, killing all prisoners, and are moving steadfastly north.

Enclosed, you will find a white gull's feather. Pray I have not left it too late.

Kirsty

Norway

Bergen

May 1306

When Isa opened the missive delivered by an Aberdeen trader, a white gull's feather slipped out and drifted down onto the rough surface of the trestle. Her chest contracted in painful spasms. With a pale, trembling hand, she reached out to pick it up, resting its cool, feathered tip against her cheek, wet now with tears. Down at the harbour, Murchadh was just finishing his supper when he heard Isa's sharp, pained call. He was to leave with the tide.

Scotland

Kildrummy Castle

May 1306

From a distance, the captain shook his curly, dark hair free of the thick, woollen cloak and surveyed the vast bulk of Kildrummy Castle. Eager for a feed of hay, his garron snorted beneath him. It looked remarkably peaceful with smoke drifting upwards from several vents. Tentatively, horse and man moved forward. The heavy gates creaked open to let in the solitary rider. Mary's cry was heard across in the Snow Tower. Disturbed from a deep reverie, her sister looked up from the large stone mortar and pestle. An aromatic mess of green herbs nestled in the rough bowl. Knocking over her stool, Kirsty leant out of the tower window to catch sight of the commotion in the bailey below. Her hands flew to her face.

A distraught breath escaped from lips, pallid now with shock. There was no time to lose.

Earlier in the day, Drustan arrived with news – the lands of Sir Michael Wemyss and the Hays were afire. As well, Bishop Wishart had been captured at Cupar Abbey. Along with Lamberton and the Abbot of Scone, all men of age, he was sent southwards in chains; only the fact that the men were in Holy Orders saved them from being hanged. Now, the English host was forging northwards at speed, killing all in its path. The household had been practising for this moment. Donald was to stay at Kildrummy, as would Marjorie; Robert, unable in the end to let his precious heir leave his jurisdiction.

Down in the crowded bailey, a fine cloud of dust rose as the party made ready to depart. Murchadh sat upon Mary's grey palfrey. The horse sidled about despite Mary's attempts to bring him to a standstill. He had been a valiant companion on her many wild rides across the hills and she would miss him. Stroking his nose for the last time, she walked away and stood within the shadows of the castle wall.

Meg slept, packed tight into a crib for which Earchann had made a special attachment to secure it to the saddle of a garron, now ridden by Floraidh. With looks of shock and fear written across strained features, Mathilda and Margaret sat bolt upright upon their sturdy ponies. A chill wind lifted the hoods of their warm travelling cloaks and fretted at their hair. Neither girl dared move, lest their eyes catch sight of a familiar face and their resolve crumble in view of all.

With her son secured in a sling, ashen-faced Marthoc rode Kirsty's placid roan. Seated upon her mount's broad back, Seonaid masked her own unrest with her efforts to calm young Ellen. The child squirmed, and the young woman crooned a soft melody whilst she adjusted the tight sash around her midriff. Several sumpter ponies carried heavy loads – the group's belongings and victuals for the long journey. Aodh, now grown somewhat in strength and maturity, had the task of keeping the ponies tethered to his own horse. He would need all his strength to keep up. On his old garron, Drustan brought up the rear. With a hostile army heading north, he was keen, now, for a sea-bound adventure. In order to give the appearance of two family groups, the young priest surprised all by agreeing to don a sailor's cap to hide his tonsure under the pretence of being a husband to one of the maids. In these troubled times, two family groups travelling together would attract less notice.

With brief, choked farewells uttered, encouragement was offered, as though the party was intent upon some happy excursion. Smiles cloaked faces, rigid with grief. Last minute admonishments were proffered – to eat their meals; wear warm vestments; stay clean; be good and not to nip at each other. With tears streaming down the creases in her face, Morag watched from a darkened doorway. Puffing heavily, Mhairi ran forward with a last minute parcel of warm pies for the girls, whilst Marjorie exited from the Snow Tower; her peg dollies and the tiny trunk of clothes in a bundled package for Ellen.

Slowly, the company moved forward. Tomas raised his hand in blessing. Ellen began to wail and Meg woke with a start. Their piercing cries rebounded off the castle walls. Kirsty fought the desire to fling herself at her children's retreating forms and kiss their precious faces one last time. Reeling, she felt Mary's firm grasp around her waist and was grateful to be held upright. Murchadh burst into a cheerful sea shanty to which young Drustan gave voice, adding a strange dirge-like quality so used was he to the monotones of monastic music. It was not at all what the captain intended for a diversion. The gates of the castle creaked shut behind them.

As the group passed the small village which had grown up around the castle, sullen faces looked out upon the lucky ones who were leaving danger behind. All knew when the Sassenach army came there would be no such happy ending for them.

Scotland

Turnberry Castle

June 1306

It would soon be time to leave. For the past few weeks, the household kept watch lest the English sneak up on them unawares. After the heartbreak of the children's departure, Kirsty rarely spoke, so despairing was she of ever seeing her daughters or younger sisters again. Mary took charge, keeping Donald and Marjorie busy with all manner of tasks and activities. Understandably, they were fractious and on edge. As well, she gathered the key members of the household together to inform them of the plans which had been agreed upon. Neither of the Bruce women wished to stay at Kildrummy any longer to be trapped like animals. Though she was desperate for the freedom of the hills, Mary refrained from speaking her mind for once. Along with Donald and Marjorie, Kirsty and Mary would go with Robert and his men when they returned from gathering an army, joining Elizabeth who had remained with her husband after his crowning.

In the Great Hall, with the shadows heavy around them to conserve the wax candles and rushes, the wary household gathered. On the surface, the news was accepted without recrimination, for all knew something was afoot.

To cover a fearful sense of abandonment, Mhairi and Earchann protested they were far too old to go rambling about the countryside. Nodding in agreement, Shona and her daughters were pleased enough to stay, knowing nought else. The garrison was needed, of course, if a siege occurred. The plan was to bring in the villagers from outside the walls for their own safety, but also to man the castle. Their leader, a blacksmith, Osbourne by name, had approached Mary one day when she was returning from the hunt with this proposition. None of the villagers desired to be outside when the English came. All would work to bring in the harvest and food would be rationed.

With Robert and his men due any day, the women readied themselves for their departure. For the sake of Donald and Marjorie, and with her boundless energy and strength, Mary made finding more suitable clothes for their ride into a game. At last, the king's army returned from the north, strengthened. Would they be able to match the colossal strength of the English host? News came – De Valence had taken Perth. With the Kildrummy party travelling in the rear, King Robert's army headed south without delay.

Scotland

June 1306

Leaving the women in Niall's care, the King of Scots proceeded to the walls of Perth, ready to engage the English commander in some kind of dialogue, preparatory to war. Robert challenged de Valence to bring out his men for combat or surrender the town and leave Scotland. The English lord demurred, saying it was too late in the day, but would consider his options upon the morrow. That evening, Robert bedded his army down near Methven on a rise. Men were sent out foraging, and others to recruit more troops for the inevitable battle.

In the early half-light of the following day, the earl and his men attacked the sleeping Scots. In the heat of the battle, the king fell from his horse. English soldiers converged from all sides. Dazed from a vicious blow to his helmet and weighed down by chain mail, Robert staggered. Chris Seton saw him sink to his knees. In a feat of Herculean strength, he lifted Robert up onto his horse. Together they galloped to safety; a few seconds more and Scotland would have been vanquished.

Some escaped with the king, but the vast proportion of his army died horribly at Methven that day. Many knights and their retainers lost their lives in the pandemonium. Young Dughall and the much older Fionnlagh, both Turnberry men, fell together beneath the hooves of a great destrier, their heads smashed to bloody pulp. Of the squires and young farm hands, clad only in padded gambesons, the English knights' great swords and axes made short work, severing heads and limbs from bodies as if scything grain in some malign harvest. Wealthy lords had value as captives with potential for ransom and land for the taking, but there would be no clemency for many of these nobles, the reviled enemies of the English king. For Sir Simon Fraser, a brutal death awaited: drawn behind horses on a hurdle to his place of execution, where crowds gathered to watch the grisly spectacle of death by torture. Many others earned the same fate as Wallace and Fraser.

After the battle, the king and his brother, Edward, made for the safety of the hills with their small band of trusted companions: Chris Seton, James Douglas, Neil Campbell and Gilbert Hay. A much-reduced contingent of troops later found them, as did Niall and his charges. Distraught at being separated from her son in the melee, Kirsty could do nought. Instead of staying at the women's camp as requested, Donald had pleaded with her to let him go with the men. Believing he would be safe with her brothers, she agreed and was rewarded

185

with the rarest of gifts – his smile. Now, for all she knew, her son lay dead or injured upon the hillside at Methven.

With the English army hot on their trail over the next few days, the remnants of the Bruce force entered narrow Glen Dochart in central Scotland. It was a key passageway to the west and the path to freedom. Another skirmish took place with the small force overwhelmed by strength and numbers – surrounded on all sides by the English, as well as Scots, hostile to the Bruce. Wedged together and riding at thunderous speed, the Bruce and his small band of warriors broke through a contingent of Macdougall's highlanders who scattered and fell before the onslaught. When the fugitives achieved a temporary measure of safety, urgent plans were set in place. Niall Bruce and Sir John of Strathbogie would take the women and all the horses northeast over the mountains to the safety of Kildrummy. If necessity demanded, they were to go even further to Orkney or beyond to Isabel in Norway. Impassioned farewells were cut abruptly short.

Before heading southwest over the mountains to Loch Lomond and the lands of Lennox, Robert and his men divested themselves of chain mail and armour; it would only weigh them down in this boggy land. In desperation, they looted the dead for anything of use: boots, weapons, food, flints and plaids. On foot and surrounded by their foes, the men turned southwards and took to the hills.

Scotland

Kildrummy Castle

July 1306

Many days of hard riding over mountainous terrain followed, down steep inclines into deep, shaded vales, fording swift-flowing burns and wider, rock-strewn rivers. Food and sleep were mostly denied them, for fear the enemy would pick up their trail. At last, the frantic spent group rode in through the gates of Kildrummy. For much of the way, Marjorie had ridden with Niall. Now he released his tight, cramped hold and she slipped, whimpering, into the upstretched arms of Earchann. His old, wrinkled face streamed with tears of relief and sorrow.

Elation and grief make strange bedfellows, but for Morag and Mhairi, these feelings were set aside as they urged the household to prepare food and beds. Once again, Kirsty blessed these loyal souls who were as family to her. All the while the villagers, who had come into the castle by arrangement, watched them, wary and fearful of change.

A short time after their return, news came – an enormous English host was almost upon them. Accompanied by the Earl of Atholl and a few trusted retainers, the women and young Marjorie led their horses, hooves slipping and grating on the wet cobblestones, down through the dark, vaulted tunnel. Lit by smoky, flaring rushes, it led to a small side gate and out onto the narrow path by the steep-sided ravine. To travel this path alone required a feat of skilled horsemanship; a faulty step could mean death in the ravine below.

Farewells were quick and muted. Fears lay unspoken, but none could hide their disbelief and raw devastation. Niall's sisters hugged him, aware only of the unflagging strength he offered in return. Marjorie clung to him in desperation. Wiping her tears away with his fingers, he pulled her close.

"Courage, lass," was all he said, before lifting her up to the waiting arms of the earl. In the eerie half-light, they escaped through a fine veil of mist and fled north. Niall remained, standing motionless, until a deep sigh escaped his lips. With a heavy heart, he made his way up once more to the battlements.

Who knew what lay ahead for any of them?

Scotland

Kildrummy Castle

September 1306

Boulders flung from trebuchets crashed, raising great clouds of debris. Beneath their shroud of dust, bodies lay angular and still. Overhead, arrows rained down: murderous, black hail, which blocked out the light. Screams pierced the great roar of battle. Sweat dripped from Niall's forehead, stinging his reddened eyes. Muddied rivulets of blood ran down his neck. The deep, sustained thud of weapons upon six thousand iron shields reverberated through every bone of his body, but when the din ceased, the silence held even greater menace. Within his belly, fear and gnawing hunger vied in an endless battle for precedence.

Over the past weeks, Niall had been valiant in his defence of the besieged castle. Now, he rubbed his eyes in appalled disbelief. Smoke and flames billowed out from the Great Hall wherein lay the castle's jealously hoarded grain stores.

"Guards, to the well!" he screamed, but none heeded his call. Another flurry of arrows was airborne. A terrified child sprinted past him. An arrow caught him midstep. Niall dived for cover.

Tomas saw that his beloved chapel was on fire. As fast as his old knees could carry him, he hastened to save the silver plate and his vestments. He knelt to pray, seeking a few precious moments of peace and an end to the panic and affright which seared his soul. With the intense light from the three tall chancel windows shedding prisms of amber and crimson upon him, he prayed for the safety of all within the castle walls. Smoke billowed around him. His throat felt dry, scorched by the searing heat. Soot and ash rained down, burning holes in his habit. Gulping for air, Tomas glanced up.

The licking, flickering flames had taken hold, consuming all before it. With an enormous groan, he realised his prayers were in vain. A huge plume of black smoke and dust rose into the darkened sky as the chapel roof crashed to the ground. Around the bailey, frantic cries of desperation and terror rose above the roar of the fire.

None knew a certain blacksmith had made a deal with the Earl of Pembroke's men. For the safety of his family and a hoard of gold, he was to create a diversion within the castle and let the soldiers in through the concealed postern gate. Soon, all lay butchered – household and villagers alike – some in the bailey; others, like Nectan, with his head smashed in, quivered in a blood-smeared stairwell. Morag lay sprawled beneath him. Upon her face, a look of fearful bewilderment was frozen in time. Talorc's screams could scarce be heard above the frantic baying of the hounds. In terror, the stallions attacked their stalls with their hooves. None could escape. Osbourne had barred the stable doors. Down in the kitchen, old Earchann defended Mhairi and Shona with nought but an iron poker, until a blade deftly sliced his belly and his pulsating bowels erupted onto the bloody floor in front of them. Shrieking in terror, the fraught women clenched their eyes shut in horror; it was the last thing they would ever see. Meanwhile, Shona's daughters crouched behind barrels in the storeroom. Before long, their desolate screams echoed around the castle.

Deep in the ravine in their prearranged place of safety, Osbourne moaned and threw himself upon the rocky ground; his children lay dead by the sword and his wife, legs and clothing askew, stared silent and accusing at the dark swirl of sky. Murderous with rage and blighted by shock, he barrelled over one of the English captains until they were both covered in blood and muck. Later, before the smoking ruins of Kildrummy, burly sergeants held Osbourne. Dust clouds formed around them as he squirmed and kicked.

Nestled within the fire's blue heat, a crucible held the precious reward, now melted into a sinuous golden swirl. The prisoner's eyes glazed in recognition, and his bowels loosened. Soon, his cries rose to the high-pitched squeal of an animal in extremis. As the molten liquid dripped and slid down his gullet, Osbourne's body shuddered and convulsed. A strange, tortured gurgle could be heard, followed by an unearthly silence.

The dung heap was to be his final resting place.

Burnt, dazed and bloodied, Niall staggered through the towering gates of Berwick Castle. His chains had long since chafed the flesh from his wrists and ankles, and his body shuddered in the grip of a fever. The prisoner knew full well what awaited him – his mind, full of bleak imaginings. Along with many others, he endured an execution so slow and precise that even the bravest of them cried for their mothers and begged for release from the ice cold blade.

When the garrison commander gave up the island castle of Loch Doon, Christopher Seton lost his freedom. His execution took place at Dumfries, whilst his brother and fourteen other Bruce adherents – including Alexander Scrymgeour, the Royal Standard Bearer – met their fate at Newcastle. Much like any vermin, the Scottish rebels were to be exterminated.

Scotland

October 1306

The fraught band of Bruce kinfolk and supporters pushed northwards through enemy territory to seaports where they might gain berths to Orkney. Now, they rode hard for the coast near Tain. Hot upon their heels came the Earl of Ross – a Balliol adherent, now on the side of King Edward. Darkness fell. They could go no further and took desperate refuge, sanctuary as it were, in the stone chapel of St Duthac. With memories still fresh in his mind of his imprisonment after the Dunbar Drave, the earl found the issue of religious sanctuary beyond his moral boundaries. Screaming in fear and outrage, the fugitives were dragged from the small chapel by the earl's men and watched, in abject horror, the slaughter of their retainers. The noblewomen and the Earl of Atholl were sent south.

According to King Edward, the Earl of Atholl deserved a most fitting punishment. Treading dangerous ground, the earl's mother pleaded for the life of her son. In desperation, she reminded the monarch they were, in fact, distant kinfolk. It would be a great pleasure, he said, to accord the earl his higher status. And the king was true to his word. Atholl's scaffold rose thirty feet higher than all others.

The female prisoners shuffled into the Great Hall of Berwick Castle, exhaustion evident across their pallid, drawn faces. Thin, hunched shoulders spoke of a brittle tension, long held. Fear wrote its own tale in hooded eyes, bloodshot and swollen from weeping alone in the darkness.

With an ermine-trimmed cloak slung across his shoulders for added warmth, King Edward sat upon an ornate wooden throne. His bejewelled hands rested on the carved leopard armrests. Off to one side, an administrator sat at a trestle, ready to record the king's judgement for posterity. His sharp eyes noted the absence of Sir Richard, Earl of Ulster, from the cluster of noisy advisors in the hall. The king raised his arm. As if cleft by a blade, silence fell.

Edward had given serious consideration to the prisoners' punishment before he laid eyes upon them. Now, they stood before him in gowns which were little more than rags. He sniffed into a kerchief scented with bergamot and lavender, but their stench assailed his nostrils. The king looked upon

Isobel of Buchan, whose expressive face betrayed a curious mix of loathing and fear. She shivered, repulsed by the soft lisp which slithered across his tongue. An eyelid drooped as if fatigue and boredom presented a constant challenge. This impression was at cross-purposes with the reptilian glint evident within his eyes, which spoke of an attenuation to fine detail and a cruelty which would not be denied.

"For you, my dear, a special punishment awaits. So eager were you to place a crown upon the head of that insolent traitor who calls himself King, that I have designed for you your own iron crown, made after the fashion of a cage, barred with slats of wood and iron; eight steps long and wide. Your little house shall be exposed to all the elements and will hang from the walls of this castle. There you will rot. I wish for the entire populace of Berwick to heap their scorn upon you. Though fed and watered, you shall be denied human companionship, but fear not, you shall have the convenience of a curtained privy; I would not give you cause for embarrassment." At this pronouncement, Isobel's grey eyes widened in horror and disbelief. Though she bit her lip so no cry could be heard, her knees sagged and the guards jerked her upright.

Overwrought by all that had happened, eleven-year-old Marjorie whimpered piteously. Edward turned his head and gave her his full attention. Caught in his fierce gaze, the child's dark eyes grew wild with fear.

"The daughter of the Bruce deserves a memorable punishment. You shall be my special guest – in a cage of your own, of course. Have you seen the high walls of the Tower before; perhaps on a visit with your father, the treacherous dog?" As Edward spoke, his voice crested upon a wave of righteous anger.

Unable to contain her white-hot anger, Mary leapt forward and aimed a gob of spittle at the king. It landed just short of his stylish leather boot. Screaming, she cursed him for every heathenish, evil act under God's sun, until the guard regained his balance and backhanded her across the face. Blood splattered from her split cheek and lips. Enjoying each pronouncement to the full, Edward continued, "Aah, yes! The sister of the Bruce! If you must behave like an animal, you shall be caged like one. I believe the walls of Roxburgh Castle will be high enough, even for you."

The king gave his full attention to Elizabeth. "There you are – blessed daughter of my dear and loyal friend! Your father would have me release you into his care, but *you* consented to be the treacherous dog's queen, his *bitch*, as it were. No, one of my manors – perhaps Burstwick near Holderness – shall be your new home. Two companions will be permitted, but elderly, not gay. We would not want you to have fun now." Edward sighed once more. A smile twisted the corners of his mouth, whilst his grey eyes burned with a silvery heat, born of hatred.

"The last of the Bruce wenches! This one is quieter, not a wailing strumpet. Therefore, I choose to be lenient and sentence you to indefinite solitary confinement in the Gilbertine nunnery of Sixhills in Lincolnshire." He paused, savouring the moment of exquisite power and devastation.

"Are you aware you are now a widow?" Kirsty swayed, close to collapse, before she was jerked from side to side by a guard. "Seton and his brother received their just deserts for murder, most foul. Believe me, they suffered. Their heads decorate my castle walls at Dumfries and Newcastle. My army sacked Kildrummy. All within its walls perished. By now, the raptors have picked clean their bones. Your brother, the one known as Niall – his head is fastened above the gates of Berwick. Do not forget to look upon his sightless face and know I, Edward, am your king!" His voice rose to a thunderous roar.

With the interview over, the king limped across the dais towards the exit. A satisfied smirk played across his thin lips. A guard shoved Kirsty in the back. Heads bowed in profound despair, the prisoners shuffled towards the studded door which led down, far below, to the dungeons – the only sound to be heard, Marjorie's choking, hysterical sobs.

Scotland

December 1306

Dearest Isa,

When I was crowned in March, Elizabeth gently mocked me and called her poor husband, the King of Summer. Now, there is no laughing, for I am the King of Bleak Winter. So many dear, loyal friends are dead, all within the past months. In late March, I was crowned at the Abbey of Scone.

"Robert the First, by the grace of God, King of Scots!" I heard them shout. What a grand sound that was, after these many years of mishap and mayhem. Grandfather would have smiled, just a little. The Bishops of St Andrews, Glasgow and Moray – as well as the Earls of Atholl, Lennox, Menteith and Mar – were present. The young Earl of Celtic Fife, the MacDuff, was held in England; his sister, Isobel, rode from Aberdeen to conduct the ceremony, as is their family's right. Her Comyn husband would have been ill-pleased. A comforting thought, indeed!

As I expected, the reaction of King Edward was swift and brutal. He sent Aymer de Valence, Earl of Pembroke, into Scotland, together with Henry Percy and Robert Clifford, and a huge host from his northern shires of England. There, they met with the Comyns and their supporters including the Earls of Dunbar and Strathearn. They killed any of our friends upon whom they could lay their hands and arrest. In Fife, they were able to seize the Bishops of St Andrews and Glasgow, although they were not murdered, but thrown into deep dungeons in the south of England. Old men forced to walk the length of the land in chains! The English, with over six thousand men, seized Perth and I rode south with a similar army to confront them. Outside the walls of Perth, I challenged Pembroke to bring out his men to combat or to surrender the town and leave Scotland. Our heralds agreed he would come out the next day and with that assurance, I retired a few miles to Methven to camp.

Well, I now know better the chivalric code of Pembroke. He led his army in a night time attack upon my sleeping men. I was almost captured by Sir Phillip Mowbray, but Chris Seton, Kirsty's man, knocked him down. A little group of us were able to cut our way out of the press: Edward, Thomas and Alexander, along with the Earl of Atholl, James Douglas, Neil Campbell and Gilbert Hay. It was a grievous defeat. From there, I headed for Kildrummy and collected the royal womenfolk who were under the protection of Niall. I had thought of getting the women to you in Norway then, but word came an English fleet was waiting to intercept them. Pembroke advanced into Mar, so I had to head for the west and the safety of the Hebrides where Angus Macdonald holds sway in his isles. We only got as far as Tyndrum where the Abbot of Inchafray and his Culdee monks granted me absolution for the death of Comyn. Copious blessings came my way for my role in upholding the ancient Celtic church. Just a few miles beyond, we were ambushed in the pass of Dalry by Macdougall of Lorne, the son-in-law of John Comyn. It was only with great difficulty we escaped because of the terrain. Indeed, I had my own cloak wrenched from my shoulder by one of the Macdougall clansmen. On retreating, it was clear the way to the Hebridean Sea was blocked. So we gave our remaining horses to Elizabeth and the women who were escorted back to Kildrummy, through his own country, by the Earl of Atholl. The plan was for them to head north to the Orkneys, once rested, and thence to you, whilst Niall held Kildrummy for as long as possible against Pembroke.

For the rest of us, it was a case of taking to the hills on foot. Neil Campbell went ahead to arrange a galley to take us from Loch Long to Kintyre, whilst we followed on behind with many men wounded. At length, we got to Loch Lomond and luckily found a rowing boat to get us to the west side and then heard the Earl of Lennox was not dead. He had escaped and was living on the islands in the loch. With his help, we got to the rendezvous with Neil Campbell and thence to Kintyre and the Macdonald lands. Since then, I have been gathering men from the western isles with the help of Angus Macdonald and Christina of Garmoran and Moidart. We have also been on the Isle of Rathlin and in the north of Ireland – briefly for the danger is great – rallying men to the cause. The intention is to begin our counter-attacks early in the new year using Kintyre as the springboard back into mainland Scotland.

Till then, I will over-winter in Orkney and hope the distance and poor weather will bring a measure of safety. We badly need respite from all this toil and hardship and I look forward to meeting up with our kin. I hope and pray our womenfolk are safely with you in Norway. I pass this letter to Svein Thorkelson who is trading for dried fish on the west coast of Scotland. Treat him well if this message gets to you – he has a mighty thirst! Pray for Scotland. It is badly needed and, Isa, for our safety's sake place this missive into the flames upon reading.

Rob

It was Svein's mighty thirst which was to prove his undoing; a man given to less avarice and bravado might have kept to his bed and waited for the skies to clear. Whilst the storm raged overhead and the waves grew even higher, Robert's letter floated to the ocean floor amidst the debris of the captain's galley.

Scotland

Arbroath Abbey

December 1306

The Dowager Queen of Norway,

As requested by your grace, I write with what I know will be deeply upsetting news. I pray the good and merciful Lord is close to you, now, as you read this epistle. Some time mid-year, your family left Kildrummy Castle to join King Robert, but his army was routed near Methven. It was put to flight.

In the care of Sir Niall Bruce and the Earl of Atholl, the queen, your sisters and the king's young daughter fled over the mountains to the safety of Kildrummy. Later, in the ninth month of this year, the castle was sacked and burnt by the Earl of Pembroke's army. The English king raised the dragon. None were spared. Niall's head rests now atop the gates. Over in the west, more were captured and hanged – Sir Christopher Seton, his brother and many other Bruce supporters. Prior to the sacking of Kildrummy Castle, the women and Princess Marjorie accompanied by Atholl escaped on horseback. They were captured some weeks later at Tain where they had taken sanctuary in the small chapel of St Duthac. They had been trying to get to the safety of Norway, or at least to the northern isles. Ignoring his sacred duty, the Earl of Ross handed the fugitives over to King Edward who imposed brutal punishments. Sir John of Strathbogie, the Earl of Atholl, was drawn, hanged, his body burned. Open to the elements and the hostile gaze of passers-by, Isobel of Buchan is now situated at Berwick Castle in a wood and iron cage atop the walls of the castle. Having vented her spleen at the English tyrant, your sister, Mary, is in a cage of similar design suspended over the walls of Roxburgh Castle in a most precarious position, if I may say so, with the winds which sweep down from the north. Marjorie, daughter of King Robert, was placed in a cage atop the great walls of the Tower of London for a month or so, until Edward was swayed from this vile and evil act by his queen. In an English nunnery at Watton, the child languishes in solitary confinement. Your sister, Christina, also resides in similar confinement, but at the priory of Sixhills in the far south of Lincolnshire. Queen Elizabeth is under close supervision at one of the English king's manors.

In case you consider I may be able to assist in some way, think again, your grace. I have no power or influence over the nunneries mentioned. All have been chosen for their passionate hatred of the Scots and their fierce loyalty to King Edward. Your brother, our king, is a hunted man and, quite sensibly, has disappeared. No one knows of his whereabouts. I am also of a mind to flee. Our beloved Scotland is no more.

Respectfully yours

The Abbot of Arbroath

PART TWO

PART TWO

Orkney

January 1307

It had been a dark and tempestuous winter. Savage gales rolled in from the west, bruising the coast. Against the shoreline and the low, rocky cliffs, monstrous waves crashed until it seemed that Orkney, itself, might disappear beneath the onslaught. Now, the low, rolling hills were obscured by a grey haar – a heavy, burdensome mist which settled over the landscape. Sometimes, the air quivered and undulated as if some unseen force had exhaled a long, deep breath.

The previous summer, an odd assortment of women, children and men arrived in the bay on South Ronaldsay, one of Orkney's southernmost islands. At the manor of Alexander, Laird of Halcro, and his wife, Cecilia, they sought sanctuary. Nestled in behind a line of sand hills, the stone-built manor was both gracious and utilitarian. Its sod roof rose, in part, to two levels. The higher section contained the living quarters whilst the ground level housed the kitchen, a large wood-panelled dining room and several, more formal, rooms for entertaining. Here on Orkney, the use of timber was a significant marker of wealth – trees do not grow well with the great winds and all wood must be imported. Outside, rough farm buildings clustered around the back of the building providing protection from the scything wind which could tear and rip at a man's cloak and reshape his ears.

Now in her nineteenth year, Mathilda Bruce returned from

her solitary walk along the mire of a fish-strewn shoreline. In the wide entrance hall, the young woman shivered as she removed her sodden cloak; it offered little protection and her auburn curls clung damply to her neck. Winter's chill brought a deep, abiding ache to her bones that rarely left her, and icy fingers of liquid now traced a slow, intimate pattern down between her shoulder blades. Enticed by the earthy aroma of peat, Mathilda would like to have knelt beside the warm hearth. It was obvious that exquisite pleasure would have to wait, for she had caught the sound of voices from the adjoining chamber.

Before an enormous fireplace, a cluster of men dressed in steaming plaids or worn, saffron-coloured tunics stood, leaning on the hilts of their large swords. Some were seated on settles or stools, bent forward straining to hear, hands stretched around mugs of ale. Though the smoke vent was open, the air was thick with the smell of peat. All eyes were upon a particularly vocal group who tossed ideas in fierce consternation back and forth, like glowing, fiery sods. Alexander Halcro, his thatch of hair and bushy brows bleached white by age, was engrossed in animated conversation with two much younger companions: Magnus Jonsson, Earl of Orkney, now approaching his sixteenth year, and Mathilda's oldest brother, Robert the Bruce, King of Scots. As a wanted man in his own country, he had sought respite here in Orkney. These isles were under the suzerainty of Norway and thus a relatively safe place for men on the run from hostile Scots and English soldiery.

Seated close to the warmth was Master Weland, the young earl's guardian. He was well-pleased with his charge. The long hours of training in the art of battle had seen Magnus grow as strong and sturdy as an ox, but he continually bemoaned the soft, blond fuzz upon his chin. Despite his youth, he possessed a keen understanding of the politics of the north and would not be denied a place in such an important discussion.

As sometimes happens, a lull came in the conversation when men pause, to consider all that has been discussed. Weland leaned forward with an iron poker and stirred the smouldering lumps of peat. A few flames flickered and took hold. The wind moaned in the eaves and the hairs on the back of his neck stood up. There was something otherworldly about a wind which roared over the land, barely tolerating human endeavour and claiming all that was not tied down for its own wayward purpose. Even the hills, upon whose bare backs giants had clambered, seemed from another time. Now turned to stone, they stood solitary and still, whilst other monoliths congregated in circles as if waiting for the wind to breathe life back into them.

After many years as a councillor to Norway's king, Weland had been rewarded with the valuable wardship of the Earl of Orkney, a minor at the time of his father's death. As guardian, he devoted his energies to the broad education of his ward in all the elements, both secular and religious, which underpinned the important role. Aside from consolidating Magnus's adherence to firm administrative practices, there was less to do now. He was coming into his manhood and held a warrior's single-mindedness. Soon, he would be making his own decisions. A long time supporter of the Bruce family, Weland had played a key role in the events leading up to this meeting. All the same, he was content to observe the strong characters before him today and would report back to King Haakon and Isabel, Dowager Queen of Norway – Bruce's older sister and widow of the Norse king's brother.

Firelight cast strange shadows across the drawn faces of the men. They continued their discussion, proposing strategies, attempting to second-guess the movements of their foes across

203

the length and breadth of Scotland. After this sojourn, the King of Scots and his men planned to return home to the unenviable task of unifying and rebuilding a nation fraught with division and conflict. What would this year bring? More failure if their ill-fortune continued or perhaps the finely-tuned use of limited resources might lead them to precious victory. Without determined help from their sparse allies, all knew the Bruce cause was doomed and an independent Scotland would be usurped by its larger neighbour.

So much had happened since their defeat at Methven last July. With a small band of supporters, Robert and his brothers fled across the wild, heathered hills, along steep mountain trails. Keeping in front of their foes by a mere hare's breath, they slipped down into shadowed vales and tracked through rocky water-ways. Their flight from danger continued when they sailed up the jagged coastline of west Scotland. That was just a few short months ago. A kinswoman of the Bruce, Christina of the Isles, risked all to offer sanctuary. Even there, deep within the Inner Hebrides, they could be hounded by enemies, many of whom were Scots hostile to the Bruce. Desperation made them brave the rough, swirling seas once more. Taking advantage of a brief spell in a blow, the fugitives forged on and made safe landfall on Orkney. They were aided by several of the Gamoran men, well-versed in the treacherous northern tides. But Robert and his brothers were driven by another purpose in fleeing to these northern isles. They knew their younger sisters and nieces lived in safety here, through the determined efforts of Master Weland many months before.

Now, they were all far away from the danger that threatened them in Scotland. With such adverse weather, this group of small islands – seventy in total – was isolated from the south. Pray God, the combination of distance and foul weather would keep them safe.

Turning away from the tableau of men with their resolute expressions and tight, hushed voices, Mathilda made her way up the stairs to her chamber. It held a less intense, but noisier, domestic scene which she shared with her sister, seventeen-year-old Margaret, and their niece, Ellen, now in her sixth year. In a small adjoining room, several pallets were set up on the floor for Floraidh, their friend and healer, as well as the sister maids, Seonaid and wet nurse Marthoc. In the far corner stood a large cradle which had been brought down from the Halcro's attic for the babies. Mathilda's niece, Meg, and Marthoc's son, Camran, were nigh on twelve months old. The latter was named for his slightly skewed nose – an unfortunate birth injury. He was a joyous child, nonetheless, and a great favourite with all who met him.

Though all this was far from ideal, they were, at least, safe and warm in this foreign abode. Here, the local people spoke Norn and lived in the style of the Norse. It was a far cry from the group's Scottish heritage. Owning lands in Caithness in the far north of Scotland, the Halcro family spoke the Gaelic with a fair smattering of French and Latin. Earl Magnus was similarly placed, being Earl of both Orkney and Caithness. The chaotic scene before her of clothing strewn about and crying children took Mathilda back in time. Her thoughts returned to the anguished parting from her older sisters, Kirsty and Mary; her niece, Marjorie, and nephew, Donald; as well as the familiar, much-loved faces of the Kildrummy household. All had been left behind. As the oldest family member, she had garnered what inner strength she could to pacify her younger companions as the group ventured forth. Given her own distress, it was all she could do to aid Murchadh, the leader of their party. As a seagoing trader with his own galley, the captain assisted the Bruce family with great devotion and never more so than on this occasion.

At times, the journey to the coast across Scotland's northeast had been alarming, especially when they skirted around villages and farmlets where it was known supporters of the Comyns resided. Under cover of darkness, Murchadh had sought sanctuary in Aberdeen at the home of his trusted friends, the Isaacs. The following day, he reconnoitred the harbour and made ready his vessel to depart on the early tide that evening.

None of them had been in a galley before and the movement was frightening. Once out in the open sea, they surfaced, pea-green and ill, from under the heavy hempen cloths. Until then, they had remained alert and stiff with fearful hearts and sour, churning stomachs amongst the stinking bales of wet furs, barrels of stock fish and spiky logs. Murchadh traded these goods between Norway and Scotland, returning with much-needed grain, wool and salt. Mercifully, the journey up the coast had been free from danger. Drustan, Kildrummy's courier priest, was enthralled with the ship's freedom out at sea. Under the captain's tuition, he stood at the helm, wind shifting his bristly, red hair, taking turns steering the craft with young Aodh. After the confinements of castle life and onerous drudgery of the kitchen, Kildrummy's scullion also found adventurous life on the high seas much to his liking.

On long watches, Murchadh tried with little success to teach Drustan sea shanties, abridged to suit his monastic role. The young priest's real skill lay in his keen eyesight which could pick out, at great distance on sun-burnished seas, other vessels, as well as pods of spouting whales, floating logs and the occasional shoals of herring. When these creatures of the sea were plentiful, Aodh leant over the side with a scoop and delivered the heaving mess onto the floor of the vessel. Then, the fish were cleaned and gutted and seared on the griddle over the soapstone hearth. For those not afflicted by the sickness brought on by the rolling sea, the succulent flesh was a most welcome change from their normal dried fare. Indeed, it was a veritable feast.

Here at the manor, Aodh undertook kitchen duties, somewhat reluctantly. He was often at a loss as to the tasks being demanded unless the action was mimed. Drustan's assignment to the Bishop of St Magnus's great cathedral in Kirkwall on the main island of Orkney meant they rarely saw the young cleric, but it was no surprise to hear of his move from the choir into alternative work tending the large medicinal gardens.

As expected, Murchadh sailed further north up to the Shetlands and Faeroes. God willing, he would return soon, en route to Norway, his holds laden with goods gathered along his usual trading route around the western seaboard of Scotland and as far south as Ireland. Any news garnered from the rebellion would be most welcome.

There had been much feasting to entertain the guests. Tonight was the last banquet: a farewell to the king and his men. During celebrations, a huge bonfire would normally be lit upon the hillside, but with their esteemed visitors' safety of paramount concern, the less attention drawn to this area was better for all concerned.

David, Bishop of Moray – a northern cleric outlawed by King Edward – sailed over from Kirkwall for the occasion. For many months since his flight from Scotland, he had been the guest of the Bishop of Orkney and was under no misconception that his liberty would be at stake without the sanctuary provided by the young earl. Such was King Edward's mighty wrath and desire for vengeance that he wrote to the King of Norway asking him to expel the rebel bishop from his lands. His request was denied. Most of the leaders of the Scottish church loyal to the Bruce, such as

Wishart and Lamberton, had lost their freedom; not only that, the aged and infirm prelates were forced to walk from Scotland in painful shackles to their places of imprisonment in far-off England. Only their Holy Orders saved them from being hanged. Bishop David's blood boiled to hear of his associates' ill-treatment. An insult to God, himself!

Meeting face-to-face once again, Robert reassured David of his royal support for the Scottish church in its own fight for independence; both suffered from being under the sway of the Popish church with its inconsistent and unreasonable deliberations in response to the political machinations of the kings of England and France.

When the time was right, the fiery bishop planned to return to his homeland to gather troops and begin the substantial task of raising the hostile north for the Bruce. With a pincer movement – Robert and his men in the southwest, and the warrior bishop in the northeast – they hoped to unite Scotland under the one banner. Sir William Bellenden offered his support to Bishop David to provide critical assistance during this precise military strategy. Until things improved in Scotland, the laird and his wife would play host to Robert's young kinfolk.

After the feast, Robert took Mathilda aside in a curtained alcove off the main hall. In the distance, the crash of waves on the cliffs sounded harsh upon the wind. An eerie howling rose and the wind shook the wooden shutters from time to time. Outside, barn doors rattled and a loose pail rolled around the farm enclosure. A servitor hurried outside to wrestle it from the wind's briny grasp.

Facing each other in the window embrasure, Robert reached out to hold Mathilda's soft hand. Her long, tapered fingers curled within his large hand, scarred from battle and calloused from wresting his double-sided sword and battleaxe. With well-rehearsed caution, he spoke of his intention to return to Carrick, to try once more to unify Scotland behind his standard. The plan involved the Bruce forces taking the country piece by piece, gathering loyal men and resources along the way. Aware of the danger her brothers faced should this strategy go awry, Mathilda paled.

Robert continued; his voice deep with concern. He hoped she and the others would remain here in Orkney. As well, he had discussed with the laird, a shift to a safer house which might prove less accessible from the northern tip of Scotland. Mathilda nodded in agreement. Her wide brown eyes fixed intently upon Rob's face. A scattering of freckles trailed across the bridge of his strong nose. Not for the first time, she noted the shadows of exhaustion under his intense hazel eyes and the deep lines of worry across his broad forehead. Covered for the most part by his thick, auburn beard, one ruddy cheek bore a jagged scar. In no way did this mar his essentially good-humoured and kindly face. Mathilda liked the way her brother's eyes crinkled when he smiled; infrequent though it was now, such was the weight of his kingship in a war-ravaged kingdom.

Rob asked of his sister that she be brave and care for the family here on Orkney. Under cover of darkness, their vessels must depart on the morrow. As long as he knew they were safe, he could continue with the complex task of regaining his crown. In the future, he may have to ask more of her as well through her betrothal to a suitable husband – to bind the latter by kinship in return for loyalty and wealth. As a female member of the nobility, Mathilda was well-schooled. She understood this was the sacrifice women must make in lieu of fighting on the battlefield. Robert nodded, pleased there was an understanding between them. They all had a job to do; each as important as the other.

Soon, it was time for Robert, Alexander, Thomas and

Edward to say their farewells. The brothers were quiet, pensive now, not as they had been in their youth, rambunctious and teasing. Each blew a soft kiss towards the sleeping infants in the adjoining room, acknowledging the maids with brief nods. With unabashed affection, they hugged their sisters and young niece. The fine-boned bodies of the girls in their night garments were squashed against musty, woollen plaids; soft cheeks were scratched by the men's beards.

To each of her brothers, Mathilda offered a keepsake: a piece of fringed linen, the colour of toasted oatmeal, with their initials embroidered in the corner. Robert was intrigued for wrapped within his gift was a small, leather-bound book. Margaret, too, had been busy constructing four sturdy necklets of brown leather cord. Each one held a single white shell, delicately holed by some creature of the sea. Now, she placed these precious amulets around the men's weathered necks praying they would keep them safe.

A gap-toothed smile spread across Ellen's sleep-weary face. From a small hemp sack, the child emptied four small, round stones. Collected from the nearby shore, each one held something unique to her eye. Into the large, calloused palms of her adored uncles she placed her precious gift, sealing the solemn action with a child's sticky kiss. Sobered and deeply moved, the brothers left to make the final preparations for their impending journey.

Into the high wooden bed with its carved finials and richly embroidered curtain, the girls clambered, snuggling beneath the down quilt. For a long time, the older ones lay awake with their thoughts, whilst Ellen slept between them – the deep, unencumbered sleep of the very young.

Scotland

February 1307

It was to Tioram – the castle of his kinswoman and ally, Lady Christina of Gamoran – which Robert the Bruce headed following his sojourn in Orkney. Braving the heaving ocean around Cape Wrath, the most north-westerly point of mainland Scotland, the galleys sailed down through the unpredictable waters of the Minch to the Isle of Skye. A close watch was kept on the dark cliffs for the bright flare of signal fires and along the wild, craggy shoreline, for hostile vessels. On through the passage amongst the many small isles of the Inner Hebrides, their vessels dipped and rose in the grey seas. At times, their skin turned bitter-blue, and the days were dismal and short.

Much refreshed and feeling the best he had for many months now they were on the move, Robert ordered the galleys into a narrow inlet, where they dropped anchor and were pulled up onto a series of rocky nousts. His overall plan was for a short stop to reconnoitre the area; seeking out additional resources of men and boats, weaponry and food. One ship containing his brothers, Alexander and Thomas, had already been dispatched to Antrim in Ireland to locate Angus og Macdonald who had been wintering there, foregathering gallowglasses and vessels in support of the king over the past few months.

Set on a small isthmus, the castle was situated in a sea loch surrounded by well-treed hills. At high tide, the spit of land became an island which offered further security. With the red rampant lion on gold flying high in the stiff breeze over the square woollen sail, the king's vessel was identified well before the craft reached the shore. Other galleys, bearing the distinctive Gamoran crest – a long black fish beneath a galley

– were lined up together. Atop a stone parapet, a lone woman stood staring out to sea. A band of warriors gathered, ready to accompany the visitors over the rocky walkway and up to the sturdy gates of the castle. Some wore plaids – claymores and dirks no doubt hidden amongst the voluminous folds of thick, woollen cloth. Others were clad in knee-length saffron tunics. Imposing swords in carved scabbards hung at their sides.

From the rough, natural harbour of flat rock, Robert and his men proceeded to the Great Hall where lavish food and drink were provided as part of the normal ritual of generous highland hospitality. Still the lady of the house failed to present herself. It was only at the end of the meal a message arrived at the high table requesting the king visit the private solar of Lady Christina. Edward offered a broad, speculative smile and winked at Robert, concluding the king would take up the good lady's offer of hospitality. At their last visit, he believed this had included a great deal more than mere food and shelter, and of which Edward, himself, would have liked to partake. With great dignity, the king ignored the ribaldry of his incorrigible brother and left to attend the lady as requested.

High up in her solar, Christina stood looking out over the sound. The shrill cries of terns and gulls were caught on the wind and the hoarse bark of seals could be heard from the far rocky shore. Upon the walls of the chamber, tapestries of powerful hunting scenes hung from thick wooden poles. Here and there upon stone flags lay the hides of deer. Over in the corner, Christina's bed was most unusual, carved as it was in the shape of a broad-based galley with a thick, heather mattress upon which lay a sumptuous mix of furs. Robert entered through the arched doorway. Christina turned.

Her expression carried such pain and sorrow it stopped him in his tracks. Tears filled her dark, almond-shaped eyes, spilling down a face that was flawless in its beauty. Free of any veil or gold filet, her long dark hair lay draped across white shoulders. She was not dressed in any definite attempt at allure but, nonetheless, Robert caught his breath at the sight of her. A saffron gown, trimmed with red brocade at the hips, enhanced her slender form, whilst leather-toggled boots graced her narrow feet.

"Sit ye down, Rob. I have dire news it is my grave misfortune to relay." With a graceful hand, she motioned to the window embrasure where two padded stone seats faced each other. At the parchment-strewn trestle, which served as both desk and table, the Lady of Gamoran paused. From a brown earthenware jug, she filled a goblet of wine and then passed it to her guest. Their fingers touched momentarily. Robert's mouth became dry. He swallowed with difficulty. Without success, he tried to harden his heart in preparation, but a slight twitch in one eye attested to his level of agitation. For interminable seconds, he waited whilst Christina sipped her wine. At last, she spoke.

"News came some time ago from the east. Kildrummy fell last September."

Incredulous, Robert leapt to his feet, knocking his goblet over at the same time, splattering viscous drops of red upon Christina's gown. At the sudden movement, a rough-haired hound dozing in a rare patch of winter sunshine rose to its feet and bayed, only to be silenced by a firm word from his mistress. An echo seemed to rebound around the chamber, doom-laden, foretelling of destruction.

"How could this happen? It is the most secure of castles. What has become of my wife, my daughter, my sisters… Niall?" A groan escaped from Robert as he fell back onto the seat. Before him, a dark pool seeped amidst the wreckage and bled across the floor.

"Just before the castle was placed under siege by the Earl of Pembroke," Christina began.

"That murdering bastard!" shouted Robert. "He attacked

us at Methven during the night, slaughtering my men, wreaking havoc. Now, my forces are scattered to the winds."

"Wait ye, Rob. Allow me to explain what happened. Just before the siege began, the queen, Princess Marjorie, your sisters and Lady Isobel of Buchan escaped under the cover of darkness out through the postern gate. You know the one on the far side near the ravine." Robert nodded, impatient now he had heard the word 'escape'. Christina knew Kildrummy as well as he did, for she had been married to his wife's brother. Both were now dead.

"They were led by the Earl of Atholl and others, hoping to reach a safe harbour whereby they could make their way to your sister, Isabel, or at least to Orkney. After some weeks, they still were unable to make it through and headed north. When they reached Tain, the Earl of Ross and his men pursued them. At the chapel of St Duthac, overlooking the sandy bay, the group sought sanctuary, women, men and horses crowding into the small stone building. The earl ignored this and took them, killing some and sending the females in an open cart with Atholl walking, half-dragged behind, to Berwick – to the king. It is said Edward now lies ill, close to death, at Lanercost Abbey."

Robert paced around the chamber. He came to one of the windows which overlooked the water. Grabbing hold of a wooden shutter, he thrust it against the wall with all his might, shattering the joints. Demolished, it fell in pieces onto the animal hide below.

"What has befallen them?" he said in a low, rasping voice. Christina paled. She licked her lips. Anxiety made her speak with more firmness than she intended.

"The queen... your wife... is confined at one of the king's manors, Burstwick in Holderness. Isobel of Buchan and your sister, Mary, are imprisoned in small wooden cages with metal bars, exposed to the elements and the jeers of the crowds, on the external walls of the castles at Berwick and Roxburgh. Isobel was punished, thus, for her role in placing the Scottish crown upon your head and Mary, for having spoken out against the king. For a month or more, Marjorie was in a cage at the Tower of London, retained in such a hideous manner just for being your daughter, but, at the request of Edward's queen, she was moved to a nunnery at Watton. There, she remains in solitary confinement. Your sister, Kirsty, is also in a convent, confined on her own, at Sixhills in Lincolnshire." Robert was shocked into a bewildered silence, but the bitter irony of the situation was not lost upon him.

"Mea culpa!" he groaned, "I attacked the Comyn at the altar in Dumfries for this accursed crown. Now, those I hold dearest have been taken at the altar of St Duthac. They are being punished – and for *my* actions." Robert's voice rose as he thumped his chest. He began to sway and collapsed onto a settle. The muscles in his jaw worked roughly. Great, gasping breaths came from deep within his chest. Leaning forward, he placed his head in his hands. With a fierce gaze, he glanced up and locked eyes with the hapless Christina.

"What of Niall and the others?" he said. Christina recited the litany of death.

"Atholl was drawn and hanged. His bowels were cut out and burned before his eyes, and his head sliced from his neck. On the west, Sir Christopher Seton and his brother, as well as many others, were executed in like manner as was your standard bearer, Sir Alexander Scrymgeour. Their heads sit on pikes for all to mock upon the castle walls at Dumfries and Newcastle."

"And Niall?" he asked again. The twitch was now full blown and a purple, twisted vein pulsed in his neck. With her heart beating sorely in her breast for this most beloved of men, Christina paused before delivering this terrible blow. She knew how much Robert favoured this brother above all others.

"The household at Kildrummy was betrayed; the castle sacked and burnt. All within were put to the sword. Niall was executed like the others but at Berwick Castle. His head hangs above the gates." With immense control, Robert rose. Deep shock was evident in his blank eyes: sighted, yet blind to all. Somehow, he remained upright as he staggered from the room.

From her window, Christina watched with increasing alarm. Ignoring the startled cries of the guards, the king crossed the bailey and passed through the castle gates. With stiff, jerking steps, he made his way over the rocky causeway to a path: it wound around the coast and on, up into the forested hills. Christina called for some of the Bruce's men, notably Douglas and Hay, to follow him at a safe distance but not Edward, whom she asked to remain behind. She braced herself for a second telling of the dreadful tale.

Robert the Bruce thought long and hard about his return to his birthplace of Carrick, the home of his Celtic ancestors. For some time, after hearing the news of the deaths and imprisonment of his loved ones and supporters, a desire for revenge burned with a red, devilish glow deep within his breast. This pervasive darkness of spirit was not a normal companion for Robert and did not sit well, brought up as he had been with the values of chivalry. In the dead of night, hot pokers of guilt caused him to lie awake, clammy with sweat, stomach churning; aware his actions in far-off Dumfries had led to the misfortunes of his family and kingdom. Grief gnawed as well, like some strange intestinal worm, upon his organs.

Robert's thoughts returned again and again to the confrontation with his rival, which had led to his murder. Not by his hand it had to be said, but many believed it to be so. Within the walls of a church, it was an irrevocable offence against God. Such a belief was like a hard, solid form within his chest, threatening at times to choke the air from his lungs. How was it his plan had gone so awry? He adjudged the site of their meeting within a sacred place to be safe, but, when wilfully goaded, his hot temper reached a flash point and ruined all. Now, he had played into the hands of his enemies.

King Edward had arranged for Robert and his supporters to be excommunicated by the Pope. There would be no blessings from the church for marriages, baptisms or burials. None could enter the kingdom of God. For the whole of eternity, all would be lost, wandering in the smoky depths. Nightmares feasted upon Robert's sleep. Daylight found him exhausted. It was this turmoil of emotions the embittered, grieving king needed to conquer – his inner demons of guilt, shame and bewilderment; the English could come later.

Was the crown of Scotland a mere siren, whose malign call was leading him towards destruction? Was it ambition and power and the fear of failure which so engaged him? Determined, Robert probed and penetrated his beliefs, delving into his core. His faith had always been a natural part of his life as a knight. Now, so much he believed essential had been denied him. Was it all folly? Without the firm foundation of the church, he felt adrift, as a ship without an anchor flounders in rough seas.

At times, his Anglo-Norman and Celtic blood had been a blessing and at others, a curse, pulling him this way and that as if he were some ill-formed puppet – a caricature in a mummers' play. He scarce knew if his words and thoughts were his own: uniquely-formed or those of his grandfather. He had tried to use his wits and take the larger view, changing sides to strengthen his position. In doing so, he was branded by some as a wily betrayer, repudiated by many of his countrymen whose aid he desperately sought. Now he had taken a firmer path and it had led to his ruin. He was isolated from all he loved by death, distance and infamy. How could he unite this land, if his own actions involved broken vows and impulsive depredations rather than his long-held, heroic intentions?

Such reflections proved a revelation for this son of feudal Scotland, where the superiority of his class was an accepted truth. Now, life had changed irrevocably for him. He saw that genuine nobility of spirit came not from birth. It was forged like the finest steel through life's furnace of pain and hardship, as he had been. In the process, old and new beliefs were melded together and cast anew, much as the strongest sword takes its final shape in the flames.

Slowly, Robert's perception of his future gained focus and clarity. His quest entered a new phase, well beyond the confines of self and family. Humility must walk hand-in-hand with courage, strength and vision. Respect and loyalty must be earned. All must be included in the final outcome, friends and enemies alike, if order and balance were to be regained. The sacrifices would be great, and he would need the strength and persistence of all the saints to maintain these high ideals – but, however rough and dangerous the journey, Robert vowed to lead his people to safety and peaceful abundance. This time, right would prevail over might, and all those who had suffered so harshly would be vindicated.

When the king said his farewells to Christina of Gamoran, it seemed to both of them that he was a changed man. Gravely, he thanked her for her support – a contingent of highlanders, weaponry and many galleys as well as extensive funds and victuals.

As Robert leapt aboard his vessel, his stern expression was implacable. With booming gongs beating time for hundreds of chanting, bare-chested rowers, the Hebridean birlinns sped like grey sea-wolves out of the loch, heading south, slicing through the waves with their curved prows. For some time, Christina remained alone, standing in a patch of fitful sunlight at the rocky harbour with small wavelets rippling at her feet. Bereft, but strangely calm, she placed a protective hand upon the small mound of her belly. Change was not only the prerogative of kings.

On the Isle of Arran in a sandy cove, which obliquely faced the Ayrshire coast, Robert watched and waited. A week before, his galleys had sailed down the west coast of Scotland firstly to the Isle of Rathlin, just north of Ireland. There, he finalised his plans for attack with Thomas and Alexander. Hundreds of gallowglasses had been hired through their own efforts and those of their ally, Angus og Macdonald. The lads were to take this contingent of veteran mercenaries to Galloway, landing at Loch Ryan, to create a diversion and wreak havoc upon any hostile forces. Meanwhile, Robert and his men would reclaim Turnberry Castle, the ancestral home of the Bruces, but only with extreme care and stealth as the mighty Percy – an experienced commander – was quartered there with his army.

Douglas and Boyd were sent across the water to check out the lay of the land. When it was deemed safe for the Scottish forces to venture forth, they would light a signal fire under the cover of the low cliffs and hillocks at Maidens Bay. It was for this signal Robert peered into the gloom, hour upon hour. Massive waves boomed and crashed upon nearby rocks. In a sandy bay, protected by Holy Isle, the king's galleys lay moored.

Around a small fire protected from view by a series of low boulders, the men leant against logs, bleached pale and smooth by the sea. With shadows rippling across his broad face and tender fingers of breeze teasing his hair, Robert read aloud from a book, a most precious gift from Mathilda on Orkney. It was a tale set in far-away France. Before the younger girls made well their escape from Kildrummy, Kirsty hastily packed the book into their saddle-bags, praying it might serve as a reminder of happier times. In turn, Mathilda hoped it would offer her brother some respite during the challenges ahead. Robert cherished this remarkable gift, for he loved to read and the book, with its worn leather cover and well-thumbed vellum pages, was a tangible reminder of his sisters. As well as being entertained, he hoped his men might learn from the chivalric principles. Though he had heard it several times, Sir Neil Campbell – a former clerk – listened well, his brow knotted with concentration as if committing the tale to memory. As usual, Edward showed faint interest and continued sharpening and cleaning his sword, his thoughts fixed on the forthcoming adventure.

The hours passed and the wind grew in strength, blowing gusty and strong. Robert retired to a makeshift cot in his tent while a few of his men maintained a vigil. He was well-blessed, he thought before sleep claimed him, to have such a stalwart band of friends around him. If necessity demanded it, he knew they would lay down their lives for him. Pray it would not come to that.

"Sire! The fire is lit!" It was Gilbert Hay who shook the king awake. Displeasure at being so rudely awakened from sleep's dark abyss was soon replaced by elation. To ward off the brisk chill, Robert rearranged his thick plaid about him. As he followed Hay to their vantage point, his feet crunched upon rocks and sand. The comforting sound of waves drawing in and out accompanied them. There it was, a fire in the far-off distance! Golden flames flickered in sharp contrast to the black horizon. Soon, it would be light. On the morrow's eve, they would attack using the cover of darkness. Till then, they would rest and garner their resources for the trials ahead.

It was a slow crossing. Some of the small fishing craft, obtained on Arran to ferry the men across, were hardly sea-worthy enough for the journey. To avoid being swamped by the heaving swell, hands and shields bailed out the freezing brine. Stars shone overhead as the multitude rowed into the small sandy bay of Maidens, only just avoiding the jagged skerries to the south, marked by spume-crested rollers.

It had been a long time since the Bruce had set foot upon his homeland. Splashing ashore in laced brogans, he reached down. Roughly grabbing a handful of small shells, sand and smooth pebbles, he brought it up to his cheek, relishing the cold, damp grainy mix. The sour tang of sea wrack burned his nostrils and scorched the back of his throat. At long last, he was home. Thankful for the dark, lest his men see the quick, bright tears and think him the weaker for it, Robert cleared his throat and waved in the direction of a small hut nestled amongst grassy tussocks beneath a hillock.

Without explanation, Neil Campbell dragged a grizzled old man from his warm cot to stand, shivering with fear and dread before the king. It transpired he knew nothing of any fires or the men Robert had sent there, but told of a Turnberry barn set on fire the previous night by drunken soldiers billeted within. The area was swarming with English, much like a nest heavy with blundering wasps. Sworn to dire secrecy, the local man returned to his cottage. This time he drew the bolt, hoping to prevent any further intrusions.

For a short while, confusion reigned. Most were braced, ready for adventure. Precious momentum would be lost with a retreat to Arran. There was nothing for it but to proceed. Robert and Edward would have no trouble finding their way. For the Bruce children, the vales and small burns of Turnberry had been an adventurous haven and, even now, the placement of outbuildings, farms, mills and granaries remained etched forever upon memory.

Robert Boyd and young James Douglas returned from their wider surveillance and gave a comprehensive report of the dangers in the area. To reduce the risks, the king formulated a new plan. Instructions were given, and groups departed in haste, each with a deadly task. Dirks in hand, the soft-footed highlanders were well-skilled at quiet, unholy slaughter. Somehow, Robert's own men, perhaps even his impetuous brother, let a man escape. Disturbed by the intruders, hounds bayed to the heavens alerting the castle in the process. One by one in the narrow castle windows, faint lights appeared. The drawbridge was lowered over the deep landward ditch, when caution prevailed. It stopped with a shudder, hovering midway as if indecision had stayed the hand of the wary gatekeeper. By night's end, hundreds of soldiers, billeted in the clusters of surrounding buildings, lay dead, sprawled askew in their beds, dark blood pooling beneath rough heather mattresses.

Gratified with the slick carnage of the night's work, Robert called his men to order. Before heading to the relative safety of the hills, they gathered much-needed spoil from the corpses: weapons, armour, flints and food, as well as horses. It was to the bare-topped mountain country surrounding Loch Doon, ancestral Bruce lands, now lit by the pallid grey of approaching dawn, they escaped. The rebellion, if one could call it that, had begun.

With treachery afoot, the plans of men can easily come asunder. Just a few days after the events at Turnberry, the Galloway expedition led by Thomas and Alexander met with disaster. When the Irish contingent landed with eighteen galleys on the shores of Loch Ryan, the clash of swords and cries of the enemy enveloped them. In a few short hours, the forces of Sir Dugall Macdowall routed the gallowglasses. An Irish kinglet, Sir Reginald Crawford, had his head hacked from his shoulders by Sir Dugall. Shackled and sorely wounded, Thomas and Alexander Bruce – the latter, an eminent graduate of the University of Cambridge and Dean of Glasgow –

staggered to Carlisle. Like so many others, they endured harrowing deaths. Freedom from oppression took its toll in flesh and blood and bone.

Once more the heavy mantle of grief lay upon Scotland's monarch and all those who loved him. He had lost three of his brothers and many friends. His womenfolk were incarcerated in appalling circumstances, far out of his reach, and it was unlikely he would ever see them again. His family had been one of the richest in the country. Now, he had no funds to speak of, no castles or lands to call his own and few resources apart from those harvested from the dead. From the interminable years of war and strife, the people of Scotland were scarred and spent. Only the most foolhardy and desperate rallied to Scotland's king. Robert the Bruce was, indeed, a king without a country.

As the woman and her entourage passed beneath them on the rock-strewn mountain track, sentinels whistled the cry of the whaup, back and forth. Sensing their eyes upon her, she looked up and reined in her mount. When she called out, they shifted slightly behind clumps of bushes amidst scattered outcrops of boulders. Loosened scree came skidding down to land on the track, raising small whorls of dust.

A small band of wild men, ragged of hair and beard, well-armed with sword, spear and dirk, appeared as if from nowhere. The smell of unwashed bodies gave early substance to their presence. Suspicious of a ruse, the men, on the run from English soldiery after the massacre at Turnberry, questioned the woman's intentions and that of her attendants. Edging around the heavily-laden sumpter ponies, they could see there were fine pickings to be had here. With perhaps more confidence than she felt, Margaret of Carrick identified herself as loyal kin to the Bruce. She came of her own free will to bring him victuals, coinage and weapons.

The watchful men motioned for the group to move on. A warm welcome from the king awaited these guests and the much needed provisions. The barrels of ale, especially, would be relished.

Racing back up the mountainside to ensure the small cohort had not been followed, the lookouts melted into the whin-dotted hillside. It was remarkable how their patterned plaids receded into the light and shadow. High above them in the pale milky sky, a raptor wheeled. An eerie call drifted upon the wind as it sought its prey.

Scotland

April 1307

Seemingly from nowhere, sharp-edged rocks smashed against the iron bars of the cage, attached to the walls of Roxburgh Castle. Alarmingly, the latticed wood and iron structure began to sway and rock. The din was shattering. There followed the dull thud of last season's wizened apples. A bevy of rotten eggs exploded with force, covering Mary Bruce in the vile, sulphurous substance and, shortly after, a volley of excrement splattered across her face. This afternoon ritual took place as farm workers returned home from the fields. The bushes beside the rough path provided a screen but, often, Mary caught the jeering bark of laughter and was ready for them; crawling into the back of the cage behind a curtained area where a makeshift privy hole had been cut into the wooden floor. It was the ideal place from which to scream virulent abuse. Today, she was caught dozing, dreaming of her grey palfrey on a hunt in the rolling hills around Kildrummy.

Mary was bone-weary. Caged now for almost a year, the extraordinary effort of will required to stay alive was taking its toll. All the previous night, a vicious north wind had blown, shaking the rickety structure. Fear and pain kept her awake. The thin blankets did little to keep out the bleak cold. Her limbs ached interminably. Her fingers and toes had begun to twist just as the branches of trees always exposed to strong wind. Strange lumps formed on the joints and no amount of rubbing eased their throbbing. She wished for a pot of Kirsty's salves. Lest bleak despair overtake her once more; Mary forced the thought from her mind. Blankness was the only way to deal with this evil.

For a long time, she had cursed everything and everyone. King Edward and his armies took pride of place in her litany of hate, closely followed by the Earl of Ross. Her family did not miss out either upon her vitriol – Grandfather for his false dreams of kinghood and Robert for taking the Scots crown as his own, placing them all in such jeopardy. Spoken in anger so long ago, it seemed St Malachy's curse might have rent the curtain of time once more. Now, fate had brought the Bruce family to its knees; they would all wither and die.

Within her accursed cage, Mary focused her angst upon those enemies closest to hand. Lice crawled in her lank hair and over her body, finding homes in damp, dark places. Rough splinters in the wooden planking dug into her bones and sharp burrs in the thin woollen covers scratched at her skin. At night, the nipping, teasing fleas, which infested her bedding, made her scratch and rip at her skin and by morning her sores would fester and weep. Frigid air whistled up through the hole of her privy, piercing her most private regions with its icy, probing fingers.

In these, the middle years of her womanhood, Mary longed for the warmth of human touch and words softly spoken, but her only friends now were the sparrows and other tiny birds which could fit between her bars. They came to eat the crumbs of dry crust from her dinner or the shattered pieces of fruit or egg. On the floor of her cage, Mary lay quite still with her face as close to the tiny creatures as possible to absorb the lightness of the warm, feathered bodies and fragile legs. In their bright, beaded eyes, she saw the wild freedom of the skies. They were so dear to her, more familiar even than the faces of her own family. She named them all. Chittering and chirping, they spoke cheerfully of trips made far and wide and gratefully drank the hot tears which dripped from the end of Mary's nose, pooling onto the rough furs.

The prisoner had watched as the trees down beside the river faded from gold to amber. The leaves drifted and dropped to form a multi-hued carpet below, till only the delicate tracery of bare branches remained. Now, the boughs were touched by the faintest aura of green: a new season was on its way. To escape the scant physical comfort, pain and misery, Mary's thoughts soared with the wind and rode the spirals and dips with her fellow travellers, the birds. Such freedom rendered her speechless with joy, but then she had little need for words.

Roxburgh had once been a Scots town. Now, English soldiers and their families were billeted throughout the area. From her vantage point, Mary watched smoke spiralling up out of the smoke vents of the cottages. Each day, a motley crowd straggled by the castle on their way to market. The prisoner strained her eyes scanning each passer-by. Perhaps there was someone familiar from whom she could garner information. One might even pass a message to her brothers so they might rescue her. Ever practical, Mary knew they would be killed if they came, but that did not stop the bitter poignancy of hope. At one time, on a nightly basis, she enacted her own escape in her mind. As the seasons passed, these imaginings dissipated. Out of necessity, Mary's longing to see home and family was banished to some remote corner of the soul where the sharp spikes of grief could be laid to rest, to mourn in peace. She would be here in her cage until death, her most likely rescuer, claimed her. Only then might her spirit find its way home.

Sometimes, sleet beat its fine, staccato rhythm on the iron bars and entered her small haven, sending icy darts to chill and pierce. When the sun shone, the stark beauty of the snow hurt her eyes and soul. Winter gales rocked the little house until it seemed it would be caught and taken into the belly of the howling tempest. She wished it would fling her far from this accursed fortress. Overhearing the muted conversations of her corpulent gaolers, Mary learnt they were under strict instructions to keep her alive. No more than that! Only in the fiercest weather did a few extra blankets and stinking furs come her way, shoved into her stiff, blue hands through the latched door on the side where a wooden landing had been built.

From time to time, a physician peered through the bars, proclaiming all was well. She decided he must be near-sighted or well-rewarded to ignore such misery, for she had shown him her encrusted sores and stretched her bent and twisted fingers through the bars of the cage, whimpering in pain at the effort. Nevertheless, after each visit, she would receive an extra jug of sour vinegar which passed for wine. Meat and grains would appear in her broth. When he left the castle and returned to the town, once more her daily gruel would be watered down to a grey, rancid slime. The wine she could barely drink, but she put it to good use to bathe her wounds and pour onto the lice in her hair. Obscurely, what helped to keep her alive was the fruit in varying stages of decay, wilfully thrown at her cage.

Mary's joys now were small, but offered exquisite pinpricks of pleasure. The fleeting colours of sunrise held her spellbound. Across the crevices of the castle's thick stone walls, tiny spider webs hung, festooned with dewdrops which sparkled with the early morning rays. The ascending cries of larks high overhead or a tiny, perfect robin chirping beside her caused her breath to catch. At times, it seemed the air itself shimmered with sound. If the wind were right, she could make out the haunting melodies of the blackbirds and nightingales in the thick belt of trees down by the broad, spreading river. With the immediacy of such beauty, Mary's spirit escaped her earth-bound sorrows.

The cage had been hung on the village side of the castle to place the prisoner within easy view, or aim, of passers-by. The intention was to cause maximum humiliation and distress, but this outlook offered Mary the unexpected benefit of a variety of sights. Across the wooden bridge, great ox-drawn wagons lumbered past, laden with goods for the castle. Some, she noted, were filled with grain, indicating the end of harvest. With the onset of summer, wool shorn from the fat sheep in the lush fields filled the carts. Soon, she began to recognise the villagers and soldiers and took an interest in their movements. She saw courting couples as they ran to hide behind the stooks of hay over yonder. In time, children grew from babes-in-arms to brawling bairns within some oft-seen family groups. When some of the older folk no longer wandered by, she presumed illness or death had overtaken them. Such benign thoughts helped to fill the long hours. Time meant nought to Mary and was measured only in the movement of the sun or the shifting of the dull, pewter-grey light to impenetrable darkness. Initially, she carved the days in the wooden planks of the floor but gave up that practice. Now, she only marked the seasons.

Scotland

April 1307

After the rugged events at Turnberry, there followed many skirmishes and battles. With a genius for tactical manoeuvre and the ability to use the land's shape and contours to his own advantage, King Robert enabled his small force to overcome contingents, larger and better resourced than his own. As the winter months gave way to warmer, drier conditions, advancing hostile forces hemmed in the Bruce contingent. On the west coast, Percy remained safe within the massive walls of Turnberry Castle. Geoffrey de Mowbray was stationed close by with his troops. The men of Galloway were on alert, led by Robert's old enemy, Dugall Macdowall. From the east, John de Botetourt tightened the net with seventy horsemen and two hundred archers, whilst John Macdougall of Lorne proceeded south down through Ayrshire with eight hundred of his caterans.

In the wild hills of Carrick, the king and his men lived hard and rough. Hot upon their trail, the Galwegians's bloodhounds tracked the rebels. If the hounds found their quarry, death would surely follow. A small company of sixty or so men formed the basis of Robert's band. They had not long crossed a river with steep, wooded slopes when scouts sighted a company of some two hundred troops advancing upon them. Positioning his men above a swampy morass, Bruce commanded his company to lie well-covered, whilst he and Gilbert Hay moved up a steep path to higher ground, seeking a strong, defensive position.

At the head of a gorge, Bruce positioned himself well, giving his enemies little or no foothold to cross a narrow pass. While he remained to defend the pass, the king dispatched

Hay to bring up the rest of his force. As the baying of the hounds grew louder, the hairs on the back of Robert's neck stood upright. *No man should ever experience the fear of the hunted beast,* he thought. Breathing deep to calm himself, he stood his ground. In the cold flush of the moon, hunched men crept towards him, confident they could defeat a single man even if he was a warrior king. His sharp blade glinted dully, halting only the most wary. First, they let loose the hounds which Robert despatched with ease. They were no match for a weapon such as his and their poor, ragged hides now lay quivering at his feet. Foolhardy or brave, the enemy moved forward, one by one, to battle the king. In time, bodies lay piled in grotesque positions of death until no more would face the sword. The cries of night birds echoed the shrieks and moans of the injured. Scenting blood on the night air, wolves howled in anticipation.

The Galwegians retreated, calling off the pursuit. At first light, they would begin again. Exhilarated and exhausted, Robert fell to the ground. He was soaked in the sweat of battle, and his muscles cramped as if caught in a vice. The men were shocked to find their leader prostrate, his sword arm, weak and limp at his side. Relieved to know he was unharmed, they helped him to his feet. Darkness concealed the bloody ground, but dirks were soon busy dispatching the dying heavenwards. Once again, the king's valour and personal strength had saved them. With precious time gained, the band took their chance, blending with the darkness as a thick belt of cloud moved across the moon. Misty rain began to fall. The men slipped and skidded down the scree, keeping up a steady pace to put as much distance as possible between themselves and their pursuers. It would be a long night.

Spies told of rebel forces in the rough, mountainous region of Galloway around Glen Trool. English soldiers advanced from the south, along with Thomas Randolph, the Bruce's own disaffected nephew. Confident of victory, the Earl of Pembroke's officers took fifteen hundred men up the River Cree to destroy the fledgling Scots' force. Robert's band of poorly armed and ill-fed men coaxed the English forces into an ambush. As the latter entered the elongated glen, trailing two or three abreast on horseback along a narrow defile beside the water's edge, chaos erupted. From a high ledge, boulders, hoisted and heaved down the slopes by the defiant Bruce force, rained down upon the hapless soldiers. Without room to manoeuvre, the frantic men and horses flailed, some falling into the dark, chilled depths of the loch. With unfamiliar dismay, the Earl of Pembroke retreated west to the coast. Once more, the Bruce cohort reaped their grim harvest.

The English monarch's virulent hatred of the rebels consumed his every waking hour and haunted his sleep. Rage soured his stomach and his words. Harsh admonishments rang in the ears of his elite soldiers, who had pursued the King of Scots using all the means at their disposal. But success had eluded them. They must do something different. *And who better to trap a Scot than another wily Scottish bastard,* or so they thought.

Bearing southwards, John of Lorne and the men of the Macdougall clan made fast upon their quarry. They were well versed in traversing the mountainous landscape and far better suited to this terrain than the heavily armoured English. To aid their search, the canny Scot procured one of Robert's own hounds from Turnberry; the faithful hunting dog would know his master's scent. The rebels felt the chill of danger draw close. With some urgency, Robert divided his men into three companies and devised a rendezvous some distance away.

When he recognised the brindled pelt of his old wolf hound, Robert cried out in alarm for the dog's instinctive attachment was bringing the enemy force close to his own contingent. There was only one action, he deemed, could save them and the faithful hound was dispatched by an archer's arrow. As he led his men away to safety, Robert's heart was heavy with sorrow and shame, remembering the dog's anguished yelp. Such loyalty deserved a nobler end

In May, success followed with the Battle of Loudon Hill near Ayr where Bruce – once again using the land to his advantage – won against a much larger and better-armed contingent of men. A subsequent victory was won against Ralph de Monthermer who retreated to Ayr Castle, which was then placed under siege by the Scots. This was a difficult time for Robert. Sir Ralph had saved his life, warning him to leave London before King Edward's guards came to arrest him. Such thoughts needed to be set aside. Now he was an enemy. When more English levies arrived, the Bruce headed once more to the haven of the vast Galloway Hills. Soon, the English became reticent, less sure of themselves in venturing out, believing the countryside played host to stealthy brigands wielding razor-sharp dirks; one slice from such a weapon could open a man's neck from behind or, with a brutal twist, expose his organs to the cold north wind.

As their band grew in size and strength, Sir James Douglas approached the king with a plan to seek out his vassals in Douglasdale. His castle had been bestowed upon Lord Clifford and a strong garrison now resided there. The young captain sought to travel in disguise, to observe the strength and whereabouts of the enemy to the north and inland near Lanark. It was intended as an exploratory mission only. Robert agreed, imploring him to take great care for death would surely result if he were discovered. He clasped his friend's hand and wished him a speedy return.

Days later, in the murk of a small, heather-roofed cottage,

Douglas sought out his faithful servant. Dickson gasped and held his bony, mottled hands to his chest as if to prevent his heart from leaping right out of its bloody enclosure. Fear soon turned to muffled elation. Under the cover of darkness, loyal Douglas' vassals gathered night after night at the old servitor's home, rejoicing secretly at the return of the young lord. Long had they nurtured a desire for retribution, especially since the old bear, Sir William, had perished in the Tower. To escape the harsh English overlordship, the proud, unyielding young men of the village had long ago melted into the dark sanctuary of Ettrick Forest to the southeast. Brutal consequences resulted for their small village. Made vulnerable by the ever-present famine to the ravages of disease, many of the very young and frail old folk perished. Those who were left heard of the exploits of Sir James Douglas and were rightly proud of his achievements, but, over time, despair and fear vanquished their pride.

After days of careful observation and deliberation, the conspirators established a plan to retake the castle. On Sundays, most of the garrison left the small fortress to attend the neighbouring church of St Bride. With dirks well concealed, some of the vassals entered the low stone building and sat alongside the soldiers. The impassioned cry of "Douglas!" rose above the stillness. The startled levies were attacked, both from within and without the church. Through the element of surprise, James and his loyal vassals were victorious, but Dickson fell in the onslaught. A blow from a sword severed the main artery in his spindly thigh. Beneath him, dark blood pooled and ran across the cold stone flags in the shadowed vestibule.

Onto the castle the men went, slaughtering the remaining garrison and removing any comestibles which could be carried off with ease. With the desire for revenge searing bright and hard within his breast, James ordered a mound of stored malt and corn to be raised. Barrels of ale and wine were staved in and thrown upon the pile. Then, the bodies of the remaining garrison and its captain were thrown atop and set alight. Forever known as the 'Douglas larder', the fiery mass burnt on well into the night, consuming the halls of his father's castle; the son knew the fortalice must be destroyed or it would once more provide shelter to their enemies. With some urgency, the rebel lord rode westward whilst the remaining villagers packed their meagre belongings and fled to the forest.

With these isolated military successes, the balance began to tip, inexorably. As word spread, small groups of men began to trickle in to the standard of the King of Scots.

Norway

June 1307

For many months after the appalling destruction wrought upon her family, the Dowager Queen of Norway lay abed in her darkened chamber. With a pall of sadness lying heavy upon her, Isa felt possessed from within by a desolate spirit; the raging tempests of winter had seemingly penetrated her soul and taken up residence. Despite her power and wealth in Norway, she was unable to do anything that might stay the hand of the King of England. Such powerlessness drove her to profound despair.

Persistent, intrusive thoughts clouded her mind – the torturous deaths endured by her brothers and their friends, and the depredations heaped upon her female kin. Nor could she, with ease, take food or enjoy the abundance of her life in Bergen. As the months proceeded, so emaciated did she become that royal physicians were consulted. In time, those who loved this noble daughter of Scotland made her rise from her bed. For Isa's part, guilt at the abandonment of Inga was perhaps the single motivating factor which made her greet the day once more.

A distraction was necessary. The queen gathered her friend and their young daughters aboard the royal vessel. As spring turned to summer, they sailed to the far north. It was to be an informal visit: a subtle reminder of the royal presence. Effie was a skilled strategist and would report back to her husband any untoward developments. Carefree days passed. The bracing sea air forced all thoughts of death and destruction from Isa's weary mind. As she began to take an interest in her new surroundings, her appetite returned and a constant supply of healthy morsels brought renewed vigour.

They sailed through a chain of rugged islands, past tiny fishing villages. All day, the sky remained light, for the sun never sank below the horizon. Scenes of stark drama took place as pods of white and black whales attacked groups of hapless seals around their vessel. Eagles flew above them. Icebergs floated past and care had to be taken to avoid running into their lethal bulk, hidden beneath the white-crested waves. Deep in the frigid north, Isa watched from the safety of their vessel as huge bears and their cubs, yellow-cream against the snow, were hunted upon the ice sheets by native people. The tempestuous end to the lives of these immense beasts – their blood, crimson upon the stark-white tundra – brought forth mourning for all lives brutally wasted. Isa's tears flowed: part of the natural process of healing when life's pain and grief must be endured.

Returning to Bergen, Effie found useful tasks for her friend to complete within her library, cataloguing books from the monks in Bologna. With her own translations keeping her busy, Effie garnered her friend's skills to complete illustrations for her manuscripts. Thus, despite unbearable sadness, Isa began a full recovery within the safe network of her loving friends and family.

In due course, Master Weland came to pay his respects, but it was obvious he was suffering from the ill-effects of his voyage from Orkney.

"My age is catching up with me," he said. This time, he found it harder to quell the aches in his joints and thudding pains behind his brow. Days and nights spent wet and chilled, being tossed about upon the rough North Sea, held less appeal now. No longer did he bounce back from the mariner's sparse diet of rock-hard barley rusks, salt cod and ale, and his body felt as dry and brittle as the bones of a dead fish.

Isa set herself the task of caring for her old friend. Cosseted in one of the chambers in her apartments, Weland flourished with the excellent fare. In return, he told her all he had seen of her brothers before their departure south. She welcomed news of Mathilda and Margaret and her nieces. It was pleasing to think their combined efforts had brought them to a place of safety. Out of necessity, all other thoughts were pushed aside.

Orkney

July 1307

With her head bent and face hidden by a bonnet tied loose beneath her chin, Ellen sat on her haunches upon the beach, engrossed in a search for the little jumping creatures which lived beneath the sand. Further along in the small curved bay of Skaill, Floraidh gathered armfuls of sea wrack to take back to the still-room of the farmhouse. Here, she would mix black, health-filled potions.

Subtle ripples appeared upon the slate-grey sea and, in the distance, a flurry of dark clouds raced between the horns of the two cliff-girt headlands. Running fast, Floraidh reached Ellen and swept her to her feet. Up the bank of sand and rocks, they clambered. Along the path lined with the tiny wildflowers of the machair and past the paddocks filled with small black cattle, they ran, lungs bursting for air, arriving as a flurry of sleet shot its icy darts against the barn doors.

Inside in the musty warmth, several women and an older man looked up, startled. They sat upon low stools around a large mound of hay. With hands calloused and red from their gruelling task, the workers returned doggedly to the rhythmic winding of the hay into golden skeins of rope. It was quite tricky, this winding process, as each end of the finished skeins needed to be the same thickness. The versatility of the simmans was endless. With heavy stones attached, the rope was used to tie down the thatch on the roofs of the farm buildings in the compound. As the cord grew in length, the artisans hitched the straw coil around their bodies, over one shoulder and under the opposite armpit, for greater purchase. The finished skeins were then tied into loose balls and tethered to the thick pine beams of the stone building. Above the workers, the matted rolls hung down, here and there, like the webbed nest of some enormous arachnid.

Floraidh acknowledged the workers with a nod. She could understand little of their dialect. They seemed to be plodders by nature, wary of strangers and slow to react. Ignoring the woman and child, the group chatted companionably. The man spoke with slow deliberation, whilst the women's speech rose and fell. Most likely, they were discussing the arrival of the newcomers or perhaps some local gossip. As the visitors departed and headed over to the big house, curious eyes watched their progress.

It had been many months since the fugitives from Kildrummy had sailed into the Bay of Skaill accompanied by their hosts, Alexander Halcro and his wife. Although a relatively short trip, great care was taken to pass the mountainous Isle of Hoy amongst the many submerged reefs and dangerous tidal flows. Now they were on the main island on the northwest coast, some distance from Scotland – hopefully, beyond the reach of their enemies – at a hall owned by Lady Cecilia's brother. Here, Walter Baikie lived with his wife, Maud, and their bairns: a lively pair indeed, five-year-old Caillean and Coinneach.

In the middle of the cove, set well back from the beach and nestled into the landscape, was the skaill – a substantial longhouse, extended over centuries to include two spacious wings. On the eastern side, a large barn stood beside an old walled cemetery, within which lay the boat-shaped graves of former owners. This prosperous holding contained two farm steadings worked by Sigurd Grutgar and Thorold Hammerclett and their families. These astute farmers maintained the crops of bere and oats, as well as the herds of small black cattle. At some distance on either side of the hall, the families lived in thatched longhouses with byres attached for their animals, located in and around the ruins of ancient burial mounds. Their Norse ancestors placed their homes close to these strange knowes for the protection afforded by the faeries and hog boons, they believed, resided within.

The sisters, Margaret and Mathilda Bruce, as well as their nieces, Ellen and Meg, lived in one expansive wing of the large house with their maids, Seonaid and Marthoc, and healer, Floraidh. It was separate from the main house with its own kitchen and living area and had been home to the elderly parents of the previous owners. In the warm and welcoming kitchen, Margaret assisted Aodh in the preparation of their evening meal. Senga, the elderly cook assigned to them, lay resting, having come down with a bout of chesty coughs after a drenching in the last sudden downpour; she had been trying to rescue bundles of fish drying on the triangular boards over near the barn.

It was passing strange, Margaret mused as she stood at the large, scrubbed-pine table. She now found herself, complete with bloodied hands, performing menial tasks – cleaning out the entrails of a chicken. Life had changed when they left their privileged lives behind in Scotland. Here, they were dependent on the goodwill of others; though she was aware Isa sent substantial funds for their upkeep. If help was needed, it seemed only right all should assist; besides Margaret had spent much of her childhood cosseted with Kildrummy's cooks and her knowledge of cooking was extensive – though, it was not until now she needed to turn her hand to it out of necessity.

When Margaret failed to respond to his query, Aodh threw a handful of flour at her. It splattered about her person and got up her nose, making her sneeze. Dragging a reluctant Ellen, still protesting at being so abruptly removed from her game on the beach, Floraidh entered the room through the wide courtyard doors. With a deft hand, she defused the situation by requesting Aodh make haste to the large barn and retrieve her dropped bundle of sea wrack, whilst she placed Ellen on a stool at the large table in front of a platter of floury scones, still warm from the griddle.

By comparison with the large vaulted kitchen of Kildrummy Castle, this room was small, suited as it was to a close family group. Above the large wooden beam atop the fireplace, straw ropes stretched along its substantial length with numerous fish pegged for drying. Against the rough-plastered white wall, a pine dresser displayed plates as well as mixing bowls and cooking utensils. Deep recesses provided shelves for the fish oil lamps, wax candles and a flint stone.

In front of the fire, a large crib held Meg and Camran, who sat up now eating bannock crusts, hardened and dried over the fire. Beside them, deep in thought, Seonaid mended hose; she sat in an unusual chair with a high curved back made from the coarse Orkney rope. One of the babes choked on a moistened lump. With a deft finger, Seonaid leant over and removed the sticky substance, flicking it into the fire. From her chair, she could see beyond a doorway into another room filled with several settles and chairs set around yet another fireplace. Colourful mats woven from leftover rags and old garments covered the stone flags. A corridor led off the far wall of this room to a number of bed chambers all on ground level.

When times were difficult for the group, it was to Floraidh, their trusted adult, they turned. The girls had needed her calm support to work through the shock and trauma of hearing the fate of their family and beloved household at Kildrummy. The dreadful news came to them from Lady Cecilia via the Bishop of Orkney and his contacts in the south. Of them all, young Meg had lost the most with her father, Christopher Seton, executed and her mother imprisoned, but she was too young to remember either of her adoring parents.

It was Ellen, now approaching seven, who mourned the loss of her mother, Kirsty, with a child's grief: that curious mix of disbelief, abandonment and betrayal. Since leaving Kildrummy, Ellen's behaviour had been fractured by tantrums and a return to behaviours more suited to a younger child. Now in their late teens, the sisters themselves experienced a grief which was complex in its diversity and magnitude. Long, melancholy days followed.

Not long thereafter, Bishop David brought news of Thomas and Alexander, and their deaths in far-off Carlisle. Margaret and Mathilda were inconsolable. Floraidh wished she could have shielded the girls from this pain. In time, they would tell Ellen, but not yet. Within these layers of inexplicable tragedy, the young women lost not only family members and friends, but the essence of their childhood. Fear and despair reigned in the present and, now, their future held the promise neither of happiness nor hope, only dire uncertainty. The happy memories of the past lay buried.

Sometime later, their tiny band came here to Skaill. With the change of environment, a measure of healing began. From outside, Marthoc could be heard chiding the twins, both drenched from playing in the large loch behind the long barn at the back of the house. Not long after the group's arrival at Skaill, Marthoc had taken to caring for the wild boys. It was an act of profound healing for her, having lost a son – twin to Camran.

The adventurous young lads tried to sail a small coracle from one side of the loch to the other. Instead, they were fished, like small human versions of the local brown-speckled trout, spluttering and choking from nigh drowning in the peaty, brown waters. Their saviour was Askell, the elder son of the Hammercletts, one of the Baikie's farm families. None asked what the tow-haired farmer had been doing down by the reedy loch. All knew he had taken an immediate shine to Marthoc on her arrival and visited her in his spare time. That the pretty, buxom woman already had a son seemed not to be a hindrance to the relationship, nor did their lack of a shared language.

Meanwhile, freed from the constant surveillance of mischievous children, the Skaill's maid, Astrid, was able to get on with the more relaxing of the household tasks: weeding and mulching the large, circular garden, overflowing with vegetables and herbs in the courtyard. A sheltered haven of peace, this was perfectly sited – protected from the wild, coastal winds between the wings of the house in the courtyard and enclosed by a long barn. Rough wooden benches lined the walls, and it was the perfect place to sit on rare warm, dry days to pod bowlfuls of peas and mend hose. Floraidh liked gathering her medicinal herbs, surrounded by the somnolent drone of the heavy bumblebees feasting on the wild clover between the rough cobblestones.

Privileged by wealth and with an indulgent husband, the

boys' mother, Maud, followed her own interests. During the long days of summer, she favoured driving her horse-drawn wagon over to the village of Kirkwall to visit friends. An unusual woman because of her freedom and interests, Maud had a loose network of like-minded associates; some of whom followed the unusual pastime of observing, drawing and collating items dug up by farmers' ploughshares.

By rights, as a woman, she should have been engaged in the management of her household, but sitting at home doing embroidery and such was not to her liking. Besides, she scoffed, there was plenty of time in the dark days of winter to be a recluse; the staff of her small household could manage the daily routine, and food was always on the table for Walter when he returned from supervising production on the farms. All they needed was provided by the hardy farm families they employed. There was plenty of soapstone for bowls and household items, either on the island or imported from Norway. Looms and spinning wheels were commonplace in the longhouses, and all the materials required for spinning and weaving were near at hand. Meat was butchered on-site and the sea was a plentiful source of fish, which could be dried or preserved in brine. Indeed, Scotland's feudal system did not exist here in Orkney. Many of the farmers were Udallers who owned their own land, as well as the shoreline. These versatile local men worked both the land and the seas.

With the arrival of the Bruce cohort, Maud found a willing helper in Floraidh who took on the task of seeing to the health of the various households around the farm. Mathilda was keen to accompany Maud on her adventures. Today, a visit to the broad circle of stane blocks on the farm of Olaf Brodgar was underway. Maud sat upon a stool and loosely sketched on parchment the shape and alignment of the massive stanes.

Waiting for the older woman to complete her inspections, Mathilda glanced at the scudding clouds. In tune with the ephemeral nature of the wind, her thoughts skittered here and there until they settled, like drifting leaves upon the many changes in her life since their arrival in Orkney. Concentration was etched upon her fine features, as she delved and prodded. Had they remained in Scotland, she and Margaret would have maintained their roles and a respectful distance between mistress and servant with one such as Aodh, despite their warm childhood relationships. With all they had experienced during their escape, those lines had blurred. Now, they seemed more like the farming families who surrounded them in Skaill. The sisters shared the tasks once considered beneath their status, but were essential to the smooth running of the tiny household. In doing so, relationships were altered irrevocably.

Orkney proved an enlightening experience for Mathilda, to live in the home of Maud and Walter and witness the easy closeness of their relationship as well as a wife's freedom to follow her own interests. For all their wealth in Scotland, Mathilda had lived with constraints – the invisible boundaries of class and culture. She found the personal freedom here invigorating. As well, Orkney was ruled peacefully by the young earl and his guardian. In far-off Skaill, there was no fear of attack or reprisal and, when darkness fell, sleep came easily to them all. Over time, Mathilda felt the tight coil of tension within her unravel. She took pleasure in the peaceful rhythms of farm life and the rolling seasons. High overhead, the windswept piping of the oystercatchers emphasised this infinite sense of freedom within such an unencumbered existence.

England

Priory of Sixhills

July 1307

Kirsty raised her head from under the thin cover on her bed of rough planks. For the better part of a year, this cold, damp cell, which lay deep within the walled compound of the priory of Sixhills, had been her prison. From here, there would be no escape.

She slept little. As usual, the nips of lice ate away at her sleep and she scratched determinedly at the contemptible hair shirt beneath her rough tunic. Today, distant sobbing fractured the silence. It rose to a strong, strident ululation and then faded away. Intrigued, Kirsty placed her feet upon the stone flags and took a few tentative steps, before diving for the stinking chamber pot in the corner of the room. Floating on the froth-scummed surface were the brown pellets vacated from her bowels several days ago. As steam rose from the full pot, the sharp, malodorous whiff assailed her nostrils. The overflow – a putrescent, yellow rivulet – ran across the sloping flags towards the bed, soaking into the coverlet which she had let fall carelessly to the floor. Kirsty had longed for the warmth of summer. Now, it brought with it a rise in the obnoxious stench. Stepping with care to avoid the puddles, she made a deliberate effort to breathe through pursed lips. Emboldened, she pressed her face against the bars of the grate in the thick oak door. She paused, to listen for more of the strange wailing sounds.

Normally, she would have been roused before dawn and forced to kneel before the ugly crucifix which hung on the wall; a long, painful vigil on knees already red and swollen. If she showed the least resistance, her clothing was stripped from her by stern-faced nuns and her back flayed with a leather switch, whose vicious knots left her bruised and bleeding. Buckets of icy water were thrown over her crouched body. Even now, she could feel the painful welts rubbed raw by the multitudinous spikes of hair. No one came. The day wore on and hunger began to gnaw at her insides, though why she could not guess, for the food she was offered bore little resemblance to anything she had known in her previous life as the Countess of Mar. Steps sounded outside and the heavy door creaked open. A red-eyed crone, dressed in a long, trailing black habit, carried a bowl of slops. Kirsty had long ago given up asking questions. This time, however, her expression of enquiry was met with an unexpected response.

"The great and masterful King Edward is dead!" the nun croaked as she placed the bowl on the trestle near the door. A look of pure malice crossed her shrivelled features. She leant forward and delivered a gobbet of white, slimy spittle into the bowl before turning on her heel. It was only when the door clanged shut Kirsty realised she had been holding her breath. For the first time in a long while, a smile of pure joy creased her thin, pinched features.

Scotland

August 1307

Hidden within the Galloway hills, Robert and his men ate well, feasting on the plump hind. They had hunted and killed the beast several days earlier and left it to hang in the cool confines of the cave in which they sheltered. Wine skins, dried beef strips and hard-crusted loaves of oat bread were shared amongst the gathering, courtesy of a troop of English soldiers foolhardy enough to have wandered into their territory. It made an enormous difference from the meals the men ate on the run: raw oatmeal, mixed with warm blood tapped from a vein in the hind leg of a cow – if they could find one; otherwise, they chewed oatmeal, moistened with icy water from a burn.

With great relish, they set about celebrating the death of the hated English monarch and none more so than Robert, King of Scots. Someone produced a small set of hand-held pipes and began to play a lively tune.

In a state of near madness, King Edward bound his son with a deathbed oath to boil his bones and place the skeleton at the head of his army, so he might inspire the troops to greater ferocity against the hated Scots. His son, Edward II, was considered a lesser man, given his penchant for games and mixing with richly-dressed young men. However, the insouciant young king gained some credibility when he ignored this bizarre oath and took his father's body to Richmond, handing it over to the Archbishop of York for burial at Westminster Abbey.

A month or more later, he proceeded into Scotland before a great army and up into Ayrshire in a token gesture to his father's obsessive hatred. Thankfully, he lasted but a few weeks before returning south to his home comforts in England. As the army left the borders of Scotland, Robert gave the orders for the harrowing of Galloway, to an extent never before witnessed. Such sweet revenge did little to erase the pain caused by the ignominious deaths of his brothers. Regardless, many Galwegians paid a heavy price. So fierce was this ravaging, the young King Edward granted formal access requested by the refugees from this unfortunate land into his own forests in northern England.

From then on, Robert left the southwest in the capable, but sometimes reckless, hands of his brother, Edward, the Earl of Carrick, overseen by the 'good Sir James' Douglas, whilst he headed north to conspire with Bishop David of Moray, newly returned from Orkney.

Orkney

October 1307

Bumping along in a cart, Aodh sat on the wooden bench beside Hlodvis and Svein, the sturdy sons of Sigurd Grutgar. They were making their way over the high ground to the peat bogs. The lads – who were in their late teens – had begun to mix as the Grutgar longhouse, situated as it was on the left hand side of the bay facing the sea, was within walking distance of Skaill House. On the opposite arm of the bay, the Hammerclett longhouse lay nestled within the mounds. After almost a year on Orkney, Aodh was fluent in Norn though on occasions missed the fine nuances of the local dialect. The lads chatted about the night ahead and the feast to celebrate Hallowmass, when spirits walked their halls.

Today, their task was to gather the dry peat, cut and stacked in summer, before the onslaught of winter tempests. The old horse pulling the wagon was used to the heavy load. From under fringed, woollen hoods, heavy and damp from a fine mizzle, the boys looked out, searching for old bushes of heath for the bonfire. As they pulled and twisted the dead plants from their roots, the lads piled them in and around the rectangular pieces of brown peat – the rotted earth which could be burnt for fuel. It had been one of the early Vikings – Einar, 'the turf cutter' – who reached this masterly conclusion. In the drier months of a cool summer, Einar and his warriors had lain around fires which had burnt through the night. The following morning, the ground itself continued to smoke and burn. Such a discovery was indeed momentous for the fuel-scarce isles.

Sometimes, the lads came across the long runs of voles in the moorland grass and startled the small creatures into making a run to safety. High overhead, birds of prey, elegant hen harriers, made opportunistic swoops and dives upon the furred animals, crushing them with their claws as they took flight. Aodh took an interest in the land around him and relished the different varieties of animals and birds he saw along the way.

Traditionally, the role of preparing for Hallowmass – one of the great fire festivals held on the last day of October – fell to the boys of the district. Once the cartload of peat had been delivered and stored undercover at the back of Skaill House, the lads took the cart on up to the headland. Here, the bushes and leftover peat were stacked into a massive pile. For weeks beforehand they had been gathering fuel and now the stacked tinder was thrice their height.

Grey light melted into the bruised purple of dusk. Darkness settled over the land. Carrying swaying lanterns, family groups from farms across the low lying hills and fields beyond the loch began to filter along the paths and roads. This time the festival was to be marked at the home of the Grutgar family. There would be fiddling, dancing and much drinking late into the night. The Bruce women were attending their first local event. After living on Orkney now for over a year, they had grown close to their quiet, thoughtful neighbours.

The peculiar, shy silence between them was broken one summer's day. Margaret had been gathering clothes from the drying line when a strong gust whipped them from her hands. Sailing across the fields like errant clouds, they dropped, as the wind slumped, at the feet of the young farm lads who were busy planting a crop. Surprising even herself, the youngest Bruce sister leapt onto the low stone boundary fence, only to fall headfirst with heavy skirts asunder into a sodden runnel. In the end, she trudged across and arrived with a minimum of grace, mud-spattered from head to foot and with an odd clump of spindly grass clinging to her neck. In response to Margaret's haughty expression, the boys shrugged an apology.

The capricious breeze sprang to life. It flipped a pair of linen clouts, Svein had bent to pick up, out of his grasp. The garment flew off to be caught like some jaunty standard, flying atop the Grutgar's longhouse, hooked on a corner of the protruding smoke vent. The lads' father was witnessed scratching his head before taking a long hay fork leaning against the side of the building, to poke at the offending piece of intimate attire. It refused to cooperate and vacate its post. Amongst those watching, deep-throated chuckles turned to laughter and then to piercing shrieks.

Later, Sigurd's squat, rosy-cheeked wife returned the undergarment, laundered and mended, and accepted a warm drink beside the fire. Once the social niceties were out of the way, Fridr proved quite loquacious. Margaret learnt there were many Norn words to describe the moods of the wind. It seemed, today, a fickle breath of air had blown the precious gift of friendship their way.

Within the longhouse of the Grutgar family, the central feasting room was crowded with locals standing or seated around the wooden planking skirting the perimeter walls. In the centre of the room, Sigurd's daughter, pretty blond-haired Heidrun, turned a calf on an iron spit set within an open hearth. Fat dripped and sizzled into the flames. Off to one side, a deep cauldron filled with an aromatic meat and root vegetable stew rested upon a trestle. Warm loaves of bere bread lay in a loose pile. There were platters of freshly fried fish, porpoise and whale. Haunches of air-dried meats leant against bowls of seabird eggs, collected by the fearless Hammerclett sons from the cliffs and boiled in great vats of water. Visitors from beyond the loch brought numerous skin-crisp brown trout upon platters. With an abundant supply of hares in the area, Senga offered crusty pies that Aodh had only just carried across from the main house. Copious amounts of ale flowed and food, consumed with relish. Soon, the empty platters and soapstone bowls were removed and trestles stacked against the wall. Cheerfully inebriated, Sigurd reached for his fiddle and toes began tapping to the lively tunes.

After another round of food and drink, it was time to light the bonfire – much to the delight of the children and young folk. As the host, it was Sigurd's task to lift a burning peat from the hearth with iron tongs and carry it in an age-old ritual up to the headland, where it was thrown onto the great mound of tinder. When the pile began to crackle and spit, faces within the crowd became distorted. Sparks flew upwards, searing the darkness. All cheered. As the fire grew in gusting, flickering height, youngsters danced and cavorted. Older lads began to spread the conflagration, dragging torched clumps across the hillside, setting alight tufts of tough, wiry grass here and there, then leaping over the low flames like demons of the night. For as long as any could remember, this had been the pattern of wild behaviour on bonfire nights. Soon, misty rain and low-lying swirling clouds enveloped the hillside and the many small fires were merely smoking cinders, glowing red-eyed in the darkness. The land had been cleansed.

Having collided and fallen on some hot peats, the Baikie twins departed with Floraidh, accompanied by Ellen who was overwrought with excitement and fatigue. Maud and her thin, balding husband, Walter, stayed on for a while enjoying the festivities and catching up with families in the area. At one stage, Askell Hammerclett and Marthoc disappeared, wandering off, as did many of the other young couples.

Sensible folk stayed close to the fireside on Hallowmass, for spirits of the dead wandered the earth. Most at the bonfire feared the trows: some of the enchanted folk who lived within the ancient mounds. Not quite the size of a small man, they had blunt features and round, sallow faces; lank hair cast sinister shadows upon heavy jowls. Their fearful habits included thieving innocent babes and replacing them with their own blighted offspring. Humans, whose infant failed to thrive, believed their child to have been spirited away. To the changeling left behind, parents refused to show nought but fear. In time it would be placed outside to die in the cold, thus ridding the family of the infesting evil.

The Baikie's guests were advised to take special care of their infants, young Meg and Camran. Family groups lit their lanterns and rushes from the bonfire, a symbolic as well as practical gesture, to ward off the spirits and light their way home along the dark, muddy tracks. As Svein and Hlodvis escorted Margaret and Mathilda home, the wind began to whine and wail like some demented soul from the underworld.

When Aodh was asked to stay behind and help with cleaning the large greasy platters, his heart sank. In a great cauldron, water steamed from the stones lifted from the fire and dropped therein. Reaching for a handful of rough sand, he began to scour and rub until his hands were red and grazed. He was still unsure where he fitted within this new land. At times, it felt as if his thoughts and ideas mattered and then, once again, he became the scullion boy, invisible to all. Not knowing his place was confusing to say the least. Though abandonment had been his greatest fear, Aodh now craved the freedom and independence of the young lads who befriended him.

Looking up, his troubled brown eyes met the intense blue gaze of young Heidrun. Her dimpled smile sent his bodily senses reeling, sliding off-balance as if hit by the mightiest wave. Suddenly aware of unforeseen possibilities, his thoughts skittered nervously about his head. An irritating tic made its home in the corner of his left eye. Aware only of Heidrun's musky presence, the lad breathed deeply and bent his head to finish the task at hand.

Scotland

December 1307

With the southwest in the capable hands of his lieutenants, the Bruce headed north with a small force to link with Bishop David of Moray. Upon his return from Orkney, the valiant cleric raised the north in the name of the Scots' king. He was aided in this task by the competent Sir William Bellenden. This pincer strategy worked well with the bishop's able handling of the situation, for it allowed Robert and his captains to concentrate on bringing the southwest into a manageable state of submission.

In the far north, Inverness Castle was reduced to ashes and the town's English incomers decimated by the bishop and his men. However, it was in the lands of the Earl of Ross – supporter of the English king and the man who orchestrated the capture of the Bruce women – that Robert gathered a formidable army of three thousand men. Prior to this, he captured Inverlochy and went on to Loch Ness, site of the great Urquhart Castle, before crossing to the northeast coast, attacking the castles of Nairn and Elgin on the way. Bruce threatened the Earl of Ross for tribute lest his lands and property receive the same treatment. Ross sent an urgent appeal for help. With time short and the distance far, aid was not forthcoming. Could it be that English monarch lacked interest in the convoluted machinations of the far north? Inevitably, the earl capitulated to the Scots' king who, to ensure ongoing compliance, took several of his adult children hostage. Bruce then sent a force over to the east to take on the Comyns. Once again, Edward proved a liability to his brother, exacting a violent retribution far in excess of what Robert anticipated.

It was around this time news filtered through from the Scots' diplomats in France regards King Philippe and his attempts to annihilate the Knights Templar. In order to pay for his costly wars with England, he had borrowed heavily from their organisation and now sought to erase these debts. It was a time-honoured strategy; with the loan merchants removed – more often than not by mobs incited to violence – all debts ceased to exist. But the French king had a far broader strategy.

During the time of David I, the Knights Templar developed a preceptory and grange at Balantrodoch, in the Lothian area of Scotland. Given some had fought under Edward I at the Battle of Falkirk and the ongoing, fluid political scene in Scotland, investigations were set in place to ascertain where the Knights Templar stood in relation to the present conflict in Scotland. With the passing of the hated Brian le Jay, their commander who favoured the English, circumstances changed. None knew exactly, but it could be said the preceptory flourished around this time; a substantial stone church, marked by its Templar cross, was built on the lush banks of a burn, adding to the many grange buildings.

In France, the warrior monks accumulated great wealth and power and were answerable to the Pope rather than to the king. In challenging King Philippe's authority, and his vanity, their position became increasingly precarious. As the crowned King of Scots, Robert found himself in an intriguing position: Scotland was impoverished from almost two decades of war and he would have liked the financial backing of the local Knights Templar. But for many years, the strategy of the community of the realm had been to consolidate an alliance with France against England. In addition, numerous forays were made to influence the Pope and enhance Scotland's legitimate claim as an independent nation. When the Pope at Avignon came under the sway of the French king, the Order lost its Papal safety net.

With great secrecy, Philippe put in place a masterful plan: a nationwide neutering of the organisation. On Friday 13th

October, all Templar commanderies were attacked. The leaders as well as many knights were imprisoned. In one fell swoop, the king hoped to catch in his web the great wealth of the Templars, but it was spirited away beforehand from the shores of France. The refugees sought sanctuary in England, Portugal and, some say, Scotland. Many others remained behind in the dank dungeons of Chinon Castle and the like, to await their fate. In most countries, Templar property passed to a rival order, the Hospitallers. Being subject to an excommunication decree, King Robert was not overly inclined to enforce this and, quite wisely, left his options open.

CHAPTER TWO

Orkney

March 1308

The tempest raged. In desperation, Floraidh hung onto the whin and heather beside the path which skirted the cliff. If she slipped, her fate would be sealed upon the jagged rocks and foaming sea a long way below. Grey tendrils sought to escape, but were held tight within her scarf. One hand gripped her shawl at which the wind, intent on seeking it for itself, twisted and tugged. Margaret followed, almost crouching, clinging as she went to the dripping bushes; her nostrils, assailed by the briny-sweet herb scent, whilst sharp spines tore at her skin and clothing. At times, her smooth-soled leather boots failed to find purchase on the wet grass and she felt herself sliding. Only her tight grasp on the bushes, their roots pushed deep into rocky crevices, saved her. They had passed the home of the Hammercletts where Thorold and his wife, Flota, lived with their sons, Askell, Asliefar and Asgeirr and daughters, Nessa and Brynja. From the low-set stone house, peat smoke billowed and twisted with the wind gusts. Margaret knew the dwelling stood empty for the door flapped with dull, repetitive thuds. Once they reached the huddled family group up on the cliff's edge, the story began to unfold.

In the heavy morning darkness, a calf separated from his mother wandered too near the cliffs. Just as Asgeirr placed a rope around its neck, a giant skua, the largest seabird on Orkney, dived close to the pair. In fright, the disoriented calf leapt forward. Both fell, down onto a rock-strewn ledge far below. A whole day passed. The young man lay in misery and pain out in the cold and wet. Beside him, the calf's limp body offered much-needed warmth. Asgeirr's family thought him gone to visit friends past the loch and cursed his laziness. But as luck would have it, Nessa caught his faint cry on the wind. Troubled by an ache in the jaw, she had paced along the cliff top, trying to distract herself from the gnawing maggot; most Orcadians believed, as did their Viking ancestors, tooth pain to be caused by a small, insidious creature feasting upon human flesh. After clambering down to the narrow ledge, the brothers tied the simmans in a makeshift sling around Asgeirr and hauled him up.

When Brynja pelted into the kitchen at Skaill House, frantic and gasping, hair plastered to her forehead and rain running in rivulets down her cheeks, Floraidh had leapt to her feet in her eagerness to aid the injured man. Now, she paled, though none witnessed it in the wavering light of the lantern when she saw his queer, misshapen shoulder. By this time, Asgeirr was delirious with pain and fever, calling out, seeing demons where none existed. His anxious family hovered beside his prone form. Floraidh bent forward and, with all her might, twisted and heaved the shoulder back into its rightful place, ignoring the agonised scream. Placed upon some boards looped together, the young man was carried down from the cliff top. The group wound their way between the knowes, the grassy mounds, to the protected area around the farm.

Within the longhouse, choking peat smoke swirled about the room and stung their eyes. At first, the ripe smell of the byre teased their nostrils, but they soon grew accustomed to its presence. Margaret watched as Floraidh took a leather pouch from her hemp shoulder sack. Into a soapstone mug, rainwater was poured along with the ingredients from the pouch. The mixture was pounded and stirred. With gentle hands, the healer lifted Asgeirr's head and began to spoon the bitter liquid between his lips.

"This should help him sleep and soften his pain," she said. She asked for a length of cloth, which was twisted with Thorold's help around his son's body, binding the arm into a folded position with his hand high up near his chin. He was to remain like this until the swelling went down. Rest and warmth should aid his recovery.

Floraidh turned to young Nessa and inspected her mouth. The gum was red and swollen. It was to Thorold she murmured the treatment required. A long thin piece of simmans was produced and tied around the offending tooth. Nessa squirmed and cried, but her brothers held her firm, whilst the long tie was attached to the door latch. Then Thorold slammed the door shut with great force and the bloodied tooth flew from Nessa's mouth, landing in a slimy trail upon the stone flags. Bloody spittle streamed down her chin and angry tears flowed upon her cheeks. Flota pressed a warm cloth upon Nessa's painful gum until the bleeding lessened. Within a short time, the fracas settled. Ale was handed around in mugs, though Nessa found it hard to drink with her jaw so swollen and sore.

Some days later, on a wet and windy afternoon, Floraidh and Margaret paid a visit to the Hammerclett longhouse. They were pleased to see the young man sitting up in a cot beside the fire. Though pale, he was in better shape than when last seen. Nessa, too, seemed much improved. Her jaw had returned to its normal size and the pounding pain was but a memory. Invited to sit around the central hearth on small, wooden stools, the women watched while Flota produced a warming drink and sweet buns, freshly baked by Brynja. Thorold graciously thanked the healer for saving their son's life. He enquired as to how the family was settling into the area, though refrained from asking, through natural shyness, why they had come to this locale.

257

As the wind howled and rain battered the door, the man of the house sought to fill the gathering dusk with storytelling. In quiet reflection, he filled a mug with ale, cleared his throat and his deep, melodious voice began to hum an old tune. His family followed suit. Whilst the fire flickered and rose with the rhythm of the baleful wind, the longhouse settled within its ancient stone foundation soothed by the sweet melancholy. In the quiet space that followed, Thorold relayed tales of the different islands of Orkney. Some even had their own fables and ways, unique to them.

Next, he spoke about Teran, the spirit of winter, its voice heard in the screaming fury of the winter gales. His own voice rose, and his waving beefy hands fought the ocean, for Teran battled the Sea Mither who granted life to every living thing, bringing warmth and calm seas to Orkney. This was happening outside right now, he said, as the Sea Mither yearned to bring peace to the islands. Margaret perceived that Teran must be winning, as monstrous waves could be heard crashing against the cliffs. Outside, spray drift covered everything in a fine mist and even here, amidst the warm peaty fug, Margaret felt her skin, damp and sticky from the salt air. Within this chaos, the Sea Mither sought to offer abundance.

The door flew open. Bellowing with excitement, Askell and Asliefar entered, letting in a great gust of frigid air and shattering the peace. Driven in by the huge seas, a leviathan had beached itself upon the sand and rocks below in the cove. Leaving Asgeirr to Floraidh's careful attention, the family took down the long knives from their secure place high up along the beams and proceeded with haste through the machair, clambering down a rocky incline to the cove. Crested boomers rolled in from the pewter-grey ocean. Spray stung the eyes making clear vision difficult, but there upon the dark sand lay an immense grey whale; its smooth hide shimmered in the strange half-light.

By this time, an alert had gone out. Locals streamed from farms all around the area. Most carried lanterns and lights that bobbed and swayed along the paths to the beach. Hempen sacks were flung across shoulders along with looped coils of simmans. Knives glinted dully in the dim light. From the low cliffs at the rim of the cove, Margaret watched the bloody slaughter as men and women hacked hunks from the carcass, stuffing the slippery flesh into the sacks. Shouts of excitement could be heard over the wind's mournful cry. Soon, all that remained was a skeletal mess of bones and skull. With great difficulty, sinews were hacked and sliced. Individual ribs were prised apart to be carried off over the shoulders of the strongest and, last of all, the enormous skull was claimed by the Hammercletts. Up the steep narrow slope and over the grassy hillocks, the brothers hauled the prized load to the family's barn, whilst the waves rolled in and cleansed the shore.

Nothing would be wasted. They would feast tonight. The blood-dark meat would be eaten freshly cooked over many hearths. Some would be dried and preserved, and the dense bone crafted into any number of objects: farm implements, needles, knife handles, spindles and clothes presses. From the tough skin, waterproof jerkins and capes would be fashioned and worn ropes replaced. This great creature was a most welcome gift from the generous Sea Mither.

England

Priory of Sixhills

August 1308

Kirsty lay shaking with the rigors of a fever. Angular shards of ice thrust upwards into her brain. Beneath her milky-white skin, pale-blue veins mapped strange, liquid paths over ridges of bone and tight sinew. At other times, her organs felt as if they were being fried upon some internal hearth and her skin, red and livid, seared by flames. In pain and dire thirst, she cried out, though her voice, cracked and weak as it was, barely rose above a low, anguished moan. She had been unable to eat for many weeks now and lived in a strange, shadowed existence peopled by those whom she loved.

Christopher was there, as were Garnait and her brothers, Niall, Thomas and Alexander. They smiled, coaxing her to go with them. Mostly she looked for her children who somehow eluded her search. Kildrummy was empty. Where was everyone? Shadows followed her footsteps. Sometimes she saw her mother laughing with her father in his solar at Turnberry. Far off, her grandfather's voice boomed. It felt so enticing to wander with those she loved and to see their smiling, happy faces. Up and down the endless, dark corridors and stairwells of Kildrummy, Kirsty searched for her children. Then, she remembered. It was a game. They would hide and she must seek. She was so tired. She called them; her voice thin and reedy. They would not come. Waiting for the cold to claim her once more, Kirsty slipped into a dreamless slumber.

A dense cloud of foul breath, rank with the stench of rotting teeth, made her gag. A wrinkled visage loomed before her. Unseen hands shook her, then pulled her from her cot and dragged her limp body along a stone floor. Pain meant nothing to Kirsty; her head knocked against the wall several times on this journey. Darkness claimed her, until a vile liquid seeped through her lips. She choked, spluttering. Fingers forced her lips apart; a long soft tube was placed in her mouth. A hideous substance dripped down into her gullet. Before her eyes, a new face came into focus, then blurred into a haze. Though her head ached, Kirsty slept.

In the morning room, Aethelrida mixed her potions. With a gentleness born of compassion, she cared for those who fell ill at the nunnery. When Mertha and Eriface, two nuns of the most callous and bitter dispositions, dragged the prisoner to her chambers, delirious and close to death, Aethelrida was appalled at such a heinous act of cruelty towards a child of God. Angry words ensued. The king would hear of this, they hissed. This would not augur well, but she was beyond caring. When Aethelrida cut away the hideous hair shirt, fleas and lice jumped upon her arms. She threw the repulsive item upon the fire. The hiss of insects meeting their death in the flames was audible and the taint of burning hair scoured her throat.

The long nightshirt, stained with shit and blood, she set aside for disposal in an outside pit. When she turned the prisoner's skeletal body, the nun gagged at the smell of rotting flesh. Blood oozed in places amidst a criss-cross of raised welts filled with green and yellow pus and across the shoulder blades, the white of bone was visible. The young nun ran to her window. Leaning well out, she gulped at the clean, crisp air beyond.

Kirsty's eyes opened wide, surprised at the colour that surrounded her. Sunlight streamed through a large chancel window and fell upon the thick coverlet over the cot in which she lay. She had no wish to move, such was the rapture that filled her body. Her belly felt strangely full. No longer did she shake, for a soft bed of wool held her, safe and warm as any womb.

"How feel ye, my child?" Kirsty stared, surprised an angel would speak thus to a mortal. The sun shone around the shining countenance within its multi-hued halo. Never before had she seen anything so striking. Such beauty pierced her soul's core. The prisoner caught her breath, but could not hold back the flood within. A scalding river of tears cascaded down the ravaged terrain of her once-beautiful face.

A hand held hers. Kirsty sought to withdraw. So much had been denied her she was afraid to trust that anything good and wholesome lived in this foul place. The smooth, warm flesh held firm. For so long, she had felt like flotsam adrift in a turbulent sea. Anchored now, Kirsty dared open her eyes. The young nun was moved by the look of fear and continued stroking the fragile veined skin of the woman's bony hand.

"Ye are safe now," she said.

The prisoner turned her face to the wall and slept. Death no longer stalked her.

Scotland

September 1308

In the far northeast, there were battles to be won, but the Bruce could do nought. Snow covered all the land. The atrocious conditions of more than two years of life on the run in Scotland's harsh climate had blighted his health. Weakened by sleeping rough in damp, frigid conditions, ill-fed and often in a state of high, festering worry, Robert had succumbed to a debilitating disease. Now, he lay ill.

To those who watched over the King of Scots, it seemed death's grey pall hovered. In time and by pure force of spirit, he rallied from his sick bed to lead his forces, borne at first on a litter and later upon horseback. With his astonished men holding him upright, they took Balvenie and Duffus Castles. Onto Tarradale, they raged and back to Elgin Castle, which again proved impregnable. In the early part of the year at Inverurie, not far from his own lands of Gairloch and those belonging to his sister at Kildrummy, the Bruce's army won a decisive battle against the Comyn forces, coercing its leader into permanent exile.

In the far south, King Edward II had gone to France to marry Isabella, daughter of Philippe, so it was unlikely there would be any large incursions from the English this year. Robert was well-pleased. Somehow, he had regained his strength and could get on with the business of clearing the land of his enemies. If they succumbed and joined his peace, well and good; otherwise, they would be slaughtered. With the host gathered by the persistence of Bishop David, Robert now had the confidence to pursue his enemies on a broader scale. Aided by the brave men of the north and his erstwhile followers in the south, the Bruce altered the political landscape of Scotland.

For King Edward II of England, the year of our Lord 1308 held mixed fortunes. Following normal protocol, he had been forced to take a wife, but his long time companion, Piers Gaveston, was shunned by the English parliament. The irate monarch sought restitution of his friend's rightful place as a power broker at his side. Deeply dissatisfied with her husband and his sycophants, Edward's young wife was powerless.

Mid-year saw Edward Bruce lead a savage assault on Galloway where many were killed or put to flight, although the English still held a significant number of castles in the area. As the trees changed from green to vermillion and the air grew crisp, Robert's forces overran Argyll. Soon, the three counties hostile to the Bruce were overwhelmed, though the castles in the area remained in enemy hands. With the change in his fortunes, Robert now resided inside the buildings they had taken, rather than sleeping on cold, sodden ground. He received sufficient food and herbs which, along with rest and warmth, aided his recovery. Troubled by recurring bouts of a debilitating skin disease, Robert fought his physical weakness, not always with success.

In October, the King of Scots sat at a trestle at the royal castle of Auldearn near Nairn. Faced with the man who had sent his kin to Edward I, Robert acted with a generosity of spirit with which he even surprised himself; especially when his hands itched to squeeze the earl's scrawny neck. He took a deep breath to steady his nerves and looked into the sad eyes of a man, his enemy no more. Relief stole across the strained features of the Earl of Ross. Bishop David acted as a witness to a treaty which he considered was far more generous than the earl deserved; his lands were returned to him as well as an additional grant in Dingwall and Sutherland. With a weak flourish, Ross appended his signature to the document. One of the aspects of this treaty pertained to his son, Hugh. If the earl remained steadfast, then the king would betroth his sister, Mathilda, to the young man. This gesture was perhaps the most telling of all, that the families of Bruce and Ross might be linked by blood. The two men clasped hands. Finally, it was done!

It was through these momentous times, and earlier, that Edward Bruce consolidated his friendship with Hugh's brother, Walter. What had started as a dalliance with Isabella Ross blossomed on Edward's part into a much stronger commitment. He was besotted. This brought with it a grave and complex challenge for the Bruce family. Edward already had a long-term relationship with Isabel of Strathbogie, daughter of Sir John, Earl of Atholl, who had lost his life in the Bruce cause. Now, Edward publicly spurned the anguished woman and her brother, David, the new Earl of Atholl, became his sworn enemy. Impulsive and headstrong as ever, Edward could not be persuaded from his path. The Strathbogie family were kin to the Earls of Mar and their lands bordered on Kildrummy. Not long ago, they had been allies. All this was in the past. Robert was displeased. The disaffected young earl had transfigured into a dangerous enemy with a score to settle.

Just as Kildrummy was a damaged shell, so too was the Bruce family, broken, but not yet destroyed. 1308 saw the king's fortunes wax, whilst those of his enemies waned to the point of extinction. Dugall Macdowall was forced to flee and his kin, slaughtered. John Macdougall of Lorne was laid low, confined to his bed for six months or more. Like the Earl of Ross, he beseeched King Edward for assistance. In its absence, his family entered into a wary peace with the Scottish monarch. Not long thereafter, Sir John Comyn, Earl of Buchan, died in England. Crippled and ill within her iron cage at Berwick Castle, Isobel could only rejoice at her husband's passing.

Scotland

September 1308

After more than two years in her cage perched on the high walls of Roxburgh Castle, Mary Bruce was perilously close to madness. Her body was riddled with pain and disease, whilst her thoughts were a tangle of mismatched memories, pierced occasionally by a frightening return to reality. From time to time, she would screech and flap her arms as if she would fly from her high nest. Villagers gathered at a safe distance on the road watching, laughing nervously at her outbursts. When she cursed them and their vile prodigy, they jeered and pelted her with stinking refuse. The following day, a vicious storm flattened their crops. From then on, they quailed in fear whenever they had to pass her cage.

Mary felt choked by humiliation and rage. She yearned for space, the comforts of her former life and all that to which she had been accustomed. The suffocating blackness at night frightened her, but she longed for it as for a lover; only then could she sink back into her old life and wrap her precious childhood memories around her like a warm, protective cloak. Sleep was no longer a natural state for the prisoner. In the biting cold, the nipping insects, which scurried around her person, kept her wide-eyed. To sustain her precarious hold on her sanity, Mary began to work her way through the past. It took concentration, and the dark velvet of night was best; as a parched soul gulps water from a precious spring, so too did Mary gain sustenance and exquisite pleasure from her night time dreaming. To recall these joys brought searing pain and tears with the light of day, but necessity demanded she develop this skill. To drift and fall effortlessly upon demand through time's lucent barrier was her only path to freedom.

The sharp tang of burning wood in the guards' iron brazier up on the parapet set Mary's memories tumbling back to the aromatic fires lit with driftwood on the shore near Turnberry, where she joined Edward and Robert as well as her sisters, Kirsty and Isa. Stars pierced the dense, black raiment above them. Away from the castle and village, the air was fresh, overlaid with brine. Upon a makeshift grill, fish caught earlier that day turned brown and crisp. Juices sizzled in the heat. Cheeks grew hot as the salt-laden wood hissed and shot out sparks of iridescent blue. Ravenous after the day's activities, the siblings heaped slabs of flaky white flesh onto oatcakes. Edward dropped his, muttered a quick curse, brushed off the grit with soot-blackened fingers and devoured the lot – much to everyone's amusement. So vivid was the image in her mind, that Mary's senses were activated. From within her belly, a low growl rumbled and she began to salivate.

Breathing deep within her trance, Mary heard the comforting murmur of waves rippling upon the rough sand. Rob told stories of Roman legions and tales of Viking warriors, creeping up on them in the dark. Edward wove visions of deathly-pale spectres arising from wrecked vessels to gather upon the rocky shore. As he approached, Earchann cursed the rough ground, giving the youngsters time to scatter around the rocky shoreline. With his lantern swinging, he searched the shallow caves until the girls' smothered laughter gave them away. All were rounded up to the sound of fierce Gaelic scolds. To prevent any further escapes, the stocky serving man used all his strength to drag Edward and Robert ignominiously by their ears, back through the castle gates. No doubt he would have liked to take a switch to their backsides as well. Enduring Earchann's wrath, the girls followed dutifully behind with the lantern. But they knew Mhairi would have a warm drink and honey cakes waiting for them down in the kitchen and, up in their chambers, their beds would be cosy from the warming stones placed there earlier by Bethoc.

Mary recalled when they were young that their maid often sang them to sleep. How strange it was – her eyes grew soft at the sight of her wild charges, whilst others blazed in frustration and fury. Whenever the girls came in with skirts torn by brambles or covered with smuts, the young maid said nary a word. Quietly, she would gather up the discarded garments from the floor to wash and mend once more. Nothing seemed too serious or onerous back then and the future had held such promise.

Something reminded Mary of an escapade. A deep, slow chuckle breached the darkness. For the young levy, half asleep around the brazier, the hairs on the back of his neck stiffened. He stirred, casting his eyes along the parapet walk. From his vantage point, he saw with some relief the prisoner remained curled up beneath her covers. The wind was playing tricks, he chided, and the tension slid from his face. Yawning, he scratched idly at an armpit. Taking a swig of ale, he glanced at the heavy night sky, pulled his thick cloak about him and huddled closer to the flames.

Mary's thoughts trailed back to a happier time. Beneath closed eyelids, her eyes flickered back and forth. With Edward's scant regard for safety and her daring, the two youngsters were a mischievous pair of imps whose behaviour was the talk of the household. On numerous occasions, the captain of the guard had ordered them not to climb on one of the exterior walls being repaired. Beyond the wall, carts often rumbled by along a narrow track en route to the entrance. On this particular day, she and Edward climbed, swift and purposeful. Before long, a wagon loaded with newly-shorn wool was moving towards them along the external track. Timing was everything. Leaping up, they each let out a screech. The captain and his men looked up from their tasks. Looks of exasperation turned to white-faced horror, when the children overbalanced and disappeared from sight. Their gurgling screams ended in deathly silence.

On the other side of the wall, Mary and Edward lay buried in the soft wool, biting back hysteria. The driver, a thick-headed lad, laughed out loud, deeply amused that two bairns would fall from the sky like a pair of befuddled pigeons. As the ironclad wheels of the cart rumbled to an abrupt standstill, his smile soon faded. Their grandfather and his entourage had returned from the hunt and seen the whole sorry event. Wild with rage at their ill-conceived game, he spurred his steed. Within the thick pile of wool, the children knew nought until he dragged them out of the cart, one under each arm. Once through the gate, he dropped them in a battered pile in front of the guard. "If ye are so keen on this wall, ye can help rebuild it!" he bellowed. And that is exactly what happened. For days after, they carried rocks to the wall until their hands were blistered and raw. Not one soul took pity upon them.

Mary's first love was a horse, a pale stallion. It belonged to her father and when he was away, she mourned the loss of this mighty beauty. Upon his return, she crept into the stables at night and showered him with withered apples stolen from the barrels in the kitchen storeroom. Mary's fantasy that she was Rhiannon, Celtic horse goddess from a faraway land, clothed her in golden armour. Brave and true, the warrior woman experienced untold adventures whilst protecting her people. Her mother told this story often to her wild, unruly daughter, so like herself in many ways. Sadly, the noble beast died from a compacted bowel; its carcass, butchered for the hounds.

It was strange though, how she could hear the horse whickering still and its hooves strike so sharply on the cobbles. Abruptly, the dream ceased. Beyond the water-filled ditch, a chestnut palfrey carried its rider along the road. Mary forced her eyes to focus upon the horse's canter and realised it was struggling.

"Your horse will be lame if you keep on it like that. See to its back leg!" she called out, as loudly as she could. Startled, the woman looked up. She rode on. The prisoner cursed her own foolishness. Why should she care?

Next day, the woman rode by, chatting with the driver of a wagon transporting barrels of ale. This time, her horse was of a mottled hue. When she passed Mary's cage, she raised her hand to her face as if brushing away an insect, or perhaps in salute, Mary could not be sure. Either way, the guard failed to notice. After the storm incident, children of the district had taken to pelting her with stones. Some clattered up onto the parapet and the garrison commander took exception to this. A helmeted soldier was posted beside the prisoner's cage. The guard, for each day he was different lest one form an attachment, often cast a speculative eye upon the prisoner. Inevitably, the look became one of awe and horror. Mary was in no danger, for the smell alone was enough to turn a man's stomach.

In the early days, blood dripped and ran down her legs each cycle. Flies gathered, and a rat found its way somehow up through her latrine hole. Imagining its pointed, yellow teeth biting into her in the night, she beat at it with her hands and stuffed the aperture with rags. Now, her courses were insignificant, as starvation ate away at the goodness within her body. Once more, Mary wondered when this vicious calumny would end.

Orkney

October 1308

Up on the headland, Mathilda Bruce relished the isolation and peace as she leaned back against the grey, lichened rocks. From time to time, black and white tannymories flew past, close to her. Their wings thrummed and whirred as if belonging to fat, blundering moths in desperate panic. In flight, their arched beaks offered a fleeting blue-edged streak of russet. The comic creatures waddled around on the grassy cliff's edge, but today, the lass could not raise even a smile at their antics, such was her despair. To calm herself, Mathilda closed her eyes, concentrating on the sounds surrounding her haven. Overhead, oystercatchers and skylarks piped and sang in competition with the ascending calls of seabirds. Terns, gulls and razorbills dived and fished amidst the choppy waters of the sea, which stretched off into the haze. Before her, streaks of rose and pale saffron cloud stretched thin, elongated fingers towards the low westering sun in eloquent farewell.

It had been an unusually clear, calm day which began peacefully enough until a vessel entered the bay. Aboard was

Bishop David of Moray, emissary of her brother, the King of Scots, who had recently brought warring parts of northern Scotland into his peace. Taking her aside after his entourage landed, the bishop read out the contents of Robert's letter, not knowing Mathilda could have read it for herself.

As the message contained within became apparent, the young woman paled and her breath came in short, painful gasps. Pressing her nails into the palm of her hand, she made herself focus on the prelate's deep, strident tones. Robert had arranged her betrothal to Hugh, son of William, Earl of Ross. He requested Mathilda trust his judgement despite all that had happened in the past, for Hugh was a fine man, well-favoured in looks, manners and ability who would one day become the Earl of Ross in his own right. Hugh and his siblings had been given as hostages to King Robert by their father for his part in a treaty as a pledge of his good faith. During this time, Mathilda's brother, Edward, developed a deep friendship with Hugh's brother, Walter, and was now enamoured of his sister, Isabella. This, of course, was problematic as Edward was already handfasted to Isabella of Strathbogie and had two sons by her. Bishop David frowned as he read the last few comments. He was not fond of the king's impulsive brother.

For so long, she had railed against the Earl of Ross for his brutal treatment of her family when he breached the sanctuary of St Duthac. Her dearest kin sought in vain to escape, but he delivered them to King Edward. The horrendous manner of their imprisonment weighed upon her mind, and she doubted she could bear to be in the earl's presence, let alone take on the mantle of wife to his heir. At this point, she was unsure whom she hated most: the Earl of Ross or her brother for asking such a thing of her. It mattered not what kind of man this Hugh was, nor that Edward found Walter and Isabella Ross agreeable company. She was sickened to her soul by the request. Mathilda bowed her head and asked to be excused. Numb with shock, she walked from the chamber. A blast of cold air revived her. Ignoring her veil as it fell onto the muddy cobbles and oblivious to the questioning looks from all and sundry in the courtyard, she lifted her gown and ran. One man looked up from his task, shocked to see the pure anguish written across the young woman's strained features.

Sobbing, she found her way up to the headland. Wrapping her shawl tight about her shoulders, she sought shelter beside a clump of boulders. Anger coursed through her veins. How could Robert ask such a thing? How could he make peace with a man who had caused them all so much pain? She thought of young Ellen grieving for her mother. Then there was Meg, who held no memory at all of Kirsty and would never know her father.

For hours, she sat and pondered her future with such a family. A sense of duty and obligation to her brother for all the hardships he had borne in the battle for the crown of Scotland, vying with pure visceral hatred for the Ross family. It was not only that, Mathilda decided. She had grown to love Orkney: the deep, pensive rhythms of sea and land; the freedom of her life here amidst the ancient markers; the light and dark; the wildly contrasting seasons; and the gentle acceptance experienced by her family amidst the precious warmth of this tiny community. She had made friends here and did not want to leave.

Deepening dusk and bracing cold caused her to stand stiffly, brushing grass and grains of sand from her gown. As she turned towards the lights of Skaill, she observed a stocky, dark-haired man standing some distance away from her. In his hand, he held her veil before him as he came closer, a peace offering as it were. Bowing low, he introduced himself: Hugh, son of the Earl of Ross.

For some days now, the heir to the Ross earldom had been the esteemed guest of the Baikie family. He was young and handsome, Seonaid commented to her sister and Murchadh – the captain who had brought them to Orkney all those years ago. In the warm, homely kitchen at Skaill House, they sat around the large wooden table.

Welcoming the opportunity for some respite on his journey as well as some much-needed home cooking, Murchadh was on his way back from trading around Scotland's west coast. In a day or two, he planned to venture on to Norway. Marthoc joined in the conversation, pointing out the young lord was still a part of the hated Ross family and would not be forgiven for taking Mathilda away from them. It was quite surprising then, for someone who was so self-focused, that she noticed Murchadh looking at Seonaid quite strangely, as if for the first time. She wondered what the captain could possibly see in her sister. His taste was obviously in question, or perhaps his eyesight, for had he not bypassed Marthoc's own comely wares which had been freely on offer in the past.

Bishop David went onto Kirkwall to confer with Earl Magnus and would return in a week or so prior to departing for Scotland. The sister maids were busy making a wedding gown for Mathilda. King Robert had sent many ells of fine rose-gold silk and gold braid. Mindful it would be a winter wedding, he also sent a cape lined with miniver, no doubt purloined from some wealthy trader in Aberdeen. The wedding would take place in far-off Ross and Cromarty, near Inverness. In the meantime, another celebration was imminent, that of Marthoc's wedding to her beau. Askell had courted the sonsy lass from the moment she arrived in Skaill. Now, Marthoc looked forward to moving over to his family's longhouse around one curved arm of the bay. Though she was with child, all remained silent on the issue; the villagers were fearful, lest the trows or fairy folk learn of it and bring harm to the mother and unborn child.

Between the two sisters, Marthoc and Seonaid, there were some fraught moments. Both loved Camran with a passion. With his mother's focus on her husband-to-be, the lad was just as happy to stay where he was with Seonaid, his aunt, who treated him like her own, and with Ellen and Meg; both of whom were like sisters to him. For Marthoc, this public betrayal was as hurtful as a dirk thrust into her breast. Both worked away in a tense silence which spoke volumes, intent on transforming the silk into a magnificent gown. As the day wore on, Marthoc's thoughts wandered to the ritual blackening.

Midafternoon, Askell and his brothers sauntered forth from the family farm. Friends waylaid the groom, half-dragging him in reluctant good humour around the bay to the Grutgar's barn. Here, to the ribald calls of the all-male crowd, they stripped him to his braies. In a large wooden pail, tar had been mixed with soot, flour and feathers collected from the clifftop resting nooks of seabirds, and the twiggy nests of ducks and goslings from around the loch. The unctuous mixture was stirred with a large paddle and the cold, sticky mess slapped upon Askell's bare body from head to foot.

Blowing whistles, shouting and banging sticks on drums, family and friends crowded around their blackened victim who looked like a shuddering, hunched bird. Aodh looked on askance for he was to wed the pretty, nubile Heidrun, next year. Up till now, he had been unable to believe his good fortune at finding a niche for himself – with friends, a home, and a family of his own in this new life in Orkney. No longer would he be Aodh, the scullion boy. Here, he was seen as an equal. In light of such good fortune, Aodh looked forward to living in the Grutgar longhouse with Heidrun, sharing duties across the farm and Skaill House. Now he was not so sure.

Dusk brought a chilly end to the proceedings. The men herded Askell down to the shore. Most ended up with him in the waves and were covered in as much muck amidst the floating mess of blackened feathers. The shrieks of laughter and jeers almost drowned out the squawking cries of the gulls overhead. From the low cliff which rimmed the small bay, Margaret and Mathilda watched in amazement. Out of the corner of her eye, Margaret caught the approach of Hugh Ross across the machair. Subtly, she moved to go down by the shore, leaving Mathilda engrossed in the spectacle on the thin strip of beach below her. As Hugh came to stand by her side, she turned, sensing his bulky form. It was hard to stay angry with this personable young man who had shown her nought but kindness, allowing her space and time to recover from the shock of their betrothal. Amused at the antics of Aodh as he dashed forward throwing pails of water over the gathered crowd, they both laughed and then fell into an awkward silence. With skin, smeared black by the oily tar, feathered bodies staggered out of the waves and ran for the warmth of the Grutgar's barn and a welcome bonfire. The celebration would continue into the night with much ale consumed in the revelry.

"Walk with me?" Hugh requested. His quiet, encouraging manner was hard to resist. Mathilda complied, dutiful as his betrothed though reluctant. She had no desire to speak with him at all, such was her confused state of mind, but she recalled their first meeting. Up on the clifftop, Hugh had apologised for his father's actions in capturing her kin. After being imprisoned in the Tower for seven long years following the Battle of Dunbar, the earl pledged allegiance to King Edward in order to gain his release. An oath, once given, required a firm commitment and he fulfilled what was asked of him to the letter. Despite this, Hugh knew his father's allegiance had always been to Scotland. Traditionally, the Ross family were Balliol supporters, being kin to the Comyns. When her husband had been imprisoned, Hugh's mother – a powerful, persuasive woman – sought to gain King Edward's patronage. To some, it appeared Lady Euphemia had fallen under the sway of his magnetic personality. She worked passionately for the English cause and in the end her husband was released from the Tower. He returned home to Ross, unwell and weakened by his incarceration. Hugh knew his father could not face such an experience again. Indeed, it would have been the death of him.

Deaf to the pleas of the wives whose husbands languished in his prison after the Dunbar Drave, King Edward was ruthless to his enemies. Many a family lost all and starved. Earl William found his wife's stance had protected the Ross lands – Hugh's future, in fact. By her pragmatism, she saved them from ignominious poverty. The earl returned home to find his wife both in charge *and* a confidante of the English king. Grateful for all she had achieved, it was easier and safer to continue enjoying the king's patronage. *Aye right!* Mathilda thought with some irony.

Growing up as heir to the Earl of Ross under these circumstances was a curious experience for Hugh. He had lost his father through imprisonment for much of his young life whilst his mother's temerity in embracing the English cause, brought them under King Edward's protection – on friendly terms as it were, but at his beck and call. In many ways, it was as strange as the situation in which Mathilda now found herself: a much younger Hugh had been forced to tolerate relations with a sworn enemy in circumstances beyond his control. With her betrothed's insight into her confusion, it no longer seemed imperative to Mathilda to spurn his polite, tentative advances. Furthermore, Hugh's father had joined, albeit under pressure, with her brother, King Robert. It was time to end the blood feud over the death of the earl's cousin, John, the Red Comyn. Bruce and Ross found their measure and consolidated a respectful alliance. Mathilda knew her brother sought peace rather than war, and strategic forgiveness and mercy gained far more than any battles for the relatively small price of pride-filled anger. It was a lesson she was struggling to learn, but learn she must.

With all these considerations, Mathilda found herself warming to Hugh; the hard core of ice within her heart melting despite herself. Not for the first time, she wondered what he would be like as a marriage partner, but she held deep reservations regarding the powerful matriarch, Lady Euphemia. By week's end, they would depart in the Ross galley which lay anchored in the bay. Mathilda's sadness now focused upon leaving her family behind in Orkney. For this sister of the Bruce, it was a time for farewells and grand beginnings.

Norway

December 1308

For once, Isa was dumbstruck. Murchadh had brought her several bags of salt from the Solway near her home and a bale of fine Scottish wool for spinning, all from his latest trading venture across the North Sea. Seated by the cosy hearth sharing a goblet of warmed wine, he imparted news garnered during his latest visit to Orkney and spoke of Mathilda's betrothal to Hugh, heir to the Earl of Ross. Frowning with irritation, Isa rose and began pacing around the solar, oblivious to her guest. A spray of sleet battered the thick glass windows of the dower apartments. All day, rain had obscured her view of Bergen. She shivered and nestled into the fur lining of her cloak.

"It beggars belief Robert would sacrifice his own sister to such a family!" she said, forgetting her own betrothal to the

Norse king only a few decades after the Battle of Largs. Murchadh nodded, but added he had met the man in question and he seemed a sound fellow. Perhaps her brother knew what he was about? Isa shook her head disconsolately. The accursed crown of Scotland! How much more pain and sorrow would their family have to endure in its pursuit? Apart from this diabolical news, she was pleased to hear all was well with the rest of her kinfolk on Orkney and prodded Murchadh for a detailed description of their health and wellbeing, the quality of living conditions and the environment in which they flourished. For the past year or so, he had brought her the latest news about the rebellion as well as that of her family, enduring this inquisition of questions at the end of each voyage. He enjoyed her grace's patronage; his loyalty, beyond question. Deep within his being, he knew he would go to the earth's end and beyond for this lovely woman, grappling the great sea serpent bare-handed if she asked it of him.

Realising their meeting had come to its natural conclusion, Murchadh moved towards the door. At the sound, Isa turned. Gracefully, she moved across the chamber, thanking the captain once more for his dedication and kindness; his efforts had saved her family, those now on Orkney, and for this, he deserved her undying gratitude. He bent his head and made ready to move through the low doorway. Isa placed her hand on his arm to slow his departure.

"I have another favour to ask of you." She spoke with some earnestness. "The queen requests my presence at the Yuletide festivities in Oslo. My vessel is in need of repairs, and Kettil has a swollen leg. He cannot sail until full healing has taken place." Of course, Murchadh agreed, changing his plans without a moment's hesitation. Their departure would take place after he traded his goods down at the Bryggen wharf. Despite the miserable weather, it was busy with preparations being made for the annual fair.

A few days later, a small group – Isa and Inga and their maids – departed in Murchadh's trading galley. A cold mizzle fell, obscuring much of Bergen in the dense, heavy darkness. Rather than spiralling freely up into the air, the resinous pine smoke from the many hearths lay in a flattened layer across the shingle and turf roofs. Within the cramped shelter, the women sat upon their trunks of clothing and gifts; damp cloaks pulled tight about huddled forms. Since hearing news of Mathilda's betrothal, Isa had felt out of sorts, in a dark place of old, painful memories. Overwhelmed by despair, she hoped the trip away and Effie's usual good spirits might cheer her. As well, she looked forward to seeing Akershus Festning, which had recently been completed. The fortress was situated on a headland overlooking the new royal capital: a small community by Bergen's standard, for the citizens numbered a mere three thousand. King Haakon preferred Oslo's strategic location from which to monitor the fractious royal families of Sweden and Denmark, who were often questing at each other's throats, causing much instability for Norway.

As they sailed into Oslo's harbour, the rain cleared. Billowing white clouds rolled in from the northwest. Galleys with carved prows and furled woollen sails spread out across the choppy waters. Some sported royal emblems and flags. Isa looked up. There upon the headland stood a great hall. It was similar in design to the one in the Holmen in Bergen. By the time their goods were unloaded, Effie was waiting down by the wharf. She waved madly: her effervescent spirit, a great boon, lifting all those around her. Linking arms, the two women began the climb to the castle, followed by their entourage and a cart laden with belongings. Having decided to go on to Denmark to trade the remnants of his Scottish goods, Murchadh would return in a week.

They passed through the stone walls still under

construction. Isa was incredulous at the broad expanse of water and curving coastline which lay before her. Princess Ingeborg took Inga by the hand and the girls ran off to see her latest acquisition, a pet bear cub named Bruno. Much later, in a large, rug-strewn solar filled with comfortable settles and a trestle or two, the women sat by the fireplace. Flames licked greedily at the pine logs. A resinous haze filled the chamber. As if enacting their own tale of drama and woe, fleeting shadows rose and fell across the wall tapestries and the vaulted stone ceiling. Outside, there were no sounds at all for it had begun to snow. Bringing her good sister up to date with her news, Isa relayed all she knew of proceedings in Scotland and Orkney. A cloud of emotion darkened her face. She touched upon Mathilda's betrothal to the son of the reviled Earl of Ross. Effie's astute blue eyes focused upon Isa's expressive face and she grasped her friend's hand. Exposed to the daily pragmatics of royal politics, she knew Isa would have to come to terms, painful as it was, with the actions of her brother. They would soon have other things to consider for the great Yuletide festivities were to begin on the morrow. A massive banquet was to be held to celebrate the completion of the fortress and the queen hoped her good sister would be too caught up in the light-hearted frivolities to be consumed by dark thoughts.

In the Great Hall of Akershus, the crowd gathered in high expectation. Amongst the guests were many of Norway's magnates and their wives; the royal dukes of Sweden – Eric and Valdemar who sought sanctuary with King Haakon from their foes both in Sweden and Denmark – and the bishops of Bergen and Oslo. Master Weland had sent his apologies; recent developments in Scotland kept him in Orkney, but he hoped soon to journey across the seas to Norway. The castle and all its outbuildings were spotless, having been cleaned from the basement storerooms to the highest tower. A sheaf from the last crop of grain hung in the Great Hall – testament to the rituals of thanksgiving and renewal. All was in readiness to welcome the forthcoming year.

The nobles and their ladies were dressed in magnificent style. Tonight was a time of celebration and the guests looked forward to the feast and the lighting of the Yule Log: it now rested within a fireplace so large several oxen could be roasted within its shadowy confines. The trumpeting of animal horns heralded the arrival of the king. With the muscular figure of a warrior and a wild mane of fair hair, his looks belied his keen, erudite mind. Haakon entered the hall accompanied by his blond queen and the dark-haired widow of his deceased brother. Along with the royal dukes and the bishops, they sat at the high table.

Effie arranged the seating so she and Isa might sit together. In wide-eyed silence, the pair gazed in awe at the sight before them. Armed guards lined the walls behind the many trestles filled now with seated guests. Huge beeswax candles lined the centre of the tables granting the cavernous stone hall a warm festive glow. Greased rushes in their cressets smoked in the fresh gusts billowing up from the nearby fjord. Guests dipped silver goblets into the bowls of warmed glogg, an infusion of wine and aromatic spices. The noise levels rose and in the far corner, a pair of hounds jostled and growled at each other. King Haakon motioned for silence and servitors kicked the dogs into submission. A huskarl came forward; a fiery pine branch held high in each hand. To great acclaim, he paraded around the perimeter and then lit the gathered kindling around the log. When the flames caught and held, all cheered. It was a grand augury for favourable times ahead. Goblets were raised and hearty toasts made to the mighty Yule Log. The cheering reached a crescendo. Heralds blew their horns once more, marking the arrival of the feast.

From various doorways, servitors filed into the Great Hall.

Platters were held high, loaded with ribs of pork, baked hams, sausages, massive chunks of roast venison and all manner of wild game. Others carried elaborate serving dishes with creatures from the sea: smoked salmon, crustaceans, poached sturgeon and the black flesh of whale; next came smaller tubs of herrings along with several cauldrons of lutefisk. Later, bowls of almonds and candied fruits from the orient appeared to tempt the sated appetites of the guests. At this stage, the bishops rose in unison and made a timely, dignified departure from the hall with King Haakon's blessing.

To great applause, servitors carried in a favourite treat on a broad platter. It was a large pig, the symbol of Freya, goddess of abundance, made with sweet white almond paste. When most of the food had been cleared away, the festivities could commence.

Jesters wound their way through the revellers accompanied by tiny, liquid-eyed monkeys on leashes. Squealing with high-pitched excitement, the latter grabbed at the nuts and fruit and soon became a general nuisance. One leapt upon the shoulder of an elegant matron, ignoring her screams as it plucked and pulled at the coils of silvered hair looped around her ears. When it let loose a series of noisy spurts, lumpy-brown and vile-smelling, down the front of her gown, she fainted into the arms of her irate husband, one of the king's administrators. Effie and Isa exchanged looks of horror, whilst the king and many others, suitably inebriated, roared with laughter. The chattering primates were led away to the relief of the crowd and a substantial space was cleared for the dancing bear, musicians and jugglers.

In time to the beat of a drum, the lumbering creature rose up on its hindquarters and swayed, lifting one leg then another. When a nimble jester ran at the animal almost knocking it off balance, the drunken crowd applauded. The monster roared and lashed out at its adversary with a paw that came dangerously close. Women gasped in fright. With a thick leash attached firmly to its trainer's wrist, the black bear stumbled over to an exit en route to its large pit in the bailey. At his hindquarters, the king's hounds followed, nipping and yelping. The bear turned and with one swipe of a well-aimed paw, silenced a large brindled hound, knocking it to the ground; its claws, which had been ground down, hardly drew blood.

Cymbals clanged – the signal for the boisterous revelry to become even more frenzied. Into the fray came a being, so strange women shrieked and men cried out in mock alarm. The creature was dressed in a goat's skin with a horned head upon his massive shoulders. Representing the totem of the powerful god, Thor, he butted seductively at the females in the crowd and then, when attacked by warriors, feigned death after a lengthy battle up and down the length of the hall. He lay upon the stone flags and was mocked by all, then leapt up, once again vigorous and strong. The crowd cheered. This rite, symbolising rebirth, was repeated annually to ensure a good year would follow the dark, cold winter with fertility and abundance. Yuletide had begun in earnest.

Scotland

December 1308

How Mathilda had missed the rugged landscape of her homeland and the comforting familiarity of the life she knew best. Above all, she relished the fact that, soon, she would see Robert and Edward at her wedding to the heir of the Ross earldom. After the long journey, the galley sailed into Cromarty Firth through twin sentinels. The craggy mounds of the Sutors were so-called, Hugh told his betrothed, because of the legend that two giant soutars shared their shoemakers' tools, throwing them back and forth across the narrow channel. When the ship reached its destination, the relieved crew cheered. Some distance from the shoreline, Delny Castle proved to be a substantial stronghold set on a great mound. Good grazing land rose to the south. To the northwest lay the densely wooded hills of Ardross.

In the Great Hall, Earl William received Mathilda. Grey of hair and skin, the earl grasped her hand, beseeching forgiveness for all that had happened to her female kin. Mathilda was taken aback. He was not as she imagined; age and illness had left its mark on the old warrior. Showing signs of irritation at his abject apology, an autocratic woman of some elegance stood beside him. Lady Euphemia towered over the earl. Three of Hugh's four siblings were in the welcoming party – Isabella, Dorothea and John. Another brother, Walter, Mathilda later learnt, was absent; studying as her brother, Alexander, had done at the University of Cambridge in deepest England.

Though all were silent whilst the formal introductions were made by Bishop David, Mathilda caught the fleeting expressions of amusement upon the faces of Hugh's sisters. At first she bristled, believing she might appear dowdy in her russet, homespun gown and be mocked for it, but she was relieved to see that, apart from the countess, the daughters wore clothing suitable for riding and hawking. With Scotland at war and in the absence of an established king's court, following the clothing fashions of the continent had been relinquished in favour of practicality. Indeed when Isabella rolled her eyes at her mother's frostiness, Mathilda knew she had an ally. She was grateful as well for Hugh's steadfast support. He stood beside his betrothed, his arm linked with hers, and stared at his mother until she relented and smiled at her son. Purely by chance proximity, Mathilda was caught within its radiant expanse of warmth and love.

As if some stray urchin in need of a home, Mathilda was

escorted to her chamber. Along the way, Hugh's sisters talked and laughed, pointing out items of interest. Even so, it was hard for their guest to get her bearings. They walked along several corridors before entering a curved stairwell leading up several flights into a corner tower of the castle. The large chamber was quite chilled and a serving maid busied herself lighting blocks of peat in the fireplace. In a corner stood a large, comfortable bed; its curtained surrounds richly embroidered with the Ross emblem. Against one wall, a trestle served as a table and desk. Tapestries lined the rough-textured walls. By the hearth, a settle and several stools were conveniently placed. A large window embrasure, with its padded stone seats facing each other, looked out onto the narrow waters of the Cromarty Firth and the long, dark bulk of the Black Isle. The sky was filled with a mass of heavy clouds. Rain was on the way.

Servitors brought up Mathilda's trunks. Isabella and Dorothea wished to see their guest's wedding gown and praised the rich fabric and lavish trim. It seemed Mathilda's fears were unfounded for the Ross family had fallen on difficult times, as had many families with Scotland's decade or more of war. That the young women were impressed raised Mathilda's confidence. Isabella tried on the silk veil over her rich brown hair. It was obvious marriage was much on her mind, for she had mentioned Edward's name several times already in their brief conversation. Mathilda loved peace and the quiet joy of her own thoughts, and this fascination with herself as a newcomer proved overwhelming. She realised, however, to survive she would need the girls' friendship and sisterly confidences as well as the support provided by Hugh, upon which she had come to depend. Her first meeting with his mother had been daunting, glacial even, but she reminded herself, she was a Bruce, first and foremost, and a sister to the king. She could and would, determine her own future.

Advent would begin soon and fasting would be the order of the day, at least whilst Bishop David was in the vicinity. This meant the wedding and its feast had to be concluded within a few days of their arrival. Mathilda was exhausted by all the introductions to family members, visitors and the large household. Despite this, she had a great sense of expectation, of waiting for something momentous to happen. And indeed it did! Whilst the household gathered in the Great Hall to await dinner, a commotion occurred outside. Guards shouted. A large contingent of men rode across the drawbridge and into the bailey. Horns sounded as the stallions were brought to an abrupt standstill. The courtyard filled with onlookers who watched as the earl and his countess welcomed Robert, King of Scots, and his armed guard. There was a certain masculine glamour to the group of dishevelled, hard-bitten soldiers, as they trooped into the Great Hall. It was to Mathilda that Robert strode. Casting all protocol aside, he lifted her up and swirled her around, much to the amazement of the household. Edward was right behind him grinning from ear to ear. It had been two long unhappy years since they had last seen each other in Orkney, during which time tragic events had overtaken their loved ones.

After a hasty meal where pleasantries were exchanged at the high table, Robert excused himself for important negotiations were necessary with the earl and his heir. Flushed with success, he was keen to discuss his recent victory over the Macdougalls at the Pass of Brander. Mathilda's dowry also required further examination. In addition to the lands the earl had been given and which later would fall to Hugh when he became earl, Robert granted the lucrative burgh of Nairn. Dingwall Castle was in his care, and he outlined his wishes for Hugh and Mathilda to live there. His sister was to be the chatelaine of her own castle rather than live within the domain of her mother-in-law, subordinate to her will. He would formalise the transfer of its ownership to Hugh as soon as the treaty between the two families was consolidated.

Mathilda relaxed by the warm hearth in her chamber, enjoying the peace after the hectic newness of the day. A firm knock sounded upon the heavy door. Somehow, she knew it would be Robert. With all formalities forgotten, the siblings greeted each other with much affection. Upon the trestle stood a jug of wine from which Mathilda poured two goblets, one of which she handed to her brother. In the soft firelight, she examined his face. It was lean, worn even, with care and past illness, but his eyes held the same warmth and intensity. He began to talk, whilst Mathilda breathed deeply of peat and the nearby sea. From up on the tower roof, a solitary owl hooted and the nearby sounds of the castle faded into the distance. She saw the battles and troubles as Rob described them. Tears flowed down her pale cheeks when he touched upon the deaths of their brothers and many dear friends. He reached across and, with his strong fingers gentle in the moment, wiped the tears away.

It was almost too painful to go on, but go on he must, for he needed her forgiveness. He choked upon his words, unable to describe his shame that his actions wrought such infamy upon their kinfolk; bodies and spirits now crushed beneath the heel of their enemy. To then betroth Mathilda to the son of the man who had brought about this devastation – he could only imagine her hurt and confusion. Mathilda nodded, for the pain was still something with which she was trying to come to terms. He might be a king, but he *was* her big brother and these wounds lay deep.

For a time, they watched the flames as each block of peat smouldered and caught, but it was clear from Mathilda's expression she had moved through her anger and confusion. Marriage to Hugh Ross was now something she relished –

given her betrothed was a fine man in all respects, except of course his family name. Once more, Robert cursed the war which had driven so many families apart. He thanked his sister for her compassion and understanding. It was more than he could hope for, he said. Mathilda disagreed vehemently on this point. He would make a great king and deserved nothing less than his family's full support.

The joining of the Ross and Bruce families heralded a time of profound healing. All in Scotland needed to see the Bruce was genuine in his desire to bring the Scots together. Old scores were to be set aside so they could move forward as one nation.

The following morn, Mathilda and Hugh exchanged their marriage vows before Bishop David. At the family chapel at Fearn, some miles to the north of Delny Castle, a cold wind blew gusty and strong off the Firth and the bride was well-pleased with her fur-lined cloak. At the conclusion of the ceremony, the vibrant young couple turned to face the expectant crowd. Hugh grasped Mathilda's chilled hand in his. Happily, they raised their arms to salute family and friends. The retinues of Earl William and Robert Bruce, King of Scots, cheered and applauded. Many understood and appreciated the deep symbolism behind this action.

CHAPTER THREE

Scotland

March 1309

It was an inclement day as only the east coast of Scotland could devise, unsure of its future from hour to hour. *Much like my own kingship,* Robert Bruce mused to himself. He had never quite lost the feelings of anxiety which had been his constant, unwanted companion for so many years.

The motley collection of wattle and daub buildings that made up the town of St Andrews was situated on the low North Sea coast and thus was influenced by all its capricious moods. The grey, choppy waves and heavy drift of cloud did nothing to dispel Robert's mixed emotions for, today, the first parliament of the Bruce government was being held at the great cathedral. An uneasy mix of fear and elation churned in his gut as he glanced back from the low cliff to take in the melee that surrounded the imposing church. It was by far the biggest structure in this sacred place, but it was not yet complete.

Flags and coloured banners displayed the emblems of the Earls of Ross, Caithness and Sutherland as well as many of the Scottish nobility. For the most part, they represented the north and western parts of Scotland. The south was still making up its mind as it were, for there the presence of the English was strong, ensconced in their great fortifications. Many of these fortresses were impregnable to all but the largest siege engines. Robert considered the task ahead of him, knowing full well it would take years to oust the English host from Scottish soil.

His blood burned to achieve his goal, but there were so many obstacles.

Looking out to sea, the king paused, inhaling the briny freshness to brace himself before facing such an influential gathering. He had used tenacity and force to strengthen his crown. Now, he needed wisdom to bring the assembly to his cause: a unified, independent Scotland free of the burdensome Sassenach yoke. Two men came to stand by his side. Bruce welcomed the Earl of Ross and his heir, Hugh, congratulating the latter on hearing of Mathilda's pregnancy. She was well, and Dingwall Castle would make a fine home for the young family. Once his most reviled enemy, now he counted the earl as a friend and the kinship ties were strong with his sister married to the young heir. He took heart from this encounter.

Striding over to the cathedral, the men passed groups of tethered horses, food carts, and stacked weaponry and armour. Fires burned here and there. Aromatic wood and peat smoke added to the odours of sea wrack, horse dung and human effluent. Such a large gathering always ended up smelling like some foul midden. As he passed, the men of Argyll scowled. Some even hissed quietly, hooded eyes filled with menace and the venomous dislike of the powerless for the powerful. For men such as Alexander, Lord of Lorne, the Bruce was still the enemy. Following the defeat of his forces last year at the Pass of Brander, he was here under sufferance.

As Robert entered the cavernous abbey transept, he was met by the pervasive odour of incense. Passing down the central isle, he saw turned towards him, the open, expressive faces of his dear friends, all as family to him now. In the crowd, he caught the broad, ruddy face of young Earl Magnus and smiled, acknowledging his presence with a wave. Beside him sat his mentor, Master Weland, who had relinquished his formal role as guardian. Here was a man to whom he was indebted, one of many if truth be known. A warm smile touched the king's eyes as he inclined his head, greeting his old friend. Present also were the bishops and significant clerics of the land. They were an essential part of this parliament, for most were well-versed in law and administration. Their support was imperative given his enemy, John Comyn, had been killed on the sacred altar of the Kirk in Dumfries. He would not back away from this. *What's done is done,* he thought to himself, *and nothing, neither my shame nor deep regret, can change it.*

He could sense the discordant tones within the crowd. Some jostled for the best seats. Others held to the back, old enmities surfacing here and there in a low, angry snarl. The king headed to the front and turned to face the throng. He exhaled his pent-up tension and consciously relaxed the muscles in his chin and jaw. In a move of studied bravado, he unclenched his fists, thrust out his chest and placed his hands upon his hips as he surveyed the gathering, front to back. A cursory glance suggested his supporters outnumbered the detractors.

"Welcome, all of you! I stand before you as your king, crowned now for some four years, but a humble man all the same. I was once advised to live cautiously. Had I done so, I may have missed opportunities and failed by default. I cannot step away from my actions for they have defined me and my kingdom.

"It has been an extraordinary experience to fight against implacable odds and succeed by stratagem rather than strength, for you all know Scotland is but a flea in the ear of the English kings, an annoying irritant which needed to be crushed. We stand today proud of our achievement. I thank my friends and supporters who stood by me in the darkest of hours, for these men I value above all the wealth of the Orient. Your strong will, courage and discipline saved me when my body and spirit failed me." Before him, a large group of men with worn features and battle-hardened bodies nodded their assent. One or two smiled in appreciation as Robert caught their eye.

"Some of you may think this is about my private ambition and the desire for power and wealth. It may have been at one time, but is no longer so. I have been tested by great adversity and shamed by the great heroes who have died, tragically, for our country, my brothers included. I now stand shoulder to shoulder with their spirits who live on in us, in truth and honesty.

"My only desire is that this country of ours becomes one. As we seek to rebuild our shattered lands, we must stand together, steadfast against our common foes. Scotland has never lost its greatness, but it has been weakened by war and the division of our people – family fighting family." Robert paused and drew a deep breath, surveying the crowd of faces, fascinated by the theatre of history taking place before them. He raised his arms to encompass the gathering. His deep voice rose to an impassioned roar. "Join with me! Let us put the past behind us and travel the path to peace and abundance *together*. Let us unite this kingdom!"

A tumult of roars and cheers rose to the immense heights of the vaulted oak ceiling. Despite this emotional oratory, not all were convinced. The past hurts were embedded within the fissures of the nation's psyche and could not be healed by words alone. Scotland's king did not expect forgiveness. However, he would grasp with both hands the wary, tentative acceptance of changing times and an end, for now, to the hostilities.

The time had come for the parliament to get down to the task of running the country, so long in disarray. Two items of business required urgent attention by the community of the realm. Firstly, the resumption of communications with the

French king, who had been seeking a truce between England and Scotland on behalf of the Scots, was raised.

Master Weland rose before the assembly. In his role as royal councillor in Norway, he was known to have had many formal dealings with King Philippe. Beneath his bushy silver brows, his blue eyes twinkled. He added his own unique perspective. "One must be able to see round corners when dealing with the French king." Some laughed, but many of the prelates nodded. Naturally, he said, this assistance had strings attached as Philippe, alleging his great affection for the Scots' king, wished the Scottish people to support him in a crusade. Vigorous discussion erupted. Over many years, much had hung in the balance, but all agreed France's support for Scotland lacked real substance. "France always looks to its own and so must Scotland," the old man added firmly. The parliament's response to the French request remained wary and reticent. When Scotland was free, her liberty preserved, then and only then, would consideration be given to such a venture. Certainly not before!

Secondly, there was the need to establish the formal mandate of King Robert through the deep and abiding support of the Scottish church and the great barons of Scotland. To achieve unity, more work needed to be done, but the considerable attendance at this parliament was a significant and promising start.

For the community of the realm as represented here in this assembly, it was a transformative and revelatory experience: to once more administer their own country without the interference of others. At last, the long, bitter struggle had brought independence within reach. For many in the gathering, freedom was experienced through almost every human sense. They glimpsed its form and perceived how it might shape their land and people. As a country thirsting for its own systems and beliefs, they tasted its coolness upon parched lips. Spirits made heavy by grief and war were touched by its lightness. They heard from the king it was their right as an ancient nation. As a people deprived of so much, their hearts rose: joyful at last, resolute in their desire to meet the challenges ahead.

Norway

Bergen

April 1309

Dearest Mathilda,

I pray this missive finds you well and content within your marriage, and that you found favour with the wedding gifts. Have they proven useful? Perhaps you might write and tell me about your new life. I must admit to being nonplussed, angered even, by Robert's betrothal choice. It cannot have been easy for you, my dear. Though the years have passed, you are never far from my mind. Murchadh remains my eyes and ears across the seas, so I have kept abreast of events at home and on Orkney. The kindness of Earl Magnus, and the generosity of the Laird of Halcro in keeping you out of harm's way, warms my heart. I am forever in their debt. Master Weland is another who deserves my heartfelt gratitude. Now the earl has come of age, the king expects his councillor to return soon and resume his duties. I look forward to hearing all the recent developments in Scotland.

Perhaps you might like to hear my news? Your niece, Inga, and her cousin, Ingeborg, daughter of King Haakon and Queen Euphemia, are now betrothed to the royal dukes of Sweden. The girls need to grow and develop, especially Ingeborg who is quite young still. My Inga believes she is old enough to make her own decisions. She is often restive and argues with me, especially when I ask her to do something that she finds irksome. She thinks me in my dotage and the affairs of life are beyond my ken. When she has to answer to her husband and manage her own domain and family, her views may soften, reshaped by harsh reality.

A few months past, we were invited to Oslo for the Yuletide celebrations where I met Valdemar and his brother, Eric. Warriors both, the men are tall and fair-haired and handsome, as are many north men. Always, they seem to be caught up in some drama with their brother, King Birger, from whom they are trying to wrest the throne. At one stage, they captured and imprisoned him. Next he escaped and, now, they seek sanctuary with the court of Norway. Chaos seems to follow them.

In his wisdom, King Haakon seeks to bind these wild adventurers more closely to Norway through kinship. I would have wished for someone with greater insight for my Inga, but she finds Valdemar amusing and light-hearted in his cups. His nature is blunt and forthright whilst his brother, Eric, the strategist of the two, is the more subtle. Being older, the latter was betrothed to Princess Ingeborg who has the higher status.

To be more responsive to the divisions between Sweden and Denmark, King Haakon built the great fortress of Akershus in Oslo and moved the royal court there. Currently, Denmark is supporting King Birger. At times the alliances have shifted, much like a bear in a balancing act. It is a wonder Norway's king can keep up.

Dearest, I miss our sisters, Kirsty and Mary, and all our kin who have suffered so cruelly, more than I can say. I cannot bear to think upon it. Pray God holds them in the palm of his hand.

Isa

England

Priory of Sixhills

May 1309

Kirsty stretched, sinuous as a cat, upon her cot. Her thick blankets slipped down and landed upon the stone flags. On a trestle, a jug of ale and a half loaf of bread remained from the previous night's meal. A knock sounded at her cell door. A whispered voice bid her good morn. Kirsty rose, a smile upon her face. Aethelrida had some task for her.

Through the grill, a thin scroll was pushed which Kirsty was to translate. Only a few of the nuns had been taught the art of reading or writing in Latin. Strangely, Aethelrida was not one of them. Upon the prisoner's trestle lay the accoutrements of writing: a few sheets of vellum, a feathered quill, a horn scraper and container of ink. At a quick glance, it seemed this treatise spoke of skin complaints and the foods which would aid the skin's healing. Aethelrida heard the approach of the novices on their way to nones and bid Kirsty farewell. She must hurry. It did not pay to be late for the early morning ritual of prayer. Once more, Kirsty thanked the good lord for this angel who had saved her life and made her life in the nunnery bearable. Now, she had warm bedding, wholesome food in her belly and tasks to fill her day.

It had been a long time since neglect and harsh treatment saw Kirsty's skeletal body riddled with infection. Aethelrida's bitter complaints to the prioress saw some, though not all, of the restrictions set by the previous king reduced. The prisoner's sentence of solitary confinement was to remain in place until alternative orders came. Aethelrida made it her business to reduce the harshness of Kirsty's punishment. This led to a running battle with two brutal nuns: diminutive, wrinkled Mertha and lanky, hatchet-faced Eriface. From observation it seemed, to Aethelrida, the pair operated as one, for neither was particularly bright on their own. When she first became aware that Kirsty was literate in French and Latin and could manage her letters, she suggested to the prioress the prisoner be given the difficult job of translating the medical treatises. The last nun who had this capacity died of a stomach complaint not long back. Since then, the prioress had lost her sight for reading – words blurred into a muddle at her every attempt, causing her head to ache – and she was quite agreeable. It was most timely. The aged woman was keen to conceal her poor eyesight. Thoughts of being replaced by a younger, more able nun were often in her mind. Upon consideration – as long as no conversation occurred – she supposed this also would meet the essence of the king's punishment. There was nothing to say the prisoner could not earn her keep in the nunnery. And was it not true they were all expected to contribute?

Mertha was rancorous at what she perceived to be special treatment offered to the prisoner and made every effort to hinder Kirsty's work, by slopping food as it was delivered onto her trestle. Sometimes, she shoved her victim at the same time, spilling ink across the parchments. Whenever Mertha and Eriface arrived together, Kirsty knew the outcome would follow a more vindictive pattern. Somehow, Aethelrida developed a sixth sense and managed to outwit them. It became a game of fox and hare. A message would be proffered by a smiling, guileless Mertha, for the infirmary nun to attend the prioress urgently. Aethelrida would feign interest. Shortly thereafter, she would catch the women in the act of some hideous brutality: either forcing Kirsty face down into her latrine pail or whipping her senseless for some alleged misdemeanour.

The prisoner was caught between the two extremes: one

kindly and the other, brutal, but strangely, she found she could cope better with her incarceration. Now, it felt less hopeless with Aethrida's endless compassion as well as the mental stimulation of the tasks that came her way. When Kirsty's translation showed that the consumption of fruit – in its dried form of course – and vegetables as well as increased cleanliness would stop the carbuncles, which so plagued the nuns, the prioress softened. It was obvious Kirsty's skills could be of great benefit to the community. She permitted the prisoner to be moved to a cell nearer to the infirmary for convenience. Most importantly for Kirsty, it was within hearing distance of Aethelrida's chamber. Only then did some of the more obvious harassment come to an end. Instead, subtle punishments emerged. Tight balls of grey, matted hair, thick-ridged toenail clippings or the occasional rat's tail, sliced of course, appeared in her bowl of food at night. Kirsty had taken to examining each spoonful before allowing it to touch her lips. This, too, backfired upon the offenders. Late one eve, Kirsty gagged at the sight of small pellets of dung floating in her thin stew. Aethelrida happened to be passing the chamber. Quickly, she came to her aid, and the offending food was shown indignantly to the prioress. The malicious nuns were given a choice: either eat the food themselves or clean the latrines on their hands and knees as if they were junior novices.

In the corridor, Aethelrida caught the sounds of a high-pitched, nasal whine. She peeked around the corner of the lavarium. Tiny, she may have been, but Mertha held sway over the hapless Eriface who lay hunched upon the floor. "Ye great lump, I warned ye to mash the pellets!" Mertha's weapon of choice was a foul cloth. In her fury, she slapped it against her companion's bowed head. Wet shanks of hair flapped across pallid skin, adding to the woman's misery. Her snivelling could be heard down the corridor. Several novices shuffled towards Aethelrida and she departed hurriedly to the infirmary. In a low voice, she delivered a compelling account of the events to Kirsty and was rewarded with a rare dimpled smile. Neither could hide their gleeful satisfaction. They must be on their guard even more for some heinous act would surely follow this public humiliation. Indeed, one could almost hear the duo's thick minds calculating their revenge.

It was a strange time for the Scotswoman. All these events were but light relief from a greater drama. At a deeper level, she felt unhinged from her own reality as if she had never lived her previous life, nor loved those whom she knew she had lost. Perhaps, in time, the memories of home and family might even fade altogether. In the night especially, numbness entered her being; grey melancholy followed, seeping into the vacuum where feeling had once lived so warmly. She feared this place – the stone of its edifice – would feed upon her body and soul, till she perished old and wizened like Mertha. Death would claim her and she would be buried out in the icy ground to lie forever in English soil. For a noble daughter of Scotland, this was the final, pitiless twist in King Edward's cruel punishment.

It was a natural progression now that the prisoner began to ask questions of her confidante, to seek a tentative link with the outside world. Aethelrida looked at her blankly. *Of course,* she thought to herself, *Kirsty would have no knowledge of the priory's history.*

Many years ago, an English monk, Gilbert of Sempringham, initiated priories which were loosely based upon the Cistercian model. It was quite an unusual arrangement, the nun granted, for the Gilbertine priories housed monks and nuns in their own separate, cloistered chapter houses with a mix of lay persons, both male and female, to carry out the basic tasks such as farm work and laundering. Even the church itself was divided down the centre by a wall and the monks passed the sacraments through a small window to the nuns on the other side.

Apart from the receipt of the treatises from Brother Robert, who had a special teaching role, this was a closed nunnery. Surely, the Scotswoman realised this? Dolefully, Kirsty shook her head. Aethelrida had no idea what was happening in the outside world and, in all honesty, she did not care. For the prisoner, white-knuckled desperation set in. All that existed lay within these thick stone walls. She would be entombed here forever, lost to her family and her world. Once more, Kirsty's night terrors raised their spectral heads.

Scotland

Dingwall Castle

June 1309

Dearest Isa,

Your news was well-received. It would give me much pleasure if we might continue to correspond. Murchadh found us. At Delny Castle, he was redirected – quite tersely it seems – by the lady of the house. Nor was sustenance offered to one who had made first landfall after a long journey. Hugh raged at this breach. His mother continues to find ill-favour with my family, but I cautioned him on speaking to her thus. I seek to build bridges, not have them burnt before my eyes by his temper, albeit in my support. Indeed, Robert's request we live in Dingwall Castle is evidence of his great foresight. Had I to live under the demanding gaze of the Countess of Ross, life would be miserable indeed.

Nothing I do is right, though it matters nought for it is rare we meet. Recently, I gave birth. Hugh was so relieved the babe and I survived the ordeal, his disappointment at the lack of an heir soon passed. Now, he is besotted. I am sure you of all people will understand this. However, an even greater misdemeanour has been committed, for the child bears not the name of Euphemia. This earned Hugh a sound reprimand. He would not allow me to read the letter, but threw it in the hearth. By the look on his face, the message already had sufficient fuel to fire the page.

It shames me to say that I have become quite fond of Hugh's father. He seeks respite here from his lady wife. I feel sure it must have been at her insistence he captured our family. He fears her wrath far more than any English king. It is said she was rewarded many times over for her support. Some infer she was the king's paramour, though Hugh doubts it, for she saw so little of him in person. Nevertheless, the earl adores Marjorie and comes often to bounce her upon his knee and sing silly ditties. How could a mother not warm to such a man?

Whenever possible, our wayward brother, Edward, visits Dingwall to meet with Hugh's sister. This is another cause for the countess's dislike of our family. I am sure she wishes for a more suitable husband for Isabella and in that, I cannot blame her. He comes embroiled in scandal having repudiated Isobel of Strathbogie. Now, *her* brother, another supporter of the English, seeks revenge for his sister's humiliation and distress. The countess does not seem to mind Robert. He can be charming – when he puts his mind to it – and has always been attractive to women, but Edward she sees as someone given to impulsive behaviour and one not to be trusted. He desires above all else to be Isabella's lawful husband, but some problem with consanguinity has come to light, which must be addressed with the Pope. Though mightily frustrated by these events, our brother is set upon this path. Isabella dotes upon his every word, which is difficult to take as you might imagine.

Now to more important things! Floraidh came to help me

with my delivery, courtesy of Murchadh. Her knowledge and patience assisted me through my travail. She brought news as well. I had hoped she might remain here to tend our household, but tomorrow the captain sails north while the weather holds. I am assured my midwife will return when needed.

Hugh and I have discussed bringing the family here. Though the north of Scotland is mostly in Robert's hands, there are still serious pockets of disaffection here and there. With Argyll to the southwest of us teetering and a strong English presence in many of the castles, it is not safe as yet. Without siege engines, Rob's men must try to win by stratagem which is no small task. Banff, Perth and Dundee castles are held by our enemies and are able to have supplies replenished by sea. In the south, there are many fortifications in hostile hands: Stirling, Edinburgh as well as Berwick and Roxburgh – where Isobel and Mary are believed to be held – just to name a few. Galloway, Ayr and Carrick are riddled with our enemies. So it is not yet safe.

By all accounts, our family continues to be as happy as I was on Orkney; such a peaceful, comforting place, though the weather is frequently foul. The freedom of the big skies, the wind-driven clouds, the sea visible at every turn and the birdsong could bring joy to the weariest heart. I miss our family, but for the moment I am caught up with my husband and child and managing the castle here. Hugh is a dear man whom I adore, though I must admit it was not always so. I was fearfully angry, anguished to be more precise, with Robert's choice, but our brother is wise beyond his years and a strong judge of character. He and Sir William have become friends as well and, on occasions, he has stayed at the earl's hunting lodge.

Many thanks for the gifts sent earlier this year. The great white fur we have upon our bed. It keeps us warm when the north wind howls across the marshes. The knives with fish teeth handles we use for special occasions. Hugh thanks you for the gift of the falcons. Our brothers will enjoy hunting with them when they visit. You will understand I have not taken to hunting or hawking, as it was not the usual practice in our community on Orkney; the farms provided all our provisions.

My wedding was memorable, for our brothers attended. I was relieved to be able to make my peace with Robert beforehand. In doing so, he shared with me his beliefs which form the cornerstone of his kingship. Most challenging of all is the concept that revenge will never end a war. At times I would wish it otherwise, for our family has been sore hurt, but Rob says Scotland cannot continue at war, divided as we are. We have neither the strength nor resources, which is why he chose to make his own peace with the earl and entwine our families through kinship.

Our brother believes the mark of a great king lies in his capacity to show mercy. Diplomacy will always win out over the sword – fine words indeed, but it goes without saying our opponents need to lay down their weapons. Rob is no fool and his decisions are based on logic and good reason. He knows the unhappiness his decisions cause, but neither will he veer from his path. There was sorrow when he spoke thus and I accepted his admission. We speak of men growing into their manhood: our brother has grown into his kinghood. All must be done for the community of the realm. I have never seen him so impassioned. Of course, it might help if he kept his temper under control; Edward seems to get a tongue lashing on a regular basis for one thing or another.

There is much to tell about my life here. Hugh is away so often in Rob's service that I must see to the needs of our large estate. Having spent much of my life in a small community, I am ill-equipped to do so and must rely heavily upon our household. No doubt I will learn in time to be more of a chatelaine, especially if I am to be the future Countess of Ross. Kirsty always made it look so easy. Forgive me for mentioning her name. My heart is heavy, knowing she is in such peril. Pray, she and Mary, and all our dear kin, are still alive.

My good sisters visit from time to time. They are light-hearted and always bring a welcome smile to my face. Feeding our guests, whether they be fifty or five hundred, is my biggest challenge though we have several cooks – sadly none like Mhairi or Aonghas. For the most part, I am well content. It would be far worse if my lord husband were old and feeble – though perhaps I could outrun him! As it is, I am fortunate indeed for I have no desire to run from Hugh. We send our good wishes to you all.

Mathilda

Scotland

Roxburgh Castle

July 1309

Mary Bruce lay as dead upon the floor of her cage. Many hours passed and the guard moved over to take a better look. Through the bars of the cage, he prodded the prone form with his spear. A rook cawed sharply on the wall of the castle. The levy cursed it soundly for the fright it gave. He turned on his heel and hurried along the landing to the curved stairwell and disappeared. The echoes of clanking armour followed his departure. The rook, a black sentinel, stood silent watch. Clouds gathered and dispersed in the strong gusts of wind. Scraps of ragged, stained clothing lifted in the wind to show the bluish bone of a leg, smeared here and there with a streak of bloody faeces. A thin, reedy pulse beat faintly in the neck of the prisoner. A shiver passed for a breath.

The captain of Roxburgh's garrison appeared, puffing and heaving from having run up several flights and along the twists and turns of the corridors. The wind took his breath away. Heights were definitely something he did not favour. If truth be known, he preferred to be no higher than upon his horse's back.

"Open the door," he commanded, gasping once more, this time from the stench. *It is inhuman,* he decided. *The wench would be better off dead.* However, his position depended on keeping her alive. Otherwise, he might be moved north where the heathen Scots roved in vicious, murdering bands.

"Cretin! You should have come to me sooner rather than sleeping on duty! Remove the prisoner and take her below!" He shouted as if the man was not only incompetent, but deaf as well. The guard picked up the comatose form. His stomach turned and he cursed loudly; brown, watery shit dribbled down into his leggings. Wherever he touched the hideous creature, lice skidded and leapt onto his skin. Blood welled beneath his hands as her thin covering of skin ripped and bled beneath his touch. He held his breath and stumbled towards the doorway. It was if he grasped the air. There was no substance to her. The rook watched, then brazenly flew in through the open door of the cage and began to pick at the sparse debris upon the floor, before calling to its companions.

Days later, Mary woke to find herself in a stone-walled room. The infirmary was overly warm. Her breath caught, not used was she to the thick, earthy aroma of peat. One of the guards was attempting to force a broth between her lips. She ate hungrily, slurping from the rough-carved spoon, drooling onto the coverlet as she did so. Exhausted by the effort, she fell back. Again, she slept dreamlessly.

Mary's ragged gown had been replaced by a tunic of sorts.

It was none too clean and much too large, but a thousand times better than her ragged shift. The coarse blanket scratched her skin in places. No longer did she bleed.

"Your name?" Mary's voice croaked with the effort.

"Dafydd," he whispered with a strange inflection at the end. The youth looked away furtively to see if any had heard the exchange. "You should be dead, my lady, given what they've put you through…"

"You know who I am?" He nodded. "Then tell me, for I scarce know myself," came the hoarse reply.

Much later, Mary stared in wonderment as the Welshman washed her face and hands. Human touch was like a strange, unearthly miracle to her. She watched, dry-eyed, as the cracked and bitten nails on his thick, calloused fingers went into the bowl of grey water and came out with a rough, homespun cloth. The cold, greasy fluid dripped and ran down her neck. It was beyond bliss. Dafydd began to tell his story. Under duress, he had been rounded up back in Wales whilst out hunting and taken away from his land and family. He was only thirteen. No one knew where he was. Mary nodded, knowing only too well what that was like. He was an archer in the English king's army until wounded. A scar ran down his face across his right eye. Only then did she realise, when he looked at her, his head tilted to one side. His left eye gazed firmly in a forthright, honest manner upon her. "They put me to work in the infirmary instead," he said, "and, now, I heal people rather than kill them." A shy smile spread across his ravaged face.

It was mealtime. Dafydd brought a knife with him to cut up the chunks of bread and thickly sliced venison. Mary's teeth were weak and her gums sore. As one did for a babe, he chewed the tough meat and placed the moistened pieces in her mouth. It bothered her not, for without his help she knew death would have claimed her for its own. Sometimes, his pockets held a treasure: a handful of raisins stolen from under the cook's nose. With his good care, she was visibly improving.

"You know they will make you go back," he said one day. Mary nodded and rolled over to face the wall. Her back heaved with silent sobs. He pulled her back to face him, ignoring the look of despair and horror. "I have a plan," he whispered. The bright blue bead of his good eye was vivid with hope and anticipation. Promptly, he raised the knife to his upper arm, slicing through a small blue vein. In a moment or two, blood dripped down and he smeared great gobs of it upon her mouth, chin and neck. Pulling his tunic down over the cut, he stood up and cried out in alarm.

"Look! The wench bleeds!" Mary coughed convincingly, spraying blood across Dafydd's surcoat. Soldiers, brave in the face of a sword, ran for the door. All recognised the evil sickness. Later, it was agreed by the captain – from a distance – Dafydd, alone, should tend the prisoner, for all had seen her blood sprayed over his face and hands. He was charged to keep her alive for as long as possible. Pray they would live through this. The captain knew such a sickness could travel faster than a soldier on his way to a whorehouse! Dafydd was left on his own to man the infirmary. Food was left outside the door, as were ale and blankets. He only had to shout for something to appear. For once, the Welshman was in charge of his own domain. Over time, the archer answered her tentative questions. In total wonderment, Mary heard her brother, Robert, had come back, as if from the dead, and now was in control of much of northern Scotland. It gave her hope he would come for her.

When Dafydd told Mary of the deaths of her younger brothers – some here in the guard had been at Carlisle Castle – her grief was painful to watch. Throughout her anguished mourning, the young man's undemanding presence proved a great solace. Mary grew well under her guard's care, but would lay back gasping and moaning should anyone come near the door. How long this subterfuge might work, they did not know. Each experienced a precious, miraculous freedom so full of wonder and joy neither wished it to end, but end it did. In time, they were caught out.

Sobbing, Mary pleaded with the captain. At the point of a spear, the prisoner was bundled back into her cage. Screaming, she fell upon the floor and, in her torment, began to retch. The captain averted his eyes, uncomfortable with such a spectacle. Bleakly, Dafydd watched on. His wretched face was etched with pain and sorrow. Calloused hands, gentle in the care of his patient, were clenched white now in futile anger. Not for the first time, he wished he was back in the gentle green vales near his farm, away from this barbaric land. Shortly thereafter, he was sent north with a contingent of soldiers on their way to Stirling Castle and he knew he would never see his homeland again.

Orkney

October 1309

It was harvest time – when most Orcadians were caught up with age-old traditions. Some of these involved the gathering of grain for the harvest bannock. Standing by a low stone wall, Margaret Bruce watched in anticipation. A race occurred to the finish and a scythe was thrown at the young man making the final unfortunate cut. Now the last sheaf had been made homeless, punishment must be meted out. Hodlvis knew the sharp implement would fly in his direction. Somehow, he dodged injury. Carrying the special sheaf into his family's barn before the many observers, he collected the grain, which would be ground in a large quern stone and made into the harvest bannock to be eaten. In some areas, the sheaf was rubbed on the bare buttocks of the unlucky offender. Fortunately for Hodlvis, this part of the ritual was uncommon at Skaill.

The ceremony was completed just in time. Thunder rumbled in the distance. Thick, charcoal-grey clouds were building on the horizon. Jagged lightening spikes sparked an ominous light show within their shadowy, rolling mass. It was some way off yet, but Margaret scanned the dark, oily sea. She wondered how the local lads, the Hammerclett brothers included, fared. Late yesterday, they had taken a vessel out. The herring were running.

Sighting nought but white-crested waves, Margaret turned away and continued her solitary walk up along the shoreline. *It had been a confusing year,* she reflected, chewing her bottom lip. Mathilda's betrothal to Hugh Ross had seen her dispatched to far-off Scotland and the small family group could do little but mourn their loss. To all who would listen, Margaret espoused she would never accept the marriage. Since then, time had dulled her high emotions. Then some months back, Murchadh arrived with an urgent request for Floraidh to accompany him to Ross: Mathilda needed the midwife's sure hand at her birthing. This was understandable, but, without the reassuring presence of their wise woman, the remaining members of their group in Skaill felt adrift. Even the local farming families missed her healing hands as injuries happened so often by accident or neglect.

Margaret tried to fill the void though she lacked the healer's breadth of knowledge and experience. She did her best to keep up the supplies of potions based upon sea wrack and other herbs and even assisted at Marthoc's delivery of a bonny, fair-haired girlchild. She pondered upon it now for it had been quite an odd experience. Around the time of the birth, the local women began acting in a peculiar way.

When prodded, Flota, the babe's grandmother, gave this explanation. During birthing, a woman was at her most vulnerable. Fear pierced the heart of the community, for the trows – those sinister mound dwellers who brought only harm by their presence – desired above all else to mate with a mortal woman. Should the woman die in childbirth, it meant she had been taken to the nether regions. There, she would give the male trow the healthy child he desired and later help the trow women as any midwife would. A likeness might be left behind. Such was the community's terrible fear of death they held to these unusual beliefs. To counter the menace, the family stuck a blade firmly above the door of the home, for all knew the trows to be afraid of metal.

To Margaret, the Hammercletts need have no such fear. Marthoc made enough noise to scare away the most powerful of the fairy folk. Like any new mother, she was given the best food and ale in the house and basked in the family's care, but the community of women were reluctant to leave mother and child unprotected and did as they always had done. For several nights after the birth, neighbours took it in turns to stand watch and rock the cradle. No babe could be stolen, nor changeling enter a home thus protected. Once mother and babe flourished, a number of celebrations took place when visitors came to congratulate the family. In time, a private feast was held by Marthoc's immediate family to mark her return to household duties.

Mathilda had also birthed a little girl, another dark-haired Marjorie. In light of so many dangers, Margaret wondered how they fared. Poignant thoughts arose for Robert's Marjorie. Now, she was lost to them. None knew where.

As she peered out to sea once more, a frown took up residence between Margaret's fine hazel eyes. Visible upon the far horizon, the clouds continued to build. It was an oppressive day. Occasional heavy drops of rain fell upon the young woman's upturned face as she searched the heavens. On her journey back to the house, she noticed the birds were preternaturally quiet. Pausing in her deliberations, she lifted her long dark hair, rolled within its fine snood, away from the clammy dampness of her neck. So many things had changed for her here. Indeed, she helped with the harvest along with all the others. As the seasons followed each other, all were preoccupied with the basics of survival, which included feeding and clothing the families that lived around Skaill Bay. The old traditions provided protection. Now, they needed to be carried out with passion and greater attendance to detail, for the old ones warned the land was not as productive as it once had been. It was becoming colder and the growing season shorter, they said. Fear of starvation was a great motivator. It brought the community together.

The evening sky darkened. A storm boomed overhead. At Skaill House, Seonaid comforted the younger children, whilst Ellen quietly practised her letters on a slate at the kitchen table. Soon, it was time for bed. All toys and writing equipment were put away; the fire, stoked up. The adults sat listening to the great drama as it played out overhead. Flashes of lightening ripped through the darkened room. All shivered in apprehension, thinking of the vessel which had not yet returned home. In time, the women went to their beds and the storm abated.

Next morning, the sun rose incandescent in the sky. Leaves glinted silver-bright, like new minted coins. Thatch, weighed down with overnight rain, dripped incessantly. A crowd gathered by the shore. Mothers held shawls tight around their faces, eyes only for the empty horizon. Marthoc comforted her crying bairn. The day wore on and still they waited, to be joined later by the older menfolk. Anxious lines were etched on faces, worn now with fatigue. Someone noted a signal fire upon the headland. A boat had been sighted. It grew larger. Hearts rose and then, with cries of dismay, dipped; it was not a vessel from this bay. The galley drew in closer. A clear-sighted one screamed and fell to the ground. There on board were the missing men, grey-faced with exhaustion. Their journey had not gone well, but they were alive.

To their families, nought else mattered. A calf was slaughtered and a feast took place that night to celebrate the men's rescue from their capsized boat. It should have been a joyous occasion, but there was confusion aplenty. Several of the local women had heard a clicking sound some nights earlier. Another saw a raven on the roof of a hall. One heard the sound of a cock crowing at midnight. A bird was witnessed striking a windowpane and falling stone-dead. All of these events were the known precursors of death. Perhaps the men given back from the sea were just doppelgangers – beings who had returned in place of the men. Though none spoke of it, a strange uneasiness settled upon the community.

The following evening, old Grutgar fell from the roof of his barn, whilst attempting its repair following the storm, and broke his neck. In unison, the wise women of the area breathed a sigh of relief. This they could understand. All gathered to help the family in the great human struggle: the cycle of life and death.

Scotland

Dingwall Castle

December 1309

Dearest Isa,

I pray all is well with you. Robert and his men have joined us for the Yuletide celebrations. In preparation for the great feasts, the castle is buzzing with energy and action. Thankfully,

Hugh is back. I have sore missed him and he, our dear child. It will take some time before she settles with him, but I urge him to be patient.

Down below the castle mound, the village is alive with revellers and music. Fire twirlers light the darkness with swirling, golden flames. Acrobats and jugglers make their way about, as well. It has all the atmosphere of a fair. Boars roast on spits, filling the air with tantalising aromas. There are games for the children and wrestling for the men. The rain has held off; it is cold and thick white clouds settle over us. A change is on the way.

Our brother holds little trust that the Macdougalls will keep within his peace. Thus, he has been busy showing the royal presence in the Ross galleys, all the way from Loch Broom down to Argyll and Dunstaffnage Castle. This time, our men had sufficient food and warmth, and Rob returned in fair health. His men worry about him and the sickness which ails him. Hugh says the king can ill-afford such weakness; our enemies will regroup and forge ahead in the knowledge. On his way, Rob visited Christina of Gamoran who was kin by marriage to his first wife. On previous visits, it seems she welcomed him most generously, Isa, for she has born a child to him, a lad called Alexander.

Edward says the widow is beautiful and a powerful aura surrounds her presence. In a castle by the sea she lives alone, but for her clansmen. Though he is king, I dared ask our brother about his visit. Strangely, he was not loath to discuss it as first I feared, but seemed almost relieved to talk of the fair Christina. He esteems her well, too well perhaps, which is a problem in itself. After the dreadful defeat at Methven and the long months fleeing danger, despair brought him low for all that had gone so awry. When she offered herself freely to him, he was sore of body and spirit and badly needed her support, which made him wary of giving offence. A man needs no such excuse and most certainly not a king. Though Rob loves Elizabeth, he fears they will be parted forever. Perhaps this will be so. Even now, there seems no way forward. In quiet moments, I have seen raw anguish upon his face, but he brushes me aside should I make mention of it; so I let it pass. No easy choices present themselves. I cannot bear to think we will never see our loved ones again.

It seems the old king met his match in Robert. No doubt he expected him to capitulate and seek terms of surrender in order to ransom his family. Rob said as much, but knew in doing so his life would have been forfeit, not to mention the Scottish crown. Rob says the only way forward is to win this war; then we will be in a stronger position to negotiate our kinfolk's return. He holds as stubbornly to this as a drowning man clutches at a reed. To me, it all seems a long way off and these plans may never come to fruition.

Otto will take this missive tomorrow and run the gauntlet of the English blockade once more. Reports abound that King Edward is irate his embargo is being ignored. He even complained to the Count of Flanders about aid being sent to Scottish rebels. Indeed, Rob is most appreciative of the clothing, armour, weapons and food that arrives from Bergen and will send more of our fine Scottish wool that is so desirable.

The English king issued a military summons for all to gather next year to wage war on us once again. He sent his leaders to Berwick and Carlisle, but the men concluded a truce with Robert until January of next year. They lack the heart for a fight, preferring instead to squabble with Edward over his infamous paramour, Piers Gaveston. What must his French queen think about it all? At least it seems the barons are not keen to fight us, knowing full well there is no food for the horses or their men. They are not as foolhardy as their king.

Scotland and all her people are subject to another period

of excommunication for 'persevering in iniquity' and supporting our crowned king! At first, it was worrisome, but now we have accepted our continued disfavour. One would think the Pope would not deign to concern himself with our small country; he continues to bicker with Rome and the French king. For some here, it is a dire punishment, but our brother has the support of many prelates within the Scottish church.

Snow is falling. The hours seem to slide and disappear and it is time to dress for the banquet. There are so many guests to feed and entertain, I must admit to feeling on edge. Having lived such a quiet life in Orkney, I am unused to large crowds and ceremony. Now, under pressure, my wits desert me! Two of my maids are a great help. Mirin tends my wardrobe, whilst Janet has just taken Marjorie away to her cot. I am being harried now. Rob and Edward send their love, as do we all. Blessings to you for a happy Yuletide

Mathilda

Norway

December 1309

It is said an ill-wind brings no good and so it was this autumn past. King Haakon grew more and more irate with his councillor and his failure to return from Orkney to recommence his duties. He sent messages to the earl, but was sore-hearted to hear that his royal councillor's ship had left as arranged. Master Weland and his crew never made landfall.

CHAPTER FOUR

Norway

Bergen

March 1310

Dear Mathilda,

Yester eve, Otto arrived safely, though he described a few tense moments trying to outsail an English ship. With the enemy close by at Banff, danger is everywhere on the seas. The precious cargo of wool was welcomed by the king. You will have heard by now Master Weland's vessel was taken in a gale last autumn. King Haakon was shaken by this loss; he put much store by his councillor's astute assessments. I miss my old friend's generous support and dry wit more than I can say. Our family owe him much.

At a service held for him in the Kristkirke, a surprising number of the local traders and craftsmen attended as well as many dignitaries. Not all had been his friends, but he was well respected. Henry, his brother, passed away some years ago in France so there was no family present, though Earl Magnus spoke of his old guardian – as a son, of a father – such was the closeness between them. I prayed the many candles might light Weland's way home.

To your news! I am heartened your marriage to Hugh is a happy one and that young Marjorie flourishes. Inga gives me such joy and I wish the same for you. It is many years since we have seen each other. You were but a child back then. I recall your red curls and expect you still have these. I, on the other hand, am now a mature matron and cover my greying hair quite willingly.

How are you managing in your role as chatelaine? It seems to me that women are so often alone and in charge, adeptly overseeing great estates and large households, but when the menfolk return, we must become servile again. Forgive my perverse wanderings! It is as well you have your own domain, for the countess sounds a formidable creature.

Being so far away, I am hungry for details of your life as well as that of our brothers. I imagine Rob perceived just winning the battles against the English was enough. Now he must finish the task he started – to win the hearts and minds of our people. The twists of fate are strange and bewildering; if only he had not gone to confront the Comyn.

Soon, Inga and I shall travel to Oslo. Effie has finished her final ballad and wishes to discuss it – meaning, I must listen as she postulates upon each word. Whilst her friendship means much to me, sometimes my enthusiasm wanes. All are well here and send their love.

Yours aye

Isa

England

Priory of Sixhills

April 1310

A light breeze shifted the parchment and teased the herbs drying upon the trestle in the morning room. Absorbed in her task, Kirsty worked diligently in a peace so quiet the heavy, somnolent drone of bees could be heard from outside in the herb garden. All the nuns were away to their prayers in the chapel. After four long years, the prisoner was permitted to leave her cell; only for prescribed times, mind, to attend to the manufacture of salves and lotions. The latter were described in the medical treatises that she translated – only she could determine their meaning. To speak of them was still forbidden, so it was quicker if she made up the mixtures herself. Kirsty was not unhappy with these precious periods of freedom. Any time away from her small, cold cell was relief indeed.

Once given the role of being Kirsty's main provider, Aethelrida had saved her from some of the worst privations and abuses administered by two of the most hardened nuns. Sometimes, she broke the rules around silence and whispered to her of small things: what to do about Sister Mary's ingrown toenails or the prioress's painful piles and poor digestion? Ofttimes, it was gossipy chat: who had slept late and was now in dire trouble or how old Sister Agnetha had broken wind in Mass, mellifluously and at some length, and the censure which ensued. For the young novices who giggled irreligiously into their wimples, punishment was to be administered. God had sent them here to learn humility, the prioress stated emphatically, and so they forfeited Sister Beatrice's cooking that night. All knew she was going blind and did not know her cumin from her peppers. It was scarcely a punishment. One memorable time, the old woman put a cupful of their precious salt into the bread, mistaking it for flour.

Humming an old, half-remembered Gaelic tune, the prisoner pounded and mixed, stirred for a while, then added some angelica. The mixture took on the right hue and texture. Dipping a fingertip into the foul brew, Kirsty screwed up her face and then gave a wry smile. It was perfect! Just then, the oak door swung slowly open. A monk stood in the darkened doorway. He squinted into the brighter light. "Sister Aethelrida?" he queried. Kirsty shook her head. "And ye are?" he asked.

"Christina, though some call me Kirsty, sister of the crowned King of Scots." These words were spoken far more boldly than she intended. She was unsure of this man, and what harm might befall her for speaking thus.

"Ah yes... the prisoner. I was hoping we might meet one day. Are ye permitted to speak?" Kirsty shook her head once again. She was unused to formal conversation and was in no hurry to see what this monk – the first man she had seen in years – would say. "Then I shall speak, and no rules will be broken. My name is Brother Robert. I was known by the name of Mannyng and knew your brother at Cambridge. I joined the Gilbertines many years ago. It is I who send the treatises to the prioress." At the mention of Alexander, Kirsty's face lit up. Any news of her brother was as welcome as rain upon a parched seed. The canon paused. He seemed shaken for a moment and then proceeded.

"Your brother was a fine scholar, the brightest ever to achieve so highly in his studies." A shadow fell across Kirsty's face for the monk, this acquaintance of her brother, couched his words as if Alexander was no longer. Noting her confusion, he paused, searching for the right words, but gave up for there were none. "I am sorry, my lady, but your brother was killed several years ago. On the orders of our king's father, he was executed, along with your brother, Thomas. They were part of an attack upon Galloway with a band of Irish brigands."

Kirsty slumped against the trestle and the heavy pestle which she had been using rolled slowly off, landing with a thud upon the stone flags. Its haphazard momentum continued until the leg of a stool blocked its path.

Cursing himself for his off-handed and thoughtless way of delivering such news, the monk leaned over and picked up the implement, laying it back in its place. As he did so, dust motes, drifting in a patch of sunlight, caught his eye. "Your brothers, Robert and Edward, continue to be the scourge of

England," he said as if this might in some way compensate for her loss, but then gave up, nonplussed. The room smelt of the earth, layered with moss, leaf and bracken. It reminded him of the last burial he had attended. Outside in the corridor, there were hushed, hurried voices, the flurry of rustling habits and the slap of leather sandals. As the monk turned to depart, pain and sorrow could be seen etched across his face. The words he spoke came as soft as a scattering of leaves upon a grave, "I truly am sorry. Alexander was an exceptional man. I, too, mourn his passing."

When Aethelrida returned from her duties, she found Kirsty curled into a tight, pale ball in the corner of the chamber, weeping piteously; her brothers, whom she had imagined for so long in high spirits and robust health, had been dead for years.

Scotland

Dingwall Castle

July 1310

Dearest Isa,

The skies are clear today. I can hear the harsh squawking of the black-backed gulls. They sit upon the parapets and torment the guards when they try to break their fast. One even stole a bannock straight out of Tom the archer's hands. Believe me; they are as impudent and as hungry as the urchins in the village. After this long, gruelling war, many families have lost a father or several brothers and no longer have the capacity to feed themselves. Near the castle walls, there is a lazar house, built long ago by King David. Apart from the leprous ones – kept strictly in one section – all manner of ills and injuries caused by the war are treated by the monks. As well, they see to the poor and homeless. Hugh is considering moving the hospice to the outskirts of the village, for the rabble attending there grows larger by the day. Empty bellies will strain even the best spirit. Somehow, we must find ways to feed and clothe them.

I can hear the grunts and curses of our garrison, practising manoeuvres down in the bailey. The English are poised to move into Scotland. Who knows what may transpire? Several times, truces were in place, only to be extended again. This is due to the exertions of our French friends, but also Edward's barons who are less than enthusiastic about another war. Word is the English king is now in Berwick and sends a contingent by sea to support his Perth garrison, many of whom are from Gascony.

In Hugh's solar, a war council was held. I remained in the window embrasure, intent upon my cross stitch. On a trestle, a large parchment lay open. Upon it was inscribed a rough map of Scotland marked with the castles that already had been taken in the south – Cupar, Forfar, Rutherglen, Dumbarton to name a few. England is in control of the Solway and, throughout the centre of our land, has a powerful hold with the impregnable castles: Stirling, Edinburgh, Roxburgh, Jedburgh and Berwick, as well as a range of smaller strongholds. We lack the large siege machines to batter the walls; the skilled men to operate them; enough sappers to undermine and fire the walls, and the massive supplies necessary to keep a siege army operating for months. All we have are grappling hooks and ladders which are a boon being portable, relatively light and easily assembled in the dark.

Rob says it is imperative the supply lines to the English-held castles are controlled. The fortresses on the coast are most troublesome. They continue to flourish. Banff is a good example and evidence of our enemy's maritime power. Our

Irish supply routes must be maintained to allow us to threaten the Isle of Man. This action serves as a powerful diversion, for the isle would be a strong base from which to threaten the west coast. Our brother exhausts himself searching for different paths. The surprise effect of almost impossible attacks here and there strike fear in the heart of the English. Such a strategy requires all to stay on guard. Then our men disappear; only to reappear in some other area or even to strike once, twice or thrice in the same place. These actions unman our foes.

The Welsh used similar tactics, but they were destroyed by the ring of great castles in which the English made their nests, like pestilent rodents, and were nigh impossible to shift.

Rob is adamant the most pressing task to hand is the taking of the Scottish castles held by our enemies. These must be patiently invested, starved and seized by a mix of strategy and daring. Here Rob's captains come into their own, for they seek local men with knowledge to lead our troops along unknown paths and up to the weaker points of a castle's walls.

A small group of men found their way into Linlithgow Peel using the device of a hay wain with men hidden inside. Once through the gates, the men leapt upon the guards and opened the gates for our troops to enter. You might query what happens once a castle is taken, for surely they would be useful. Rob is convinced they are a danger to our independence. These fortresses can be retaken and then the war goes on. No, he has it in his mind to win this war and he says we will have but few opportunities to do it. Therefore, the castles must be destroyed, first by fire and then dismantled, stone by stone. It is a gargantuan task, but many a town expands as a result of such effort.

On a broader front, our commercial and diplomatic links with the continent require further development. Edward returned from Ireland where he had purchased goods including sorely-needed iron and weapons which had come from England. It is a shame he could not find a siege engine or two. Bellies must be fed and food is so scarce: the corn and meat will be well-used. Meanwhile, Rob received heartening news. The clergy have come out in force at a General Council to support him as the rightful king. Soon, our men go southwards where the most resistant centres occupied by English soldiery will be their targets. I will miss Hugh. As usual, this missive is sealed with lead. Murchadh knows, of course, what to do.

Yours aye
Mathilda

Scotland

Roxburgh Castle

July 1310

Mary Bruce sat, blank-faced and quiet, beneath the watchful gaze of her armed guards. The manacles on her ankles hurt mightily. King Edward was not taking any chances. As the wagon passed through the castle's massive gates, she saw her cage fall to the ground, just missing the water-filled ditch. It was dispatched by cheering guards high up on the parapet who were keen to see it gone. Below, a farmer waited. Avarice tightened his already-narrow features, for he had been promised the cage for his sow.

As if to send them on their way, a vagrant wind lifted the prisoner's long, matted hair from her hunched shoulders. Gritty, choking dust eddied about them. The sergeant shouted and the wagon jolted forward. She was being moved to a new location. A nunnery in Newcastle had been touted, but audacious Scottish raids in the area put paid to that idea. Mary was beyond caring.

Though her body pained in many places, a bleak smile forced itself upon her ravaged face. Four long years in a cage and she had survived! Since Dafydd's departure many seasons ago, the garrison captain had not wanted a repeat of her near death. Her rations were increased and any salves or furs supplied without question. On rare occasions, water and soapy herbs were forthcoming. Mary's strength had returned and, with it, her identity.

Viscerally relieved though she was to be away from the bars, the open air proved frightening now to the prisoner. The surrounding abundance overwhelmed her. To narrow her vision, she focused on the muscular hinds of the horses; swaying rhythmically, their voluminous tails swished at bothersome flies. During the journey, which progressed slowly along the rutted tracks, she upbraided herself for her weakness. For so long she had craved space and the freedom to move about. Now, her heart hammered loud within a chest made tight by fear and tension. *Breathe,* she told herself; *breathe, Mary lass!* As the journey progressed, her cramped muscles loosened. With unfettered vision, she saw the trees and byways, but from a different perspective – at ground level. Strange new sounds caught her attention. A low branch snapped as it brushed past the wagon. She reached out, grabbing at the leaves. Crushed, they gave up soft aromatic oils and the prisoner pressed her hands to her nose. It was a simple enough pleasure, but it had been so long denied her.

Denied the luxury of water before her journey, Mary's own musky smell became omnipresent. However, the skies looked like they might open and pour down God's own showering rain. Not that she believed in that foolish nonsense anymore! How could a loving God treat one of his children as she had been? No! She might be manacled, but her spirit was free. No one would ever tell Mary Bruce how to think or feel ever again. If she had been well enough, she might have seen the humour in that statement. Carried away by the strength of her internal argument, she saw herself haranguing any priest who came proselytising.

As for the good King Robert, when she saw him again, she would shower him with angry, bitter words. He had placed her in harm's way, and then neglected to rescue her. He deserved her ire! And after that? Most likely, she would hug him till her bones hurt, for her longing to see him once again and hear his warm, powerful voice welcome her home, tore at her heart.

Orkney

August 1310

Margaret Bruce was unaccustomed to her new role and her muscles felt as taut as rope. She steered the vessel, moving its rudder this way and that, as she and Maud crossed the sea through a long channel from the largest island of Orkney – the mainland as locals called it – to the isle of sand. A strong, dry wind filled the sails and whipped Margaret's brown locks out of its covering, sending the wispy web of fine silver threads tumbling into the sea. It floated momentarily and, then, was swallowed by a crested wave.

Upon a low rocky outcrop, long-snouted selkies sunned themselves, ready to mate and, in time, birth their white pups. Their companion, a farmer by the name of Ottar Comlequoy, informed his two passengers that some selkies gave birth to their pups in the ocean, and straight away the young ones could swim. It was indeed a miracle, he said. His eyes, barely visible beneath spiky, seal-grey tufts, crinkled with delight. Perhaps the wondrous Sea Mither granted this ability to save them from the hunters? As they neared their destination, Ottar began testing his woven creels for weight in the shallow water, but to no avail. The pots were empty. Once more, the old man took the rudder.

They were on their way to a small farm steading on Sanday, to visit Maud's brother who lived there with his wife. Of late, Margretha had been unwell. In a wicker basket was packed enough food for a week or more, though they were not planning a long trip. Sheep dotted the isle, but Alfr's main food source came from fishing the bountiful seas, as well as gathering the plentiful whelks, limpets, mussels and rock-bound oysters. Ottar helped with the pots, catching crabs and lobsters, and shepherded the sheep to the stonewalled shearing pens, gathering the waxy clumps of grey wool caught on spiky tufts of grass along the way. When the herring were running, others came to benefit from the sea's rich harvest. Sometimes, a small pod of whales cast themselves upon the beach, caught within the shallow furrows of the bay's sand-ridged floor. A leathery-skinned turtle came ashore but once, to lay its eggs.

Treading between green, furry lengths of weed, Margaret saw brittle-spiked stars and slimy brown sea slugs. Ottar pointed out small blowholes of the spoot, the razor fish with its long hinged shell. Clusters of these lived in the broad stretches of sand and could be dug out with a knife at low tide. "They are delicious, cooked quick in boiling water," he claimed, smacking his lips together. Margaret frowned: she had found them tough, like white strips of old hide when cooked by Aodh in the early days of their arrival at Skaill.

A large flock of grey gulls hove into view. In the clear sunlight, their underbellies glimmered stark white. They swooped down to land upon the wet, mirrored sand and their black-tipped wings folded in unison as if to some silent command. Disturbing a pair of oystercatchers, they began to forage along the shoreline, causing an indignant army of tiny, opaque crabs to rise on pale-russet claws and scuttle for cover. The clamour of squawking birds rose as squabbles occurred over fish heads and other briny treats. Overhead, gannets circled and dived into the fresh clear waters, laced here and there with white crests. A solitary black cormorant watched their progress – hunched, full of gloom upon his rocky outpost, as if out of sorts with the intrusion.

Damselflies and their dragon mates flitted across the freshwater pool of the nearby burn, where the occasional otter was known to frolic and feed upon fish and crabs; its sharp claws and teeth would make short work of the latter's shell.

"There!" the old man cried, as he pointed out an otter's five-clawed, webbed footprints leading down to the sea. "Perhaps the wily creature raided my pots," he said, shaking his shaggy head of grey hair. A holt, home to its young, was likely to be close, but Ottar's nemesis was nowhere to be seen.

From a small rise upon which stood several sod-roofed stone buildings, Alfr waved a hearty greeting. Visitors were always welcome to their isolated home. Maud's brother had the rounded red cheeks and broad-boned facial structure of his Norse ancestors. Dusting floured hands upon her smock, Margretha came out of the main cottage, the fragrance of fresh-baked loaves wafting from within. After a tour of the small steading, they moved inside to escape the chill of the rising wind. It would be light for many hours. A simple meal of bannocks with hearty slabs of fresh cod grilled over the fire, and a rich soft cheese made from ewes' milk sated all appetites. Alfr opened a cog of ale which he had brewed himself.

Talk moved to developments across the isles. Relations with traders from Scotland had deteriorated, and squabbles often erupted in the alehouses. Earl Magnus was called upon to mediate between disgruntled traders and the visitors. Conflict escalated when one group believed the other to have insulted their business practices or questioned the quality of goods traded. Most of the Scots Ottar knew were quick to take offence and even quicker to reach for a dirk, he said. It was thought the worsening relations would get out of hand. All nodded sagely. Margaret spoke of Murchadh who traded his goods between Norway and Scotland. She would have heard if he experienced any difficulty. It seemed not, but then he was a peaceable, steady man who had lived away from his homeland for many years. She said no more. Apart from Maud, none here knew of her relationship with the King of Scots or her royal sister in Norway and she saw no reason for it to be otherwise.

The peat shifted and settled in the hearth. Aromatic smoke hung low across the room. Slow, purposeful sips were taken from thick mugs of ale. The wind rose to a pained shriek and the sounds of waves booming upon the shore could be heard. Ottar fell back upon a time-honoured conversational device, for it was a rare soul who did not harbour an opinion about the weather. He commented how the old ones felt in their bones the winters were getting colder. The farmers, too, claimed their crops were not as productive with the shorter seasons. Maud nodded. She was sure Walter would agree. There was less available to trade after each season, though nought had changed in how the land was farmed.

The wind howled across the wide bay and sand whipped against the shutters, making a strange tapping sound. Alfr rose to check the door. Ottar cried out. "Leave it, man, for it will but be the finfolk searching for their kin." Focusing his rheumy eyes upon the flames, he supped upon his ale, cleared his throat and began to tell the tale. His old, reedy voice rose and fell with the cadence of the born storyteller. Sometimes, Ottar looked askance over his shoulder, his eyes wide, arching his startled brows. In case the fairy folk should take offence, he lowered his voice to a barely-audible whisper. Instinctively, his

328

audience leaned forward to catch his words. Soon all could see take shape before them, a magical world which harboured a mystery older than time itself.

Finfolk were strange beings who could live between lands. Their winter home lay beneath the sea, surrounded by bright coloured grasses which streamed with the ever-moving current. Decayed beams of old wrecked ships rose upwards like towers; their chambers lit with the phosphorescent lanterns of minuscule sea creatures. Smooth-shelled limpets served as household furniture and could be moved about just by a finwife's sharp tap. Empty crab shells served as beds, softened with neatly snipped barnacle fur. It made for a rich and comfortable life, but all was not well. The finfolk also had a summer home. It was lush and green and warm. One day, this glorious isle was stolen by humans. The old ones, wise in the ancient ways of sea and land, could scarce believe the heavy tread now upon their beautiful summer land. Lessons must be taught and so the finfolk exercised the sea's magic, held so easily within their bony grasp. They stole away mortals for their winter land by entrapping vessels within a thick bank of fog. Ottar warmed to his tale and digressed.

"Should you see a strange craft, half-hidden by the haar, beware! The finfolk can row from here to Norway and back faster than a rainbow can bridge the mizzle." He waved his arm in a generous wide arc to the east. In response to the rising wind, peat glowed in the hearth.

"Listen closely," he sighed. "Within the wind's voice, you can hear the moans of the poor wee lads who will never return home." Margaret shivered and pulled her thick woollen shawl close.

The tale continued, richly brought to life. If a finwoman marries a finman, she broods and grows ugly. In time, she is sent to the shore to search for silver – the great joy of the finman – taking on all manner of arduous labour. To avoid this fate, it is far preferable for the lovely daughters of the finfolk to marry humans and so they sing sweet melodies to entice young fishermen onto the skerries. Far, far down, they take the men to remain forever in their domain beneath the sea.

"Now, it is said many an Orcadian mother blames these mermaids for the death of a son at sea. But men bewitched by the beauty of the young maids can also be led astray upon land. A long time ago, there was such a young man enchanted by a maid he met down by the shore not far from here." Margretha and Alf nodded. They knew of the family's croft, long gone now.

"The bonnie lass curved her shimmering, pearly tail about her as she sat upon a rock, combing the fine sea grass from her silken locks. When the lad appeared, fright caused her to drop her comb – a jewel-encrusted starfish. With a cry, he snatched it up. Caught in the fateful web of love, he refused to return it despite her tears, unless she wed him. This she did, but not before she bade him promise to release her back to her sea home. Seeking advice, the young man confessed all to his mam who warned him from the match, for trouble would follow surely as night follows day. He would not listen, and his mam wrung her hands in despair. She watched and waited. For seven long years, the couple lived happily together. The maid bore the lad seven sons, but each day she mourned her homeland and her heart grew heavy.

"When the end of the time approached, the old mam who cared for her son's youngest took him – some say cruelly, others not – and burnt the shape of a cross fair across his backside whilst the child yowled and struggled in vain. Next day, the family readied themselves to depart. The mermaid called out for her babe, but the heat from the Christ's cross seared her pagan breast when she bent to lift him. Again and again she tried until, with hands blistered, she gave up, weeping in despair. When the family sailed with the tide, the mermaid wailed in anguish at leaving her child behind to live on in the human world without her. Cared for by his old gran, the bairn grew up strong and true. Fortune smiled upon him and the lad lived a long, fruitful life. He is long since dead," Ottar whispered, "but his mother knows not… and so her search will continue till the end of time."

Margretha wiped away tears, thinking only of her son born too early a few short months ago. Alfr cleared his throat and reached for his fiddle. Whilst Maud rose to move the iron kettle closer to the heart of the fire, a plaintive tune, rich with longing, filled the tiny cottage. Margaret's thoughts turned to Kirsty in her convent prison far away. Ellen barely remembered her mother and Meg had been a babe when they escaped so many years ago now. The children were happy, even so, and well cared for at Skaill, but Margaret yearned now to hold the bairns; their mother had loved them dearly, but they were lost to her.

With the peat smoored, all readied themselves for sleep. Waves rolled in against the shore; the timeless, rhythmic heartbeat of these ancient islands. Snuggled within the warm folds of his cloak, Ottar began to snore. The deep nasal rumbling left the occupants of the small chamber wide-eyed in the dark, alone once more with their thoughts.

Scotland

Dingwall Castle

December 1310

Dearest Isa,

The Sassenach king is at his wits' end, trying to engage our forces in open warfare. Rob leads him a merry dance with tactics which frustrate and tease. English foraging parties come to grief and, by the time a larger force arrives, the Scots have disappeared. Our bold captains – Douglas, Randolph and Boyd as well as our brother Edward – are savage in their attacks upon the enemy-held castles.

At a recent meeting, Rob met with two English envoys at Selkirk. Another meeting was planned, but treachery was afoot and negotiations ceased. Some wonderful news came from the initial meeting. In the course of his assault upon our land, Edward II proceeded to Roxburgh Castle. There, it is said, he saw Mary and took pity upon her state, releasing her from the privations of her cage; now, she resides in Newcastle's mighty fortress. Rob is sure he was only told this information to tempt a rescue, but our brother is no fool. That our sister is alive is hard to believe. Isobel of Buchan was also released from her cage and is now in the care of the king's cousin at Berwick Castle. This does not auger well. Edward Beaumont married Alice Comyn earlier this year. Thus Isobel is now in the hands of John Comyn's daughter. With such an opportunity for revenge, her imprisonment will continue to be harsh.

Meanwhile, Hugh's brother, Walter – a student at Cambridge – sent news of Kirsty. Robert Mannying, a lay brother at the priory in Lincolnshire, told his associates at the university he had come across her at the nunnery. She is frail but well and has been put to work translating medical treatises which he supplies to the prioress. What joy this news has brought us this Yuletide, though we have heard nought of Rob's Marjorie, apart from the fact that she is in a convent in Yorkshire. I wager Elizabeth will have fared well by comparison, being the daughter of an earl.

I am with child again due mid-year. Hugh frets he will be away when most needed and bade me seek Floraidh's services again. This will give him some comfort. Perhaps Murchadh might pass on the message when next at Orkney.

As ever
Mathilda

CHAPTER FIVE

Norway

Bergen

February 1311

Dear Mathilda,

It seems my last letter did not reach you. I entrusted my parchment with the captain of a trading vessel from Holland. It was en route to trade in herring in Orkney and, thence, to go south to Aberdeen. The galley never returned to our shores. Some say it was caught by the sweep of the great sea serpent's tail. More likely, it went down in a gale. The dangers of the sea are many, as witnessed so often by the traders here at Bergen.

Words cannot describe the joy I feel to know Kirsty and Mary are alive. After all they have been through – it is beyond belief! And your news is most welcome. Murchadh will do as you have asked and seek out Floraidh. He stands by now to take this missive. God keep you safe, dear child.

Isa

England

March 1311

Mary stood before the tiny Gascon commander of the Newcastle garrison. Guillemin de Fenes looked the prisoner over. He gave a disdainful snort. "Your request is denied. The priest is here to hear your confession and so, Mademoiselle, CONFESS!" Exasperation sounded in his tone. He believed himself a brave soldier and chivalrous to a fault, but this woman tried his patience to the limit. Any other prisoner might have been grateful for the opportunity to divest his soul of his sins, but not this one. If the brother was anything like his sister, then God help England, for there was no pleasing her.

In her current state of imprisonment, Mary received far better care. Her lodgings, as she preferred to call them, were clean and spacious. At her request, fresh gowns and warm covers for her bed were provided, following receipt of a small beneficiary from a stranger in Kelso, the village near Roxburgh Castle. The commander knew nought, but that a purse of coins was handed to the captain of the escort by a woman the night before their departure. She was known to run the local alehouse where most of the soldiers sought relief from the rigors of duty. The man kept his pledge to hand over the purse for the alewife threatened to dilute the new barrels of ale with her pee if she heard anything to the contrary. Mary would be forever grateful, but she shook her head, unable to fully comprehend such kindness – and from an Englishwoman!

Rubbing his fingers through his fine goatee beard, the commander ruminated on the prisoner's unending demands. *Her food rations are sufficient. She appears well enough. Now, she has asked for hot water with which to bathe!* The latter request was refused. Exasperated, Guillemin's thoughts were brittle and on edge. *This is not some roadside hostelry. She is a prisoner for God's sake. Merde! What did she expect?* The trouble was Mary reminded the little commander of his mother, back home in Gascony, who ran her household in a sanctimonious, forthright manner. Truth be told, he even joined the army to get as far away from her as possible. Now, this waspish, high-born wench was manipulating him in exactly the same way with her clever logic. All he sought to do, kindly he believed, was meet her spiritual needs.

"Why should a priest hear my confession? It is he who should confess to me that he is a fraud and the God whom he purports loves and cares for me does not exist!" Mary spoke slowly, but firmly, as if to an imbecile.

Yes, that was exactly the scathing tone his mother used when she spoke to him. "I am not an imbecile," he said under his breath, adding an oath or two for good measure. His left eye twitched annoyingly. "Take the prisoner back to her cell, before I have her lashed for such statements." He attempted a bellow, but managed no more than a shrill snarl. Before entering the chamber, the curious guard altered his expression from an amused smirk into blank submission. All knew their glorious leader was an empty, puffed-up vessel of a Frenchman, whose mother just happened to be kin to Piers Gaveston, the king's favourite. Otherwise, he would never have received such a prestigious, safe posting.

Mary sat down upon the hard bed. Had she won that battle? Perhaps not, but she would burn in hell before she would ever again confess to a priest.

England

Priory of Sixhills

May 1311

It was commonplace now for Brother Robert to seek out the prisoner. Looking the prioress squarely in the eye, he informed her that he felt compelled to bring the woman's heathen Scottish soul to God. Unabashed, he told himself later that it was just a small departure from the truth. Perhaps the Holy

Father would understand, knowing his intentions were honourable? Aethelrida knew, of course, the monk had some prior knowledge and interest in the Bruce family, but intuitively never divulged this to her superior.

Thus it was, Kirsty held regular private discussions with the monk whenever he visited. Over time, she learnt – through the intermediary of Walter Ross – that her children were safe and well in Orkney. Her relief was palpable and it brought some pleasure that he could offer positive news. Regards Mathilda's marriage to the son of the hated Earl of Ross, she remained shocked. It would take time to reflect upon this development, though the news was several years too late for any real vitriol on her part. She learnt the earl was now one of Robert's greatest supporters – all down to the strategy of reconciliation Rob set in place so many years ago. She was intrigued by the news that Walter Ross was one of Edward's closest friends and Isabella of Strathbogie, the mother of his children, had been set aside in favour of Walter's sister. Kirsty remembered the last time the poor lass visited Kildrummy, so happy was she to be seeing Edward during a rare period of respite from the war; it always seemed to be the women and children who suffered most in these tangled unions.

Piece by piece, the monk filled in the missing years. It brought Kirsty some satisfaction to know her brother was making slow, steady gains. Perhaps in some small part, it made her sacrifice worthwhile. Of her family and children, there were only memories and even these were fading. Her health had suffered most grievously. Indeed, she had lost her past and, in all likelihood, her future would be stolen from her too. She had to hang onto something, for often it made no sense – no sense at all.

Scotland

Dingwall Castle

September 1311

Dearest Isa,

Floraidh arrived to birth my son, some weeks past. William flourishes with the aid of a young girl from a small steading near the village. Some months ago, she came to us for help. A common enough tale in these unstable times! Last year, the youngster was ravaged by a band of brigands, many of whom roam the land without any lawful purpose or connection. Her parents tried to save her but were killed; their home, burnt to the ground. Though we feed so many from our kitchen, Hugh took her on to help in the launder room. Soon, it was apparent she was with child. After a torturous birthing, the babe perished, but now the lass acts as wet nurse and will have a better life than before.

The war progresses slowly for the English. With his Lord Retainers blocking his every move, the king seems to be in a muddle; they avidly dislike his favourite and the power he holds. Whilst Robert made incursions into Galloway, Gaveston arrived in Perth early in the year. Later, the Earl of Cornwall was dispatched to block the Scots from bringing in aid and troops. May saw the English defend the Isle of Man to prevent incursions being made there as well. The tactic worked, depleting the enemy's resources in Scotland. Rob says he will defend himself with the longest stick and means to reach well into English territory.

Our men moved into upper Tynedale, crossing the Solway fords to burn and pillage. Random attacks drove fear and confusion into the heart of the enemy. Unable to fight such an elusive foe, the English withdrew. Our raids continued into

Cumberland and Westmoreland. Now, Rob's lieutenants only have to threaten to attack and the town burghers pay a generous tribute for a truce. It worked for the Vikings, why not for us! These riches go into the military chest to fund our war.

The English still hold many castles. Sieges are taking place such as the one at Loch Doon. It was relieved by David of Strathbogie who fights for our enemy, but Rob is optimistic the strength of the great castles will diminish if we persist. Now, our spies say John Macdougall of Lorne leads a naval expedition against the men of Argyll and the Hebrides – those who have gone over to the Bruce. Operating from a base in Ireland, he acts as admiral of a special fleet of dissidents. Is it not dissimilar to a board game with strategic moves to counter and check the opposing forces? King Edward knows not how keen an opponent he has in Rob, nor how rarely he is beaten.

News has just come to hand – Kirsty's lad is alive! After Methven he was imprisoned; then admitted to the king's household as a page. How old would Donald be now? Not yet beyond adolescence, but I wager efforts were made to turn him against us all. Though his mother will be overjoyed to hear her son is alive, it will be an ongoing tragedy if this proves to be the case. No news of Mary or the others. Pray they are safe and well.

Mathilda

Orkney

December 1311

Down on the dark shore, the unsettled villagers watched and waited, their faces lifted to the burgeoning flickers in the night sky. With fur-lined capes pulled snug about them,

Margaret stood with Ellen; now grown taller since reaching her teens. Beside her, Meg snuggled into Seonaid's warmth. Unable to keep still, Camran sprinted up the beach to the Hammerclett family as they clambered down the rocky path. Excited voices drifted upon the breeze. More gathered to view the spectacle.

A great display burst forth in the heavens above them. At times it faded and then washed across the sky, sending arcs streaking in all directions. Transfixed, the villagers stood in awe of the otherworldly grandeur of the Merry Dancers. It was a clear night with the rhythmic swish of wavelets and a distant rumbling, the only sounds to be heard. Shimmering reflections drifted upon the still sea.

Occasional gasps of pleasure tinged with fear came from the gathering, for none knew what the dancers in the sky might presage: message delivered, the lights drifted back into the dark velvet and stars sprinkled the black plenitude. Beneath a silver sliver of moon, the subdued crowd made its way home and the spae-wives gathered to determine the auger.

Whilst Seonaid put the children to bed, Margaret and Floraidh conversed companionably. To ward off the chill, they drank warm spiced wine before the hearth in their solar. Some weeks ago, Floraidh brought back much in the way of news from her visit to Dingwall. Reports had come that Mary, Kirsty and Donald were alive. A cherished hope bloomed – that some day they might be reunited. Margaret wished she could have heard the news firsthand and shared that joy with Mathilda and her brothers. By some feudal convention that held no meaning here on Orkney, but to which the small group still ascribed, it had been decided the youngest Bruce sister should remain behind. The younger children required supervision even though Seonaid provided abundant nurturing and care, and was senior in both years and experience. Fortunately,

Margaret's short trips away with Maud on her occasional sorties around the island were deemed to be within acceptable limits.

Walter and Maud's twin boys were strong young lads, full of the vigour of life. After having survived their childhood, they were considered to be remarkably accident-proof, but Astrid and Senga struggled to keep them in line when Maud was absent. In time, their father stepped up to the task. He was now involved with their training as the management of the farms would fall to them. Caillean and Coinneach were also learning their letters with the help of a tutor-priest, who had come over temporarily but stayed to assist Walter with the administration of the large estate. Old and gruff, Father Anselm knew well how to handle the ways of lazy lads, keen to avoid their duties. None doubted he would whip them into shape.

In need of a change from the confines of cathedral life in Kirkwall, Drustan – friend and past courier of the Bruce family at Kildrummy – accompanied him. In his wisdom, the bishop had decided the growing community could benefit from a small chapel. Margaret wondered if the substantial number of folk adhering to the old beliefs might have influenced the decision and, of course, there was the potential income in tithes to be gathered by an incumbent priest. Nevertheless, Walter was paid good money for a small plot of ground not far from the Hammerclett's longhouse and the community would be expected to offer their services in the building of the church. Having found his calling in stonework and carving, Drustan was to be in charge of the project. Winter was too cold and wet to start. By next summer, the plans should be ready for the project to commence or so the bishop assumed, unattuned as he was to the vagaries of rural life. In their quiet methodical way, the villagers knew they would be far too busy until at least late autumn. The bishop and Skaill church would have to wait.

For the small Bruce enclave, it was a delight to spend time with their old friend and hear about his life, working in the medicinal garden at the bishop's palace. He seemed to have changed little, apart from added girth around his middle – due, he said, to the tempting treats left over from feasts for dignitaries: Earl Magnus, the royal seneschal from Norway and visiting prelates from across the seas. Floraidh and Margaret wished to obtain cuttings, in time, from Drustan's herbs and to learn their particular qualities. As they wandered around the bay and loch, the priest pointed out plants that might prove useful, taking advantage of Floraidh's knowledge as well. Proudly, she showed him the sea wrack potions, rich in nutrients, though many refused to swallow the black brew. Those souls brave enough, were kept well with her ministrations.

When pressed to try it, Drustan, unwisely, took a large swig and only with great effort managed to swallow it. In the process, sweat broke out upon his brow and his jowls wobbled before turning the palest shade of green. It was, in effect, the foulest liquid ever to have passed his lips. When Floraidh insisted he take a bottle back for the bishop, Margaret could not help smiling at the expression on the priest's face and his desperate efforts to avoid giving offence.

To Drustan's surprise, he learnt Aodh had married. The priest was quite taken with the playful innocence of young Heidrun. The scullion boy from Kildrummy was long gone and Aodh was enjoying his life as a farmer, especially since old Grutgar had passed on. The small black cows were his joy. The lad boasted he could name each one, though to Drustan they all looked remarkably similar.

Marthoc showed him her new daughter and he met her great hulk of a husband, relishing the latter's tale of survival from the gale a few years back. Being a fisherman on Orkney held many dangers with the wild weather and huge sea creatures. Given other circumstances, Drustan felt sure sailing would have been his calling. Seonaid had not changed much, he declared to her delight. In response, she fussed about him even more, pressing tasty morsels upon him. Drustan rubbed his belly and nodded. Surely another helping of stovies would do him no harm at all!

When he saw Ellen, he was taken aback, for she was so like Kirsty in looks and physique. He perceived a wistful air which hovered about her person, just out of vision, but it was present nonetheless. It was obvious the lass had never recovered from the loss of her parents. *Some folk,* he thought to himself, *carry their grief like a banner streaming in the wind overhead.* Such a one was Ellen, though she was unaware of doing so. When he met Meg and Camran, Drustan's heart lightened. The babes had grown into bright, happy bairns, uncomplicated souls with lively dispositions. Later over a meal together, news was shared of their family over the sea. Much that had happened held tragic elements. However, in his priestly role, Drustan reminded them that surely it was God's blessing they were here, safe and well after their adventures.

Mixed feelings were evident amongst the expressions of his well-wishers at his departure to Kirkwall. In his saddle-bag, there lay an innocuous-looking horn container from Floraidh. Once on his journey, he hoisted it far into the bushes and sent a brief prayer heavenward.

Afterwards, Margaret took herself off to the shore. Such visits, raising the spectres of the dead and missing, were particularly disturbing. The backs of her eyes felt worn and tight with the strain of fighting off tears. White ridges lay where her fingers had been clenched. Talk of God's glorious beneficence had this effect upon her. For much of the time, she lived in the present and enjoyed her life – but, when the past was brought back into focus, it made her feel vulnerable again, like the lost child she had been so many years ago leaving Kildrummy. Having experienced so many calamities in her life, Margaret envied the solid lives of the farming families here; the way no one left except in death and all stayed living closely together sharing the timeless seasons. With the small, steady highlights of the festivals to look forward to, as well as the joys of births and marriages, it was companionable and safe. Nothing happened quickly. Indeed, Margaret was certain she had begun to fit in.

She had learnt to talk in the villagers' slow, measured way, often glancing up to the sky to check the weather or looking out to the far haze on the horizon. Over time, she had grown fond of Heidrun's brother, Hodlvis, and knew he liked the look of her. Her glossy brown hair and long, graceful limbs made her stand out from the local fair-haired women who were short and rounded. For a time, Margaret pondered what it would be like living here as the wife of a solid, hard-working farmer. To think upon this would only cause her pain.

She knew eventually she must leave and go back to Scotland. The facts spoke for themselves; she was the sister of a king. At some stage, her brother would betroth her to someone of his choice. Out of necessity, Margaret began to avoid the young man's company and could not bear to see his hurt expression, for she was unable to offer a satisfactory explanation. Now, his normally open, friendly face was closed to her and she missed the stillness and quiet strength of his physical presence.

Until recalled to resume her former life with its structure and expectations, she would walk the paths lining the cliffs and watch the great auks fly overhead. On clear summer days she might wander the shore searching for treasures, or lie down in the machair to observe the tiny wildflowers up close, watching all the while for butterflies that twisted and turned

343

in elegant courtship. Overhead, birds would capture her imagination as they freewheeled about the expanse of sky. Quite possibly, she would drift asleep in the sun, lulled by the sound of the murmuring sea.

CHAPTER SIX

Norway

Bergen

April 1312

Dear Mathilda,

I pray this missive finds you and the children well. Once, I wished Inga would grow up, but now in this, the year of her marriage to Duke Valdemar, I would have those childhood years back in a trice. Enjoy your bairns, dear one, though it may be tedious and difficult. All too soon, they will leave you to seek their own destinies. Alas, I sound like an old woman alone in her dotage, but it is not so. I am just regretful for all that has passed so quickly.

Because the girls were betrothed to brothers, it proved sensible to have a joint ceremony. Effie and I are immersed in the planning. It will be a lavish occasion, but quite traditional all the same. It will take place in a few months in the Mariakirken – not as prestigious as the Kristekirke here in Bergen, but the convenience of Oslo, being closer to the Swedish border, suits King Haakon and the dukes for political reasons.

What to wear is my major concern. I wager I will be attired in whatever the queen suggests, as she likes us to be in unison. Are we not good sisters? Over the years, I have learnt it is far better to go with the flow of her mood – though I love her dear company and we have had many happy times together. However, she can be like a river, swollen in spate, which sweeps all before it. On the grand occasion of a double royal wedding, the wealth of our nation must be witnessed by all and so, once more, a hoard of gold and silver chains and medallions will cover whatever gown I wear. As well, the girls are to become Swedish duchesses, so their husbands will wish them to be veritable walking treasure chests. Such extravagance would be frowned upon back home.

The banquets here are lavish at the best of times, but Haakon will spare no expense on the occasion of his daughter's wedding, especially with so many foreign dignitaries invited to attend. At one stage, he chanced upon the idea of Arabian dancing girls who wear belts with gold coins around their bellies, which they shake in time to sinuous music. Effie put an end to that. She is bringing the finest chefs poached from the royal court in Paris and means to impress with large figures, hewn from ice, glass goblets and Italian wine: all of which she has learnt about through her continental manuscripts. For my part, I am looking forward to the outcome, though am sure many of our nobles will prefer Norse food and drink. Our girls do not seem to care either way and, quite wisely, will accept whatever is on offer. At least Effie and I are in agreement on one thing: there will be no monkeys at the feast!

There has been much talk lately of Haakon's trip to Scotland, planned for later in the year. He and our brother have had discussions over many issues arising between our countries. Robert was invited to attend the wedding and the diplomatic talks could have occurred here. However, the need for his presence in our war-torn country has caused him to decline the honour. It would have given me such pleasure to have him celebrate this special occasion with us. In his place, the Archbishop of Arbroath – Bernard Linton, Robert's chancellor – will attend and also hold preliminary negotiations with the king. I pray he will be neither pompous nor arrogant like some of the clerics here. Perhaps, he might even share the latest news from Scotland with me. Since Master Weland's passing, I have heard little in the way of detail.

This news will surprise you, Mathilda! The king has done me a great honour in asking for my assistance in a mediation process. Conflicts have arisen between Orkney, Scotland and Norway, as well as Shetland. They are the talk of the court, and the king's ire has been aroused. None should forget – at their peril, in fact – that Norway was once a violent nation. When offence is taken, Norse blood boils and rages. The magnates are calling for vengeance. In case you have not heard of these events, they are as follows:

Pirates kidnapped the Seneschal of Orkney, a knight of Norway. He was held for ransom for both himself *and* King Haakon's revenue. Then several burghers from St Andrews arrived in Norway for the purpose of trading. Their goods were seized. Lengthy imprisonment followed, where the men were treated as hostages before being allowed to sail home, empty-handed. A similar raid took place on Shetland when a Scottish esquire, named Patrick Mowatt, was arrested by a royal bailiff. The poor man was beaten, robbed of his goods and forced to pay a ransom of forty merks for himself. All of this has caused much debate. The king is none too pleased to have to deal with these diversions when he is so concerned with the instability on Norway's eastern border. Perhaps, the lithesome coin-shakers might have served as a useful distraction to settle his temper.

Indeed, I have been given permission to travel with Archbishop Linton as a representative of the king – an honour even here in this country – to discuss these issues with the injured parties. This will take place over summer prior to the royal meeting in mid autumn. I see Effie's hand in this. She knows how much I have missed my family. Pray God I shall be able to meet with you all sometime this year. It cannot come soon enough for me, but first I must supervise the making of the wedding gowns, in line with Effie's vision of sublime elegance.

Isa

England

Priory of Sixhills

April 1312

In the vaulted infirmary, a body lay supine, as if dead. It was so diminutive one might almost believe it to be a child's form. Kirsty knew otherwise. Fuelled by venomous hatred, the patient opened her eyes and glared through narrow slits, like an adder about to attack. It was painful to look upon her, for she was a glowing shade of saffron: even the whites of her eyes were tinged thus. As Kirsty moved to adjust the covers, Mertha spat full in her face. Wiping the slimy gobbet which dripped from her cheek, the calmness of Kirsty's voice decried her inner turmoil, "Why do ye hate me so?" In spite of her pain, Mertha turned her body to face the stone wall with all the frigid vitriol she could muster.

Aethelrida approached the cot with a pan, a sharpened knife and a container. When Mertha saw the leeches, she began to shake. As each one was set in place, she began to shriek in terror, for she had an unholy fear of the slimy suckers feeding upon her soul as well as her blood. Whilst the leeches became engorged, it was necessary to hold the tiny nun down with force. This went on for days without halting the bright pigmentation of her skin. One morning, Mertha was found, eyes open, beseeching her God for peace. Eriface snivelled into a dirty nose cloth whilst she prepared her friend's body for burial. As the white shroud was wound from head to foot, Kirsty watched on. When it was over, the prisoner came to stand by the lanky nun.

"Tell me, why do ye hate me so?" she demanded. Eriface focused her reddened, rheumy eyes upon her foresworn enemy. She paused in her task as if to speak, then thought better of it. Roughly, she shoved Kirsty out of her way before leaving the chamber. Choked sobs echoed down the hallway.

Much later, the prioress shared the tale which she had known in part, but gleaned more fully from Mertha as death approached. It seemed the tiny nun's dislike of the prisoner had its poisonous roots far back in the past. As the story unfolded, the older woman's austere eyes glistened; black beads in a pale, wrinkled face. None here liked the Scots, and Kirsty was barely tolerated by most. It was the reason they had been chosen by the old king to perform their role as guards. Of this, the prioress was justly proud. Most important of all, the Gilbertines were a totally English establishment and as such, the prisoner would have no redress about her treatment. Speaking with a cold, hard voice, the prioress relayed the nun's story.

"Mertha's nephews were at their lessons in Hexham when that evil rogue, Wallace, came raiding. In sheer terror, people ran about, and families became separated. The Scots fired the town. Unable to save his sons, her brother hung himself, and the boys' mother died, Mertha said, of a broken heart. Given she had neither the face nor body to live by her wares, Mertha's only option was to enter the priory in Newcastle. After a time, she was relocated here along with many others." Abruptly, the prioress rose. It was clear she too had her own story of hardship caused by the Scots and their terrifying border raids; no doubt, Eriface, if pressed, would have her share of hate-fuelled tales. As she tidied up the infirmary at the end of the day, Kirsty ruminated upon the face of war. For so many, it represented pain and misery, whilst for some – a precious few – it was the path to glory

Scotland

Dingwall Castle

May 1312

Dearest Isa,

Your news brought great excitement. Hugh has not long returned from the south. He tells me our force landed at Ramsey on the Isle of Man and placed Rushden Castle under siege. It capitulated soon after, and Rob was well-pleased.

I long to see you, but fear your visit may be ill-timed if our brother is not here. We shall entreat him to return by midsummer. Our best wishes to dear Inga upon her marriage. I look forward to a full report.

As ever
Mathilda

Orkney

June 1312

They had all gathered to welcome a precious family member to Skaill. Isa drew her sister close but could sense her unease. Margaret held no memory of Isa; she had been a mere babe when her eldest sister had departed Turnberry, those many years ago. Now, within the warmth of Isa's embrace, her natural shyness began to melt. There was something indefinable – a touch, a chink of laughter – which played at the edge of her consciousness, but try as she might she could not bring it into the light. For Isa's part, she never wanted to let go again, but she must; the past had held sway for long enough. Ellen and young Meg both stood apart, their bodies stiff and slightly formal. Camran watched on, aware of the confusion but unable to comprehend its source or meaning. Much to Isa's surprise, the young lad flung his arms around her waist and the generosity of his welcome sweetened the atmosphere.

There was much to catch up on, but so little time. Isa had come from a series of robust discussions with Earl Magnus and his irate subjects here on Orkney. The seneschal who had been attacked required more than an apology and the money stolen from King Haakon would need to be returned. All agreed the pirates should be brought to account for their actions. Some considered they might be in the pay of the English to bring instability to the region or, quite possibly, they were just outright brigands. Isa suggested word be put about down at the trading harbours that the rogues would suffer mightily at the hands of the Norse King, whose ancestors had practised the 'blood eagle'– where a man's lungs would be ripped out through his back and upturned to represent wings. Perhaps, just the inference might put a halt to any further piracy. "Is that not a myth, your grace?" The young earl raised an eyebrow and was rewarded with a wry smile.

Regarding the attack in the Shetlands upon Patrick Mowatt, the Scottish esquire, he would require an apology and restitution of his stolen goods. Earl Magnus agreed to take the necessary steps to gain reparation. This bad blood had been building over time and its cause required exploration to prevent further incidents. The Orcadians blamed the Scottish traders for their savage tempers and a turn of mind, fraught with ill-conceived suspicion. Upon Isa's suggestion, Earl Magnus agreed his seneschal would supervise trading arrangements in the future to ensure fair trade occurred on both sides. Any disputes were to be brought before the earl rather than allow hostilities to fester. In addition, if negotiations could not be resolved at a lower level, the earl agreed to hold formal discussions with Scottish representatives. The discussions ended amicably, for the earl was well-known to Isa. She owed him a grave debt of gratitude which she could never repay. Later, over a glass of excellent Gascon wine, which had somehow found its way to Orkney, he relayed a recent development regards an English ship bound for occupied Scotland. It had been seized by German traders and taken to Aberdeen, where they sold the cargo and proceeded to take the captured hull all the way to Stralsund on the continent. "So," he concluded, laughing at his own joke, "one man's pirate is another's impudent hero!"

At Skaill, a simple family meal together was Isa's greatest wish. Seonaid and Marthoc grilled a huge fish, caught fresh by the Hammercletts that morning, and Aodh provided his own contribution. In memory of his days as turn-brochie within the great oven at Kildrummy, he dedicated himself to basting the lamb, grown fat and tender on Skaill's lush pastures. Floraidh fussed about filling mugs from the cog of ale, which she had helped make over in the Grutgar's barn. In the peaty fug of the kitchen, they squeezed around the old wooden table and talked of all that had happened since their departure from Scotland. Camran and Meg even fought over who might sit next to their honoured guest.

Ellen remained slightly aloof, spellbound by many of the stories regaling happier times. She remained silent. No words could even come close to describing *her* memories: they were inconsistent and as fragile as a moth's wing – a flash here and there of some out-of-focus face or a voice, at once familiar but unrecognisable, calling her name from afar. Now, Ellen felt herself edging closer to capture every nuance of Isa's expressive face; the sparks of light which lit her blue-green eyes from within and, most extraordinary of all, the mother smell of her. An innate desire to take Isa's hand and put it to her face, skin to skin, almost overwhelmed Ellen – to absorb its soft warmth and smoothness naturally as a child might, sitting beside its mother. It was exciting and frightening in the same breath and the desire for her own mother was so physical she could have wept with the pain of it. Without knowing, Isa had tapped into a vein of Ellen's most precious memories, which had been so long buried she had negated their existence.

Kirsty and Isa were so alike in looks and mannerisms that Ellen was not the only one unnerved by the parallels between them. Margaret too was swimming in a clear fresh pool of memories: some as bitter as any of Floraidh's potions, but others as sweet and pure as the nectar they had sipped as children from the first spring flower. When Lady Marjorie died, Kirsty and Mary became surrogate mothers to Mathilda and herself, and the mourning for their sister mothers ran deep from the terrible day they fled Turnberry.

For her part, Isa desired the occasion to be cheerful and light. Indeed, Ellen had a subtle effect upon her, but the reverse, for she was so like Kirsty. Determined to lift all their spirits, Isa regaled them with tales of her life in Norway: her wedding and coronation; seabound adventures up to the far north where she saw walruses with their great 'fish teeth', the long-horned narwhale and enormous white bears which stood higher than the tallest man. Even Princess Ingebjorg's pet bear, Bruno, rated a mention because he had eaten one of the king's best leather boots. Only her tearful pleading saved him, but that was after the servitors chased him through the royal wing. It was most unfortunate for all concerned that with all the noise and clamour the sturdy beast sought refuge atop the ornate hangings of the royal bed in which the king was sleeping off the previous night's banquet.

The most recent news concerned Inga's lavish wedding – a great success until a fight broke out between the Swedish and Danish representatives. Someone called Effie had been distraught, when her precious glass goblets shattered in the melee. Once peace was restored all continued smoothly, until a dwarf jester inadvertently insulted Duke Valdemar who had him thrust into the bear pit. Almost in unison, Camran and Meg both gasped. Isa's eyes twinkled with merriment. The two youngsters hung upon her every word. Perhaps he was just banished, she could not be sure.

Truly, Isa thought, it was by far better to tell tall tales that tweaked the truth than dwell upon sad and bitter endings. When her vessel departed the following morn for far away Scotland, Isa took with her the faces of her kinfolk, etched forever on her mind, as they stood upon the small, half-circle of Skaill Bay.

The young woman ran bare-headed, all the way up to the headland. Her efforts were rewarded. Isa's vessel was just leaving the confines of the bay and sailing out into open waters, safe under the royal flag of Norway. At times, the galley rose up as if spat out and then was swallowed back into the belly of the rolling swell of the great western ocean. From this distance, it seemed so fragile and Margaret worried it might never reach its destination. With both arms outstretched, she waved. There was no response. Below the cliff, seals lounged on an outcrop of rocks and their hoarse bark rose on a shoulder of wind to compete with the gulls overhead. Shivering in the breeze, she watched as the ship's sail shrank to a small dot and was lost to view. Her gaze turned upwards to the clouds, which ran a race across to the east. Crouching down amongst the tussocks, she snuggled within the voluminous folds of her cape, seeking shelter and warmth. Of comfort, there was none. Margaret wondered if she would ever see her sister again and the tang of brine upon her lips mingled with her tears. She heard someone call her name and looked up to see Ellen threading her way towards her.

Scotland

Dingwall Castle

September 1312

Perhaps it was because they had cursed the great northern winds, that now they were cheated of its helping hand. The bare-chested crew chanted and rowed for all they were worth. Sweat dripped in rivulets from Kettil's brow down into the furrow of his scar, as he beat the great gong and roared in unison with his men. It was enough. The galley moved along the narrow Cromarty Firth to its head, reaching the small harbour which serviced Dingwall Castle. It came to a groaning standstill against the rough wharf and a burly sailor threw a rope to a Ross man who looped it several times about a bollard. Sea birds, which had been following the vessel, sank down onto the rippling water and began to clamour amongst themselves over refuse floating before them. Watched over by a bevy of guards, the wharf was crowded with villagers: some hale of figure and voice; others wizened and bent over. Between them all ran small, snot-nosed children; fleet of foot and hand, intent on scavenging food and other treats.

Isa could have kissed the filthy decking such was her relief at having reached safety. Even thinking about their crossing of the dangerous Firth, which separated Orkney and Scotland made her weak at the knees and want to weep once more with the horror of it all. The harbour was noisy and smelt of tar, smoke and fish much like the Bryggyn, and a contingent of fair-haired traders from the continent gave substance to that impression. The large stature and jovial natures of the men made them stand out, as they shared occasional banter with the guards. Standing around braziers, ale pots in their hands, they gave the appearance of being relaxed, but nothing could have been further from the truth. Their keen eyes observed the unloading of cargo from the galleys, whilst scanning the wharf for undercurrents of trouble from their volatile hosts. All seemed to be well with minimal damage noted.

The pathway of wooden planks to the harbour was a stream, flowing with folk coming and going. The hood of Mathilda's cape slipped back and her curls, caught in the fitful sunlight, glinted like burnished copper. At that moment, Isa recognised her second youngest sister amongst the crowd. The awareness was accompanied by an unsettling shift of perspective, as if an unseen hand had torn the curtain of time. Isa pinched herself to ensure it was not some cruel dream. Over the years, many of these had fractured her sleep. As if to reassure her, a gull dropped a warm message from on high. It caught the edge of her cloak. With a smile, she wiped the excrement onto a nearby bale waving away the servitor who rushed to her aid. At last, she was home and nothing could mar the pleasure of this long-awaited homecoming.

For Mathilda's part, she felt sure she would recognise Isa by sight as well as by instinct; the Bruce women all had a similar look about them being dark of hair and medium height. It was also their good fortune to have strong, firm bodies and robust health. With bright, attractive faces, they could never be described as pretty. Such a word held a softness which could never be ascribed to their fine looks. Sharp intellect shone through in pale, upright foreheads and their eyes often had, in happier times, sparkled with wit and merriment. Isa began to wave and both women fought back tears. It had been nineteen years since they had last laid eyes upon each other, though of course Mathilda carried no memory of this. Then she had been a bairn, new to walking. Now, she had children of her own. In her arms, she held a squirming chubby infant. Beside her, a small auburn-haired mite hid within the moss-green folds of her mother's velvet cloak.

Once upon land, Isa knelt down to say a quiet, "Hello there!" to Marjorie, who clasped her mother's legs and hid ever deeper. Leaning forward, Isa tickled young William till he smiled. Shyly, he melded his body as if one with his mother's and then tilted his head just so for a quick peek. Both women laughed; he was an engaging, little soul. After a lifetime apart, neither tongue nor quill could describe the delight the sisters felt in their long-awaited meeting. Kettil placed Isa's trunks and accoutrements in the cart provided for the purpose and, with her maids in tow, followed the sisters up from the harbour, through the village of rough wattle and daub huts to the stone castle perched on its mound overlooking the surrounding countryside.

Above the hovels, lazy spirals of smoke twisted in the air. The pale blue sky was laced with fine mackerel clouds. Gulls swooped and dived, their repetitive cries adding another layer of sound. A pair of fat white geese ran across the muddy walkway, honking with alarm, chased by their young herder who was desperate to catch them before they ended up in some pot. A foolish goat butted Kettil before it was roughly booted aside, scattering several scrawny chickens. Near at hand, a thin hound gnawed at a bone, stolen from the flesher's stall where flies buzzed around carcasses suspended from hooks on wooden poles. Off to one side, Isa noticed a low building within whose walled courtyard a crowd of grim-faced men in stained tunics milled. Around an open hearth, women huddled over a large, steaming cauldron, whilst several well-grimed bairns ran about in circles fighting with sticks, stopping occasionally to scratch at their lank hair. That was the lazar hospital run by the monks, Isa was told, and these were the growing number of poor and homeless.

In Mathilda's solar, the pair sat side by side on a settle. At first, the conversation was hesitant as each gauged the other's desire for disclosure, but soon Isa took the lead and reached for her sister's hand. "From the beginning," she said, "let's start there."

Though they had corresponded, it was different face to face with words spoken from the heart and there was much to learn and understand. In time, the Ross family came up for discussion. The extent of their land holdings reached all the way to Skye and beyond. Indeed, Mathilda's good sister, Dorothea, had not long become betrothed to Leod, Lord of Lewis in the Outer Hebrides and would soon be moving there. Isabella, of course, was spoken for by their wild brother. Had the countess softened towards Mathilda? Her sister offered a wry smile. A few weeks back, Hugh had taken the children to visit the matriarch and Mathilda held high hopes for some kind of reconciliation – Will being Hugh's heir and a charmer to boot. But instead, he managed a feat of Herculean proportion, sending the contents of his last meal hurtling across the family solar towards a favoured tapestry, spraying the countess and several maids in the process. Marjorie proceeded to complain of a sore belly and spent the afternoon whining. Needless to say, Hugh was advised to come on his own next time.

In turn, Isa spoke of small things. How her maids, whom Mathilda remembered from the letters read to them by Kirsty all those years ago, had each gone their own way with her blessing. Eithne, the daughter of Irish thralls, was lady-in-waiting to Inga, now a Swedish duchess. Potentially, this fine position offered the maid increased prestige and the opportunity to make a good match. Poor Kettil's heart was broken in the process. He had come on this journey to recover both his sea legs after a recent injury and his composure.

Isa's favourite, Bethoc, had found happiness with Erling Kappen. They lived on the side of one of Bergen's mountains with expansive views over the inlet and had a small steading. Each morning, the craftsman loaded up his cart and made the short journey into the marketplace to his stall. Bethoc managed the farm on her own, caring for their animals. She milked a few goats and sheep and made her own cheese and butter. Gathering herbs down by the stream was a favourite task. Some were used to dye the wool. Indeed, the process from the sheep's back to a thick vest or brightly-coloured rug involved hard, engrossing labour, but Bethoc had found her niche and, best of all, Isa laughed – there was no one to tell her what to do!

Strangest of all, Aoife had married the thin, balding jeweller and was now running his stall with some success, allowing Ottar the opportunity to craft more of his beloved jewellery. Perhaps Isa's former maid was a little less critical, now that she saw herself as the wife of an important gold and silversmith in Bergen. If truth be known, she had found the perfect person to harangue. Her words barely touched her husband before sliding off into the moist Bergen air. Truly, he was a chameleon and his innate ability to fade into the background served him well. The couple were becoming wealthy for few could pass the jeweller's stall without being called to account by Aiofe, whose skills lay in discovering titillating news. As a result, folk would gather around to hear the latest gossip. Rarely were they permitted to leave without making a purchase. She had so much to occupy her time she rarely mentioned the sea monsters now, but Ottar was always sent if they required anything from the harbour-side traders.

Isa's little companion had died in his sleep upon his velvet cushion by the hearth. She missed Solas almost as much as she missed Inga: a terrible admission for a mother, she claimed, but it was so nevertheless. The wee dog had seen her through some rough times and his friendly, uncomplaining presence had indeed been her solace. This trip was a godsend – she needed other things to distract her mind from the melancholy contemplation of all the changes in her life. The talk moved on naturally to their brother and his whereabouts. Robert would not be present for some weeks because of his commitments elsewhere, but he had sent Hugh in his stead to welcome Isa, given she was the formal representative of the King of Norway. Isa was much taken with the rugged, charismatic Hugh and was overjoyed to see the young couple revelled in each other's company. Indeed, another child was due next year sometime and Mathilda was aglow with good health and happiness.

A date had been set for King Haakon to arrive in Inverness for the signing of a new treaty with Scotland. It was to be at the end of October. Rob assured them he would make it back in time, but had taken personal command of the attacks upon the castles of Dumfries, Caelaverock and Buittle. Under Edward's command, things had stymied, for he was better suited to chasing down a moving force than sitting patiently planning a strategy to topple a rocky fortress.

Hugh brought news of the most recent developments. More and more towns were paying tribute to the Scots' king to prevent the infliction of damage. This suited Rob full well for the money, cattle and corn were essential to Scotland's needs. The impetus started with a raid in Durham. Midsummer, the Scots powered into the northern bishopric on a market day, burning the town, killing many and inflicting great destruction. A few leading gentry undertook to act upon their own initiative to purchase a truce and met with the king in person at Hexham, buying a full year's worth of peace.

Leaving the command to his capable lieutenants, Robert journeyed to Ross, accompanied by Edward – the latter, proud in his role as the Lord of Galloway – and Thomas Randolph, son of their older half sister. After the battle at Methven six years ago, Thomas had been captured, imprisoned and much later released on the proviso he fought for the English king. This he did willingly, for the idealistic young man was appalled at the egregious direction the war had taken with the skirmishes and ambushes initiated by Robert and his men. All this seemed totally outwith the chivalric code which Thomas believed essential to civilised warfare, if there could ever be such a thing. Later, Thomas was captured by the Bruce forces and many soldiers slaughtered. After robust examination of their differences, Thomas returned somewhat reluctantly to the Bruce fold but, Rob judged, with an increased insight. One of the pivotal issues concerned the style of warfare instituted by Wallace, which Rob argued was both valid and necessary to the Scots' path to victory, given their lack of arms and men. Over time, Thomas's loyalty was well-proven and Robert sought to reward him, for his nephew was possessed of a formidable intelligence and a forthright, honest manner. Thomas accepted the prestigious role of guardian to Andrew, the young Earl of Moray.

Much to Isa's amazement, a banquet was held in her honour by the Ross family. The countess was impressed by Isa's powerful mediation role: such an honour for a noblewoman was unheard of in feudal Scotland. Prior to attending the great occasion, the Bruce siblings gathered together for a reunion in Mathilda's private solar. Isa was swirled about by her brothers until she was almost too giddy to stand. Elation and sadness were a curious mix and the light-heartedness they assumed in response lacked substance. To Isa, it seemed the chamber was filled with the shadows of their loved ones; Robert and Mathilda also caught the illusory echoes of voices past, but given that Edward was likely to scoff at such fanciful ramblings, all remained silent on the issue.

The Scoto-Norwegian Treaty of Inverness was concluded to the satisfaction of all. It was to be the first piece of international diplomacy of Robert the Bruce's kingship. This new treaty was to rectify negligence on Scotland's part, in fulfilling its commitments from the Treaty of Perth in 1266 – Magnus VI of Norway had ceded the Sudreys (the Hebrides and Isle of Man) to Scotland in exchange for a payment of four thousand marks and a permanent annual payment of one hundred marks, which was to secure peace between the two countries and put an end to many years of war and strife. However, Scotland had lapsed in making the annual payments. Over the course of the past few weeks, representatives of the King of Norway – Haakon had been unable to attend – and Scotland's king repeated the terms of the original treaty and adjudicated the various conflicts which had arisen.

Based upon Isa's arrangements which had been agreed in principle, the relevant parties would make appropriate reparation. The treaty also confirmed Norwegian sovereignty over Shetland and Orkney. Important signatories to the Treaty included William, Earl of Ross, and Bernard of Linton, Scotland's chancellor, who had returned from his trip to Norway. All were pleased with the outcome. Robert, in particular, was keen to build strong international links. Who knew when Scotland might require assistance from their great neighbour to the north?

England

Newcastle

October 1312

Mary Bruce continued her verbal battle with the diminutive Gascon captain. She badgered him into allowing her a daily walk under guard along the battlements of the castle; it was something to look forward to in a long dull day and, from atop the castle's high walls, she could see down into the town along the narrow festering lanes and across to the busy harbour. Her health would suffer if she was not permitted exercise and, to emphasise the point, she had waved the crippled joints of her hands at him, wincing in pain. Her feet she assured him were similarly damaged and needed to be exercised to reduce the swelling.

Mary was well-pleased and congratulated herself. For his part, the wily commander believed the prisoner might prove useful to him in the future if the wild men from the north came raiding south. Then, the harridan would find herself most useful tied up on the battlements. Indeed, had not the brigand, Wallace, attacked Newcastle many years ago? Now, the depredations at Hexham and Durham had been the talk of the market place. Should he need to negotiate his own escape, the prisoner's improved wellbeing and good opinion of one, Guillemin Fenes, might prove a distinct advantage.

All this manipulation and folly came to a sudden end. Piers Gaveston, the captain's kin and mentor, was executed by King Edward's recalcitrant barons. Pale and sticky with despair, the little Gascon was sent to Roxburgh Castle, ever closer to the Scots' hordes.

The prisoner would miss the prickly little man, but she did not know how much until the next garrison commander arrived. A brutish stickler for rules, the blunt Yorkshire man would not tolerate any discussion or leeway with the prisoner. Like Kirsty, Mary was put to work in the infirmary. Had she been placed in the stables, as she requested, she would have seen to the horses quite happily, but the captain was no fool and would not allow her the opportunity for escape near any of their fine animals.

Mary loathed having to treat the men, injured in raids by the Scots to the north and west of them. It repulsed her to wash filthy, lice-ridden bodies and dress pus-encrusted wounds, which later turned black and evil-smelling before the wretched men died in agony. From her hands, she could not rid herself of the smell. She loathed leeches and the sight of their engorged bodies made her gag. The image of fat maggots feeding on rotted flesh haunted her dreams and, in the half light of early morn, when white shrouded bodies began to wriggle towards her from the shadows, she began to scream.

Scotland

Dingwall Castle

December 1312

Dearest Isa,

We have missed you. Will crawls into your chamber and hoists himself up, hanging onto the bed's counterpane. Then, his wee face crumples and he begins to wail. I want to join in his despair. Marjorie, too, is lost without your devoted attention.

Recently, our brothers returned from the south and, now, I have much news to impart. Rob led a raid upon Berwick Castle. They were doing well, he said, creeping in the dead of an icy night up to the walls and using grappling irons to hoist their ladders up onto the ramparts. A hound barked, disturbing the dozing guard, and our folk had to run for their lives. It was a close call, indeed, and they returned here badly in need of our care. With the men away, food has been scarce – but last week, Edward and Hugh went hunting with Earl William over near his hunting lodge, bringing back several fine deer and two massive boars. Thus we will eat well over Yuletide and have enough to share with the villagers.

The weather matches my mood: the grey skies are bleak and the rutted tracks filled with iced puddles. At night, hot stones in our bed are most welcome. Until the fires are lit in the morning, the castle chambers are especially frigid and I am tempted to lie abed for longer.

A subtle increase in warmth this morning brought a covering of snow. Looking out through the arrow loop, I can see the village below; it looks pristine – crisp and white – rather than the usual mess of muddy walkways and dark habitations. Staying by the hearth is by far the best option now. My embroidery keeps me busy. The coverlet for William's bed is nearly complete. You were right about those colours: they look much better than the ones I had chosen. My maids, Janet and Mirin, are working on a similar one for Marjorie. How fortunate you are living in Bergen with such choice of fabric and thread. Little comes our way here apart from the most basic of goods. The English ships at Banff continue to waylay many of the trading vessels.

Hugh oversees the building of new stables; a heavy load of ice weighed down the roof of the old one and it was close to collapse. The bailey is in greater disarray than usual with items stored here and there. Horses stand about while the repairs continue. The men have gone out today to find a Yule Log. Over the next few days, supervising all the preparations for the feast will keep me well occupied. It will be a happy time with our brothers here.

Edward and Isabella are besotted with each other. Much of the talk is about when they might marry. Though it comes via the church, I feel sure the countess has posed this consanguinity issue to slow the talk of marriage. Perhaps she believes Isabella will come to her senses if given enough time. I do hope the pair will join in the festivities and Rob is well enough to do so. His rash has returned which is unsettling for all of us who bear the brunt of his temper. The physicians apply the leeches, but this makes him tired and wan. He fights an overwhelming desire to scratch and paw at his skin, ere it becomes raw, whereupon evil-looking crusts form. At such a time, public life is a terrible ordeal for him.

Bishop David and his large entourage are expected by week's end. All the rooms must be aired, new rushes laid down, cressets renewed and pallets set up with fresh heather bedding. Last time he complained of fleas, so all had to be thrown out. The cook was here not long ago to discuss the menus. I recalled the bishop was most partial to roast swan, so Hugh and Edward plan to go fowling on the marshes.

Marjorie loves to feel the rolling movements of the babe. William is convinced otherwise, for one of our wolfhounds has just delivered a squirming set of six, and he expects I shall do the same! Hugh choked on his wine when I told him. Rolling over at night is getting more difficult and going to the garderobe so often is most tedious. My belly craves sustenance at all hours and will not let me rest. Nothing will satisfy but the strangest concoctions – poached heron and savoury possets, of all things, in the dead of night! Hugh is not impressed, I have to say. Neither are the cooks or servitors, when shaken from their warm cots. We all send our love.

Mathilda

CHAPTER SEVEN

Norway

Bergen

March 1313

Dear Mathilda,

Our journey back proved eventful. A pair of galleys, which I conceived were pirates, came close enough to see our flag. Always keen for a bit of drama, Kettil laid hammer to gong and the crew, roaring in unison, rose up beating their shields. As if by a miracle, the vessels drifted away, disappearing off into the haze on the horizon. They would need to be brave indeed to attack a ship bearing the flag of the Norwegian king. Had they taken a closer look, they would have seen that our motley crew, apart from the captain, were beardless lads. Afterwards, we broke into nervous laughter. Upon my orders, Kettil opened a barrel of mead to celebrate our success and then the men put their backs into rowing for all they were worth in the direction of home. My maids, Hilda and Rannveig, envisioned being sold at a Byzantine market and made a great fuss of Kettil. He seems to have made a remarkable recovery from being heartsore over dear Eithne.

A few days past, Thora called by with her two children: Halldora, now a pretty blond maid, and young Holfr, the image of his handsome father. They are more used to the peace and quiet of their fjordland home and have since departed; their ship laden with all manner of goods.

Murchadh brought me an unexpected gift, a young pup, which he found on his last trading journey. She was mistreated in an alehouse, he told me. In looks, Frith is quite similar to Solas. It took time before I could get close enough to clean her wounds and brush the tangles from her pelt. Now, she rests in fine comfort before the fire.

Though I despaired at leaving you all, I feel blessed to have such warm memories of my journey. Pray it will not be another twenty years before we see each other again.

Your loving sister

Isa

England

Newcastle

July 1313

The men suffered from what looked like the leper's disease and the stench was horrendous. Reddened skin peeled from their bodies, leaving patches of raw flesh behind. Mary Bruce fought off bouts of nausea. At times she remained in her chamber and had to be carried out by her guard, such was her great fear. At one stage, the physician slapped her, shouting that she must stop this foolishness. If truth be known, Mary would have traded places and gone back to the safety of her cage. But after a week or more, she checked her appendages and saw all were securely intact. Relief coursed through her veins. Only then could she settle to the vile task of tending the diseased men.

It was in the infirmary that she overheard two of the cavalrymen talking about the horses; the stable was littered with bodies; they were dropping like flies.

"Perhaps it is something they are eating," she said, and bade them check the hay. Sure enough a weed, noxious to equines, had found its way into the feed. Once dried and bound within the bales, it all looked the same. Immediately, the feed was disposed of and fresh hay sought; not such a simple task, when all was said and done, for many of the farms had been burnt repeatedly during Scottish raids. With urgent instructions to forage what they could, a large contingent was sent south. Over time, the issue was resolved. To the prisoner, a measure of reluctant respect was awarded and, in due course, the wary commander nodded to her request – to visit the stables, but only under secure guard.

Amidst the ripe, earthy fug of fresh manure, animal sweat and hay, Mary walked in wonderment. Taking care to avoid being bitten, she stroked the protuberant, arched noses of the war horses offering withered apples as inducements for their cooperation. Despite being trained to attack, they accepted her quiet, confident gestures and relaxed as her questing hands explored their smooth, firm hides. Nestling into the soft neck of a smaller palfrey, Mary rested her cheek, wet with tears, and felt his sweet, grassy breath against her hair. As she caressed his large velvet ears, the horse whinnied with delight and blew a gust of warm air through broad, hairy nostrils. Mary watched as the grooms brushed and plaited the manes and long tails. Others lifted the immensely heavy, tufted forelegs and hooves of the great destriers, checking for stones, whilst a small army of servitors cleaned and mended the equipage, until all was in glorious, shining order.

In the silent space of her chamber at night, Mary dreamt of her days hunting and hawking across the hills. Once more, she could roam her heartland with the wind in her hair. At long last, her life in prison became tolerable.

Orkney

September 1313

Using a large shell, Seonaid dug into the girnel of oatmeal, packed hard to prevent the wriggling of mites. She planned to make oatcakes and the iron griddle would soon be hot enough. Outside the wind howled; a sound that rarely seemed to leave them. Thick, icy drops battered the windows. Around the walls, fish hung drying, pegged to ropes. It made for a pungent life, but they were used to it now. The kitchen felt cosy and peaceful, and the soft faded colours, smudged brown over the years by peat smoke, spoke only of warmth and comfort. Humming quietly to herself, Ellen practised her letters on a slate. Meg put her rag doll to bed, tenderly pulling up a tiny, patched quilt within the small cradle near the hearth.

Beside her, Camran hovered with his spinning top. It spun close to the fire. To retrieve it, he leaned forward. The thin sleeve of his kirtle caught on the edge of a glowing peat. An innocent spiral of smoke curled upwards. Instinctively, the child shook his arm. A frantic shriek rendered the still air as the garment erupted into a hideous conflagration. Seonaid turned sharply, registering with horror the smell of burning flesh. Colour drained from her face and the floury mixture fell from her slackened fingers, scattering across the stone flags. In her haste to reach Camran, she slipped, sprawling onto her knees. Ellen and Meg wailed and shrank back from the writhing, screaming form on the floor. From the next room, Floraidh rushed to gather the flailing child in her arms; his back, arched now, stiff with pain. From some inner well, she found the strength to stagger outside and hold him up to the sky as if in offering to the gods. The healer knew enough to know rain would not only put out the fire, but the severity of the burns might also be lessened. Tears and rain streamed down her grey face as she comforted the struggling bairn, fraught as he was with terror. In time, she struggled back inside, the child whimpering in her arms. Removing the blackened clothing, she plastered a salve upon his charred skin. By the time Margaret returned from Kirkwall, both Camran and Floraidh were abed, shivering from shock and fever.

Leaving her young bairn with Askell's family, Marthoc took turns with Margaret to tend both patients. Seonaid was too shocked to be of much help. For much of the time, Floraidh shook with rigors and screamed if anyone touched her blistered arms. With widespread burns across his upper body, as well as the sickness, the boy began to wane. As the days wore on, Camran became as limp as Meg's doll, unable to even lift his head. It pained him to swallow. On the fourth day, he breathed his last. Drustan rode over from Kirkwall to attend the lad's burial in the small cemetery beside the barn. His soft words fell like meaningless dross upon their ears. The smallness of the mound was mute testament to a child's life extinguished so quickly.

Camran's death ripped and tore at the heart of these good folk. Haggard with exhaustion, Marthoc attacked the women at the small ceremony, wailing that her sister had stolen her son from her and the healer failed in her duty to save him. For all at Skaill House, it was a bleak, unholy time. It fractured the small community and forced alliances to form where there had been none. Normally, the villagers would have attributed such a death to an external force, but Marthoc's influence was strong in her new family. She held no truck with trows and the like, and thrust the blame onto Seonaid and Floraidh. For the two women, daily life was now affected; they were vigorously shunned by the Hammerclett family. It was a grievous blow.

Scotland

Dingwall Castle

September 1313

Dearest Isa,

I pray this missive finds you safe and well. Rob's exploits have lifted our spirits.

In early January, the men carried out a siege at Perth. The town is surrounded in part by a turreted wall built by the English invaders. A water-filled moat and the silvery river, the Tay, add further protection. Our brother bade his men to appear as though they were departing the area, and the inhabitants believed the siege had been lifted. That night in complete darkness, Rob led his men carrying light weapons and scaling ladders through the refuse-ridden moat. Using a spear to feel the water's depth, he pressed forward. At one point, the putrid liquid rose up to his neck. Once over the wall, they surprised the Gascon knights and the men of the town surrendered almost without a fight. The subterfuge proved successful.

A month later, Dumfries Castle – its people close to starving – was surrendered to the King of Scots by his old enemy, Dugall Macdowall. What a moment that must have been to see such a man debased! I was aghast to hear Rob let him go free. Hugh remonstrated with me. It seems being magnanimous takes much intestinal fortitude. How our brother must have wanted to cleave the Galwegian's head from his shoulders for the part he played in the deaths of Thomas and Alexander. It seems Rob's desire for unity is paramount and even our most despised enemies must be brought into his peace. My dear husband looked askance at this exchange! It seems I have a short memory. Soon afterwards, the castles of Caelaverock and Buittle fell. The tide has turned!

Further south, Rob advised the burghers in the north England towns that if fresh truces were not purchased, they would be raided. Just the mere threat was enough to bring promises of payment from most, but for Cumberland, who failed to pay, they suffered the consequences. In a coup of sorts, English barons seized back the Isle of Man. Next, the men of Dunbar won a temporary reprieve from a Scottish raid for one thousand quarters of corn. Edward prefers stronger action, but for the most part, killing is uncommon, though it does happen from time to time. Robert holds that his main objective is money, cattle and corn, not slaughter. The campaign of fear has been successful.

By midsummer, our brother, Edward, laid siege to the great fortress of Stirling. Sir Phillip Mowbray, the garrison commander, asked for a year's respite: he was dreading running out of supplies. If no English army came within three miles to do battle for the castle in that time, then he would surrender and open the gates freely to the Scots. Edward agreed, caught up in the chivalry of the moment. Missing the folly of such a plan, he had not counted upon the sharp rebuke and rollicking he got from Robert. King Edward and his barons would never ignore such a public challenge.

Rob is now compelled to do the very thing he has striven to avoid, to face a massive, well-equipped and highly-trained army on an open field of battle. Edward comes here seeking support from Isabella for his actions. For his part, Hugh is tight-lipped around them. Having none of Robert's prudence, Edward cannot see how his actions will not work for the good of the nation and refuses to budge from his position. So often he courts calamity and offers nought in the way of contrition.

It is fortunate Rob has cooled since their altercation. Even in the most adverse circumstances, he sets his angst aside and, with calm logic, arrives at a position of strength. Somehow we must rise to the challenge. He holds onto the hope that the men of Scotland, even those whom at one time gave their loyalty to others, will follow him into pitched battle. To ensure Scotland's survival, it is a battle they must win.

Apart from these tidings, I can only relay that all is well with our family. My belly grows bigger each day, as round and firm as a ripe apple. Knowing Floraidh is on her way gives me confidence all will be well. Pray she arrives soon.

Mathilda

Scotland

Dingwall Castle

September 1313

Dear Isa,

I write in haste. Camran has perished from hearth burns. Murchadh arrived with Floraidh, but she was scarce in a fit state to help me with my birth. Despair holds her firm within its grip. My daughter, Lillias, arrived with a vengeance and my own health suffers as a consequence. Murchadh tells me Seonaid is stricken with grief, even more so since Marthoc lashed out at her most cruelly: Camran was in her care at the time. Ellen and Meg witnessed the tragedy unfold. Margaret struggles to hold all together and begs our help. We dearly need your wisdom and strength.

Mathilda

Norway

Bergen

October 1313

Isa received the missive from Mathilda. It was hard to believe such dire news. As with any shock, she felt herself slide off-kilter. Initially, she wanted to make the trip to Orkney herself to help her youngest sister, but in all conscience, she could not. Inga was newly with child and a return message about a forthcoming visit had already been dispatched. The solution came to her next morning.

By a cruel twist of fate, Bethoc's husband had died some months ago. On the way back from a visit to his sister, something – perhaps a wolverine – spooked his horse in the twilight. Erling was thrown from the wagon; his neck broken upon impact. Much later, his body was found, barely recognisable. Since then, Bethoc had locked herself away. To Isa, she seemed lost, lacking purpose and direction.

As a young maid at Turnberry, Bethoc cared for Margaret after the death of her mother. Now, with these events, Margaret required nurturing once more. With her wisdom and strength, Bethoc felt sure she could ease the conflict between Seonaid and Marthoc and bring joy back into the lives of Ellen and Meg. She agreed to help, believing the journey might offer much-needed distraction from her own troubles.

Without delay, she packed a small bag and departed with Murchadh.

England

Priory of Sixhills

December 1313

In the viscous murk of a winter's morn, the prisoner lay upon her cot awaiting the bell to rise. Thoughts criss-crossed her mind in fleeting patterns of happiness and despair. She had awoken from a dream, rich in hue and filled with laughter. Ill-focused and stunned, the miasma of changing realities now left her reeling.

Kirsty felt an unassailable gulf existed between herself and her children, whom she had not seen for nigh on eight years. Some time past, she learnt to her relief that Donald was alive. For so many years she suffered dreadful recriminations believing her negligence precipitated his death on Methven's bloody slopes. When she heard of his imprisonment and role as a page in the young king's court, she still suffered, caught up in the clinging web of a mother's guilt, and was filled with foreboding. Donald was, by nature, a difficult child and Kirsty could well imagine how the bitterness within his dark, melancholy spirit might have festered without the counterbalance of her nurture and love.

Ellen was now a young woman. What might she look like? How did she dress? Kirsty longed to know how her daughter felt about the mother who had sent her away so long ago. Was she angry or, worse, had she forgotten her? Of Meg, Kirsty could only remember a faint outline. In her mind, she had created a fantasy child – similar to her father in looks with fair hair and open smiling features. Kirsty knew she had never allowed herself to fully mourn Christopher's death. He was the joyful centre of her universe and had been taken so brutally from her. Their relationship was cursed; how else could one account for what had happened? With his passing, all happiness and hope was extinguished, but in her dreams they were a family once again. So often though, dreams shattered in the harsh morning light, turned her waking life into a nightmare. Lying upon her bed, she pulled the coverlet over her head. The tears came in a torrent of grief, which would drown her if she let it.

Hearing the muffled sobs, Aethelrida entered the cell and sat down upon a stool, her back to the stone wall. Cold blue light streamed in from the narrow window. Rearranging her woollen habit for added warmth, she closed her eyes and began to pray. When Kirsty needed her, she would be there.

CHAPTER EIGHT

Scotland

Dingwall Castle

April 1314

Dearest Isa,

It surprised me to see Seonaid arrive with Murchadh, but she brought good news! Your plan worked well. Bethoc chose to stay on and this strengthened Floraidh's resolve to return, even though Marthoc's recriminations are still in evidence. Such ill-feeling festers and grows in a small community, poisoning all who let it.

Under the circumstances, Seonaid felt free to accept Murchadh's longstanding offer of marriage of which we were none the wiser, though I think Marthoc may have suspected, fuelling her jealousy even further. Most grievous of all, Meg is lost without her companion, but Ellen occupies her with games and the like.

Margaret received news of her betrothal to Sir William de Carlyle, one of Robert's adherents in the south near Lochmaben. A solid support base in the south will not go astray. After June, all will be made clear as to which path the war has taken. Rob is cautiously optimistic. But Hugh says, if we lose I am to sail immediately for Orkney with the children. We may all end up on your doorstep even yet! Though I would dearly love to see you again, I pray with all my heart that this does not come to pass.

Earlier this year, Rob turned his attention to two of our

most formidable castles, Roxburgh and Edinburgh, to try and break the English hold on the south. Our 'good Sir James' led a brilliant raid on Roxburgh and took the garrison by surprise. They were well occupied, drinking and dancing, during a celebration. All the while, the Scots, under dark hooded cloaks, approached in stealth, crawling on hands and knees up to the castle walls. When a sentry saw the moving shapes, he commented to his fellow guards, loud enough for our men to hear, that the oxen in the fields were moving about. Once over the walls, a local man, Sim of the Ledows, put a dirk into the bewildered guard and our men clambered up the rope ladders unhindered. The little Gascon commander – injured, with neither food nor ale – shut himself into a small tower. The following day he surrendered, and he and his men were allowed to go free to England. Now, Roxburgh Castle lies in ruins. This will please Mary.

Three weeks later, our nephew, Thomas, led an impossible raid on Edinburgh Castle. How could anyone break into such a fortress so high on its rocky peak? A man, whose father served in the castle, showed our men the way up the slippery face of the crag to the ramparts. It was nothing short of a miracle that no one fell to their death, for the night was as black as tar. The garrison were focused upon defending themselves from a frontal assault. When the insurgents encroached from behind, they surprised and killed many. The commander, another Gascon by birth, saved himself by changing sides; a short-lived reprieve, as he was later executed for treason.

In April, our brother, Edward, ensconced himself in Rose Castle in Cumberland; the foolish folk refused to pay their tribute. From this base, he ravages the countryside. Any towns without immunity are plundered. Robert needs to fill our military chest, for the war is about to escalate.

News has come – King Edward amasses his host across the

379

border. June is not far off. Robert continues to train our men to fight in pitched battle. Indeed, twenty-one clans pledge to fight. Though he remains on edge, he is mightily pleased morale is so high. The sound level of discipline is reassuring; they will need this to hold their ground. Pray for Scotland, Isa. If we are not successful, it could well be the death knell for our country.

Mathilda

Norway

Bergen

June 1314

Dearest Mathilda,

As I write, a contingent of huskarls, commissioned by me, are heading across to join forces with Earl Magnus and his men of Caithness. Of course, it is with the king's blessing. He will not offer his full support directly, loath as he is to enter into such a conflict. His sights are set eastwards. I pray daily for a Scots' victory.

Isa

Scotland

Stirling Castle

June 1314

My Dearest Isa,

Praise be to God! We have had a mighty victory. Firstly, I

must thank you and the kingdom of Norway for your men. They came to me as a company with Magnus and the men of Caithness. I now release them from their service and return them to their homes in Norway. This letter will reach you from the hand of Kettil Haakonson. The stout warrior stood with me throughout the battle. No doubt, he can amplify my poor account. We have also given thanks for the souls of two of your men who died, with many another good man, on the field of the Bannockburn. Scotland thanks you for your many services to the cause of freedom.

As you know, Edward II of England was duty bound to relieve Stirling Castle and its English garrison by midsummer's day. On 17th June, a huge English host rumbled over the border from Berwick and Wark. I sent companies of light horse under Robert Keith and James Douglas to observe them.

Over two hundred wagons drawn by horses and oxen, stuffed full of food, armour, weapons and many comforts for the knights headed towards us. However, they had left their muster too late and now they only had a week to make Stirling. I was hopeful their forced march would tire the mighty host of over eight thousand infantry and two thousand archers, mostly from Cheshire and Wales. However, their main strength lay in knights who were heavily armoured and mounted on great war-horses, the like of which are few in Scotland. Fortunately, many of the great earls of England are at feud with Edward and were not present. Chief among these were Lancaster, Warwick, Arundel and Norfolk. However, Edward brought knights from Aquitaine, Ireland and Bayonne, along with the remnant of the Comyn faction, prominent amongst who were John Comyn, the younger, of Badenoch and the de Umfravilles. All told, the English had at least fifteen hundred knights and men-at-arms.

This huge host reached Edinburgh on 19th June, and waited two days there to receive further supplies brought north by ship. On 22nd June, they force marched twenty hours in hot weather and reached Falkirk. The next day, they moved forward a further eleven miles to within three miles of Stirling, where we waited for them. They were hot, tired and dusty, and midsummer's day was the 24th June. I had spent all spring and summer training our army, knowing this moment would come. In particular, I knew our only hope was in the schiltrons, the closely packed formations armed with long spears. These would need to move and not be static. If they stood still, the English archers would destroy them as happened to Wallace at Falkirk. This time we would have to take the offensive and to move a schiltron takes much training.

We had three of these formations with about twelve hundred men in each. As well as the ordinary folk of Scotland, I commanded the lords and knights should dismount, and we all fought on foot. These schiltrons were commanded by myself, Edward and our nephew, Thomas Randolph. In addition, I kept two forces of light cavalry mounted under Robert Keith and James Douglas, each of five hundred. As the crisis neared, many new troops arrived, either from the Highlands (mostly without spears) or from the burghs (mostly untrained). These I held in reserve, and they may have numbered up to two thousand men.

We met the English late afternoon on the 23rd June, two miles east of the castle of Stirling. The road passes through the New Park, which is woodland planted over a hundred years ago. I expected the English to try and force their way through, but knew they would find it hard to deploy there. I also ordered the flat, clear land between the ford over the Bannock Burn and the entry through the wood be filled with concealed pits. To the east, the only way around, for many miles, is an area known as the carse. The wooded plateau of New Park drops steeply towards this boggy area, which in turn runs into the Forth. If the English could not force the road through the wood, then they would have to move eastwards down into the carse by crossing the defile of the Bannock Burn, then north through the sodden ground and cross another stream in a deep ditch, the Pelstream, before heading the mile or so to the castle. The English were warned by messengers from the castle that we were dug into New Park woods. However, they determined to ride our infantry down and the English vanguard advanced at a trot.

I advanced my schiltron to where the old Roman road entered the woodland. In front of me were the concealed traps and caltrops, and then the ford over the Bannockburn. Beyond this to the east, a dusty English van under the Earls of Hereford and Gloucester began to spur towards us. It was a hot day, and as yet I was not in armour, but riding a small grey palfrey, and was busy ordering the ranks of our men. Suddenly, one of the English knights raised a yell and galloped over the ford of the Bannock straight for me. There was nothing for it, but to turn and face the oncoming rush. Fortunately, he was a brave but rash young man and I easily avoided the point of his lance. More than that, I was able to rise in my stirrups and hit him with my battleaxe as he passed. Poor Sir Henry Bohun, nephew of Hereford, was dead before he hit the ground. It cost me my good axe though. The rest of the English vanguard then charged across the ford and we waited on the far side of the traps which broke up the charge. We pressed the English back down to the crossing point and nearly captured young Gloucester who was unhorsed.

With the Stirling road now blocked, the English decided to send three hundred knights across the carse and head for the castle. If they had reached it, then they and the garrison would be a considerable threat in our rear. I advanced Edward and his men to watch them from the east edge of the wood. Our enemies rode past them, picking their way over the soft ground in a northerly direction. They attempted to cross the

Pelstream by the road ford, which lies on the flank of the wood, but Randolph and his schiltron were there, blocking the way between the trees and the burn. The English were hemmed in and their charge failed. Pressing forward in groups, they began to throw their axes. When Douglas and his men dismounted to give support, the enemy pulled back.

It was now evening and the English had twice failed to force their way through to Stirling. Our enemies were determined to push northwards, and they chose to cross the Bannock Burn at several points by filling it with thatch and wood, and thus advanced their whole army into the carse land below the wood. They had the Pelstream to their north, the Forth at their backs, and the Bannockburn to the south. To their front was the wood, but before this was a dry area of grassland rising out of the bog, and it was up this they planned to charge and break us. Alternatively, if we did not appear to face them, they could then cross the Pelstream unhindered and the castle would have been relieved. They wanted a pitched battle and, now I had them on a down slope with a bog and the River Forth at their back, so did I.

That night, I sat around a fire with Edward and our closest supporters. Then Alex Seton appeared through the gloom. He had left the English and came to tell me they were poorly rested and fed, and their confidence was shaken by the day's fighting. Not only that, he reported the slope onto the dry field in front of the wood was much narrower and steeper than it appeared. However, Seton was not the only Scotsman astir that night. David, the Earl of Atholl, full of hatred for our brother, Edward, crossed the Forth to the north and attacked our supply depot at Cambuskenneth Abbey. He killed Sir William Airth before retreating northwards.

In the early morning of midsummer's day, we emerged from the wood and advanced eastwards onto the top of the dry field. Below us, the English camp lay sprawled out, half active, in a fitful state. The English ordered their knights to the front, and faced up the slope to where our three schiltrons waited for them. Mine was in the centre, with Edward to the right and Thomas Randolph, reinforced by James Douglas and Walter the Stewart, after their hard fighting of yesterday, to the left. Robert Keith and his light cavalry guarded our left flank, and behind them on Coxet Hill, our reserves, mostly Highland clans, waited with Donald of the Isles. We braced to receive their charge, but first offered up prayers. Quickly, the English heavy cavalry pushed through their throng to the front, and then with a yell, they galloped towards the waiting spears. Our men held firm, and the months of training began to pay off. After the failure of the first charge, the English knights lost cohesion. They were at a standstill. Now, we attacked down the slope, ever pushing them backwards into a greater mass of men. Their infantry only served to get in their way, and gradually down the slope, we forced them into a massive, grinding mass.

Finally, the enemy managed to get some archers out onto our left flank, and things would have gone ill for us had not Robert Keith seen his chance and ridden them down before they could turn. Thereafter, there was nothing noble or chivalric about the fight. Our reserve came charging down the slope, and I saw the great war galley banner of Somerled enter the fray on our side. The cry went up "On them, on them, they fail!" and at length so they did. The whole press went into the boggy ground at the back of the English, and then they broke and ran in all directions. Some drowned trying to swim the Forth; some died in the defile of the Bannockburn, and many just died in the crush. Edward II was led from the field by Pembroke, and escaped with Despenser and Beaumont. I understand they were chased all the way to Dunbar by Douglas and his Borderers. The slaughter was great, and the pursuit lasted for two days. The Bannock Burn was filled ten deep with English dead. In total, thirty seven English lords were killed, and I am sad to say this included the Earl of Gloucester, who I would have wanted taken alive. More than that, we have many prisoners including the Earls of Hereford and Angus, and over one hundred knights. I promise you their ransom should bring our women-folk back to Scotland and safety. Too long have they been in English hands and subject to their cruelty. I can do nothing about the past, but perhaps the future might be kinder to us Bruces? We have lost two brave knights in William Vipont and Walter Ross. I grieve for their passing. Now my intention is to take the war into England and force a peace, which this kingdom richly deserves. I will write further when time allows, but your men are eager to return home and their ship waits below Stirling Brig.

As always
Your brother
Rob

Scotland

Cambuskenneth Abbey

June 1314

The English Goliath had fallen. Bodies lay, piled high, on the marshy slopes of Bannockburn. Crows and raptors flew about their grisly business. Men searched for loot. The lucky ones, those worth ransoming, were rounded up. To far-off Dunbar, King Edward fled with his closest knights on a desperate ride to the southeast, abandoning all in his humiliating retreat.

It had started with a fortuitous display of skill and courage. King Robert killed a knight who charged at him from the English ranks before the commencement of the battle. As de

Bohun's body toppled to the ground, a great cheer rose from the Scots' side who perceived it to be a favourable omen for victory. The men were spurred on by their king's strength and bravery, whilst Robert's anxious captains gritted their teeth in dismay at his rashness. With the strategic use of bog and hillside, the Scots' army maximised all in its favour and Robert proved himself, once more, to be a superlative general. The English suffered defeat at the hands of the lesser-numbered Scots, but this time, the king's regalia and personal goods, a prestigious haul worth over two hundred thousand pounds, fell into enemy hands.

All through the night, Robert sat alone in the abbey, fighting exhaustion, ignoring his own wounds and mourning a shrouded corpse. His cousin – the Earl of Gloucester, an English knight – lay still, silent and accusing. Elsewhere, Edward Bruce grieved for his friend, Walter Ross – a good and kind man, wasted.

Waving away a monk, Hugh chose to attend to his brother's corpse: washing the dried blood from his wounds, remembering their childhood scrapes and choking on his own grief as he did so. He tried hard not to imagine his mother's brittle anger and his father's sad confusion. He would bear the news as he must. There would be no need for words. One look at his face would tell them all they needed to know.

In the hiatus after two hideous days of battle with valour showed by so many on both sides, the human cost was now being counted. Amongst those dead were Clifford and Percy as well as prominent Scots loyal to the English – another Sir John Comyn and Edmund Comyn, Lord of Kilbride. Those lucky enough to be ransomed included the Earls of Hereford and Angus, John de Segrave and Ingram de Umphraville, all of whom languished in the dungeons of Stirling Castle. Bothwell Castle now belonged to the Scots, for the garrison commander changed sides on the eve of the great battle and imprisoned his own troops. Some like Phillip de Mowbray, commander of Stirling Castle, went over to the Scots' king who welcomed his decision. Robert knew winning a battle was a significant step, but it was the hearts and minds of his enemies he sought to capture now. Scotland was a long way from being recognised as an independent nation.

England

September 1314

Newcastle harbour bustled with ships. Unfurled masts jostled and clanged, made uneasy by the rising breeze snaking along the river's broad path from the North Sea. In the ice-blue light of early morn, curs and rats were underfoot. Men-at-arms shared wineskins, warming reddened hands over flames which flickered weakly in the iron braziers. Curses erupted from bitter mouths and one unfortunate hound, a ragged bundle of bones, was kicked for coming too close to the fire. Generous warmth of spirit was absent here. Beneath the heavy mantle of defeat, a brittle, chilling bitterness festered. Small bands of hungry, injured troops, such as these, had trickled back into England having evaded the Scots in their roundup after the battle near Stirling Castle. This surly bunch was to sail to Berwick and return with ransomed knights.

On the wharf, a trader gutted fish and threw entrails to a flock of gulls: their white necks, arched in aggressive, demanding display. When one of their brood gathered a bloody beak-full and flew off low across the murky water, the remainder hissed angrily and their flapping, outstretched wings made walking a hazard. As Mary Bruce and her escort pushed through the milling crowd, the aromas of human effluent and acrid tar rose up to meet them. Along the galley's uneven wooden planks, a guard followed closely behind the prisoner. When the ship rocked, he instinctively placed his hand at the small of the woman's back and then, aware of the eyes upon him, quickly let it drop. All knew it was the sister of the Scottish king being exchanged for some rich, landed knight. Below, the ill-tempered soldiers looked up at the prisoner and spat contemptuously upon the greasy wharf, before turning back to the fire. Tugging painfully at the frayed edges of their minds were memories of young comrades, empty of wealth, land or title, decaying now in the stinking, Scottish mud. They had not been so fortunate.

Pulling her fur-lined cape tight around her, Mary shivered. She turned to look up at the walls of the city and her prison: the great castle with its battlements and soaring towers, enshrouded in mist. A bitter smile creased her strained features. She had cheated death, both here and in her cage, and was, quite justly, proud of the fact. Though her health was much improved and she had filled out during the last four years of her imprisonment, her twisted joints were a constant reminder of her time in the cage. She rubbed at them now. They throbbed and ached in the cold. Just a few years shy of forty, Mary gave the appearance of a much older woman for her back held a slight stoop and her hair was no longer a rich brown, but stark white. Despite a mesh of fine wrinkles, her face was still attractive, though at times, in repose, her expression gave silent voice to the grave disappointments she had experienced in life. Many women died before they ever reached this age, Mary considered. Under the circumstances, she had done remarkably well, but it was fortunate indeed she had not the benefit of a mirror and knew not the ravages of pain and suffering upon her face. That would come later.

Once news of the English defeat at far-off Bannockburn reached Newcastle, the garrison commander became edgy as if a horde of wild Scots would appear from nowhere and attack the castle. The watch was increased, and the garrison undertook more rigorous daily manoeuvres. All had heard of the retreat of King Edward and his flight in an open boat from Dunbar, sailing into Berwick, bereft of all trappings and bickering like an old maid with his men. Most of the soldiers passing through Newcastle on the way to the battle had been cocky about beating the Scots. Many were English, but a good proportion of the unfortunate levies had been from Wales, Flanders and Gascony. Mary wondered if Dafydd still lived. She would never know, of course. How strange it was that a young enemy soldier had saved her life and been her only friend. Perhaps life was not as clear-cut as she always believed.

Since the ignominious defeat, Mary received more cordial treatment from the garrison commander, for she was now part of the ransom for the Earl of Hereford. The quality and quantity of her food rations increased overnight, and her requests for hot water for bathing were approved. To her great delight, she was no longer required to work in the infirmary and could walk freely around the castle ramparts. For this journey, she wore a gown and veil suitable to her position. The mantle of prestige was hers once more. Now, she was Lady Mary Bruce, sister of the victorious King of Scots and men of breeding bowed before her. As the ship moved out into the river, Mary felt the shackles, which bound her spirit, fall away. An icy wind teased her hair from its confines and brought with it an exquisite freshness. In time, the vessel breasted the rough, incoming waves at the river mouth. Mary laughed as she caught the beads of spray full-on. She was going home, and her heart soared higher than the raucous gulls following in the ship's white, frothy wake.

Wet and chilled, the prisoner was directed to a curtained enclosure, within which the huddled shapes of two women and a thickset man were barely visible. One of the women gasped.

390

She stood up and her hood fell back revealing fair hair, now tinged grey. Tears streamed down her pale, lined cheeks. The younger of the two women cried out in shock. With arms outstretched, she launched herself towards Mary, stumbling as the ship swayed. Marjorie was now a grown woman of nineteen years. Though her build was fine-boned like her mother, Isabella of Mar, none could mistake the look of her father.

"Marjorie! Is it really you?" Mary cried before the pair came together in a gut-wrenching embrace. For a time, only muffled endearments could be heard until Mary disentangled herself from her niece's desperate grasp. With one arm around Marjorie, Mary held out her hand to Elizabeth, Queen of Scots. The latter raised it to her moist cheek. It was a gesture of the deepest affection and respect.

Though she had suffered the painful separation from her husband and the loss of her freedom, Elizabeth had not endured the dreadful privations of Mary's incarceration. No words could express her abject sorrow for her good sister's horrifying experience. Seated in the shadows against the panelled wall, Robert Wishart, Archbishop of Glasgow, held his peace. Though he was blind and infirm, he knew from the sounds around him a miracle was taking place. God had granted these souls, torn apart in the direst of circumstances, their freedom. There would be plenty of time for talk later.

Scotland

October 1314

On the banks of the River Tweed, a temporary camp of tents and pavilions had been up for several days. Banners streaming in the wind told all the King of Scots was present with his entourage. Two hundred or more horses and numerous wagons stood off to the side. They were a sufficient distance from the town of Berwick for safety, but Robert was not taking any chances. He paced up and down the green, whin-dotted bank of the river, hearing the rippling water over the rocks and in a quieter stretch, the occasional splash of trout. Under normal circumstances, he might have tried to catch the latter for his supper, but not today. He was too preoccupied and food was the last thing on his mind.

Overhead, grey banks of cloud floated eastwards. Out of the blustery, chill wind, a group of nobles sat, shackled, inside several tents. The Earl of Hereford and several lesser knights were to be ransomed in a formal exchange and were under tight guard during the tense wait for the kinfolk of the Scots' king. They were keen to escape their incarceration and make the trip to Berwick, where a ship would take them south to London to report, firstly to Edward, their disgraced monarch. Then, the knights would go home, for they too had anxious families waiting for them.

Sometime earlier, Robert had sent his trusted lieutenants to survey the land around them. Never trusting the word of the English, the king was of a mind to hack off a few heads himself if the women did not arrive soon. The interminable waiting gnawed at his brittle patience. A vein – a twisted blue cord – pulsed rapidly in his neck and his right eyelid flickered, imperceptibly. His stomach felt as if he had swallowed a honeyed flagon of wasps and, from time to time, an ominous ringing sounded in his ears.

A large group of riders and several horse-drawn litters hove into view. Relaxing his clenched jaw, Robert exhaled a sigh of sheer relief. At last, they had come! At the river, the escort pulled up sharply. In his desire for haste, Robert was already across and stood ready to meet the cohort. Concerns for his safety alarmed the bulk of his men who followed, splashing across the low, rocky ford, swords at the ready.

"What took you so long?" Robert snapped at the men who rode up alongside the litters. Hay, Douglas and Campbell had endured his irritability many a time. On this day of all days, no offence was taken. Having followed their supreme commander and friend for more than a decade, these intuitive souls had observed his many moods, both grim and light. Today was not a day for stating the obvious. Sir James recounted the pitfalls which slowed the journey, as relayed to them by the leader of the escort. The ship carrying the prisoners was almost caught on a river sandbank coming into Berwick. As if that was not enough, the wind dropped and the crew, a ragged group of surly men-at-arms, had to row their way into the harbour. A second litter needed to be requisitioned for the ailing Bishop Wishart and Lady Isobel of Buchan, her health being exceedingly poor. James leaned forward to extrapolate upon this, but was cut off abruptly by the agitated king who failed to notice the deep lines of concern on the man's face.

As one, Gilbert and James moved the curious men-at-arms, both Scots and English, away from the spectacle of the king's reunion with his family and began to ready the ransomed knights for their journey home. Only Walter, the Steward's son, and Neil Campbell remained to assist their beleaguered king. They knew guilt at the fate of his loved ones and an inability to rescue them had eaten away at his soul like a canker for the past eight years. In vain he had cried out in his sleep to his brothers and those tortured souls who had died for his cause – the crown of Scotland. Awaking in a lather of sweat, their king rose most mornings haggard with exhaustion. Was it any wonder he had been so unwell over the years, for he punished himself more than anyone else ever could? Today, he came seeking redemption. Having conversed briefly with some of the women, Robert's men feared it may not be forthcoming, today or ever.

From the first litter, a young woman stepped down and looked bleakly at her father who scarce recognised her, so changed was she from the ungainly eleven-year-old he remembered. He scooped her into his arms, murmuring his gratitude to God for returning his precious child to him. If he had expected her to cling to him, he was disappointed for Marjorie held back from any display of emotion. She was a stranger to him and her silence was unnerving. Perhaps, he hoped, she was waiting for a more private time. For an uncomfortable space, Robert stared deep into his daughter's eyes, praying a seed of forgiveness might lie within their chilly brown depths, but saw none. Crestfallen, he handed her over to Sir Walter who came to his rescue. Carefully, as one tending a wounded animal, the gallant young man led her off to one side.

Next, a gaunt, white-haired woman emerged. Robert gasped in shock at the sight of his sister's altered appearance. Mary walked with slow, purposeful steps towards her quarry. Her fists rose as if to pummel his chest. Robert grabbed them; it would have been unseemly, as well as treasonable behaviour, for his sister to strike the king in full view of all. When she cried out in pain, he let her hands drop. Clearly, she had it in her mind to castigate him, but this was neither the time nor the place and both knew it, though nothing as spurious as protocol had ever stopped Mary Bruce.

"Why did you not come, Rob? I waited so long." She spoke loud enough for all to hear the harsh rancour in her voice. It was not her purpose to humiliate her brother, but far worse, to wound him. She desired that he feel the keen bite of her pain, as she had done for the past eight years.

"Welcome home, lass." Robert spoke without a trace of irony. These words held such a weight of sorrow and despair that Mary paused, her face crumpled and with it her fierce self-control. As she collapsed into her brother's open arms,

Robert's face worked hard to control his own emotions of grief and surprise.

Only a fool might believe all would be well between Mary and her brother, but she did indeed hug him till her bones hurt. On many occasions to come, both public and private, he would bear the brunt of her ire, but for now it was enough. Neil Campbell came forward and with the utmost respect for Mary's dreadful ordeal led the weeping, crushed woman away to stand beside the silent daughter of the king.

Another woman, fair of hair and body, departed from the litter. Robert bent his head and knee before her, both out of respect and love for his queen. At last, here was a woman who welcomed him with open arms. Deep within her blue eyes, he witnessed the depth of her love and sorrow. Robert experienced a rush of relief, for this was the test which brought the greatest anxiety. If Elizabeth rejected him as well, he would have been crushed to the point of annihilation. All would have been for nought. The men turned away to offer a small measure of privacy for the couple's anguished embrace.

At the last litter, Robert went to the half door and peered inside. Within its shadowed interior, he recognised Bishop Wishart, now balding and frail. From the intense concentration of his expression and the way he tilted his head this way and that to identify sounds, it was obvious the man was blind. Feeling overwrought from the day's emotion, Robert cleared his throat, which was painfully tight, to signal his presence. He took the old man's hand in his. "Welcome home, old friend."

Beside the bishop, the wan body of Lady Isobel of Buchan reclined, propped up on several pillows. In response to his voice, her large grey eyes wandered vaguely over his face, but no recognition showed. "Isobel lass, it's Robert," he protested. Her eyes lit upon an insect as it rested on her cover. Quickly, she snatched it up and ate it. An odd, fey smile spread across her fine, withered features. She lay back upon her pillows and closed her eyes. The unmistakable acrid smell of fresh urine rose to meet the nostrils of the two astonished men.

"Sire, she has uttered nary a sound since we left Berwick. Her gaolers said her mind turned when she was caged. They were pleased enough for her to leave." Bishop Wishart spoke with great sadness, for the onset of madness was a terrible blight on one so brave and full of life. In retreating so far from her world, Isobel would require care for the rest of her life. *It might have been kinder if she had died,* Robert thought, but was doused almost immediately by another massive wave of guilt. As one does when one is overwhelmed and can never rightly make amends, he arranged for her to be taken to her family in Fife, effectively removing her far from his sight. The bishop would go on to his home, what was left of it, in Glasgow. Apart from paying for the care of these two damaged individuals, there was nought else he could do. At least with Marjorie and Mary, perhaps, over time, he could rebuild their shattered lives.

One further, sobering aspect of this reunion concerned Robert's nephew, Donald, Earl of Mar. The young sixteen-year-old was included in this exchange, but, upon reaching Newcastle, declined to go any further and returned to Edward II's retinue at York. It was obvious to all the young earl remained under the English king's sway since having been placed in his household at a tender age, following his capture at the Battle of Methven and six months imprisonment at Bristol Castle. *Another cruel blow to Kirsty,* thought Robert, as he leapt upon his horse and rode across the rocky shallows of the ford, home to Scotland. His men noted his obdurate expression and stayed well clear. Disloyalty within the royal family was not to be borne lightly. It would be up to his queen to soothe him this time and use all her wiles to restore his temper.

England

Priory of Sixhills

October 1314

In shock, Kirsty sat down upon a nearby stool. Brother Robert had just delivered the most astounding news. She was to be ransomed for some English knights and was to leave for London under escort in a few days. From there, she would go by land and ship, home. Home to Scotland! It was beyond belief – a miracle! They were in the prioress's office, to which Kirsty had been called with some urgency. The prioress herself was in the infirmary for her indigestion grew worse. Unable to eat and with a distended stomach, her days on this earth were numbered. Aethelrida tended her as if she were her own mother. The monk watched as the news filtered through the miasma of shock. It was the first time he had seen Kirsty since the Scots' victory at Bannockburn. He thought again of the death of Walter Ross; another promising man cut down in his prime by the hideous war. At least now, Kirsty could return home, for he knew how much she had suffered during her time at St Mary's.

Kirsty rose. "I must tell Aethelrida," she cried. A fleeting look of sadness touched her eyes.

"Ah yes, Gwladys," mused the monk, as he gazed out of the narrow window at the murky autumn day.

Kirsty turned on her heel. "Why call her by that name?"

"Of course, ye do not know. Sit ye down, for it will be as well if ye hear her story." Kirsty settled back upon the stool and looked up at the monk whom she had come to trust.

"Many years back, a babe was brought here by the soldiers of old King Edward. She was removed from her mother after her birth and a wet nurse found until she could be weaned. The prioress named her Aethelrida, a good Saxon name, but her birth name had been Gwladys: she was, *is*, a princess of Wales. Her father, Dafydd, grandson of the great Llewellyn, Prince of Wales, was executed; her brothers imprisoned in Bristol Castle. Gwladys does not know of any life but this one, and believes herself to be English. It would serve only to cause her immense and unalterable pain if she knew otherwise. She is doomed to spend the rest of her life here, for she is as much a prisoner as ye are, *or were*, but she knows it not." Brother Robert spoke the latter as he saw the indignant, angry bile rise in Kirsty at the appalling injustice done to her friend.

"Why tell me this now?" she demanded, her voice rough and broken, choked with tears.

"Because it is important to understand how immeasurably lucky ye are, to have a family and a home. Just know there are many tragedies in this world and yours is, but one. Let the bitterness fester and it will poison the rest of your life. Think well on this. Leave your anger here. Do not take it home as part of your baggage. I wish ye well, my child."

With that, Brother Robert shook his head as if to release himself from the bonds of knowledge. It was no wonder he had chosen the benign sanctuary of the priory leaving behind the harsh cruelty of the outside world. He rose, loosening his stiff limbs as he did so, and placed his hand upon Kirsty's bowed head. A whispered blessing crossed his lips. His task complete, he turned and without a backward look, ducked beneath the arched doorway and disappeared down the darkened corridor to the infirmary. The sound of his leather sandals slapping against the stone flags receded into the distance. Kirsty sat, stunned. There was so much to take in all at once. She glanced up at the bent, agonised figure of the Christ on the cross. It left her cold. A bleak residue of pain crossed her flushed face. Anger was futile, she saw that now.

In time, her breathing became more regular. Sadness and joy mingled in a solitary, painful heartbeat.

Slowly, she rose. A stray shaft of bleak sunlight entered the chamber through a narrow window niche. Dust motes, stirred by her rough woollen habit sweeping the floor, danced upwards and were caught in her vision. So little, and yet so much, had happened to her here. Only nebulous shadows of her past remained. Could she ever put it behind her? When the chapel bells began to toll, Kirsty started from her reverie. She rubbed her chilled hands together. A slow, secret smile lit up her fine, strained features. Shivering with anticipation, she departed the empty chamber. Before her, the vaulted, stone-walled corridor stretched out into the darkness.

Kirsty took several tentative steps through the narrow opening between the heavy oak gates. A malodorous, damp smell hung in the air from the nearby drains. Beneath her coarse woollen cape, the wind teased her hair, now streaked with plentiful strands of grey. Overhead, thick white clouds drifted, tarried and hurried on, causing shadows to cross her face. At any moment, Kirsty expected someone to run after her and draw her back into the walled confines of the priory's large cobbled courtyard. Her legs felt soft and boneless. Her breath caught in her throat. Ragged, hot gasps seared the chill air. On the rough road outside, a litter bearing the royal emblem of England waited to carry her to the Tower in far-off London. From one prison to another, she thought and frowned. Would Brother Robert have lied to her? Mistrust and doubt had been her constant companions for so long. It would take some time for that habit to leave her.

She shook her head, forcing herself to believe well of the monk's cheerful goodness of spirit, for he had shown her much kindness over the past years. Bright tears scalded the back of her eyes and blurred her vision. Kirsty raised a pale hand to her face and smoothed the pulse beating erratically at the apex of her temple. Over to her left on a hill, she managed to make out the sharp towers of Lincoln Cathedral piercing the Lincolnshire sky. The last time she had seen them had been eight years ago when she arrived hollow with fear and shame.

Now, she tasted freedom, and sniffed at it on the air like an animal released from its pen. The irony was not lost upon her. For a fleeting moment, the sun emerged. The vivid clarity of light startled her eyes, so used were they to the shadows of her stone-walled chamber, whose vaulted ceiling was now replaced by the panorama of the sky. Kirsty stretched her head back to look well upon it. Indeed, it was a most glorious sight! As if on cue, she heard the sound of the monks singing the requiem mass for the prioress. Their monotone voices lifted, blended and soared. Pulling her heavy cloak about her, Kirsty breathed deep to quell the sick, fluttery feeling in the pit of her stomach. Then, tapping into a half-forgotten well of fortitude, she straightened her back and walked purposefully forward.

Orkney

October 1314

It was fortunate for Margaret Bruce that she had time to come to terms with the details of her betrothal. A brief missive arrived some months earlier from her brother advising she was to marry a knight of his choice, Sir William de Carlyle. His family were well known in the Annandale area and lived not far from her grandfather's castle at Lochmaben. Robert reassured Margaret that Sir William was a man of honour. He hoped the couple would act as guardians in the south for him to watch out for dissension in Galloway. Anxious flickers of fear began to niggle at her mind's edge and a faint coil of nausea unravelled within her belly. There was an unwritten proviso to this betrothal. It would only go ahead as planned, if both Robert and Sir William were still alive after the battle to be held against the English.

Strategy and statesmanship had been on Robert's mind in making his selection and he failed to mention if her betrothed were young or handsome, essential facts, which might have softened the news. For now, Margaret would have to trust her brother had her best interests at heart, but she cursed his single-mindedness nonetheless.

To Margaret's utter relief, the Bruce-led Scottish forces defeated their vast enemy. The waiting was over. Now they were going home! Margaret was overjoyed at the prospect of seeing her kinfolk once more for Kirsty, Mary, Marjorie and Elizabeth had returned from their years of harsh confinement. After these many years, to lay eyes once more upon her brothers as well as Mathilda – and meet her sister's children for the first time – was beyond belief. So much had been taken from them that could never be regained. In every respect, it was a jubilant but achingly poignant time.

On the day of their departure, the small group boarded the rolling galley out in the bay. They were wet through already; waves crested in from the western ocean and the small fishing boat, which had taken them out to the larger ship, struggled to get past the early breakers. With difficulty, the brawny Hammerclett men hoisted on board the various trunks and boxes using a system of pulleys. Squawking gulls flew above them and a sleek pod of white-nosed dolphins breasted the waves.

Floraidh and Bethoc fussed about Meg, as if she were a chick to be petted and kept warm. The child was on edge and fractious. Orkney was the only home she had ever known and she did not want to leave. Her blond hair blew about her open features, obscuring the deep anxiety within her expressive blue eyes. The experience held a sense of unreality for the ten-year-old child and the many goodbyes proved overwhelming. Feeling disconnected from the events occurring around her, Meg relished Floraidh's mothering all the more, clinging to her like a wee sea creature to a wave-swept rock.

Ellen, on the other hand, was much older. Scotland held a faint resonance within her, but resentment and yearning vied for purchase as she tried to imagine seeing her mother again after all these years. She knew they had left Kildrummy for their own safety, but she could never fully comprehend how her mother could have sent her away. Obtusely, she believed she must have done something terribly wrong to have brought on such a rejection, but no memory remained of her dreadful misdemeanours. For so long, doubt and sadness had been her constant unwanted companions.

When the galley heaved in response to the swell, an agonised cry rose above the crisp slap of the waves. Asgeirr's hand lay crushed between two trunks, which had slid along the deck, their weight adding to the force of impact. In immediate response, Floraidh delved within her hemp bag, producing a container of salve and a small roll of linen. As she bandaged his damaged fingers together in a makeshift splint, Asgeirr grimaced with pain, watched over by his brothers. After the family's recent ill-treatment of the healer, the men managed a few shamefaced words of thanks, before the fishing boat returned to shore. The women waved farewell, grateful as ever for the men's help. In readiness for their departure, they settled against the smooth, tarred wood of the ship's frame, to look back in earnest.

On the shore, the small community of brooding, grim-faced figures gathered in silent farewell. Aodh stood side by side with the sturdy members of the Grutgar family. Tucked in beside him, Heidrun nursed her new babe, well-swaddled against the brisk wind. The former scullion boy of Kildrummy was torn, unsure of how to feel now his Scottish 'family' was leaving him behind. His future lay with his pretty young wife here on Orkney and he placed a protective arm around Heidrun's warm, rounded body. She smiled up at him, relief evident across her broad, rosy features that he remained true to his word. Not far along the beach, a hound nosed at several bloated cod whose eyes reflected the pale, milky sky. Further along, a flurry of clamorous terns fought over the remains of a strange sea creature. With its grey-brown tail, long and whip-like, the speckled, angled form lay stranded amidst the uneven line of sandy froth. All had been washed ashore in a blow some nights back. Now, a salty reek rose upon the air. Aodh willingly took in a great whiff and smiled to himself. It was rich and ripe and real, and smelt of home.

The Baikie family stood upon the low cliffs. Maud raised a hand to her face, brushing away tears which rolled down the natural crevices of her lined cheeks. In an effort to lessen the tension, Caillean and Coinneach began to wrestle each other and edged over towards Senga and Astrid, who stood off to one side. Walter spoke sharply to the lads, but his words fell upon deaf ears until Father Anselm cuffed both boys with a beefy hand. This had a far more salutary effect. They fell into a heap and he hoisted them up by their ears, almost banging their heads together in their process.

Off to one side, Drustan stared out into the hazy bay, barely making out the ship as it dipped in the swell, resolute in the knowledge God would take good care of his friends. He had come back for the family's farewell dinner and to begin work on the bishop's chapel. As the thought entered his mind, he looked over to his right and was heartened to see some young men hard at work, digging the sodden foundations; much needed to be done before the winter gales roared in. He sensed his presence would be required, for there was a notable lack of enthusiasm on the part of the adults in the community. He sighted Marthoc coming along the path with the female members of the Hammerclett family and was pleased she had showed some generosity of spirit with the softening of her grief over Camran's death. She had attended the farewell dinner, managing a few brief words to Margaret as she warmly hugged the younger girls. Floraidh received a silent, firm nod. Time alone would heal this wound.

As the ship ventured forth towards the headlands, Margaret looked back towards her home of the past eight years. The dear forms of her companions were a distant blur. Skaill House was visible; its low bulk nestled into the landscape. Amidst the lush pasture, the cows shrank to mere black dots and the stubbled fields, empty now of their harvest, glinted soft gold in the patchy sunlight. Peat smoke rose above the homes in curling swirls, dissipating with the gusty breeze. There were so many memories, mostly happy, they had shared with the occupants of the longhouses scattered around the bay. The seasonal celebrations, registering the changes in the life of this small community, had brought much joy, as did the many trips around the islands with Maud. High overhead, an enormous skua and several black-backed gulls breasted the wind. The honking cries of geese floated high above them. Entranced, Floraidh looked up. In true arrow formation, the large-bellied birds, now distant grey-brown smudges, flew south with strong, rhythmic beats. With a quick, bright smile, she nodded at Margaret who also saw the significance in nature's sign. The galley rose and swayed. Soon, only the green headlands on either side of them remained in fleeting sight.

Margaret's heart skipped several beats. High on the cliff top to her left, she glimpsed the huddled, solitary form of Hodlvis. She was inordinately pleased that he had come to bid her farewell; his absence duly noted from all the village celebrations. She raised her arm, registering as she did so a sharp spasm of regret. Wretched and alone on the headland, the young man returned the bleak, wounded gesture.

Leaving the relative protection of the small bay, the galley breasted the fast-running currents of the open sea. Straining on ropes and oars, the crew shouted to one other. The thick sail snapped taut with a loud crack as it caught the wind. A shock of frigid water cascaded over the deck and Margaret's attention was drawn immediately to Ellen and Meg. The passengers withdrew to the sparse wooden shelter at the back of the boat, huddling within their sodden cloaks. Clutching her limp rag doll to her chest, Meg began to cry, heartbreak melding with sheer terror. With its thick sails outstretched, the ship powered along.

A great plume of spindrift covered them once again and the dear, familiar landscape of Skaill was no more. With the ever-present danger of tidal roosts and the many submerged skerries along the coastline, the galley headed to deeper, safer waters. On the shore, many prayed the great sea monster would spare these dear folk and that the Sea Mither would calm the wilful seas.

It would be many years before the bishop's church would be completed and, even then, little would change. The small community would make welcome the gentle, red-haired priest into their midst. Joyfully would he partake of many platters of fish and stovies at their table and grace the local weddings and funerals with his presence.

As for centuries past, the villagers would cherish their ancient beliefs. On dark, driech evenings, songs would be sung and tales told with wide-eyed relish. In time-honoured fashion, the changing seasons would be acknowledged. As always, the honest, hard-working villagers would walk with studied, gentle care amidst the bones of their ancestors and the fairy folk of the knowes. All would be well in Skaill.

Norway

Bergen

November 1314

Dearest Mathilda,

Rob's letter brought such joy and relief. Effie and the king joined with me in a quiet celebration. Kettil gave a thrilling, firsthand account. Haakon was most impressed with Robert's battle strategies and our men have been rewarded with land hereabouts. For the huskarls who lost their lives, I visited their families and will support them with land and money, though this will never compensate for the loss of their sons. The lads' fathers were pleased they died in battle and are now in Valhalla at Thor's great drinking hall – a warrior's version of heaven. Wrought with sadness and pain, the faces of their mothers told a far different tale. As ever, war wreaks a harsh, punishing toll upon the living.

Though many lives were lost, Rob succeeded in his endeavour to win against England. So long has he fought and conspired against all odds. Grandfather's spirit may well have cause to smile. Our brothers are still alive, and for that I give thanks, but of late we have endured much sadness here.

When the men returned, I had not long come back from my trip to the island of Oland. Some months earlier, Inga sent word she had lost her babe. Duke Valdemar has been away plotting in the south. As would be expected, he is a warrior and has little time or inclination to provide her with the care she needs. Inga was hurt by this, but will get used to it in time. Cruelly, his councillors tell her she must work harder to produce an heir when the duke returns from his duties. When she succeeds, they say, he will shower her with wealth. It is not wealth she needs, but his support and understanding. As so often happens, Inga's babe came too soon and she is filled with guilt she did something ill-conceived and harmful. The shame that she cannot fulfil her duty is overwhelming. Over the course of my visit, we talked much about this for my trials were similar. Strangely, this dreadful hardship brings us closer together. I knew how much I missed Mother and wanted to be there for my own daughter.

By now, our kinfolk have been released. I am in dire need awaiting this joyful news.

Your loving sister

Isa

Scotland

Dingwall Castle

November 1314

Dearest Isa,

At last, they are free! Accompanied by old Bishop Wishart, now blind and infirm, Marjorie and Elizabeth were shipped from Hull to Newcastle where they collected Mary, newly-released from the great fortress. From there, they sailed to Berwick to gather Isobel of Buchan and onwards, under guard, by litter to the border. Robert was most impatient and insisted he be there to greet them when they stepped back upon Scottish soil. Sadly, our brother came back shaken and humiliated. Many pitfalls lie ahead, for Marjorie is as cold and silent as a wraith and Mary, on occasions, cannot hold back her hot, spiteful bile. Eight years is a long time to have nurtured deep grudges. Much to our dismay, Donald refused to leave England and remains at the English king's vile court. Rob railed at the lad's ill-chosen action, but has no power to alter this nor could he shield Kirsty from the pain of this most dire betrayal. Through all these added traumas, Elizabeth holds steadfast in her support and love for Robert. It will be the saving of our brother.

Poor Isobel of Buchan has lost her wits and no longer speaks. Imprisoned within her cage at Berwick Castle, she paid a high price for her loyalty. Rob was appalled. Once again, he rages at the old lion and his vindictive punishments. They achieved the effect Edward wanted – to injure and maim in the short as well as long-term. Elizabeth has passed her prime for having children so this is injurious in itself to Rob – he sorely needs an heir, particularly with his poor health. In haste, I travelled to Stirling Castle and saw them as they arrived home.

Mary is much changed. Her hair is white; her skin wrinkled and mottled-brown. Being exposed as she was in all seasons, she tried to keep her face from getting chapped in the wind and cold and could only use the grease which congealed on her food to rub upon her skin. It worked for a while, until she grew fearful of rats gnawing upon her during the night. Her knuckles and joints are perpetually swollen and sore, and some of her fingers are misshapen. I wonder if she will ever be able to ride again; not that I disclosed my thoughts, for it is her greatest wish she will hunt once more. Little by little, she talks about her ordeal and made mention of the kindness of a Welsh soldier. After all the butchery of the past months, I expect the young man is dead.

Our sister is much quieter and gives the appearance of being kinder, but I think it is more that she only occasionally offers an opinion, used as she is to silence. Towards Robert, she can be quite caustic and understandably lacks compassion for all he has suffered and achieved. I believe in time she may thaw, but until then we take great care about what we say within her hearing. It is not wise to make mention of anything positive in the past for there is much our sister has missed out upon. I made the mistake of complaining irritably of tiredness after William had been up all night with the heaving sickness. My maids have it as well. Mary took me to task in front of Elizabeth and some visiting noblewomen. I was lucky to have a child and a family, she said; it was my choice to have him and so on. Her voice was low, filled with icy, bitter shards which were meant to wound. You could cut the air with a dirk, but Mary carried on her acrimonious tirade regardless. Elizabeth commanded her to leave the chamber. Thankfully, she did. It seems she has some respect for our queen. I was furious, mortified at such a public shaming. It distressed me as well, for our sister has suffered so cruelly. At times, you can look into her eyes and see she is lost somewhere in a dark vale filled with sorrow and regret and unfathomable pain.

One of Mary's most devoted followers is Sir Neil Campbell, a widower with two adult sons. Do you recall him at all? A gruff, silent man, he is tall, almost saturnine in appearance. Robert is considering betrothing Mary to him for his devotion and loyalty. I have a sneaking suspicion our brother wishes to move Mary on, so the tension can ease at Stirling. Our sister may be agreeable to this betrothal. She is keen to make up for lost time. No match was made before because of her outspoken ways and she often rejected her suitors. She could outride most men and in many instances was far braver, though some saw this more as merely reckless behaviour. Of course, men often faltered in their pursuit after hearing her forthright opinions of them. Then the war came. Sir Neil knows her of old and feels immense compassion for her ordeal. A woman who does not chatter constantly would suit him well. Yes, Rob may be right. The match may work.

By comparison, Marjorie is distant, removed from all of us. Though she has the physique of a woman, she gives the appearance of a wounded animal and is deathly pale and thin. She startles easily as if ready to dart off into a glade for safety at any sharp sound. With Robert, her silence has chilly undertones, which makes those near at hand feel uncomfortable. Often, she is vague and hard to engage in conversation. Confined to her cell, she had little in the way of human companionship. The nuns, her gaolers, spoke only of how worthless she must be for her father and countrymen to abandon her. These barbs wounded Marjorie's soul. The scars remain, perhaps forever.

The prioress at Watton boasted to Marjorie of an event in the past. One of the young novices there had lain with a lay worker at the nunnery. The couple tried to escape, but were captured. The nuns made the novice cut off the man's genitals; these, they stuffed in her mouth as punishment. Her lover died and the girl lost her babe. One of the monks declared it a miracle, saying God had removed her sin. Marjorie told Elizabeth she was terrified of the nuns after that. She believed them to be monsters! Constantly cold, underfed and lacking stimulation, she retreated within her mind. Now, she finds it hard to deal with noise, especially laughter. Young Sir Walter Stewart, son of the Steward, is being considered as a husband, which would strengthen the link between our families. Hugh said it is too much to ask of him, but it seems he is an ambitious young man, keen to become the king's son-in-law with all the status and monetary gain this would bring him. At the same time, I can see he would be a gentle husband. Lord knows, he would need to be!

Regards Elizabeth, you will recall I have not known her as an adult, but remember Kirsty speaking of her kindly. She always saw herself as Rob's equal. Apart from grief over the enforced separation and the normal process of aging, Elizabeth is much her old self: not having experienced the same level of hardship or deprivation as the others did, nor was she demeaned in any way, thus preserving her identity and status.

I wager being the daughter of the powerful Earl of Ulster would have provided ample protection from any ill-treatment.

Some time back, I mentioned Christina of Gamoran and her child to Rob. I wondered how our brother might handle this situation. Elizabeth told me Rob made reference to it soon after her return. He did not want her to hear it from others and gave an account of himself, poorly no doubt. At least he has not set Elizabeth aside as so often happens. Never one to shirk from a difficult task, she asked for Christina to be invited here, so she could personally thank her for looking after her husband so well whilst she, the queen, was unable to do so! The young lad will also be acknowledged. How galling it must be for her *and* for Christina! All know Elizabeth is desperate to have a child, an heir for Robert. I pray it happens soon. I am not sure if Rob feels humiliated or relieved at Elizabeth's sound response. There will be no secrets between them, she said.

Some weeks past, Kirsty arrived at Stirling Castle with Bishop Lamberton. She is much changed in looks and is quite frail. I want to take her home and feed her till she bursts. Now, she enjoys a constant supply of her favourite treats. Overtime, she may well fill out.

It is quite curious! Kirsty seems different to how I remember her. Her spirit is somehow deeper. She spoke of her immense fondness for two people, exceptional it seems in their compassion: a nun named Aethelrida and a monk, Robert Mannying. Without them, she says, she would have wholly lost her mind. Of Hugh's brother, Walter, who died at Bannockburn, she was most sad, for it was through his efforts she learnt what was happening to us all.

Donald's public rejection of his family and country distresses Kirsty, but she took it in her stride given her son's peculiar streak, which she has never understood in its entirety. I am relieved she accepts my marriage to Hugh, a matter about

411

which I was most anxious. Mary was not so benign and, I fear, she and Hugh (and Isabella) will have a rocky time of it. Neither Marjorie nor Mary will ever accept the Ross family, of that I am sure.

With the family reunited, Robert lost no time in seeking redress from our enemy. The royal court travelled south through Tynedale and Redesdale where our brother took tribute from the burghers and accepted, through considerable intimidation, the submission of all notables in the area. Even the pompous prelates at Durham submitted which caused much glee amongst the Scots. Robert believed this insult might bring Edward II to the negotiating table, but the fool remains ensconced in London, oblivious to the misery of his people. With this lack of response, Rob commanded his troops to resume the pillaging of the north of England. Revenge was sweet for those who witnessed the ravages of imprisonment upon our female kinfolk. They returned to Stirling laden with goods and livestock, whilst the sumpter ponies had their panniers filled with gold and silver coins.

Rob has been left scratching his head at the importune behaviour of the English king. How can a monarch behave in such a cavalier manner towards his subjects? It is said he blames the northern lords for their failure to support him at Stirling, and thus leaves them to defend their own territories. Of course, our hothead of a brother, Edward, is keen to continue waging war, threatening England from all quarters. Rob desires only peace, but knows it must come at a price.

While most of the household travelled south, Kirsty and I went north. She was desperate to be reunited with her children and I missed my own bairns. Not long after our return, Margaret, Ellen and Meg arrived home from Orkney with Floraidh and Bethoc. What a challenging time it has been for all of us! I am sure Kirsty will share her thoughts with you. Margaret is to be married soon to William de Carlyle. His family are loyal adherents. You might recall Torthorwold Castle lies not far from Lochmaben. She is on tenterhooks to meet him.

It has taken me so long to write this missive I must now add a postscript. Mary is to marry Sir Neil who has returned from England. She and Margaret will have a double wedding at Stirling before year's end. If only you could be here, as well. Please, please try!

Mathilda

Scotland

Stirling Castle

November 1314

Isa, dear heart,

How I longed to share with you the terrible events of the past years. In my mind, I wrote a thousand letters or more to you. My heart revels in its new-found freedom, but I am fearful of it as well! You would find me much changed, but my greatest wish is to leave the past behind, where it belongs. I would speak with you, though, and plead with you to come home, as it seems you did some years back now. Isa, there is much sadness and bitterness amidst our shattered family. We need your strength and healing presence.

Your loving sister
Kirsty

Scotland

Stirling Castle

November 1314

There had been no reply from Isa. Mathilda and Kirsty began to wonder if their letters lay at the bottom of the ocean. It was a complete surprise then, when news came from Dunfermline Abbey – a galley bearing the royal flag of Norway lay at anchor in the Firth of the Forth. Robert immediately sent forth a message of welcome and provided a large escort. In the castle's Great Hall, the talk was excited – brisk and raw. Emotions ran high. When the escort clattered into the bailey, a crowd of family and well-wishers surrounded them. In the distance, the rounded tops of the Ochil Hills lay covered in a thick white veil, which drifted towards Stirling. Before long, sleet peppered the crowd.

As Isa's litter came to a halt, she almost fell from it – in relief or exhaustion none knew which – into the arms of her sisters, Kirsty and Mary. Behind them, the king and queen waited for this deviation from protocol to take its natural course. There were so many to greet. Isa knelt before her brother as he introduced her to his queen. Setting all formalities aside, he hugged his most beloved sister, long and hard.

"Welcome home, your grace!" was all that could be heard before the cheers of the crowd echoed again and again around the walled enclosure.

Thronged by her family, Kirsty linked arms with Isa and drew her into the warmer precincts of the large tower. Twenty-one years had passed since they last set eyes upon each other.

Days passed filled with talk and laughter. In time, Kirsty sought the quiet sanctuary of her chamber; Isa's arrival had brought immense joy and exhilaration, but much sadness for all the years lost to them. As she bathed and dressed for the banquet, there was a knock at the studded oak door. It was Isa whom she bade enter. Almost immediately, the sisters fell into a comfortable silence.

Isa sat upon the large curtained bed and began to smooth out the counterpane of furs. "Do you remember Kirsty, how you used to comb my hair?" she quizzed.

"Aye, but perhaps it be your turn now!" quipped Kirsty, half-smiling. Slowly and with great care, Isa began to comb her sister's long tresses, now heavily salted with wiry strands of grey. In the mirror before them, they glimpsed two women who had lost the blush of youth – one, far more so than the other, ravaged as she was by life's cruel hand.

"I feel so lost." Kirsty spoke at last. With a thin, veined hand, she wiped away a stream of tears. "My bairns are strangers to me. Donald rejects me outright and remains in the court of that royal catamite. For him to turn his back on us all and willingly serve our enemy food and drink – and do who knows what else – makes me want to rage at the injustice of it all. Ellen is cool to my overtures. Meg is frightened of me – I must look at her with such pathetic earnestness. I want to devour her, body and soul, but, in truth, she does not ken me from Eve. She runs to Floraidh or Mathilda whenever I come near. How could my own daughters be so fearful of me? It will take me years to overcome this most cruel disservice, done to me and mine. How could it all turn out this way, Isa? We were so young and full of hope at Turnberry." Kirsty began to wail like a small child frightened of the dark. Isa said nothing. Instead, she knelt down and gathered her dearest sister into her arms. Kirsty's brittle shoulders shook with each anguished sob.

In one of the larger solars, there was quite a gathering with the female kin of the Bruce household and their maids. Much needed to be done, for the joint wedding of Mary and Margaret would take place within a few weeks and the wedding gowns were yet to be completed.

Two long trestles stood by the windows to capture as much light as possible, for the day was dull. Heavy clouds filled the sky and rain pattered on the glass. To reduce the damp chill, the women tucked woollen rugs about their legs. Placed centrally on the tables were woven reed baskets, filled with sharp spring shears; a selection of the finest whalebone needles and pins; large rolls of thread and voluminous lengths of gold and silver braid. The vaulted chamber was a hive of activity. A steady low buzz of talk, punctuated by the occasional burst of laughter, added to this impression.

At one trestle the maids were getting acquainted, but with some difficulty. Seonaid sat alongside Bethoc. Both originally from Scotland, they spoke Gaelic, but had not used it in years and Seonaid was fluent in Norn from her time in Orkney. Newly arrived from Dingwall, Janet and Mirin, Mathilda's maids, were Gaelic speakers whilst Hilda and Rannveig could speak only Norse.

Mirin was an especially fine seamstress. It was she who organised the cutting out of the material. Pieces of the embossed cream silk lay here and there on the trestles. Each had their sections to sew together and then the panels would be fitted as one. Bethoc spoke in Norse to Isa's maids about their journey.

"Ya! The trip was bearable. It was impossible to sleep, and the food almost inedible," Hilda said, "but no pirates this time!" The blond, buxom lasses were a lusty pair, but drew the line at being ill-used by a ship's crew or sold as slaves in some trader's market in the Far East. Both women had their eye on the captain of Isa's vessel with his warrior's face and muscular body, though Murchadh was also receiving some interest. Seonaid looked up at the mention of her husband's name and gave a contented smile. At long last, after the traumas of the past year, she felt happy and settled. Though she now spent much of her time at sea, it bothered her little. Life was too short for them, both now in their later years, to be apart, she stated in her calm, steady voice. Bethoc bent her head as if to concentrate on a particularly difficult stitch.

Kirsty stood up to stretch her legs. She wandered over to the wooden benches, upon which lay mounds of fur trim and an airy bundle of lace. It was hard to resist the folds of velvet that lay upon the trestle and she lifted some up to her cheek, enjoying their plush warmth. How different were they from the rough, greasy homespun at Sixhills. She brought her mind back to the present. These were destined for gowns or cloaks and in a glorious array of colour. Indigo would suit Mary whilst the burnished copper was her own choice. Mathilda, she knew, favoured the deep forest green and the rose-gold would look well against Margaret's dark hair. Knowing that choice was still limited in Scotland, Isa had brought a wide range of fabrics, purchased in Bergen from a Byzantine trader. In addition, she carried with her a leather-bound manuscript with descriptions of the latest styles on the continent. Earlier, the younger women had pored over these with fascination, whilst the older ones laughed at the impracticality of the outlandish headgear.

At the remaining trestle, the Bruce women were busy decorating the bodices. Fine, silvery pearls were being attached to one whilst the other was to have an overlay of Flemish lace. Kirsty sat down next to Isa. Opposite them, Ellen nestled between Mathilda and Margaret, whilst Elizabeth and Mary shared a comfortable settle close to the hearth. In the cold, Mary's joints pained her and the heat helped a great deal. The queen, of course, required the choicest position as her status required. In a companionable silence, the two women watched as the flames flared and sank with the wind's soft breath. Elizabeth was keen to draw Mary back into a more loving relationship with her brother and sought to do this by offering friendship. It required considerable subtlety on her part, to make sense of painful events and emotions whilst encouraging a more malleable, softer focus to evolve. Not all were convinced of this, but it was worth a try.

These sociable activities were a boon to Kirsty, for she could observe Ellen without having to converse with her directly. She tried hard to fight the sour, peevish feelings she felt towards Margaret and Mathilda, and chided herself – how thankful she should be that her daughter had been nurtured and loved instead of spending her youth languishing in a cold prison like poor, damaged Marjorie. The latter was asked to attend of course, but sent her apologies. Her head ached, she said, and she wished to rest. One only had to compare Ellen's healthy glow and easy, sometimes sad, smile, with Marjorie's bleak unhappiness and flat disinterest in any social contact.

Ellen would make a lovely bride when the time was right, Kirsty mused, on a brighter note. Already, Robert was considering the options for her. Isa scoffed at this for in Norway, as a widow, she organised her own daughter's betrothal – in line with the king's wishes of course. But Scotland remained a strongly feudal and conservative country. Always there were challenges and the king wished to repay loyalty, sought to build kinship networks and position his strongest adherents in the most strategic parts of the country. For his niece, he was considering the son of the Earl of Mentieth, whose centrally-placed lands would be most useful. He felt a spark of compassion for the earl with his involvement in Wallace's capture, during a time when all of the Scots' lords had returned to the English king's peace. In reality, they all must share his shame, but, as king, Robert's greatest desire was to unify the country and, where possible, heal the hurts of the past. Kirsty understood this and approved of the choice, but Mary had argued long and hard against the decision.

Floraidh entered with several servitors bringing ale for the maids and mead for the ladies. She had been in the castle's morning room mixing much-needed lotions. On a wooden tray she carried silver goblets, a horn container of her powerful sea-wrack potion and a green-glazed bowl filled to the brim with one of her salves. She crossed to Mary and the queen, neatly stepping over Isa's companion, Frith, dozing on a mottled deer hide on the stone flags. In fright, the small canine let out a yap and snapped at her ankle, almost causing her to drop the tray. Mary flinched and cried out in alarm for she could no longer withstand sharp sounds or unexpected intrusions. Isa called out with warm reassurance, both to her sister and the pup. The latter stretched her small, white puffball of a body and plodded over to sit beside her mistress's fur-lined sealskin boots. Isa smiled sweetly at the healer, knowing how much the latter disliked her touchy little companion.

Floraidh had convinced the queen her health potion might act as an aid to fertility. Elizabeth and Mary were both disconcerted at what lay ahead of them. They downed a sizeable mouthful, grimaced and, before drawing breath, washed it down with sweet, honeyed mead.

In front of the settle, the healer placed a wooden stool. As she sat down, wiry grey hair fell across her wrinkled beak of a face. A look of grave compassion crossed her features, wizened with age and experience. Nonetheless, she proceeded to massage the joints in Mary's hands and feet. Though helpful in the long run, Mary winced; the vigorous process was painful, but she flashed a grateful smile.

Having experienced their long period of imprisonment, Mary and Elizabeth were close now. Indeed, they had much in common and had not long returned from visiting Lady Isobel in Fife. Dismayed and saddened were they, for Isobel's health had worsened. She no longer ate nor drank of her own volition. Without constant care, it would only be a matter of time before death claimed her for its own. Though each had suffered at the hands of the English, the visit rendered them speechless once more at the cruelty inherent in their punishments. When the family was all together, happily, like now, the former captives felt privileged to be alive. For Mary, it had not always been so.

A great clamour of hooves on cobblestones and the jangling, metallic clink of bridles broke the peace. A large group of men rode at speed into the bailey through the heavy oak gates. Guards called out greetings. Hens and geese flew into the air, squawking and honking. Children squealed with excitement. Elizabeth looked up with interest, but made no effort to move. She had been expecting the return of the king from his parliament at Cambuskenneth. Margaret leant out of the window, keen to gain a view of her betrothed. Sir William de Carlyle was younger than she, of medium height and build with a cheerful, open face framed by an untidy thatch of dark hair. At their first meeting, Will charmed her, thankfully, and she now looked forward to their union; all thoughts of Hodlvis banished to a quiet corner of her mind.

Soon after, a servitor thumped up the stairwell. A knock sounded on the door of the solar. Despite his shortness of breath, the man blurted out his message, regardless of all those present. "Your grace, the king requests your presence now in your private chamber... and the healer, as well."

Kirsty and Isa exchanged looks of concern, whilst Elizabeth rose, adjusting her hair and clothing as she did so. Floraidh left to gather her special lotions designed to soothe the red lesions and the unbearable itch suffered by the king. Invariably, his illness followed a similar pattern. Whenever life became too burdensome, worry would gnaw at his sleep. Then, a painful rash would flare, and all would suffer the lash of his tongue. His moods would slide into a deep pit of the darkest melancholy. The desire for food would leave him. Empty and weak, he would be bedridden thereafter for days.

As Elizabeth made her way down the stairwell, a crease deepened between her blue eyes. Normally she tried to conceal her worry. Now, she also felt a sense of disappointment and irritation for her husband's ill-health interfered with their private life. There was a sense of urgency about their lovemaking. She needed to have a babe soon, hopefully an heir. Time was running out. Even now, she doubted her body's capacity after all this time, but that did not stop her trying. With Rob's pain and discomfort, it might be weeks before they could start again. The physicians would bleed him, and he would be wan and tired. He was shamed as well by the ugly welts and thickened areas of skin, which scarred his body after each episode. It took great sensitivity on her part to deal with the physical as well emotional toll of the illness. She was tired too, for the effort drained her scant reserves. It seemed they were blocked at every turn.

One night in the Great Hall, after their trenchers had been cleared away, Isa and Kirsty relaxed alongside their siblings up at the high table. Somewhat flushed, a squire brought another jug from the large store of strong Gascon wine, courtesy of King Edward, spilling some upon the linen cloth; he had been enjoying himself far too much down in the cellars. Fortunately, the siblings' attention was focused elsewhere in recalling the family's happier times. Relieved, the squire took himself off, hoping for a quiet nap behind one of the large barrels.

Before returning to Norway, Isa desired above all else to visit her mother's grave. Kirsty admitted as much. It had been decades since they had been at Turnberry. Both began to consider whether it was possible to fit in a visit to their childhood home. Could it take place before the wedding, they quizzed, as the wish grew wings and took flight. Beside them, Elizabeth overheard the conversation. Surprising the sisters, she nudged Robert's elbow sharply enough for it to become dislodged from the table. He cursed the intrusion. Miles away in thought, he was frowning in concentration about a complaint brought to him earlier. *Like a hound with a bone,* Elizabeth mused to herself. Nevertheless, she reminded him both he and Edward had talked about visiting Turnberry when peace reigned. Regaining his composure, Robert nodded. A break from the affairs of state might do him good. Mary understood the castle would be in a poor state of repair, but the idea tugged at her imagination. Mathilda and Margaret joined the discussion. They had been infants when they left Turnberry. Visiting their mother's grave would be strange, but perhaps the experience might help to fill in the many gaps about their early life.

It was decided the entourage would ride south by the end of the week. If it were to be accomplished, there were to be neither children nor maids for that matter, with limited baggage to accompany them. Simplicity was the key. Many women would not have proceeded under these restrictions, but the Bruce sisters were a hardy lot and could do for themselves if need be. If truth be known, the protocols of court life irked them.

Elizabeth and Hugh chose to remain behind to greet any guests who might arrive early and to complete the final arrangements for the wedding, which was a mere ten days away. Given the strict time limitations, the journey would be made on horseback, though Mary might need a litter. Sir Neil proposed Mary could ride with him if she wished. All looked at Mary, believing she might take offence at this gallant offer, but she beamed. She felt sure she would be able to ride, as long as she could select her own horse. There would be no great stallion this time. A gentle, malleable mare would be just the thing, she said simply. This statement suggested a visible softening and acceptance on Mary's part; an important marker of change, acknowledged with relief by all present.

A courier went forthwith to Crossragruel Abbey to arrange short term hostelry. Located close to Turnberry, the abbey had strong links with the Earls of Carrick having been established by the siblings' great grandfather. The king requested his visit be low key, the purpose being a private family matter. Still, a small contingent would need to accompany them for safety.

After the dire treatment received from enemy soldiers during the years of turmoil, the abbey was now in need of substantial repair. Indeed, a number of monks died trying to prevent the library being fired; they were desperate to save the manuscripts stored there, some of which they had been working on for decades. Others had run off in fear, but now trickled back, demoralised, stricken by ill-health. The bishop selected another abbot and a small group of monks to take up residence. Fortunately, much of the richer paraphernalia necessary to the running of an abbey lay hidden from the enemy within the grounds. With the limited funds granted for its restoration, the beautiful old abbey might become habitable, but it would take many years to return it to its state of former glory. Much work was required with the programme to rebuild the library and the chapel. Over time, the gardens and the ponds would be reclaimed. In part, the lands around the abbey were still lying fallow. There were not enough lay workers now and war had interfered with the schedules of planting. Food was in short supply and the monks barely had enough to live on – a thin bowl of potage twice a day, a jug of ale and meat, rarely if ever – insufficient for the heavy labour required of them. Morale faltered, and the abbot rebuked the men for their lack of faith.

Standing in the ruins of the chapterhouse, the abbot scanned the formal request from the king. As he considered the appalling condition of the abbey and the substantial accommodation needs of this royal cohort, his gut began to churn. The desire to piddle was overwhelming. If he were honest with himself, he wanted to run; to head for the hills as fast as his gangly shanks would carry him. Beads of sweat formed on his shaven pate and he chewed at a brown-ridged nail, made ragged by his work in the vegetable gardens and old orchard. Absent-mindedly, he rubbed at his only habit; soiled as it was with food stains and muddy handprints; its hem rent in several places from collecting wild brambles.

Gradually, reason overcame panic and a course of action emerged. Enough cells were habitable, though the monks would have to sleep three to a cell. The kitchen and lavarium had been functioning for some weeks now. Of course, the refectory would need additional stools and extra bedding would be required. Turning to an assistant, the abbot wrote out an urgent request for a wagon-load of goods and victuals, and dispatched one of the younger monks to ride with haste to the much larger Paisley Abbey. He had no doubt help would be forthcoming; the two abbeys being the only Cluniac monasteries in Scotland.

A smile, totally lacking in guile, smoothed the lines of worry from the abbot's mottled features. Tension fell from his shoulders, and he rubbed his hands together gleefully. Surely this must be God's plan, for if King Robert saw their impoverished state and the awful disarray into which his ancestor's abbey had fallen, royal funds might be diverted towards the abbey's repair. It was the answer to all his prayers. Energised now, he hurried down to the fields to share the good news.

Turnberry Castle loomed dark against sea and sky. In the distance, the faint outline of Ailsa Craig's dome could be discerned. Staying at the abbey meant the visitors had to rise early to break their fast. Now, they rode through the early morning shadows to watch the sun breach the hills to the east of Turnberry. With the sound of hooves, a few of the farmers opened their cottage doors a crack and peered out; looks of alarm written across worn faces. To see women in the group brought instant relief. For so long, death and mayhem had followed the arrival of raiding parties. Closer to the castle, a cluster of heather-thatched huts, remnants of the old village, offered meagre protection. Small plots of ground had been dug over and a smattering of purple-tinged turnips lay grouped together. A child rushed out, grabbing a bony piglet rooting about in a bare enclosure, and ran inside. The door shut quickly behind him, locked and bolted no doubt. All that could be heard was the muffled squealing of the pig. There would be no easy welcome here. The contingent did not pause, but galloped on; to rein in where the old drawbridge had once crossed the dry moat, still a substantial land ditch but filled now with rubble. The villagers had been using it as a latrine and midden, for it was putrid with human and household waste.

Robert gathered his horse's reins and slid down slowly, as did most of the others. Kirsty and Isa paled at the sight of the broad-scale destruction. Their memories spoke of noble towers and formidable walls. The drone of flies accompanied Edward as he clambered down into the ditch and up the other side, kicking out of his way as he went, lumps of charred timber and fallen masonry. Before him, lay the remnants of the once massive drawbridge. Robert and Will de Carlyle followed in his wake. Mary was making her measured way with help from Sir Neil. Standing stock-still, Mathilda and Margaret were appalled that this great jumble of rubble and detritus had once been their home and could not even begin to imagine it in all its glory. Once inside the bailey, Isa and Kirsty made their way around to the chapel. Its roof was non-existent and the stones of its plastered walls bore blackened scars. Brambles grew over the stones covering their mother's grave, and her carved cross lay in pieces. Robert had brought his great axe with him and now began to hack at the trailing vine. Careful to avoid the spines, Will and Neil pulled away the covering and dragged it over to a mound of rubble off to one side. They busied themselves, clearing a space in the centre to make a fire.

Tears fell like warm rain down the chilled cheeks of the sisters. Here their mother had slept, alone and cold, for two decades past. Their memories held echoes of her infectious laughter, arising from the rich vein of amusement which ran through her. When she saw the humorous side of life, her brown eyes crinkled with warmth and joy. As if it were yesterday, the shock of her death still resonated. Ashen-faced, Robert and Edward turned away, silent in their grief, and made for the Great Hall, to see what was left of it. Sniffing loudly, Mary wiped a hand across her eyes. Kirsty picked up a stick and bent over, suddenly interested by what she had seen – something beside the grave. Tiny green shoots of bulbs were reaching for the light. Isa laughed and knelt down to get a closer look. She remembered planting them, she said. A rare patch of sunlight found them, for the sun had escaped the clouds momentarily. There was no warmth within its rays, but it was uplifting, as if their mother was somehow smiling down upon them from above.

Mary grew faint with the effort of the ride and the scramble up into the castle, and needed to rest. Neil busied himself arranging some logs into a seat of sorts. From his pocket, he pulled a flint. Soon, the tangled chunks of wood were ablaze, and Edward and Will returned to the horses to gather the saddlebags of food and wineskins. Thankfully, the monks had packed a generous range of victuals from the abbey kitchen: thick slices of roasted lamb and venison; capons basted with herbs; oaten bannocks and hunks of hard ewes' cheese; dried apples and pears, and handfuls of cobnuts and almonds added to the feast. Intent on devouring all they had brought, none spoke. The rhythmic sound of the ocean, laced with the arching cries of sea birds, provided a calming backdrop to the morning's clash with reality, whilst the wood smoke, mixed with crisp sea air, brought relief from the heavy, cloying smell of decay. With energies replenished, the siblings found their way into various castle doorways, as the atmosphere turned from melancholy to excited exploration.

The afternoon was spent exploring the remains of the castle. Many of the outbuildings, the doocot and the stable had been destroyed. The Great Hall had lost its massive roof, and an immense mound of stone and charred timber now lay where they once had shared family meals and danced. Surprisingly much remained intact, for the tower rooms had huge oak floors; the trees felled and milled before being shipped all the way from their southern estates. These had somehow survived the fires, a testament to their father who was determined to build a solid stronghold for his family. Now, they made their way up the turnpike stairs. Robert stopped abruptly. Frowning, he turned, barring the way to Kirsty and Isa. Skeletal forms and bones littered the stairwell and the chambers above. Scurrying creatures now laid claim to Turnberry Castle. Disappointed, the women made do with pointing out where their chambers had been in the upper reaches of the tower, overlooking the sea. Their father's solar was over there, they remembered. Below was the kitchen and launder room. None were moved to go down into the murky darkness of the great barrel-vaulted storerooms and dungeons. Who knew what they might find?

Margaret and Mathilda looked nonplussed, but were delighted all the same to hear tales of when they were tiny. How Margaret had tumbled down the turnpike stairs so often. And the time when it was thought Mathilda had toddled her way to the wharf's edge and fallen to her death in the oily waters. Instead, to the great consternation of the maids and the immense joy of their mother, the bairn was later found happily asleep in the stable amidst the hay and a mess of newborn puppies; the torment of wailing stopped and their mother danced merrily around the bailey with the grumpy, hay-strewn child in her arms.

With these thoughts uppermost, the women explored the old wharf, embedded deep within the castle's structure. With its narrow steps, worn with use and slippery now with green slime, the wharf lay within a huge natural cave. Its eternal occupant, the sea, rose and fell offering a gentle welcome indeed, and strange flickers of reflected light criss-crossed the vaulted shadows. The bitter taste of tar caught and lodged in tight throats. Old hemp ropes, with edges torn and ragged, lay limp like dead adders, wrapped around the old stone bollards. The rough walls oozed and dripped. Memories, too, flowed and pooled, cleansed by time itself. Looking down into the gloom from the arched stone entrance, Isa spoke quietly of the past. To Mary and Kirsty, it was so clear – the day Isa had been taken away from them to Norway. How unhappy and on edge they had all been – and there was their father, so stern and unbending! That he had chosen to personally escort his daughter was most unusual. *Perhaps, he just wanted to make sure I arrived safely and, more to the point, remained there,* Isa thought with a wry smile. In spite of all the heartache, she had escaped the terrible hardships wrought upon their family and it had been the start of a marvellous adventure.

In the soft afternoon light, they clambered down by the shoreline. An old, battered vessel, obviously belonging to the villagers, was pulled up beyond the high tide mark. Once again, Mary needed assistance, but she was ecstatic to reach the rocks below. Breathing great gulps of the familiar brine and sea wrack, she threw back her head and raised her arms to the sky. It was the happiest any of them had seen her since her return. Mary loved to move joyously now and often made expansive gestures as if to claim the space around her. Though it was unnerving to watch, her family accepted these peculiar behaviours. For a time, they walked and wandered, picking up shells; handling the smooth, round stones. The sound of the waves was calming and deeply resonant, having provided the background rhythm to much of their childhood – awake or asleep; it had always been there. Some stood, simply staring at the rippling sea and the reassuring, rounded bulk of Ailsa Craig offshore to the south. Each found space to gather their memories and, for a while, held them close.

Before long, Neil and Will called out. Several of the villagers were making their way down to the shore. Clearly, the latter saw no risk from the intruders now, and intended to go out fishing. Food was so scarce that they had to fish to live, they said, though the boat was not theirs precisely. It had been washed up after a storm – perhaps from over Arran way – and they had mended it, best they could.

It would have been a noteworthy end to the day if the men had been known to the Bruce family, old servitors perhaps, but alas not. Sadly, all of the original villagers were dead from either famine or war. These men were from Kirkoswald in the north, and starvation had brought them down from the hills where they had hidden with their families. When the villagers realised they were talking to the king, they fell to their knees. Word had come of a battle far away, but they knew little, except the goings on in this part of the world. Nigh on four years ago, English soldiers had been ousted from here. Who knew when they might return, more vindictive than ever?

Robert was keen to offer the men work and, as a start, gave them some silver coins purloined from Mathilda's leather purse, which always hung at her side. The men jangled them in their hands and tried to look pleased; payment in food would have been by far preferable. Now, they would have to walk all the way to the market at Ayr to spend this small fortune. However, they would, to be sure. They listened with interest to the tasks required of them. Firstly, they were to remove the bodies from the castle and bury them in the fields. Then, they were to clear out the rubble, burn what they could and, said Robert firmly, refrain from using the ditch for a midden or shit hole. The men shifted uncomfortably from foot to foot; they had seen no harm in it, but agreed nonetheless. The king promised to send men to help them.

Robert was unsure about Turnberry's future. Originally, it had been his intention to destroy all the great castles, to prevent them being used against him in the event of further war. But having visited his old home with its untold sweet memories, he found the desire to restore it hard to resist. Perhaps it could still have a place in his life – a bolt-hole when the continual duties of royal life proved overwhelming. Above all else, he desired a small galley and the opportunity to sail the seas hereabouts, much as he had done as a carefree lad. It could even be moored safely down by the internal wharf; could it not? Was this his mother's influence? It had been her home long before it was his, and she had loved it dearly. He would wait then, to decide upon its future.

Before them, the westering sun shimmered upon a restless sea. Russet streaked the underbellies of grey clouds, floating effortlessly across a coppery sky. Mounted once more, the group turned northwards. It had been a strange day: moving, painful, abundant with untold rewards. Each was pensive, treading water in a deep well of private sentiments. Isa knew she would never return. Now that she had said her final goodbyes, she could move on. However, she was keen to at least rebuild the chapel and restore the area around their mother's grave. Would Robert be agreeable, she queried, if she sent a few shiploads of timber. Her brother offered an enigmatic smile. Together, they rode on.

On the day of the wedding, the sun chose to shine in brilliant display, lighting up the chancel windows within the chapel at Stirling Castle. So few people were literate, the stories of the Bible were told in pictures for all to view. Startling prisms of light – red, blue and green – cascaded across the white-washed walls and the broad stone flags of the floor. Sir Neil Campbell and the much younger Sir William de Carlyle waited with steadfast devotion at the front of the chapel. Sir Neil, the calmer of the two, had been married before, and his two adult sons, Colin and Duncan, were present. Will, on the other hand, could barely stand still. Despite the frigid, late autumn air, sweat coated his palms and he ran his hands through his mop of hair, more as a means of calming himself rather than seeking a state of compliance.

To great acclaim and the sounds of horns, the king and queen adorned in full regalia walked side by side up the long aisle. All stood, until they gained their seats in the royal box. Queen Elizabeth arranged her new ermine-trimmed cloak around her legs for added warmth and settled to watch the growing spectacle with interest and goodwill. Soon, the chapel filled with family members and royal dignitaries. At the back there was standing room only for the maids and servitors of the household. Isa, Kirsty and Ellen entered together with Mathilda and Hugh. Now, Elizabeth and Robert acknowledged Scotland's magnates and their wives, with smiles of welcome and relaxed banter. Musicians gathered in the galley and the pure, angelic notes of harp and flute floated down upon the finely-attired crowd.

When Mary Bruce entered the chapel, there were gasps of appreciation. Her gown shimmered; the bodice of pearls absorbed the colours reflected from the great windows. Mary was aglow as well with pride and happiness. Such was her achievement, that she had survived great odds and lived to attend her wedding day. A silver filet held her long silk veil in place and, with her grey hair concealed, she looked much younger. Indeed, Floraidh's concoctions had wrought a miracle. Neil looked at Mary with a tenderness born of respect. In many ways, he was in awe of her raw courage and resilience, and inspired as always by the obdurate strength of the Bruce spirit. He knew she had a sharp tongue, but she would get short shrift if she used it on him. For the most part, he considered Mary's extraordinary capacity for silence, her greatest asset, despite its terrible origin. Sincerely, he doubted whether he could have lived through anything so perilous of mind and body.

Holding up Mary's lace train was young Marjorie Ross: normally a shy, plain child. Today, she stunned all – dressed in a red velvet gown with a garland of flowers and tiny white bows interwoven through her mass of russet curls, so like her mother's. As they reached the chancel, Marjorie gently dropped the veil and moved to stand beside Mathilda, who smiled and hugged her soundly. Hugh was flushed with pride that his daughter should be so honoured; given the child was the granddaughter of the Earl of Ross, it was a most gracious act on Mary's behalf. Isa smiled reassuringly at Mathilda; the healing power of time was taking place, though it was far too soon for absolute forgiveness.

When it became known Robert planned to invite the Earl of Ross, Mary had railed at him long and hard, but he refused to budge. She then turned to Elizabeth who felt trapped between her good sister's plight, which she understood completely, and her husband's political desires. A way around the impasse came about through some gentle persuasion. Isa and Mathilda came to the conclusion the old earl would surely not wish to be publicly berated or worse by Mary. In time, Hugh spoke with his father of Mary's continued ire and the need for him to gird his loins should he accept the king's invitation to the royal weddings. The old man wisely chose not to run the gauntlet of the most outspoken of all the Bruce siblings. Lady Euphemia supported the earl as her antipathy towards the Bruce cohort continued unabated. She would forgo this gala occasion and the opportunity to wear her newest gown. Illness was the excuse offered to save face on all sides, but it was not too far from the truth for the couple remained stricken by the loss of Walter at Bannockburn. Edward, as usual, refused to back down, and Isabella Ross sat at his side throughout the wedding. Somehow, though, the only available seating was at the far back corner of the great chapel.

Next, Margaret slipped through the grand stone archway, glorious in the flowing lines of her silk gown with its elegant overlay of Flemish lace. Her attendant followed with slow measured steps. Smiling broadly, fair-haired Meg Seton carried her aunt's veil looped over her arm. Delighted at her daughter's careful performance, Kirsty beamed through a mist of tears.

With unabashed pleasure, Will stared wide-eyed at his bride. He believed himself a fortunate man indeed to be marrying the lithesome, dark-haired sister of the king. Young William Ross brought up the rear, holding a velvet cushion upon which the wedding bands would be placed.

Bishop Lamberton and Bishop David of Moray performed the ceremonies jointly. The Pope's powers of excommunication held no sway with them. Waves of warmth and affection emanated from the crowd towards the prelates; the old diplomat from St Andrews and the fiery northern bishop. For

William Lamberton, it would quite likely be his last public act for his health was in decline after so many years of incarceration. Each couple plighted their troth in Scots, rather than Latin, and additional blessings were offered by Bishop David in the old language. For the many Gaelic speakers present, it proved to be a moving experience. The audience, many of whom spoke French, registered a remarkable shift. Honouring the old Celtic ways of the sisters' Carrick ancestors, bands of cloth were wound around wrists, symbolising the melding together of the couple. All cheered as the grooms kissed their brides; Neil with great tenderness and young Will Carlyle with gusto – much to the onlookers' delight. With the service complete, the entourage moved to the Great Hall where an immense banquet was reaching its final preparations. Dancing and drinking would carry on into the wee hours of the morning and, if the weather held, a tourney was to take place the following morn on the grassy expanse below the castle. With both brides sisters of the king, this royal occasion was worthy of pride and grace and a great celebration.

Scotland

December 1314

It was time to bid farewell. Mathilda returned to her home in the far north with her children and husband. As heir to the Ross earldom, Hugh needed to see to Dingwall Castle and assist his aging father. With all the happenings in Scotland during the last few momentous years, much had been left to administrators. Plans were afoot for a new hospital and hostelry on the far side of the town. Where the lepers were concerned, Hugh wanted them away from the village, for all knew the infamous disease could be caught through proximity. Many complaints about lawlessness had arisen in the area and it was imperative the courts be re-established with rights of pit and noose.

Margaret and her husband departed south to Lochmaben Castle. As the king's man in the southwest, Will would occupy Turnberry from time to time overseeing its repair to a more habitable state. Though Edward was Earl of Carrick, he had no intention of making Turnberry his primary residence. It was too isolated from all the action and, it went unsaid, there was not a pretty girl in sight. His duty required him to be close to the king, wherever that might be. Robert sighed at the thought. Edward was a most able lieutenant, but he needed to be kept on a tight rein.

At the completion of the wedding celebrations, Isa's galley sailed for Norway. Plans were in place for her to spend the Yuletide with Effie and the king, before going on to Inga in Sweden. As expected, Seonaid and Murchadh returned to Bergen with her.

At some stage, Mary and Sir Neil would take up residence at Dunstaffnage Castle in the west, to oversee the area ruled in enmity for so long by Sir Alexander of Lorne and his son, John the Lame. If truth be known, Mary was loath to leave the bosom of her family so soon. After so many years apart, the thought of imminent separation caused a fluttery, uneasy sensation in the pit of her stomach. It surprised her no end; she imagined herself above such weakness. For the moment, though, they remained for the Yule celebrations with Elizabeth and Robert. Kirsty and her girls had no home to go to: Kildrummy was in ruins. Perhaps in time, she would feel brave enough to venture north.

Snow lay several feet deep in Stirling's bailey. Servitors strove with shovels and carts to clear the pathways and the cobbled road up to the castle. Beads of sweat trickled in rivulets down foreheads whilst mouths hazed steam into the crisp air. As the bleak afternoon light seeped from the sky, aromas emanating from the kitchens tantalised hungry bellies. It was Yuletide and the royal household was celebrating the event with a banquet.

On the raised platform in the Great Hall, Kirsty sat at the long trestle with her kinfolk and esteemed guests. Knife in hand, she toyed with the greasy roast venison served in its trencher and had little appetite for food or gaiety. Though rich and well-formed, the wine tasted sour upon her palate. The noise of the musicians was clamorous to her ears rather than restful.

Jesters and jugglers made their way through the crowd and the king's prized hunting hounds fought over scraps careless folk let drop upon the floor. It was dark outside now, and the large central hearth could not cope with the bone-chilling damp. Gusts of frigid air blew in through the narrow window shafts making the rushes flicker and dim, casting strange shadows over the faces of those before them.

After the recent celebrations, today's festivities were somewhat of an anticlimax, with the departure of three of the Bruce sisters. The long corridors and stairwells echoed with the laughter of Mathilda's children. Kirsty felt lonely, too, without the warmth and humour of her sisters' presence. She missed her conversations with Isa and wondered when, if ever, she would see her older sister again. It was curious, she thought, how fast she could fall into a deep pit of despair and, once again, wondered if she would ever truly recover from her ordeal. Today, her spirits felt ill at ease. Castles were hotbeds of gossip and innuendo and she felt out of her depth with the complex relationships and intrigue. Not for the first time, she missed the shy innocence and kindness of her friend in the far south of England. Her thoughts drifted back to the quietness of Aeltherida's morning room: the steady, rhythmic pounding of aromatic herbs in the stone pestle and the remarkable sense of peace which was entirely absent here in Stirling. She needed to feel settled in her own space and home, but was unable to concentrate on any one subject for long, so the planning eluded her.

The mood at the table was sombre, for talk turned from past celebrations to the future. What would it hold for them all? Edward havered on about the need to engage England in war; to advance and threaten, perhaps from the vantage point of Ireland. Robert gave the discussion his full attention, but his frown indicated a level of irritability with his war-mongering brother. Whenever Edward ventured down this path, Robert became even more concerned at what kingship under his younger brother would mean for Scotland. Edward was valorous to a fault and his levels of endurance for rough conditions were legendary, but the word 'peace' was outwith his vocabulary.

After all these years, Robert knew his brother would never change, and told himself he must accept him for what he was – a brave leader of men in battle. But the ideal of prudent statesmanship was beyond him. Perhaps, inevitably, cracks had begun to appear in his relationship with Isabella Ross for she bored him with her clinging, doe-eyed devotion. Where was the adventure in that? Edward was committed to the pursuit and the thought of only one bed partner from now till the end of his days was stifling in the extreme.

Elizabeth reported she had found the lass crying in the garderobe just now. After his strenuous efforts to bring the Ross family into his peace, Robert still could not curb his brother's foolishness, despite being king. His thoughts ventured to Mathilda who would be caught in the thick of the conflict and recriminations. A curse escaped his lips when he saw Edward eyeing off one of the prettier maids serving wine. In a moment of pure desperation, he prayed for strength, whilst his fists itched to pommel some wisdom into his self-centred brother.

The evening entertainments were wearing thin. As the wine warmed his blood, Robert felt the return of the familiar, stinging itch. He shifted in his seat, uncomfortable now at the reminder of his illness and thoughts of his own mortality. Sometimes, he felt the spectre of death breathing close, whispering soft in his ear, but he would turn his head away and forge on. A sigh escaped his lips. Elizabeth turned away from her conversation with Mary. She glanced at her husband and saw the familiar look of sadness cross his worn features; he was observing Marjorie and the wretched expression etched across her face. He knew she hated these noisy, grand, social occasions. A deep pit of despair engulfed him.

Time was running out. Elizabeth was no closer to carrying a babe within her belly. Soon, he would have no choice. He would have to pursue Marjorie's marriage before she was ready. Surely, she would hate him all the more for it. Part of him wanted to shake her out of her self-imposed isolation, whereupon waves of guilt and shame would wash over him. It was not her fault! *How did it all go so wrong?* He asked himself for the thousandth time. Elizabeth reached for his hand and gave it a squeeze.

All the while, Kirsty pondered her future. She had made some headway with Ellen, though the girl remained resentful of any questioning of her thoughts. At least they could sit together companionably now, as long as Kirsty did not try to probe.

Meg, on the other hand, was adapting better than she hoped and seemed to enjoy life in the castle. Isa suggested getting her a dog like Frith, for the pair had bonded immediately and played together quite happily. Everyone was surprised at this given Frith's prickly nature, but Isa understood the child's neediness and the little dog's gift of select friendship and trust.

When Isa left, Meg was inconsolable; more for the loss of the perky little canine. Soon after, Kirsty sent out feelers in the area to see if any similar small hound could be located. Sir Gilbert Hay knew of one such breed recently obtained from a trader in Perth by one of his cousins, but was too unwell to make the journey himself. Keen to please, young Andrew Moray, one of Robert's northern adherents, offered to make the journey. The next day, he rode northeast and returned a few days later with a young pup, just in time for the Yule festivities.

Now, Meg was up in her chambers, ecstatic over her new playmate. It would not replace Camran, but at least the child could now focus on the present rather than the past. Kirsty was most appreciative of the young lord's efforts for he had travelled through substantial snowdrifts and unstable weather in his quest. She had not forgotten the bravery of his father, a stalwart supporter of Sir William Wallace, who had died from his wounds after the Battle of Stirling, not long before Andrew was born.

Upon receipt of the squirming bundle, Kirsty granted the young man, twenty years her junior, a warm dimpled smile of thanks. He, in return, bowed most courteously. The elegant, chivalric moment was broken somewhat when the pup peed forth a silvery arc onto the rushes below. As great as the River Tay, Andrew commented much to the amusement of those present. From then on, Meg and the irrepressible young Tay became inseparable. As always, the healing force of love would follow its own course.

As the banquet drew to a close, fire breathers came forth from shadowed doorways in the thick stone walls. To the tight, nasal whine of small, hand-held udder pipes and the heavy blood-beat of skin-tight drums, dancers twirled fire sticks around their lithesome bodies. Through a cloud of smoke and dusty haze, amber flames thrust upwards, sending a shower of golden sparks shooting over the crowd. Some mummers entered the fray performing lyrical movements around the hall's perimeter. Next, a mythical beast escaped from the dungeons below and the players dressed in royal surcoats, carrying Scotland's banner, brought the creature to its knees after an extended battle and sent it on his way, cowed and beaten, back to the dark pit.

The roaring crowd loved the spectacle, cheering and shouting their encouragement. The king looked on in appreciation. Such a diversion from his sombre thoughts was much needed. Some were heartened by the drama and yearned for revenge – to take fire once more to the recalcitrant south and bring England to its knees. Mary and Edward were of such a mind and cheered from the high table, likewise the many battle-hardened warriors crowding the Great Hall. Those like Kirsty, who desired peace, remained pensive: their expressions, veiled. Robert saw the drama as an omen of Scotland's continuing strength, but, out of the corner of his eye, caught Elizabeth's tight look of fear. He raised her hand to his lips. Peace was his desire as well, but only if it offered Scotland the independence she deserved. Until then, much work needed to be done.

It was a fitting end to such a tumultuous year and reminded all of the victorious battle fought near a burn not far away. The clamour chased away the doubts experienced by the king. All raised their mugs and goblets to toast Scotland's glorious future.

EPILOGUE

As 1314 came to a close, news of appalling events arrived at the royal court of Scotland from across the channel.

The Grand Master of the Knights Templar, Sir Jacques Molay, and some of his close associates had been immolated on slow pyres to maximise their suffering. Torture failed to reveal the resting place of the Templar treasure and King Philippe offered death as his final recourse. Molay issued a visionary threat, though the smoke stole his sight and the fire blistered the soles of his feet. Both of his enemies, he cried out in dire extremis, would die before the year was out. He would see they suffered the wrath of God for their betrayal.

King Philippe and Pope Clement died by year's end and Christians across the continent shivered in terror.

Another who died in far-off France at his ancestral home was King John of Scotland; he had been stripped of his powers by Edward I, but to many Scots he remained the rightful king. It was the end of an era in which Scotland and her people had suffered through tumultuous events. Now, King Robert reigned, but his nemesis had left a legacy of hatred in his son, Edward.

Despite pressure from within his kingdom by his hostile northern barons, Edward II failed to respond to repeated Scottish entreaties for peace. He played on whilst his power base disintegrated and his enemies grew strong. Thus, the future held no rest for Robert the Bruce. Scotland's independence was still very much in question.

CHARACTER LIST

* Fictional characters

Scotland

The Bruce Kinship Network
Marjorie Bruce, Countess of Carrick
Robert Bruce, *jure uxorious*, Earl of Carrick
Robert Bruce, the Competitor, Lord of Annandale
Robert the Bruce, Earl of Carrick, and later, King Robert I
Siblings of Robert the Bruce (taken from Burke's Peerage and Gentry)
- Isabel (also known as Isabella; informal: Isa (pronounced I-za); Ishbel)
- Mary
- Christina (also known as Christian; informal: Kirsty)
- Edward
- Thomas
- Alexander
- Niall
- Mathilda
- Margaret

Thomas Randolph (believed to be Robert's nephew)
Isabella of Mar, wife (1) of Robert the Bruce
Children from this union:
- Marjorie Bruce

Elizabeth de Burgh, wife (2) of Robert the Bruce, and later queen
Garnait, Earl of Mar, husband (1) of Kirsty Bruce

Children from this union:
- Donald, Earl of Mar
- Ellen of Mar

Christopher Seton, husband (2) of Kirsty Bruce
Children from this union:
- Margaret (Meg) Seton

Domnhall, Earl of Mar; father of Garnait & Isabel

William, Earl of Ross and wife, Euphemia
Adult Children from this union:
- Hugh
- Isabella
- John
- Dorothea
- Walter

Hugh of Ross became the husband of Mathilda Bruce
Children from this union:
- Mathilda
- William
- Lillias

Significant Characters
John, Earl of Atholl (father of Isobel and David)
Bishops – Fraser, Wishart, Lamberton, Moray
Comyn and Balliol families
William Douglas, knight
Simon Fraser, knight
John Macdougall, Lord of Lorne
Dugall Macdowall, Lord of Galloway
Andrew, Earl of Moray
John de Soulis, knight
Isobel of Strathbogie
Gilbert de Umfraville, knight
William Wallace – knight and legendary patriot

Supporters of Robert the Bruce
Robert Boyd, knight

Neil Campbell, knight

Reginald Crawford, Irish lord

James Douglas, knight; son of Sir William Douglas, Lord of Douglas

Isobel of Fife, Countess of Buchan

Alexander Fraser, knight

Gilbert Hay of Errol, knight

Hugh Hay, knight

Robert de Keith, Marischal of Scotland

Magnus Jonnson, Earl of Orkney and Caithness

Malcolm, Earl of Lennox

Alexander Lindsay, knight

Angus og Macdonald, younger son of Lord of Islay

Malcolm Macquillan, Lord of Kintyre

Christina Macruarie of Gamoran (Christina of the Isles)

Alexander Scrymgeour, Royal Standard Bearer

Christopher Seton, knight

John Seton, knight

James Stewart, hereditary Steward of Scotland

John Stewart of Bonkyle, knight; son of the Steward

Walter Stewart, knight; son of the Steward

Turnberry and Kildrummy Households

*Aiofe, maid (pronounced Ava)

*Affrica, daughter of Shona and craftswoman

*Aodh, scullion (English equivalent – Hugh)

*Aonghas cook (Scots equivalent – Angus)

*Bethoc, maid (English equivalent – Beth)

*Catriona, daughter of Shona and craftswoman (English equivalent – Catherine)

*Dughall, junior servitor and later soldier (Scots equivalent – Dougal)

*Dughlas, priest and tutor (Scots equivalent – Douglas)

*Drustan, courier and novice priest

*Fearghas, captain and trader (Scots equivalent – Fergus)

*Earchann, senior servitor (Scots equivalent – Hector)
*Floraidh, midwife and healer (Scots equivalent – Flora)
*Fionnlagh, farmhand and soldier (Scots equivalent – Finlay)
*Nectan, huntsmen and servitor
*Marthoc, children's maid (English equivalent – Marjorie)
*Mhairi, cook (English equivalent – Mary)
*Morag, maid
*Osbourne, blacksmith/ironmonger
*Seonaid, maid and seamstress (Scots equivalent – Janet)
*Shona, widow and farmer
*Talorc, huntsmen, stableman and servitor
*Tomas, courier, tutor and priest
Roxburgh Castle
*Daffyd, Welsh soldier
Guillemin de Fenes, garrison commander

Orkney

* Alfr, brother of Maud
*Aodh, former scullion boy at Kildrummy Castle
Walter and Maud Baikie, brother and sister-in-law of Cecilia
    Halcro
*Children from this union:
  • *Caillean (m)*
  • *Coinneach (m)*
*Camran, son of Marthoc
*Ottar Comlequoy, employee and friend of Alfr
*Drustan, priest and courier for Kirsty Bruce
*Father Anselm, priest
Sigurd and Fridr Grutgar, farming family at Skaill
Adult Children from this union
  • *Hodlvis (m)*
  • *Svein (m)*
  • *Heidrun (f)*

*Alexander and Cecilia Halcro, Laird of Halcro and his wife
*Thorold and Flota Hammerclett, farming family at Skaill
*Adult Children from this union:
- *Askell (m)*
- *Asliefar (m)*
- *Asgeirr (m)*
- *Nessa (f)*
- *Brynja (f)*

*Margretha, wife of Alf Baikie
Earl Magnus Jonsson, Earl of Orkney and Caithness

England

John de Botetourt, bastard son of Edward I
Richard de Burgh, Earl of Ulster
Robert de Clifford, knight
Hugh de Cressingham, English-appointed treasurer of Scotland
King Edward I
Prince Edward, later Edward II
Piers Gaveston, close associate of Edward II
William Heselrig, sheriff of Lanark
Ralph de Monthermer, Earl of Gloucester
Geoffrey de Mowbray, knight
William Ormesby, English-appointed justiciar of Scotland
Henry de Percy, Baron of Alnwick
Edward Segrave, knight
Aymer de Valence, Earl of Pembroke
John de Warenne, Earl of Surrey

Priory of Sixhills Lincolnshire

*Aethelrida, infirmary nun
*Eriface, nun

*Mertha, nun
Brother Robert Mannyng
*Prioress

Norway

*Aiofe, Isa's maid from Turnberry
*Bethoc, Isa's maid and friend from Turnberry
*Eithne, daughter of Irish slaves or thralls, maid to Isa and Inga
*Gundred, lady-in-waiting
Eric Magnusson II of Norway, husband of Isabel Bruce
Children from this union:
  • Ingeborg Ericsdotter (Inga) – marries Duke Valdemar
    of Sweden
King Haakon Magnusson of Norway, brother of Eric
Queen Euphemia (Effie), wife of King Haakon
Children from this union:
  • Princess Ingeborg Haakonsdotter – marries Duke Eric
    of Sweden
*Hauk, huskarl and husband of Thora
*Hilda, maid to Isa
Auden Hugleiksson, Norse baron
*Jorrunn, sister of Erling Kappen
*Erling Kappen, master craftsman and friend of Isa
*Murchadh, trader/captain (Scots equivalent – Murdoch or
    Murdo)
Bishop Narve, Dominican Bishop of Bergen
*Ottar, jeweller and husband of Aiofe
*Otto, Hansa trader from Germany
*Rannveig, maid to Isa
*Sigrud, midwife
*Thora, lady-in-waiting to Isa
Weland of Stiklaw and his brother, Henry

Glossary

Bairn: baby, young child (Scots)
Bannock: a round flat cake, usually made of oatmeal (Scots)
Battle of Largs: Scots won a victory over the Vikings in 1263; also claimed by the Norse
Bean Shidh: Celtic spirits similar to banshees, who call up the dead or wail when someone is about to die
Bere: a grain crop similar to barley
Birlinn: Hebridean ship
Bodhran: hand held drum
Braies: loose trousers or undergarments
Burn: small stream (Scots)
Caltrops: spiked pieces of iron buried in the ground's surface to injure the hooves of horses in medieval war.
Caterans: fierce highland warriors (Scots)
Claymore: large, two-handed sword used by highlanders (Scots)
Coney: medieval name for a rabbit
Crabbit: bad-tempered (Scots)
Creel: large basket for carrying peat or fish (Scots)
Destrier: a large horse trained for war
Dirk: a short dagger (Scots)
Doocot: dovecote (Scots)
Doocot pie: pigeon pie (Scots)
Douce: quiet, pleasant
Dower/tocher: the wealth/lands a bride brings to a marriage contract. It can also refer to the lands she may gain through widowhood
Dreich: dreary, bleak weather (Scots)

Drop scones: soft dough mix cooked on top of the stove on a griddle (Scots)

Droukit: drenched (Scots)

Ell: measurement

Epistle/Missive: letter

Flesher: butcher

Galley: Norse-style vessel

Gallowglasses: mercenary soldiers who formed the core of a professional army (originally from Western Isles of Scotland mid-thirteenth century; later employed by Irish chieftains)

Gambeson: a quilted, padded coat worn by soldiers

Garderobe: a toilet

Garron: shaggy hill pony known for strength and durability

Girnel: food storage container

Good sister: sister-in-law

Grange: a Knights Templar farm

Haar: a sea mist which moves over land

Harrowing: wholesale destruction of a land and its people during war

Havering: talking incessantly (Scots)

Huskarls: Norse royal guards

Jure Uxorious: by right of marriage

Justiciar: judge or administrator

Kist: chest, trunk (Scots)

Knights Templar: a powerful organisation of warrior monks turned financial administrators under the protection of the Pope

Knowes: ancient burial mounds

Lazar Hospital: for lepers

Levies: soldiers

Machair: fertile sandbanks of crushed shells on the north western coastline of Scotland and Orkney; the product of Atlantic gales

Magnate: a high-ranking man of wealth
Marischal: keeper of stables, royal cavalry
Mark: medieval measurement of money
Maw: mouth
Merlin: a small falcon, larger than a goshawk
Mither/Mam: mother
Mormaerdom (of Mar): an early Pictish leadership role, just below the king, similar to an earldom
Motte and bailey: man-made hill with a castle upon it, encircled by a wooden palisade
Muckle: big (Scots)
Mummers: travelling performers of plays
Neep: turnip (Scots)
Neep brose: porridge oats cooked in the water used to cook turnips (Scots)
Noust: rocky landing place suitable for galleys
Og: the younger (Scots)
Oxgangs: measure of land an ox can plough
Papay: an island in Orkney where monks had their cells
Palfrey: a light horse used for standard riding
Peel: palisaded-earthwork upon which a timber and clay stronghold has been built
Plowtering: to mess about with water (Scots)
Posset: form of milk pudding, similar to junket
Preceptory: organised community of the Knights Templar
Primogeniture: the right of the first born to inherit
Puissant: all-powerful
Quern-stone: round stone implement used for grinding grain
Raptors: birds of prey
Runrig: medieval term for a system of furrows
Sassenach: derogatory term for the English (Scots)
Scaup duck: migratory duck which feeds on mussels in coastal waters of Ayrshire and Galloway
Schiltron: a defensive ring of men with spears (Scots)

Scone (pronounced Scoon): ancient royal site of the crowning of the Scots' kings. Loyal subjects from around Scotland brought a pail of their soil to Scone. Here, amidst the thick forest and beside the ancient church, the king placed his foot upon the soil asserting rightful dominion of the land in a powerful ritual. With the utterance of a sacred oath by the subject, the Scottish monarch accepted homage and asserted the bond of mutual support. Over countless years, the site has grown into a low, flat-topped mound known as **Moot Hill**.

Sea Wrack: Old name for seaweed

St Margaret's Holy Rood of the Cross: Margaret, wife of King Malcolm Canmore, mother of David I of Scotland, had in her possession a venerated piece of Christ's cross, called the Holy Rood

St Ninnian: an early Irish saint who preceded Columba. He had a hermitage in a cave on the rocky shore near Whithorn in Galloway

Scullion: kitchen servant

Selkies: term for seals in Orkney

Settle: a form of seating

Shanks: legs

Siege engine: a lethal machine used in sieges to project rocks and other items at speed e.g. trebuchet and mangonel

Shieling: summer pasture with a rough hut

Shoogle: to shake (Scots)

Skellie-eyed: squint-eyed (Scots)

Slaister: to make a mess with food or liquid (Scots)

Sleekit: sly, cunning (Scots)

Soapstone: a type of rock which could be carved easily into household items such as bowls; often used by early Vikings; the use of heat hardened the stone, making it extremely durable; also used as the base of a hearth on ships and in wooden buildings.

Solar: private living area in a castle

Sonsy: healthily buxom, plumply attractive (Scots)

Stanes: large standing stones (Scots)

Stovies: form of meat stew (Scots)

Surcoat: a long sleeveless garment worn over armour or clothing

Suzerainty: overlordship

Stone of Destiny: ancient stone seat upon which the Scottish kings have been crowned

Sweetheart Abbey: built by Devorgilla de Balliol near Dumfries; contains the heart of her dead husband preserved in a lead box. Prior to her death, she carried the heart in its box around her neck wherever she went.

Tanist: the best man for the position of king was chosen within Celtic society, as opposed to primogeniture in a feudal society and hereditary selection

Tannymories: old name for puffins in Orkney

The Merry Dancers: Northern Lights

Thrall: a slave, usually well cared for and one who may achieve their freedom

Thrawn: stubborn, sullenly obstinate (Scots)

Trenchers: hollowed-out loaves of bread, cooked until hard and used as plates

Tribute: money and goods paid to ensure safety

Udallers: farmers in Orkney who own their farmland

Vassals: a retainer who answers to a feudal master and holds land in return for homage and service

Whin: gorse bushes

Villein: a serf or peasant

Yarl: Norse/Orcadian earl

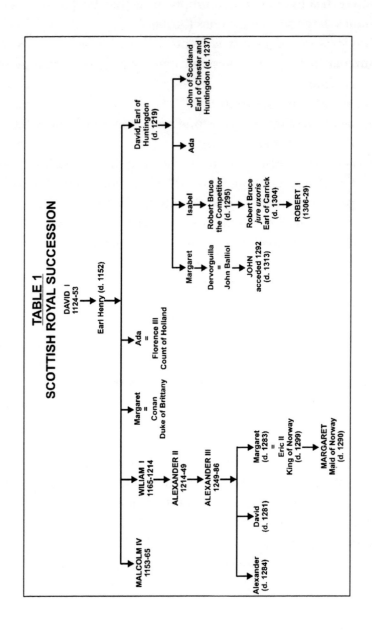

TABLE 1
SCOTTISH ROYAL SUCCESSION

DAVID I
1124-53

Earl Henry (d. 1152)

MALCOLM IV
1153-65

WILIAM I
1165-1214

ALEXANDER II
1214-49

ALEXANDER III
1249-86

Alexander
(d. 1284)

David
(d. 1281)

Margaret
(d. 1283)
=
Eric II
King of Norway
(d. 1299)

MARGARET
Maid of Norway
(d. 1290)

Margaret
=
Conan
Duke of Brittany

Ada
=
Florence III
Count of Holland

David, Earl of
Huntingdon
(d. 1219)

Margaret
Dervorguilla
=
John Balliol

JOHN
acceded 1292
(d. 1313)

Isabel

Robert Bruce
the Competitor
(d. 1295)

Robert Bruce
jure uxoris
Earl of Carrick
(d. 1304)

ROBERT I
(1306-29)

Ada

John of Scotland
Earl of Chester and
Huntingdon (d. 1237)

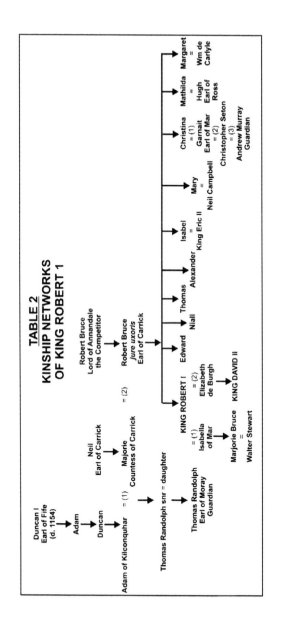

TABLE 2
KINSHIP NETWORKS
OF KING ROBERT 1

455

Scotland was a land of rich and ancient beauty, coveted by many. Its wildness was matched by its people. They were a remarkable mix of races and creeds, both ancient and new: native Picts; Strathclyde Britons; Angles and Saxons from the Germanic continent; Celtic Gaels from Ireland; Vikings and Danes from across the cold North Sea; Flemings from Flanders and the feudal Normans, the newest arrivals, from France. These warriors, traders and settlers formed a loose conglomeration of layered cultures. It is hardly surprising this ill-meshed society was torn apart, often from within by bitter rivalry between families and further weakened by external wars. By the late thirteenth century, the volatile kingdom of Scots was as brittle as dry tinder, ready for the spark which would set it ablaze. Civil war threatened and, to the south, Scotland's great neighbour flexed its muscles, flint-stone at the ready.

One bitter night in 1286, King Alexander III of Scotland crossed the storm-tossed Forth, making haste to lie with his beautiful French queen. Yolande de Dreux was his second wife, and there was no surviving male heir from this marriage. As his stallion tumbled from the cliffs of Kinghorn, so too had Scotland careered out of control.

With the death of the king, many put forward their claims for the crown. One such claimant was old Robert Bruce, Lord of Annandale, who became known as the Competitor. Rival factions threatened to split the country. The Scottish parliament appointed envoys to seek out Edward I of England in far-off Gascony, and ask for his advice and protection. For some time, Scotland's relationship with England's monarchs had been on favourable terms: respectful, but wary. Even Alexander III had been prepared to acknowledge, as did many Anglo-Scottish barons, King Edwards' overlordship. However, this extended only to their lands in England, not those in Scotland. Encroachment by their capricious neighbour was an ever-present danger. The country threatened to implode.

With the Treaty of Birgham, six-year-old Margaret, granddaughter of the deceased King of Scots and daughter of Eric II of Norway, was to marry Edward's infant son. Some objected, concerned this marriage – where Margaret was but a pawn to be used – could give the English king the pretext to interfere in the affairs of Scotland. Scottish and English nobles were sent to collect the child. During the voyage, the little Maid of Norway sickened and died. The year was 1290.

From that time on, battle lines were drawn by the attorneys and adjudicators of the thirteen claimants for the Scottish crown, delivering the complexities of claim and counter claim before a far-from-impartial judge: Edward of England. It was achieved by a piece of adroit political manoeuvring on his part, which would spell trouble for Scotland as an independent country.

Principal amongst those claims was that of John Balliol who was perceived to have the most direct, and therefore senior hereditary right of primogeniture to the throne. His claim was supported by the closely-related and powerful Comyn family. One of their territories, the region of Galloway in southwest Scotland, bordered that of their longtime rivals: the Bruce family, the Earls of Carrick and Lords of Annandale.

Legend tells that many generations before, Gilbert, son of Fergus, Lord of Galloway, bickered over land and power with his half brother, Utred. Believing he had been cheated of his inheritance, Gilbert ordered his blinding: an oft-used punishment in those times. The mutilation resulted in Utred's death. For these ill-deeds, the English king levied an enormous fee on Gilbert. Much later at Gilbert's death, the debt remained unpaid, and the king determined the land should be split. Roland, Utred's son, became Lord of Galloway, and Duncan, the son of Gilbert, the first Earl of Carrick. Succeeding generations passed and the bitterness between the two families festered, not helped as their Celtic heiresses married into the Norman families of Bruce and Comyn. Indeed, these families continued the feud with equal enthusiasm.

Rivalry aside, the Bruce claim was held to be less substantive, coming as it did through a younger granddaughter of David I of Scotland. However, Robert Bruce, fifth Lord of Annandale, pleaded tanistry in the succession dispute. The Competitor believed his claim was strengthened by an event many years earlier when King Alexander named him as his heir. Such a legend, though well known, was insubstantial, and only proven facts would do in such a controversial public arena. In Scotland, the ancient Celtic process of tanistry allowed kingship claims to be decided by the appointment of the best candidate. Failing that, bitter and often violent struggles between opposing families occurred. Deaths were a frequent outcome until only the most powerful protagonist would take on the crown. This custom highlighted a crucial difference between Anglo-Norman society and the Celtic tribal north. Within a tightly-organised feudal society, right of inheritance could only come through legitimate birth from father to son. Amongst the Celts, the clan was paramount, and the strongest person for the position could gain the throne by general acclaim.

Behind the veneer of legal convention, there lurked the very real danger Scotland could pierce its own breast. The sharp thrust of political strife was as lethal as any warrior's sword to a country's peace and security. Engulfed as they were in the mire of Scottish politics, the Bruce family was embittered by John Balliol's appointment as king.

The English monarch took this unique opportunity to pass judgement in return for recognition of his suzerainty over Scotland. The Guardians of the realm sought to deny him, but in the face of his overwhelming and manipulative power, the inevitable happened; King John Balliol and the magnates of Scotland succumbed and paid homage to Edward of England as overlord.

At one time, canny Edward seemed to foster the Bruce cause, but as they grew in strength and purpose, the king's mood darkened, and his support vapourised like a summer's mist. Now, he chose to publicly ridicule and demean. Such humiliation was beyond bearing.

To the Bruce family, their history was as vital to them as the crimson blood which pumped through their veins. Known then as de Brus, they came across the channel as part of the Norman influx. They were landed knights fresh from their estate in hilly Brix, in western Normandy; a land annexed from the kingdom of France by Vikings. The north men, or Normans as they became known, brought their families to settle and farm the rich French soil, living peaceful lives. Peace, however, was ephemeral. Duty to their powerful feudal overlord was paramount, and adventure awaited younger sons who needed to make their own way in the world. Fortune smiled upon them with lands granted in Yorkshire where they prospered; mastering the export trade of wool and iron. With extensive family patronage, William de Brus established a fine priory at Guisborough. The de Brus family had settled snugly into the English landscape, but change was on the horizon.

In the English court of Henry I, son of William the Conqueror, a Scottish prince sought refuge from danger in his homeland and became acquainted with a group of young knights. When he returned to Scotland, David requested that these loyal supporters – many of whom already had lands in England – go north with him. At King David's request in 1124, the first Lord of Annandale, Robert de Brus, established a castle at Annan, garrisoned by Flemish mercenaries, to control the wild men of Galloway who were partly of Scandinavian origin. This area had its own laws, including an archaic system: kinfolk could demand a blood price as compensation for the injury or death of a family member. Here, as in the Celtic highlands, Gaelic was spoken and laws were not written down. Hereditary judges spoke the laws of the land, stored as it was within their memory, a predominant aspect of this oral culture.

The Lordship of Annandale proved a boon to the Bruce coffers. Salt was an essential and costly ingredient for the preservation of food and the nearby Solway coast was rich with saltpans. The waterways held an abundant supply of salmon. Crops of oatmeal and barley were milled and malted using the ever-plentiful water. It was this resource which proved to be the downfall of Annan. A section of the motte and wooden bailey washed away in a flood. Moving his base further up the channel to Lochmaben, the Lord Robert of the time constructed a higher motte and a much larger stone and wood castle. Though surrounded by lochs, the new stronghold was situated away from the unpredictable watercourse. With such abundance in Annandale and their business interests around Hartlepool, the industrious barons flourished for many generations in their cross-border role. However, the complex act of keeping two masters content was a constant challenge which could only be achieved successfully in peacetime. Fortune smiled again on the fourth Lord of Annandale when he gained the hand of Isabel, daughter of King David I.

For Sir Robert Bruce, the fifth Lord of Annandale, reward for his support of the English king, Henry III, came in the form of permission to marry a thirteen-year-old heiress, Isabel de Clare. Her lack of a substantial dower was no impediment to the wealthy Bruce who needed the strength of her pedigree to supplement his own.

Lady Isabel's family line included Sir Richard de Clare, known as Strongbow, who subdued much of Ireland for Henry II. Gilbert Marshall, a landless younger son, made his name on the tourney field in France and England. As well as the hand of Strongbow's daughter, he gained his knighthood and the trust of kings and queens, including Eleanor of Aquitaine. The couple settled in Ireland becoming as many Anglo-Normans did, more Irish than the Irish. Both Strongbow and the Marshall were devout, and many abbeys and priories flourished from their patronage.

On his mother's death, Robert inherited the Honour of Huntingdon and the wealth of the royal estates of Writtle and Hatfield Broad Oak in Essex, as well as the Rape of Sussex, further south. In addition, he inherited one third of the revenue from the royal port of Dundee; its thriving port and mercantile trade, making it one of Scotland's wealthiest towns. His older son, Robert, became the Earl of Carrick by right of his wife: heiress to Niall, the last Celtic Earl of Carrick.

The Bruce family had positioned themselves strategically in Scottish and English society. Put simply, they worked hard and married well. In the absence of a royal heir, a tilt at the crown of Scotland became a reality.

AFTERWORD

This novel has developed around the lives of many well known historical characters, taken from the resources listed in the following pages.

I give credit here to the robust scholarship of many renowned authors, such as GWS Barrow, whose historical texts illuminated my path. Ruth M. Blakely is also worthy of special mention as her book details the lives of the Bruce family up until 1295. David Ross's posthumous book, *Women of Scotland*, provides an interesting perspective wherein the author describes his personal experience, visiting the actual sites where the Bruce kinfolk were held during their long period of imprisonment. I was saddened to hear of the early death of such a passionate son of Scotland.

- Some researchers suggest that Robert the Bruce had more than five sisters. I chose to follow the authoritative Burke's Peerage and Gentry for the number of siblings and their birth order.
- Many legends abound concerning the Scottish Wars of Independence and I have drawn loosely upon these. Some include Margaret of Carrick's visit to the Galloway Hills; Sir John of Lorne's use of Robert's hound; Robert's defeat of a cohort of Galwegians, and reading to his men; the 'Douglas Larder'; and Sir John, Earl of Atholl, being hung from a higher scaffold. The strange tale of the pregnant novice at Watton Priory is also reputed to be true. One iconic legend has been omitted, that of 'Robert and the spider', primarily because doubt has been cast upon its veracity.

- Some of the supplementary roles in this novel are loosely based upon real characters.
  - **Adam de Crokdak** – attorney or administrator for the Competitor and his son, Robert Bruce. **John de Tocotes** functioned in a similar role.
  - **Weland of Stiklaw** and his brother, **Henry**, were crucial characters in this period. They were known to be Bruce supporters and, most likely, would have been contemporaries of Isabel Bruce in Bergen. As noted by eminent medieval historian, Barbara Crawford, in her article, Master Weland was formerly a cleric at Dunkeld and royal chamberlain to Alexander III; and, later, an official within the Norwegian royal court and an international bureaucrat of some note across Norway, Scotland and Orkney. The article is well worth reading, especially as it gives a detailed inventory of the extraordinary trousseau delivered to Isabel at the time of her marriage in September 1293. Other notables include **Audun Hugleiksson** – a baron in Norway who was subsequently executed in 1302 by King Haakon and **Sir Bernard Peche**, the Norwegian king's representative on Orkney.
  - **King Eric II** of Norway was known as 'the priest hater'.
  - **Bishop Narve** held a key role in Norwegian political and religious life and did, indeed, hold the dying Maid of Norway when she breathed her last. He was followed by **Bishop Arne**. The conflict between the churches in Bergen has some basis in fact.
  - **Euphemia, Queen of Norway,** was renowned for 'The Euphemia Ballads' and her library.
  - **Dickson** was reputed to be a manservant of the Douglas family.
  - **Guillemin de Fenes** was a Gascon garrison commander, captured at Roxburgh Castle after fleeing to one of its

towers to escape capture. I chose to add to his role, making him commander of the garrison at Newcastle, as well.

- ○ **Osbourne, the blacksmith**, is said to have negotiated the demise of Kildrummy in 1306. The melting down of the 'reward' gold is a legend, often linked with the tale.

- Having read widely on this topic for many years, some statements remain firmly embedded in my mind. This is a process of natural assimilation. In good faith, I seek to draw attention to these matters – the description by King Edward of the cage in which Isobel of Buchan was to be imprisoned is not entirely of my construction. It has been referred to in various forms in a number of historical documents of that period. It carries the essence of a verbatim statement and has been adapted as such.

- In the sections on Norway, I chose, for the ease of the reader, to use the modern names for Bergen and Trondheim rather than their medieval equivalents, and have relied quite broadly upon the museums, books and websites listed for information on Scandinavia. For instance, a reference is made to a volva or seer and some of her tools of trade in this novel. This information was adapted from a notation in Richard Hall's book, *Exploring the World of the Vikings,* regarding the unusual tools found in an ancient grave site, presumed to be that of a seer.

- One crucial note relates to the practicalities of vessels crossing the North Sea and beyond in the winter months. Normally 'hosting', as it was called in the Viking era, was carried out in the summer period. The men returned home to harvest the crops before settling down for the dark winter months. In one of the famed Viking sagas, mention was made of a vessel returning home as late as December, which suggested to me that sailing according to the seasons may have been more flexible and responsive to weather conditions. Therefore, given the strong medieval trading tradition between Britain and Norway, I based sailing patterns around possible weather conditions at the time rather than limit transport to particular seasons. Contrary to the perceptions of modern times, oceans were the highways of the time and land travel was uncomfortable and dangerous. Historically, conditions deteriorated after 1315, but prior to this, the weather was warmer and, comparatively, more settled. Additionally, the dates offered with each letter simply indicate the month of composition. Such correspondence might have been transported to its destination some months later or even within a much shorter period than anticipated. Therefore, the continuity of information has been varied to reflect this possibility.

- Regards the folklore, history and landscape of Orkney, the website <www.orkneyjar.com> offers a fascinating repository of resource information about Orkney in general. The website's author should be justly proud of his compilation. When visiting Orkney on a number of occasions, I have heard many of these myths firsthand. Such legends are kept very much alive.

There is much that remains unknown and, therefore, is open to conjecture and literary licence. However, an author of historical fiction must, by rights, follow in the footsteps of historians absorbing their theories, nuances and biases. Their scholarship and knowledge provide the bones, the skeletal structure of a story. It is up to the writer to flesh out the facts to breathe life into richly-drawn characters and to people an empty withered landscape, long since passed. Difficulties arise when historians cannot agree upon a path and varying theses are put forward, sometimes quite contradictory in their trajectory, or facts peter out completely. Where possible, I have followed historical fact, but, at times, the sections of this immense tapestry have shown themselves to be threadbare or ill-matched. Thus, my own threads of logic and intuition come into play, based as well upon my own resource information gleaned over the years from reading extensively and visiting many of the sites associated, in my mind, with the Bruce family across France, England, Scotland, Orkney and Norway.

Readers can explore GWS Barrow's book, *Robert Bruce and the Community of the Realm*, the primary text which, very broadly speaking, underpins this novel. However, my interpretation of events during the missing months of 1306/1307 differs substantially from Professor Barrow's treatise.

Herein are two crucial logistical factors upon which this tale is based:

Firstly, the Bruce sisters, Mathilda and Margaret, and their cohort were placed on Orkney for the period of 1306 to 1314 based upon the presumption that, to avoid potential imprisonment, they needed to leave Scotland. Though sanctuary with Isa, the elder Bruce sister, in Norway may have been a possibility, this destination seemed too far away. Orkney presented a much closer, safe haven. The difficult crossing of the Pentland Firth added a further element for potential safety. Alternatively, they may have hidden somewhere in Scotland, but there do not seem to be any references in the social history of the period to suggest this. In 1306, much of Scotland's north was hostile to the Bruce and, one would presume, the danger of capture would have been great for any members of the family. However, with sufficient time and a plan in place, they may well have been able to disappear northwards across to Orkney. Under the sovereign power of the Norwegian king, it was presided over by an earl who had land and power in both Scotland and Orkney.

The likelihood that Isa had access to maritime trading connections is pivotal to this story, given she was residing in Bergen: a flourishing centre of international trade between Scotland, England and Ireland, and the continent. By this time, she was an independent, wealthy woman, widow of a former king, with strong royal and religious connections. The brief reports available comment on her wealth and powerful status, and her diplomatic skills in negotiation, which later earned her recognition in international conflict mediation. It is critical to note Isa's role would have been substantially different to a similarly placed female in feudal Scotland or England, given the latter had little or no power as a chattel of the king. It was not an impossible task then to imagine Isa setting up and providing the resources by which the younger Bruce sisters could have escaped. The avenue for this to happen was taken to have occurred by letter, especially when reports suggest Isa and her sister, Kirsty, corresponded.

Secondly, two historians differ in their interpretation of what happened to Robert the Bruce and his small band of men in the closing months of 1306. Professor Barrow argues it is likely the Bruce spent those months on the Isle of Rathlin with a brief sojourn at Castle Tioram. Dr Evan MacLeod Barron, a much earlier writer, takes the view he travelled to Orkney. A conundrum, indeed! What Bruce urgently needed was somewhere where he could regroup his forces. They had been on the run for weeks turning into months and required food, shelter and rest; primarily, somewhere safe. They also needed a wealthy and powerful supporter who would aid their cause and provide weapons, armour and galleys; based on trust, for there was no money to be had easily.

It has been suggested some of the Bruce brothers returned to Carrick to collect rents. However, the economic base of the area was virtually destroyed through years of war. How would the farmers and those lords, not dispossessed, find the monies to honour past tenancy agreements? It is also likely enemies of the Bruce might have considered the king would try to return to his homeland and support base. Edward I demanded all Bruce adherents were to be rounded up; consequently, the countryside would have been heaving with enemy soldiers.

After working through these issues, my response, albeit intuitive, is outlined as follows.

1. Lady Christina of Gamoran was linked by marriage to the Mar family, as was Robert the Bruce. The Macdougalls of Lorne to the south and the Earl of Ross to the west, who held lands nearby on Skye and the western coastline, must have had knowledge of this affiliation. It would have made sense for the Bruce to have relied on this precious kinship network, but it would not have been a safe place to spend a lengthy period of recovery given that soldiers from the south, west and east could have converged and trapped them. Also, I wondered whether Lady Christina would have had resources of sufficient breadth to sustain a band of men for such a long period of time as well as equip them for a war.

2. The Isle of Rathlin is visible from the coasts of both Northern Ireland and Kintyre and, therefore, would have been easily accessible by ship. Some historians play down the role of the hostile Anglo-Irish but, given the close proximity to Ireland, raids could easily have been carried out. Despite this, it would be reasonable to expect Bruce to have spent some time there, and legend based within the social history of the isle would support this. However with the potential for capture high, it is likely any visit might have been curtailed due to its risky location. If the hostile English, Irish and Scottish forces had landed in substantial numbers on the isle, they surely would have found evidence of the Bruce force.

3. Ireland is also mentioned as a possible location. Bruce was married to the daughter of Richard de Burgh – the Earl of Ulster – a close associate of King Edward, and one-time ally of the Bruce family. Where he stood in relation to the Scottish king is open to conjecture, especially after his daughter's imprisonment. However, a support base did exist in Ireland, and Alexander and Thomas Bruce succeeded in purchasing gallowglasses and galleys. Their adventurous raid ended in disaster at Galloway. Treachery was afoot; a force of Galwegians lay in wait for them. Spies were prevalent. As a base of extended respite, Ireland might be considered too close to the warring English and Scottish forces, for the English were based on the Isle of Man and Edward I, in Cumberland. With this scenario, the Bruce and his men may well have found themselves surrounded if they had chosen a lengthy sojourn in Ireland.

4. Some have suggested Norway as an option, given the powerful role of Isabel Bruce as a former queen, but it was a great distance across the treacherous North Sea, should Bruce have needed to take some action quickly. As a king, he may not have wanted to be seen abandoning his country in its time of need. One might presume Isa was well-placed to influence opinion in favour of the Scots. Two Scottish noblewomen, daughters of a king and an earl respectively, had married into the Norse royal family, which might suggest cordial relations existed between the two countries.

5. Norwegian sovereignty might have made Orkney a welcome sanctuary for both extended respite as well as a source of additional resources. There is a legend on Orkney that Robert the Bruce found sanctuary with the Laird of Halcro during this time. Recorded traditions often bring a new and vital dimension to historical thought. The naming of the man is also unnecessarily precise. The Laird of Halcro owned lands on both Orkney and in Caithness. The

Bruce family also held lands in Caithness beside the laird's lands, though there is no evidence to support when this neighbourly association took place. It may have occurred much later, but remains a remarkable coincidence nonetheless. It seems also that Master Weland of Sticklaw had positive leanings towards the Bruce family. If this were the case, then any potential support would have had a far more solid foundation, both in Norway and later on Orkney, than has been formerly appreciated. Jon Magnusson, the former Earl of Orkney and Caithness, was betrothed to Isa's daughter, Princess Ingeborg, daughter of the deceased King Eric II. Resources indicate that Isa arranged the betrothal herself. The earl subsequently died and the marriage did not proceed, but clearly, Isa was on good terms with the earl's family and the positive association may well have continued with his heir, Magnus Jonsson.

If the fugitive Bruce family members escaped to Orkney, this could have provided an added incentive for the Bruce to have later sought refuge, if he considered it politically and physically safe to do so. The frequency of winter gales may have further added to the safety of the sanctuary. I took the liberty of placing seamen from the western isles, who could well have known these waters and weather conditions, with the king and his men to act as their guides and to master the difficult physical conditions.

One historical argument put forward is as follows:

If the Bruce had taken this Orkney option, why would he have gone back down the west coast in February 1307 to Rathlin and Kintyre to begin an assault on Carrick and Galloway in preference to attacking via the east coast?

Another consideration, which works against this hypothesis, concerns a fiery Scottish bishop, David of Moray, who escaped to Orkney. Other Scottish prelates were captured and treated harshly despite their high religious status. King Edward requested the bishop's expulsion from Orkney. This was refused by King Haakon; a strong indicator that Norway and Orkney were not intimidated by the demands of the English monarch. It was also reported that Bishop David was present at the King Robert's coronation. A combination of these factors might lead one to consider the Bruce either had a mutually-supportive relationship with the bishop or such a bond was forged over time as the situation deteriorated across Scotland. Following his success in the south in the early months of 1307, the King of Scots then proceeded to the north where an army of three thousand had been rallied on his behalf by Bishop David to intimidate the Earl of Ross, and bring the Comyn adherents to their knees. Is it possible this successful pincer attack happened entirely of its own accord in the chaos of a war-torn country? It has all the hallmarks of a strategic plan. Given that Robert the Bruce was well known for his strategic military genius and masterly use of scarce resources, the author believes this is the more compelling and plausible scenario.

Some remarkable coincidences occurred around the Gilbertine priory at Sixhills in Lincolnshire, and the University of Cambridge.

- It was the 'home' of Gwladys, Princess of Wales, imprisoned as a babe by King Edward I following the demise (through execution of her father and imprisonment of her brothers) of her family around 1282. One imagines such an infant would have been incorporated into the daily life and running of the organisation. I took the liberty of naming her Aethelrida.

- Robert Mannying is reported to have made the statement about Alexander Bruce at the University of Cambridge. He was also at the priory of Sixhills around that time, and much later wrote a manuscript from there.
- Walter, son of the Earl of Ross, is known to have been a student at Cambridge, offering potential for a link, albeit fictional, with Robert Mannying. He was well-placed therefore to act as a conduit of information between Kirsty and her family via her sister, Mathilda Ross.

Despite the setting, this tale is as personal as any experienced today, for it is a reflection upon the potential of individuals for greatness despite terrible odds. The human variables of strength and vulnerability infuse the perennial obligation felt by individuals and nations to master their own destiny.

To obtain a country's freedom in savage and unforgiving times, countless individuals suffered and endured. These folk are rarely acknowledged, but their sacrifice forms the true cornerstone of Scottish society.

A key to the tale's humanity lies in the expression of values – loyalty, friendship and compassion – regardless of side amidst the dimensions of family life and the constraints of social class. I believe it would be fair to say the Bruce family held an array of outstanding individuals, both male and female.

This story, though a work of fiction, highlights the known facts surrounding the sisters of Robert the Bruce. The courage, tenacity and resilience of these women resonate to this day, but few know of their unique contribution to the proud history of Scotland and Norway.

RESOURCES

Book List

Allen, Tony. (2002) *Vikings: The Battle at the End of Time*, Duncan Baird Publishers

Barron, Evan Macleod. (1914) *The Scottish Wars of Independence*, Barnes & Noble

Barrow, G.W.S. (1988) *Robert Bruce and the Community of the Realm of Scotland*, Edinburgh University Press

Barrow, G.W.S. (1981) *Kingship and Unity*, Edinburgh University Press

Barrow, G.W.S. (1971) *Feudal Britain*, Edward Arnold Ltd

Blakely, Ruth M. (2005) *The Brus Family in England & Scotland 1100 – 1295*, Boydell Press

Boardman, Steven. (2006) *The Campbells 1250-1513*, Birlinn Press

Coredell, C & Williams, A. (2004) *A Dictionary of Medieval Terms & Phrases*, D.S. Brewer

Cowan, E.J. & McDonald, R.A (Ed). (2000) *Alba. Celtic Scotland in the Medieval Era*, Tuckwell Press

Coventry, Martin. (2001) *The Castles of Scotland*, Goblinshead

Hall, Richard. (2007) *Exploring the World of the Vikings*, Thames and Hudson

Jesch, Judith. (1991) *Women in the Viking Age*, Boydell Press

Magnusson, Magnus. (2001) *Scotland. The Story of a Nation*, Harper Collins

Morris, Marc. (2009) *A Great and Terrible King*, Windmill Books

Oram, Richard. (2000) *The Lordship of Galloway*, Birlinn Press

Paterson. James. (1863/2003) *History of County of Ayr. Vol 2. Carrick*, Grimsay Press

Prestwich, Michael. (1988) *Edward I*, Guild Publishing

Ross, David. (2010) *Women of Scotland*, Luath Press

Sawyer, Birgit & Peter. (1993) *Medieval Scandinavia, From Conversion to Reformation*, University of Minnesota Press

Sawyer, PH. (1982) *Kings and Vikings*, Methuen & Co

Sutherland, Elizabeth. (1999) *Five Euphemias. Women in Medieval Scotland 1200-1420*, St Martin's Press

Tranter, Nigel. (1987) *The Story of Scotland*, Lochar Publishing

Walker, Sue Sheridan. (1993) *Wife and Widow in Medieval England*, University of Michigan Press

Watson, Fiona. (1998) *Under the Hammer. Edward I & Scotland 1286-1307*, Tuckwell Press

Young, Alan. (1998) *The Comyns 1212-1314, Robert the Bruce's Rivals*, Tuckwell Press

Journal Articles

Crawford, Barbara E., (October 1990) North Sea Kingdoms, North Sea Bureaucrat: A Royal Official Who Transcended National Boundaries, Scotland Historical Review Vol LXIX 2: No 188: pp 175-184

Museums

Bryggen Museum, Bergen
Corrigal Farm Museum, Orkney
Norse Folke Museum, Oslo
Viking Ship Museum, Oslo

Significant Websites

www.historic-scotland.co.uk
www.visitnorway.com
www.orkneyjar.co.uk – folklore, culture, weather and history
www.jggj.dk/norway – The Dominican church in Norway

ACKNOWLEDGEMENTS

In bringing a historical novel to life, an author builds on the foundation work of historians. Were it not for the strength and vitality of their efforts, my own would be substantially diminished and *Sisters of The Bruce* would lack its life force and authenticity.

Throughout this challenging process, it is the kindness of family and friends which matters on a day-to-day basis. I owe a huge debt of gratitude to my closest Scottish relative, Donald Adamson, and his wife, Susan. Over the past decade, they have offered unstinting support and a 'home away from home' for myself and my family. Always with an eye to accuracy, Donald helped to ground the novel with his wide-ranging knowledge of all things Scottish, whilst his guided tours of castles, abbeys and battlefields consolidated my passion for Scotland's complex history.

My utmost thanks go to Elspeth Cameron, friend and creative advisor, whose literary knowledge was an enormous help. Her belief that *Sisters of The Bruce* was a worthy project, kept me focused and on track. Our discussions on character development, grammar and punctuation, in particular the role of the semi-colon, proved memorable. I could not have asked for a more generous-spirited mentor.

It has been my great good fortune to be part of a writers' group. The members – and in particular, the group's creator – have given me the inspiration and support that only kindred spirits can offer.

This novel would not have reached completion without the generosity of spirit shown by my family. My sons' technical knowledge and cheerful company during our adventures together were critical, as was my husband's unfailing patience and ability to multi-task, which enabled me to go on extended research trips or simply to lose myself for days or weeks at a time in the process of writing.

On a broader note, I am eternally grateful that my mother and grandmother were able to share their love of Scotland during our time together. My mother loved genealogy and writing, and I follow in her footsteps as the keeper of our family history, linked as it is to Robert the Bruce.

My final thanks must go to Robert's sisters, whose story proved so compelling that I was inspired to put pen to paper.

If you would like more information, please visit the author's blog and websites:

www.sistersofthebruce.wordpress.com
www.sistersofthebruce.com
www.robertthebruce.info